MOTHER'S HELPER

MOTHER'S HELPER

— *a novel* —

MAUREEN FREELY

Delacorte Press/Seymour Lawrence

Published by
Delacorte Press/Seymour Lawrence
1 Dag Hammarskjold Plaza
New York, N.Y. 10017

Manufactured in the United States of America
First printing

Designed by Jo Anne Bonnell

Library of Congress Cataloging in Publication Data

Freely, Maureen, 1952–
Mother's helper.

I. Title.
PZ4.F8544Mo   [PS3556.R3836]   813'.5'4   78-31482
ISBN 0-440-05928-3

To Paul

—1—
WINTER

1

Mother's helper, afternoons

Laura wanted something simple. Having spent most of her life abroad, she had never raked leaves, cleaned windows, driven a limousine, or read to the blind. She had only had two jobs in her life. The first was tutoring geometry to a friend's sister who refused, after hours of pouring water from container to container, to understand the meaning of volume. The second and more recent job was distributing linen for the university. Unfortunately she had had a few glasses of champagne at a Romance Languages reception before going to the depot, and when a group of black militants shouting insults she could barely understand came in and stole a whole pile of pillowcases, she was too dizzy, too confused to bar the doorway. During the subsequent crying jag, she had fired herself, and eighty-odd students were sent away with dirty linen.

It was not a friend but a stranger who finally came to the rescue that evening. A senior, from the look of him: the sort of person from whom she had grown to expect nothing but contempt. He sat down next to her on the floor and patted her back until she stopped crying, then listened to her story without interruption. When she asked him for advice he told her his philosophy: life was like a sieve. Everything you did, felt, or thought went in one end and drained very slowly out the other. So you had to keep faith. You had to keep digesting experience, good, bad, or indifferent, to stay alive.

Laura's father was a scientist and had taught her to believe that life was life and nothing else. But now that she was living thousands of miles away, his influence was fading. Life became a sieve for Laura, and she set about the digesting of experience with great vigor.

But some things drained away faster than others and one of them was confidence. After reviewing all the options open to an unskilled eighteen-year-old college student, she decided to find a job as a mother's helper. Not that she especially liked children. Still, she thought she would be able to cope. The only thing she was sure she had ever excelled at, now that her classmates and professors had revealed what it meant to have a truly academic mind, was being a child.

The employment office was in the basement of the library. It was not Laura's favorite place, due to the rather frightening guidance counselor at the desk, who had frizzy hair and wore a lumber jacket several sizes too big and tended to groan rather than laugh, but another friend had told Laura that the only way to overcome her fears was to face them. This she had done with great thoroughness: meeting the counselor's uninspired smiles with glares, and taking well over an hour to scan the bulletin boards. Finally she found what she was looking for in the top right-hand corner of the room. MOTHER'S HELPER, AFTERNOONS. No names, no details, no special skills required and therefore no possibility of failure. Just a fringe of numbers on the bottom, one of which Laura tore off and put into the third finger of her glove.

It was Friday, early evening. By the time Laura got outside the sky was dark blue and the ice on the quad had assumed its natural ghostly color. Her first thought was to keep out of the way. With the narrow paths and the still-unlit streetlamps she decided it would be safer to cut straight across the ice. But the surface was much more treacherous than she had expected, and somewhere near the middle she fell. While she waited for the pain in her arm to subside, she watched them move slowly through the walls of ice. The joggers. They left steady trails of frozen breath behind them, like machines.

She put off opening the door to her dormitory until the hand that was not wearing a glove was too numb to bear the cold any longer. There was no rush, no one waiting, nothing particularly attractive on what she had referred to, in more popular days, as the "evening agenda." The classical guitarists who were playing on the first landing didn't even look up when she went by, not even when she stepped on their books.

The door to her room was locked from the inside. When she knocked, her roommate sobbed and told her to go away. This had been going on for a few days, ever since Beryl had decided she was frigid. Laura was not particularly eager to get inside: despite the door she could see the whole scene. Beryl in her gray towel-robe, lying on the top bunk, her eyes red and swollen out of all proportion, reviewing the scientific facts about penetration and clitoral stimulation in a dull monotone. Then breaking into tears when she reached the part about her body failing to meet the norm. The floor would be covered with dirty socks and cat litter because Beryl found neatness depressing. Sometimes Laura felt that it was not her room at all. In the beginning of the year she had bought a poster of the Desiderata to cheer things up but, as time progressed, it was the gravestone you noticed and not the moral resolutions engraved upon it.

Jeff and Amanda were chatting over wine and macadamia nuts in the common room, but Laura did not dare join them because Jeff was still angry about her trick telephone message. Peeking through the doorways on her way down the hall, she saw that the others were all busy playing their harps and their flutes or reading with their earphones on. She did not really want company, just a place to sit down. In the end she took refuge in the telephone booth, where she suddenly became very homesick.

In the beginning she had hardly thought of home. She had been too busy going outside at four in the morning without asking anyone's permission, skipping classes, forgetting to turn papers in on time, wandering into strange parties in distant dorms, and passing out on Boone's Farm Apple Wine.

But now it was January and the novelty of breaking rules that did not exist had worn off. Exam period had come and gone and Laura had done very badly. She had followed the example of the upperclassmen in her dorm and neglected to study, not realizing that they had always been studying diligently, but behind couches or when everyone else was asleep, so that no one would say they were grinds. Just as the millionaires' sons wore torn clothes and parked their sports cars far away, so that no one would call them preppies, and radicalized athletes shunned exercise, preferring to remain inside reading Gandhi, so that no one would think they went to beer bashes or call them jocks.

Before leaving for college, Laura had planned her whole life. She was going to be a foreign correspondent, get married at age twenty-nine, have three children, and divide her time between a major capital and an undiscovered Greek island. In the security of her bedroom at home, she had felt very independent. Now she was not so sure. She had traveled with her parents to seventeen countries, nearly starved in three of them, spent long afternoons in restaurants all over the Mediterranean with would-be spies, alcoholic English teachers, failed poets, and fishermen, and been disappointed by five of the Seven Wonders of the World. So she thought there was nothing in the world that could possibly surprise her. She did not realize how different things would look without her parents standing next to her.

MOTHER'S HELPER

Laura was an only child. She might have been a spoiled child, except that her parents insisted on spoiling themselves instead. They did not believe that a child's teeth or education or clothing came first. They had never earned much money, but paydays were festivals and the rest of the month they ate macaroni. Laura was expected to enjoy the parties and endure the pasta like a soldier. It was against the rules to mention that her shoes no longer fit her or complain about toothaches. Her parents would have thought her immature. As an infant she had shocked them by crying when she was hungry and acting like a two-year-old when she was only one and a half. She had quickly learned to behave like an adult. On her eighteenth birthday she had felt so old and wise that she put her mental age at between fifty and sixty, not realizing that it was her parents' constant love that made her feel so mature, the way they worried if she was five minutes late, the way they never doubted for a minute that she would be able to buy them four houses (one in New York, one in London, one on the outskirts of Bergamo, and one in either Bali or the Caribbean) so that they could enjoy a varied retirement. Laura had always believed them when they predicted that she would be rich and famous. Now she was not so sure.

Now she would have given anything for Kathy to put down her book and say hello, or for Amanda to invite her into the common room for a glass of wine and a macadamia nut, or for Jeff to laugh and say it didn't matter when she apologized for the trick telephone message. All she wanted was a close friend. She was tired of competing with harps, flutes, stereo headsets, and illegal pets for people's attention.

Peering through the small glass window of the telephone booth, Laura watched Boris, the manic depressive, stalk the hallway. His eyes were bloodshot and suspicious, his back was bent. They said he was a brilliant mathematician but because of the way he stalked the hallway and the way he smelled, no one in the dorm ever talked to him, even though he was harmless when depressed and withdrawn to the infirmary when manic. As he passed, he nodded. She smiled at him. He looked away and continued slowly down the hall.

Laura waited a few more minutes. When she was sure there was no danger of her crying, no danger of her remembering that if she were home it would already be morning, she took the number out of her glove and made the call. The conversation was as business-like as the message on the bulletin board. The mother, whose name was Kay Pyle, gave the necessary directions to her house without even asking where Laura was calling from. She set up an interview for eight A.M. without asking if that time would be convenient. There were people talking in the background and children scream-ing. Kay Pyle kept saying "ouch," as if someone were pulling her hair. When Laura started talking about her great love of children she was quickly interrupted.

"We'll talk about that tomorrow."

— *2* —

Laura was not accustomed to early morning sunlight. It seemed to come from the wrong side of the sky. Her hair was still damp and her mouth still tasted of apples. The icy streets were covered with dead branches, casualties of a storm she only vaguely remembered. Every time she jumped over one, her head cracked open.

It was not difficult to find the house because the number and street name were written all over the fence. Leaning on the gate was a lopsided snowman with a shovel in his belly. He had a large, gaping hole for a mouth, at the back of which was a pile of seeds; two very deep nostrils, and no eyes. Pinned to his shoulder was a message: FOR BIRDS ONLY.

The instructions for entry were complicated and Laura had to read them several times before she could understand them. They were written on the gate in green Magic Marker:

1) Ring all three bells! 2) When you hear a voice on the intercom, state your name loud and clear. Children may use their code names if they wish. 3) Listen carefully for the lock combination. 4) Wait for a loud buzz, then push open the gate. 5) Proceed to the front door, punch out the correct combination on the right-hand lock, and wait for the door to open.

And then, in very faint letters near the bottom: "Sorry friends! Please bear with us while we have our burglar alarm installed."

A woman wearing a bright Marimekko robe was standing at the foot of the stairs when the door swung open. She had long, unruly brown hair and a square but very pleasant face. A wide forehead, brown eyes, a firm jaw, well-brushed teeth, and a nose just a bit too broad to be called classical. She took Laura down a long, cluttered hallway to the kitchen, a warm, almost tropical room with hanging plants, hothouse flowers, cacti, ferns. Behind the flaming logs in the fireplace was a pile of crepe paper and party hats. They smouldered quietly, then exploded, releasing hundreds of little sparks.

"I'm Kay Pyle and I'm so glad you could come," she said, removing a pile of egg-stained dishes from the stove. "Are you a tea person or a coffee person?"

"A coffee person."

"Hmmm. Do you smoke?"

"No."

She poured two cups of percolator coffee and brought them to the kitchen table. She sat down next to Laura and gave her a warm smile. "Tell me about yourself," she said.

No one had asked Laura that question for a long time. Despite her headache Laura got carried away. She told Kay the whole story, from her birth in New York City to the present. She described her early childhood in Italy and Spain, the three cold winters in Malta, the years in Lebanon, the American school in Salonika where her parents now taught. Kay was a sympathetic listener. She nodded, frowned, and smiled at all the right times.

MOTHER'S HELPER

"You must find Massachusetts very dull after all that traveling," she said, getting up to make more coffee. "I must say I am the teeniest bit envious! But tell me. I seem to remember that freshman scholarships are adjusted so that you don't have to work during that first year. I think the idea is to make sure you're adjusted to the university routine before you take on a part-time job."

Laura explained that she needed the money to go home for the summer. Actually she needed the money for the month she was planning to spend touring Europe with her boyfriend, but she decided that her case would sound stronger if she did not mention romance. (Anyway Stavros hadn't written to her since she had written the long confession about the boy she had had a temporary crush on, who had subsequently banned her from his room in the most unfeeling way and made her realize how lucky she was to have Stavros to fall back on. Stavros had very Mediterranean values. He had probably changed his mind about the summer.)

"So I take it you *do* feel you've settled down to a certain extent," Kay said, as she clattered about the kitchen making another pot of coffee.

There was something about her voice and her warm but faintly businesslike manner that made Laura want to confide in her. "I don't think I've settled down as well as I should have," she said. "For example, I spent more time fooling around last term than I did studying. And now I'm scared because I'm not used to doing badly in school."

"Did you try your hand at political science?" Kay asked, her head bent over the percolator.

"Oh, yes!" Laura said. "And it was a terrible mistake."

Kay Pyle laughed with alarming ferocity. Laura cowered, expecting to be swept out of the kitchen. "Why a mistake?" Kay asked, smiling broadly.

"I was very confused. I hadn't heard any of the names before and I couldn't believe what they said. They all contradicted each other. I'm better at languages."

"Oh!" Kay cried, coming across the kitchen, "you're a girl after my own heart!" She grabbed Laura's hand and squeezed it with affection. "I think I trust your instincts."

"Why?" Laura asked.

Another laugh so short and high that it could have been a cry of pain. "Let's put it this way," Kay said. "My husband teaches in the Political Science Department . . . Well, he's taken this term off to write a book and do some other things, perhaps, that he thinks need doing in Washington. And *he* thinks almost *all* of the courses offered by the Political Science Department are terrible mistakes! So you see why I was laughing."

Laura didn't quite see, but she said she did.

Kay glanced at her watch.

"Now what would you say if we postponed our second coffee until we've made a dent in these dishes here? The children won't be back from the aquarium until midafternoon. Let's see how much we can clean by then." She pulled open the dishwasher and began to stack the dirty dishes. There was a family of cats nestling among the breakfast plates. They were very displeased with the sudden commotion and one by one they jumped off the counter. Three kittens came out of the cabinet under the sink. They were meowing loudly, but not loud enough to drown the howls of a small child somewhere upstairs.

Kay Pyle stopped short when she heard the howls. Then she laughed nervously and slammed the dishwasher closed. "Well! That's that," she said. The dishwasher was only half full. "We might as well go downstairs. I'd like to attack the basement before lunch, wouldn't you?"

"Who's that crying upstairs?" Laura asked.

"Nathaniel. My youngest. He's not old enough for aquariums so he had to stay home."

"What is he doing up there?"

Kay frowned and said, "Thinking."

The basement was a vast gray room with windows so small that they barely existed. In the center was a billiard table with only three legs, and around it were mountains of battered toys, blocks, overturned plants, dirty underwear, dolls' heads, ravaged books, hats from the turn of the century, and a crow that took to the air as soon as the lights went on and hurled itself against the wall. There was a toilet in one corner and beds in the others. The beds were separated from the central area not by walls but by open shelves. The mobile hanging over the crib said "NATHANIEL"; the one hanging over the bed that was covered with dolls said "BESS"; hanging over the toilet was a cartoon of a smiling face. The mobile over the fourth corner, which was filled with easels, torn sheets, and pictures of horses, said SARAH: KEEP OUT. Below it dangled a second sign: NO ONE ALLOWED IN WITHOUT PERMISSION EXCEPT DADDY AND MY FRIEND LOUISE. MY FRIEND LOUISE was crossed out.

"We call this Children's Paradise," said Kay. "See if you can't help me sort out the bricks."

Laura had never seen such a place before. She had never seen so many toys. When she was a child she had lived in a room, not a paradise. And whenever she was bored, her mother had told her to use her imagination.

As she and Kay worked their way through the piles of toys, separating the bricks from the marbles, the dirty clothes from the clean ones, matching dolls' heads with the correct torsos, Kay explained the theory behind Children's Paradise. Here the children had free reign. They could act out their aggressions without adult interference. The central area was for communal playing but each child had full control over his or her bedroom area. If there ever was a problem—a nightmare, a disagreement they couldn't resolve on their own—they could make use of the intercom system. There was an intercom in every room in the house, including hallways. There were four in Children's Paradise: one in each corner.

"In a way you could say that the intercom system is my way of rebelling against walls," Kay explained to her. "It just cuts out a lot of walking and worrying if I can keep all the channels of communication open and *know* that Nathaniel is playing happily in the front hallway when I'm holed away in my study."

Laura was astounded by the things Kay told her. She had never dreamed that open shelves encouraged greater interaction with your belongings, nor had she ever suspected that a rich and unordered environment encouraged creativity. She had never been allowed to put "air holes" in her sheets, or plant shoes in flowerpots, or drop toy sailors into fishbowls to see if they could swim. She herself had never been free to act out her aggressions. Freedom, as her parents had been fond of pointing out, was something you discovered on your eighteenth birthday. Here it was different: even the crow had no cage.

The children went to a school with open classrooms where, apparently, no one was ever forced to achieve and therefore did achieve, sooner or later. Now that Nathaniel, the youngest, was going to attend its nursery division, Kay was thinking of returning to her academic career full-time. She had one big hurdle to cross before she got her degree, and that was her thesis. It was half done, but with the children coming home from school so early in the afternoon she had not been able to devote as much time to it as she had hoped. A very close friend—her husband's favorite graduate student, as a matter of fact—had suggested that she take her work to his place where she wouldn't be disturbed. That was why she had finally broken down and considered the possibility of a mother surrogate, someone with an open mind who could take her place, if only for a few hours every afternoon.

It was during the lunch break that Laura finally met Nathaniel. Kay was busy frying up some rather gray, frozen hamburgers when he peeked through the rubber plant near the door. He was a small child, about four years of age, with large brown eyes and golden hair. He was clutching the rubber plant and seemed hesitant to come into the kitchen.

MOTHER'S HELPER

"Oh, Nathaniel," cried his mother. "At last! Did you have a good think?"

"Yes, he did."

"No, Nathaniel," she said, rushing across the kitchen to pick him up, "*I* did."

"*I* did," he repeated in his high, thin voice.

"And what did you decide?"

"That it's bad to pinch other people."

"Is it good to pinch dogs and cats?"

"No, it's bad. Very, very bad."

"Oh, Nathaniel, I'm so proud of you. Give me a big kiss."

By the time she finished hugging him and returned to the stove, the hamburgers had burned so badly that only one of them was edible. Kay Pyle gave it to Laura, saying that she no longer felt hungry herself, and proceeded to make herself a thick liverwurst and mayonnaise sandwich. Even when Laura had smothered the hamburger with some suspiciously off-color catsup it tasted strange and it was only out of politeness that she finished it.

At this point there was a commotion of bells, and shouts of "Code name! Code name!" A gaunt man in a gray hooded cloak punched out the combination on the back door lock, then waited patiently for the door to swing open. The two small girls behind him were laughing and shouting, but from his expression you would not have known they were there.

"Bad news?" Kay asked him, looking very concerned.

"Mixed. I stopped by at Martin's. He'll be here in an hour."

Kay walked across the room and put her arms on his shoulders. "You'll have to tell me all about it," she said, staring into his eyes.

When the two girls saw Laura they hid behind their father's coat. They were beautiful but not, as Laura had expected, ideal. Their hair was messy and they had holes in their tights. They both looked like their mother but the older one had sharper features, restless brown eyes, and a quicker, more mischievous smile. Her sister was a year or two younger: about six, Laura decided, because her two

— 15 —

front teeth were missing. She had shiny, almost black hair and the large, gentle eyes of a child Madonna.

"Sarah, Bess," said Kay, a little too cheerfully to be convincing, "I want you to meet your new friend Laura. She's been working with me all day to make your Paradise as good as new. I feel you should go down and help her with the rest while I talk to Daddy about his work."

"Is she the one who will help out when you're gone and writing your thesis?" the older one asked.

"I hope so, darlings."

"What if we don't like her?"

"Well then, that would be a matter for Family Council, wouldn't it? Don't worry, Sarah. We'll discuss the whole issue in depth."

"When is the next meeting?"

"Let's see," said Kay, turning to the calendar on the bulletin board. The picture above January was of children from many nations playing in a circle. "Next Friday. Friday at seven P.M."

"What if we feel we've made up our minds before then?"

"Make up your minds about what, dear?"

"Make up our minds that we hate her."

"That's hardly democratic, Sarah. I feel you're just trying to make trouble."

"No, I'm not. I'm not!"

Kay turned to her husband. "Bob, why don't you try to explain. I don't seem to be getting through."

He pulled down the hood of his gray wool coat, picked Sarah up, and started to tickle her. Sarah screamed and kicked, and laughed so hard that she could hardly breathe. But her father showed no signs of pleasure. He had pinched cheeks and a hungry expression, like someone who had been condemned to hard labor. Finally he plumped Sarah into a chair. He cleared his throat twice and, putting his arms on her shoulders to keep her from wriggling, said, "What did you and I discuss last night?"

"Human rights," said Sarah.

MOTHER'S HELPER

"And what did we decide?"

"That since we are all human beings we have to give other human beings a chance."

"Who is everybody?"

"Us. Everybody who lives in Massachusetts. Even cripples."

"Now do you believe that you should give your new friend a chance? Or would you like to go upstairs and think about it?"

"No! No! I promise to give her a chance!"

"Well then," he said, straightening himself out, "off you go."

The girls had a strange way of giving someone a chance. They sat in front of her as she continued to work her way through the toys in the central playing area of Children's Paradise and, staring at her in the most unfriendly way, bombarded her with questions. Where was her house and what color was it? They were not impressed when she told them it was gray. Had she ever written a thesis? Did she know the Finnish word for balloon? What had a mouth and a fork but couldn't eat? They looked at Laura with utter contempt when she was not able to answer that it was a river.

When they had exhausted their supply of riddles, they asked her if she had ever committed a murder, and Laura, realizing that the truth would get her nowhere, said yes.

What color was the bullet? Green, Laura answered. Where had it landed? It had ricocheted. They liked that word and repeated it several times. Who was the victim? A criminal, Laura told them, a very fat man wearing a track suit who was looking for diamonds.

From then on they were friendlier. They no longer waited in silence for Laura to answer their questions because they knew all the answers themselves. Who was the only boy in the world with one blue eye and one green eye? Simon, a boy in Bess's class. Why was the Statue of Liberty's hand only eleven inches long? Because twelve inches made a foot. What should you do if you meet an epileptic in the street? Put a pencil in his mouth. Who was the only person in the world who had only one lung? The chairman of their father's department. He had had the other removed last year, and

Sarah had heard Martin say that it would have been better if they had removed his head.

Martin had long since arrived. The bells, the footsteps, the joyful greetings, had all been audible from the basement and now someone had turned on the intercom. The static, coughing, throat-clearing, and screeching of furniture muffled most of the conversation, but every once in a while Laura could catch a phrase: "no viable alternative," "Fascist tendencies," "He didn't even try and consult us." Then someone—it sounded like the father—pounded a table so hard that it sounded like thunder, and said, "By golly, this is killing me! He's taking the law into his own hands." When they heard this, the two girls looked at each other and shook their heads. They were getting so worried, they told Laura. Every time their father got back from Washington he was so unhappy. There was some sort of monster down there who kept on making their father do things he didn't feel were right.

Laura asked them what the monster's name was but they shrugged their shoulders. Just a monster, they said. Had Laura known any monsters in real life? "Tell us some scary stories that happened to you personally." Laura told them the true ones, about the rabid dog that had bitten her and the man she had seen falling off the roof of a moving house, and then, when she saw they wanted more, she told them her favorite lies. When she was a child she had had an imaginary sister who was always getting into scrapes. Now she told Bess and Sarah the story about her sister's two invisible friends who turned out to be unborn babies; the time her sister was kidnapped in the middle of the night by Sicilian gangsters and rescued by a horse called Milquetoast; the time she fell out of a prop plane and landed on the back of a whale. The two girls squealed and hid behind the open shelves when the horrors grew too great. They made Laura feel very important. No one had ever told her she had a way with children.

There was only one problem and that was the nausea she had been fighting since lunch. At first she thought it was her hangover returning, but now the cramps were so bad that she found it difficult to speak. They were like knives digging ever deeper into her stomach. She stood up, hoping that the cramps would go away, but they only got worse. Laura had to double over, and although she did not want to alarm the children, she could not help but groan. The next thing she knew she was lying on the floor and Bess and Sarah were leaning over her.

"Play dead," Bess whispered. "We'll check your heartbeat." She ran into her cubicle, knocked everything off the shelves Laura had so carefully arranged, and returned with a child's doctor kit. They took turns probing her chest with the stethoscope, which was cracked in several places, but try as they might, they could not find a heartbeat anywhere. It had moved, they decided, and that meant danger. The only solution was to put Laura upstairs in the living room on the "hospital couch" and call their mother out of the meeting. They tied a rope around her waist and pulled her gently up the stairs, laid her down on the couch next to the bay window, and covered her body with cushions to dull the pain, which was growing more intense with every second.

A few minutes later Kay Pyle removed the cushions from her face. "Tummyache?" she asked, feeling Laura's forehead. "Gee, I hope it wasn't that hamburger I gave you. I didn't stop to think whether I had frozen it before or after the children defrosted the refrigerator." She sent Sarah upstairs for some medicine and Bess into the kitchen for a bucket. She felt around Laura's stomach with the confidence of a trained nurse, her eyes full of sympathy, her mouth firm. "Two teaspoonfuls ought to do it." When Laura had taken the medicine, Kay went into the kitchen, leaving the children to hold Laura's head, and by the time Laura had finished vomiting, Kay Pyle was back in the living room with a large mug of steaming tea.

"Golly, I'm sorry this had to happen on your first day," she said. "Will you ever trust us after this? Now I want you to lie very still for an hour or two and drink this. Hot liquids always do wonders.

Children, you look after your new friend while I pop upstairs and see what's happening at the meeting. Make sure she has everything she wants and doesn't lift a finger."

Bess and Sarah pulled two chairs up to the couch. Bess held Laura's finger. When Nathaniel wandered into the living room blowing a horn, they told him that they felt he should be quiet and he complied without question. He climbed onto Sarah's lap and the three of them stared very quietly out the window. Slowly the porch, the snow, the bare trees, the sky on the other side of the bay window, grew darker. The fence disappeared and became a shadow.

Laura fell into a dizzy sleep. When she awoke, the children were prancing around the living room, shrieking. A young man wearing a long green overcoat, his ragged blond hair hiding all of his face except his nose, was twirling Nathaniel around in the air. Kay was standing in the kitchen doorway, smiling indulgently. Behind her the fire was raging again. On either side Laura could see flames.

"Laura, I want you to meet Martin," she said. "He's Daddy's favorite graduate student and *our* favorite person. Isn't he, Nathaniel?"

Nathaniel didn't answer. He was reeling around the room with his hands over his eyes, screaming that the room wouldn't stop moving.

"Martin and I are just going to pop over to his place to pick up some files Daddy needs for Washington. Children, can you cope while I'm gone? Wonderful," she said without waiting for an answer. "Now make sure your new friend doesn't lift a finger. She needs a good long rest."

Martin gave Sarah one last twirl, then Bess. "Well, kids!" he shouted, "that's it for today! The Lone Ranger is off into the night to avenge evil!" He galloped to the doorway, bowed gallantly as Kay zipped up her coat—a thick, padded orange model—threw open the door, and leapt outside. Kay followed. She popped her head round the door—the orange hood made it look much smaller —shouted "Peace!" and blew a kiss. The door slammed shut.

MOTHER'S HELPER

"She's gone!" Nathaniel screamed, rushing to the window. "She's gone forever!" He clawed at the reflection of the kitchen fire. He paid no attention to his sisters when they told him to be quiet. Only when Sarah sealed his mouth with Scotch tape did he calm down.

By now Laura had recovered slightly. She felt well enough to sit up and have Sarah brush her hair. Bess found an old compact in one of the kitchen drawers and settled down at the end of the couch to powder Laura's feet. Leaning on her shoulder was Nathaniel, his taped mouth glistening, his eyes still wet with tears. How kind they were, Laura said to herself, how considerate, for children. She gazed at the thick white rug, the rows of books, the piano, the stereo, the television set covered with a furry black bag, a padlock hanging from the end. She had traveled through many countries, and seen many strange things, but never such a house, such a family. They were so dedicated, so open, so loving, so concerned with the welfare of others. Love, Laura decided, that was it. Suddenly she understood everything: her own unhappiness, their way of life. She had been on the wrong path. She had wasted so much time. Life was so much more than a sieve.

She saw it all in a flash and then it all disappeared. For the first time she noticed how dark the room was. The children were probably scared of the dark but had not said anything out of consideration for her. Why was it that she never thought about anyone but herself? Yes, Nathaniel was trembling. Bess didn't look quite herself. Even Sarah, who was singing a lullaby, shuddered when she glanced at the blackness outside the window. There was a row of switches behind the curtains. One of them would have to be the switch for the lights.

The first switch turned on a fan and the second turned on the stereo. The third lit up the front porch to reveal two coats hugging. A thick, padded orange model and a green overcoat. Quickly Laura tried to flick the switch but she only succeeded in turning on the fan.

"Look," said Bess, "there's Mommy. Nathaniel, aren't you ashamed of all that crying? Here, let me take off the Scotch tape."

Laura's hands were trembling. She turned off the fan, then plunged the porch into darkness. Relieved, she tried the fourth switch but still no lights went on. The room filled with static and Kay's sobs.

"Oh, Martin, we can't go on like this, telling lies."

— *3* —

No one told her about the election until it was over. In a way Laura felt that this was the best way to have gone about it: although they had all done their best to make her feel accepted, the first weeks had been difficult.

So much to learn: how to boil an egg; where to find logs for the fire; how often to change the sheets in Children's Paradise; what detergent to use when mopping the floor; how to clean the windows without ruining Sarah's hieroglyphic stencils; where to find the stepladder when it came time to shine the mirror that hung on the ceiling over the parents' bed; what to feed the cats; where to record a temper tantrum as opposed to a good deed; how to make friends with the dog when it returned, snarling, from a month of mating in the country. Laura had been pathologically afraid of these animals ever since being bitten by a rabid German shepherd, and it took many days of unsuccessful overtures before she could pet Grosvenor without becoming dizzy, or realize that when he bared his teeth it was to smile, not growl.

Throughout the trial period Kay had been an ideal teacher: she never gave orders, only suggestions. Laura learned by trial and error. For example, when Bob Pyle and Nathaniel were having an intimate conversation about feces in the bathroom one evening, and Laura turned off the intercom, Kay didn't asked her directly to turn it on again. She just mentioned in passing that it would probably be better if Laura did not tamper with the channels of communication in the future. "We tend to be pretty open about everything," she explained. When Laura turned the intercom back on, she gave her an encouraging smile.

Kay only seemed to use her new office in the mornings so was always on hand when the children came home from school in the afternoons. Laura watched the careful way she handled domestic crises, and from these experiences she drew valuable lessons. When Nathaniel emptied a large box of powdered milk on the kitchen floor and started adding water, Kay laughed instead of getting angry. "What were you trying to do, my little chickadee?" she asked. He explained that the kittens were thirsty and needed something to drink. While the kittens crawled out of the mountain of white powder, leaving hundreds of tracks behind them as they scurried up the stairs, while the puddles of milk became rivers and flowed quietly across the floor, Kay explained to her son why liquids had to be kept in containers.

Then there was the time Sarah said her father loved her the most and had never wanted Bess to be born. Bess said that if Sarah tried to say that again she would tear out her eyes. They started kicking each other, then went for each other's throats. Although they were screaming when Kay came down from her study, she didn't have to raise her voice to calm them. She explained it was natural for two sisters who were close in age to be jealous of each other, but did Sarah really want Bess to die? Whom would she play with if that happened? And did Bess really want to have a sister with no eyes? She suggested more constructive ways to vent their anger, and for the rest of the afternoon there was peace and quiet in the house. Sarah brought up her paint set and sat at the kitchen table drawing caricatures of her sister, who sat opposite, oblivious to the fact that her likeness was being burned at the stake, boiled by witches, and devoured by wolves, so intent was she on sticking pins into a doll called Sarah.

On three or four occasions, when the children had fights and refused to resolve them as their mother suggested, Kay took one of them upstairs with her for a good think. Laura was not quite sure where they went to do their thinking. But she assumed it was in Kay's study because she could never find them in any of the other rooms. Sooner or later the child would come downstairs with an apology. Laura was impressed by the absence of punishment in the Pyle household: no child was ever forced to withdraw for a think unless he or she wanted to, nor were they ever pressed for an apology when they returned. But when they did apologize they were rewarded with warm hugs from their mother, as was Laura whenever she did the ironing without being asked, or made some coffee, or laughed instead of screaming when Nathaniel cracked an egg over her head.

She got to know the children as individuals, and like their mother, she learned to accept them. Sarah: bright, aggressive, sometimes cruel; a prolific painter and a tomboy, fond of climbing bookcases and jumping off refrigerators. Bess: rather sad, more thoughtful than her sister, more considerate of other people's emotions but a loser when it came to rough games. Nathaniel: inquisitive, never silent, fascinated with animal behavior, with an astounding vocabulary for a boy his age. In a way they became the brother and sisters Laura had never had.

And the house—she fell in love with the house, too. Throughout her life she had carried on relationships with inanimate objects—pillows had personalities; clothes (and she had never had very many of those) were close friends. Here in the Pyle house, it was just the same. Whenever she was alone in the house she would go up to Kay's study and leaf through the books in the bookcase: the heavy tomes on the sociology shelf—Weber, Durkheim, Marx, Hobbes, Daniel Bell, Irving Kristol; the paperback editions of Freud, Jung, Skinner, Piaget, and Lorenz; *War and Peace* in Russian; *To Kill a Mockingbird; Soul on Ice;* Dr. Spock; *The Greening of America; The Diaries of Anaïs Nin.* On the wall were photographs of Kay with the children as infants; Kay waving banners in demonstrations; Kay, much younger and wearing a cap and gown, arm in arm with her stern-looking parents. And over her desk was a poster of what Laura was fairly sure was Ché Guevara.

Laura grew very fond of this room with its fluffy carpets, African curtains, cassette recorder, stereo system, back issues of *Time* and *Newsweek, Ebony* and *Consumer Reports.* The filing cabinets were full of raw data for Kay's thesis on children's rights (she was working for a degree in sociology) but in the bottom drawer Laura found a collection of cassettes: "Scandinavian Christmas Carols— Sarah and Bess," "Caucus on African Nationalism—Bob's speech," "*Hedda Gabler*—Fred's production," "Ravi Shankar— Weatherby Hall, February, '69," and "Nathaniel's first words."

Next to the telephone on the long mahogany sideboard that served as Kay's desk was a UNESCO appointment book where Kay kept a record of luncheons, meetings, the children's activities, Laura's comings and goings. Looking through the book one day, she saw that someone called Judy always came on the two days Laura did not work. She didn't think much of it because no one had given her any reason to believe her position was in danger. She was far more interested in piecing together the different clues on the walls and the bookshelves so as to better understand her foster family.

She also spent hours in the father's study, examining the framed diplomas; the pictures of him shaking hands with various presidents; reading a book in a tropical setting; standing on a mountain peak next to a flag; standing on a yacht holding a large gray fish;

the books about American politics and European history on the
shelves, two of which, *The Politics of Peace* and *Urban Ghettos: A
Legacy of Guilt* were by Bob Pyle himself; the books about religion
piled haphazardly on the floor, indicating a strong, but now abandoned, interest in theology; the thick folders containing completed
chapters of his next book—*The Road to Legitimacy: The Emer-
gence of Ethnic Pressure Groups in the United States 1850–1940.*

Laura was impressed by Bob Pyle's many accomplishments but
puzzled by his attitude toward spare time. Did he ever enjoy himself? He had such a strained expression on his face in those vacation
photographs: the smiles were forced. The view from the mountain-
top, the large gray fish, nothing seemed to give him pleasure. In the
picture of him reading in a tropical setting, his back was to the sea.
Sacrilege, her parents would have said. But Laura had decided they
were wrong.

Her parents were very cynical about America. That was why
they had left when her father got his degree. He had vowed never
to return, even if it meant teaching in overseas prep schools for the
rest of his life. They had followed American politics from the
various Mediterranean paradises where they lived. One of Laura's
earliest memories was watching her father throw down a newspaper in disgust. How many cocktail hours, how many gorgeous
sunsets had been ruined in this way, Laura could not hope to
remember. The villains changed: Democrats tended to be better
than Republicans. But her parents' general view was that the country was crazy. The liberal gun laws, the crime rate, the racism, the
obsession with cars and lawn mowers and smell-free toilets, the
Puritan ethic—you could never relax in America, her parents told
her. You were always in danger of losing your sanity.

Laura realized that much of their anger derived from their background. It was the kind of background Bob and Kay would have
described as deprived. The only reason her father had been able to
continue his education was because of the G.I. Bill. When it had
come time for Laura to apply for a scholarship at a university

(there had never been any question about Laura returning to America for a university education) her mother had told her: "The rich in America have been putting down the poor for centuries. Now they're feeling guilty about it, so now it's time for us to collect."

Laura found the idea amusing at the time but now, in the presence of the Pyle family, she felt guilty. They were the very type of people her mother had been talking about: wealthy, established New Englanders. According to Sarah they could trace their ancestry back to the *Mayflower* on one side and Salem on the other. Pyle Hall, one of the largest buildings on the campus, had been built by a relative. Laura could not see the Pyles as a rich family turned guilty. No, their lives and the lives of their ancestors had been dedicated to good works because they were responsible citizens, eager to make America as close to the original ideal as possible. Not like her parents, who had run away. The Pyles had to be commended for their efforts, not laughed at. Laura was proud, very proud to be in a position to help them.

Of course she might have felt differently had she known that there was another mother's helper competing for the same job. When Laura came in one afternoon and Kay informed her that she had won the election, she was as stunned as if Kay had slapped her in the face.

4

"I'm sorry we couldn't tell you beforehand," Kay said, handing her a cup of instant coffee. "We just thought that foreknowledge would make you feel insecure. And all for nothing! I knew in my heart the children would eventually accept you."

The contents of Kay's filing cabinets were stacked in boxes next to the door, and a student Laura had never seen before was lugging them out to the station wagon one by one. Kay explained that now that everything had been settled, she would be taking all her work over to her new office. From now on Laura would be on her own. Why didn't she take it easy today? Just play with the children, paint with them, or make up stories? She could mop the kitchen floor if she wished. Or take the covers off the furniture in the living room and throw them into the washing machine, but only if she found the time.

"I can't tell you how happy I am that everything has worked out so well," Kay said. "Everything is falling into place. The children love you, I love my office. My thesis is approaching climax and if everything goes smoothly, I'll be able to turn it in this spring!"

"What then?" Laura asked, but Kay was already on her way out the door. "Peace!" she cried. And slammed the door.

The children were not due back from school for another hour, so Laura made herself another cup of coffee and wandered over to the bulletin board. Tacked to the bottom, under the stick drawings of animals and children, the memos, the old invitations, was a typed report:

Minutes of This Week's Family Council Meeting
Children's copy

Agenda: (1) Nathaniel's sleeping habits
　　　　(2) Daddy's new part-time job
　　　　(3) Election of a tenured mother's helper

(1) It was decided that since Nathaniel was still under five and therefore deserving of more parental attention than Bess or Sarah, he would still be allowed to sleep with Mommy when Daddy is away. *Voting record:* Mommy and Daddy for, Sarah against, Bess and Nathaniel abstained.

(2) Since Daddy's new part-time job will mean his spending four or five days a week in Washington, it was decided that everyone should have more time to think about it before taking a vote. Vote postponed until next week's meeting.

(3) The records of both candidates were reviewed. It was decided that Judy was a hard worker but had no sense of humor. Bess pointed out that she got angry when they played noisy games, and Sarah pointed out that she smoked too much and would probably die soon anyway. It was generally agreed that Laura, on the other hand, reacted positively to the children's needs and understood the importance of Children's Paradise. Nathaniel said she had the best face and Bess said

she had the best feet. Sarah brought up the story about her alleged murder but then retracted her statement when she remembered it was a criminal and hadn't taken place in Massachusetts. Mommy and Daddy expressed their doubts about it being true. Then Daddy suggested that if Laura was elected, would someone please explain to her how to dry Permapressed suits, as he had had to wear a wrinkled one to a very important meeting. Sarah pointed out that clothes were not important. Daddy agreed. Bess suggested that there be two votes, one for the tenure of the mother's helper, and one about their feelings about Mommy's plans to work outside the house. Mommy explained the importance of returning to a career when a mother's children were old enough to cope with a surrogate mother. She stressed that if the children gave her a vote of no confidence, that meant they wanted her to be a dummy for the rest of her life.

It was decided that Laura should be given tenure as mother's helper.
Voting record: Laura 5, Judy 0

After the vote Bess asked for the definition of tenure. Daddy explained that it meant that Laura could work for them forever so long as she kept up her good standard of performance and committed no crimes. Sarah suggested that she had committed crimes but was booed down.

It was decided that Mommy should be allowed to work outside the house whenever she liked.
Voting record: Mommy and Daddy for.
        Sarah, Bess, and Nathaniel against.

It was decided to review the bylaws of Family Council at the next meeting. Sarah and Bess pointed out that if they were old enough to cope with a mother surrogate, they were old enough to have more than half a vote. Nathaniel asked for the definition of "half" and Mommy explained by drawing a line down the middle of a sheet of paper.

The meeting was adjourned at 7:30 P.M., EST.

Signed,
Martin Wallace
Interim Secretary

Laura collapsed into a chair. All the confidence she had been building up over the weeks had drained away. To think that they had been testing her, watching her, waiting to see if she would make a mistake. To think that they had been talking behind her back. What did they really think? She was sure that during their weeks of secret observation, they had discovered all sorts of terrible things about her, things she herself didn't even know.

She searched the pile of papers near the telephone for more evidence, with no success. She looked under the furniture in the living room but all she found was a pile of graduate school applications and a few toys. She leafed through the papers on the desk in Kay's study but found nothing petty, nothing personal. There was an unfinished letter in the electric typewriter. "Dear Mirabelle," it began, "I was so impressed by your article in the fall issue of the alumnae magazine. The core of the problem is something that has been plaguing me ever since the Civil Rights Movement began. Why is it that the American people close their eyes to the sanctity of the individual and place so much importance on his creed and color? I must say, sometimes I find it very difficult to keep faith . . ."

Somewhat relieved, Laura went into the master bedroom for a rest. There was the usual number of what she supposed were condoms on the floor, and wads of hair, and discarded clothes, but Laura did not have the energy to go downstairs for the broom. Today was for resting and calming down. She lay down among the cushions on the enormous bed and stared at her face in the mirror on the ceiling. It was a new technique: in the old days she had never been able to keep still in front of a mirror. She would try out hundreds of smiles and try to find poses that concealed her stomach. It was always disappointing when the smiles and poses did not come out as well in photographs.

When the children came home she was feeling better, if not totally recovered from the shock. While she prepared their afternoon hot chocolate, they ran around the house with Grosvenor, leaving a trail of coats, boots, mittens, and socks. "You've got tenure, did you hear?" Bess told her when she called them to the table. "We voted you in five to nothing."

"I know," Laura answered. "I was so surprised."

"You were?" she said. "I wasn't. The moment you got ill on the first day, I knew you would win."

"Tell us another story about a crime you've committed," Sarah shouted. "You're supposed to play with us today and just relax."

But Laura was not in the mood to tell any more stories, to add to the already substantial collection of her imaginary misdemeanors. Besides she could not think of any. She had already pretended to have spent a month eating raw meat in a cave, escaped from fifteen prisons, including one that was owned by the Chinese, been swallowed by a fish and cut her way out of it . . . and it was getting harder and harder to convince them that what she said was the truth. They asked her embarrassing questions about where she found air for breathing, where she got the knife if the prison guards had taken everything away from her.

Instead she offered to play Hangman. Bess and Sarah found this game amusing but since you had to be literate to play it, Nathaniel soon got bored. He crawled off his chair and went to play with the cats. When Kay was at home, he played with them gently, but today he was throwing them on top of each other.

"What are you trying to do, Nathaniel?" Laura asked.

"Mate them," he said.

"Mate them how, Nathaniel?"

"Mate them so the male's penis goes into the female's vagina so they both howl and then they both wait for the sperms to go from the male's penis to the female's vagina so then the female gets fat and has more kittens." He picked up one of the cats and threw it across the floor. "See what I mean? She's howling and that means she is in heat and that means that she is ready for kittens."

"No, Nathaniel, I don't think the cat's in heat."

"Yes, she is! And so is the other cat." He picked up the other cat and threw it against the wall. It howled and jumped on the mantelpiece, where it sat, glaring, and licked its paws. "Give it back to me!" he cried.

"No," Laura said. "You were hurting it."

"Give it to me! Give it back! I want to mate them." He started crying and jumping up and down. Laura felt like hitting him but instead she tried to think how Kay would deal with this situation. "I feel you're being very selfish," she finally said.

"No, he's not, he's not!" Nathaniel cried.

"*I'm* not, Nathaniel."

"I'm not, I'm not!"

"Well, I feel you are."

"And I feel . . . I feel . . . I feel that if you don't give me that cat so that I can mate it right now . . . I feel I will hate you!"

The girls gasped. "Nathaniel!" Bess cried, "how dare you say that to Laura? Apologize to her right away."

"No! Nathaniel won't!"

Bess went over and took him by the shoulders. "And do you know how stupid you are, Nathaniel? You were trying to mate two females. Now how stupid can you get?"

"I feel I hate you too!" he answered. Bess gave Sarah a meaningful look. "Maybe we should send him to the Thinking Room," she said.

"No! Not there! Please! Please!" He started screaming, clinging to the leg of the table. But Sarah and Bess put together were very strong. They succeeded in pulling not only Nathaniel, but the table, the plants, the swaying cups of lukewarm chocolate, and an obstructing chair. It was developing into much too big a fight, so Laura decided to distract them. It was a technique she had seen Kay use successfully many times. She sneaked into the living room and put a record on the stereo of the Supremes singing with the Temptations, full blast.

This had altogether the wrong effect. Grosvenor got very excited and began to race around the house. Whenever he skidded back into the kitchen, he bumped into the table, and on the fourth or fifth round he knocked over Bess's cup. The cup rolled off the table onto one of the kittens. Meowing wildly, the kitten ran around in circles. The children cheered. Laura went out to the porch to get the mop. By the time she returned, all the children were running after the dog, up and down the stairs. They were stark naked. Their clothes were lying on the floor among the puddles of hot chocolate.

Laura did not know what to do, because the children had never run around naked when Kay was home. She sat down and tried to fit together the various bits of knowledge she had acquired about child psychology since her arrival. Shouting at them was out of the question. If she got angry they would think they had done something wrong and become ashamed of their bodies.

Sarah and Grosvenor came careening into the kitchen. The dog slipped and fell on the wet tiles. Sarah jumped on top of him, grabbed his legs, and started to wrestle with him. It was some kind of sexual aggression, Laura decided. And Sarah was hurting the dog, so it had to be wrong. But how could she be absolutely sure? Perhaps sexual assault of animals was just a stage. Bess and Nathaniel had come back into the kitchen and were cheering Sarah on. "Get him! Get him!" they shouted. Laura watched them, mouthing the words to "Ain't No Mountain High Enough" in order to conceal her shock, so it wasn't until the grandmother had slammed the kitchen door that any of them saw her.

Laura could tell it was the grandmother because of the imperious way she disposed of her cane and flicked the stereo switch, and the angry way her bony hands worked to undo the buttons of her gray wool hood.

"Someone," she said in a loud, quavering voice, "and I don't know who, left the gate open. *And* the back door. I understood these things were to be closed at all times." She strode to the middle of the kitchen floor, where she took off her spectacles. "Well! What in the name of the Lord have you children been up to? Sarah? Bess?"

"Playing," they said.

"Playing? With no clothes on? Shame on you. And what was the name of this disgraceful game?"

"Catch the Dog."

"You evil, evil children. I've a good mind to give the three of you a good hiding. Whose idea was this in the first place?"

"Nobody's idea," said Sarah, "it just happened."

"Well, if one of you doesn't speak up and admit to it, I'll have to punish you as a group. It's sinful the way you children are allowed to behave."

Sarah's teeth were chattering. Bess, who had her hair in her mouth, was humming: a preface, as Laura now knew, to tears. Nathaniel whimpered and covered his penis with his hands. As the youngest he would be the hardest hit by his grandmother's words. And all because of her own inaction. She had to do something quickly, before their grandmother ruined years of work and made them ashamed of their bodies.

She stepped in front of them and tried to look very firm. "It was my idea," she said to the grandmother. "They were only following my instructions."

The grandmother gave her a sharp look. "And who are you, may I ask?"

"Laura."

"She has tenure," said Bess.

"Ah, the new housekeeper. Well, well, well. And is this the way they teach children to behave in Ireland?"

MOTHER'S HELPER

"I'm not from Ireland."

"But you *are* the housekeeper."

"The mother's helper."

"I see," she said, adjusting her spectacles. But Laura could tell that she couldn't see at all. "Well, children, let us put an end to your naughty games. Off you go to put on some warm things. Scoot! Scoot!" She slapped their bottoms and herded them to the stairs. "I assume this is the number at my daughter-in-law's new office," she said, picking up a large piece of construction paper, on which was written, "Do call me if you feel the need! The number is 262-3587. Love and kisses, Kay." Next to the signature was a hastily drawn smiling face.

"Yes, it is," Laura answered, but the grandmother waved her hands impatiently. When she had dialed, she turned to Laura and said, "Yes, thank you, I would love some coffee."

"Hello, Kay? This is your mother-in-law here . . . Yes, I dropped by, and I'm so glad I did . . . The children were running around the house stark naked. Stark naked, did you hear? . . . I'm afraid I don't quite understand. Kay, sometimes you shock me! I respect your wishes to return to your career, but you are being far too slaphappy about your arrangements for the children . . . I must remind you that I have offered time and time again to take care of them . . . But I don't see that she's doing a good job at all . . . She herself admitted to having instigated the whole game . . . I see . . . I see . . . Well, if that's the way you see it . . . Certainly . . . I'll certainly call you then . . . If you really feel strongly about it . . . Fine. Good-bye till then."

Sighing heavily, the grandmother sat down at the long wooden table. She searched among the plants and unwashed mugs for the coffee Laura had prepared for her. "Oh, dear, it's instant," she said. "I've told her time and time again that it's just as fast to use those Melitta filters, but she just won't listen."

Laura didn't say a thing. She leaned against the kitchen counter, staring at the woman who had just challenged her tenure.

She examined her features for signs of meanness and found them everywhere: in the creases at the ends of her mouth, in her hollow cheeks and the firm jutting lines of her chin, in her icy blue eyes. Her eyes had softened somewhat: in the way she patted her short white hair there was the slightest hint of a wounded animal.

"Are you new in these parts?" she asked.

"Fairly new," Laura answered.

"It's difficult to find jobs these days, isn't it? The factories are all laying people off. Our church committee has done everything it can to help, but we can't combat this recession single-handed, I'm afraid."

"I've never worked in a factory," Laura said after a pause.

The grandmother looked surprised.

"Oh? But I thought Kay said . . ."

The children had come back into the kitchen. They were holding hands and glaring at the ground. They had draped their sheets around their bodies like togas. Bess was wearing a dried-up wreath; Sarah was holding a whip in her free hand; Nathaniel was clutching a Raggedy Ann.

"Now, that's better, isn't it," said the grandmother in a shaky voice. "And I had better be going. I promised to let the women's group have four devil's food cakes by seven o'clock and here it is going on three thirty." While she was putting on her coat, Nathaniel crawled under the table, leaving most of his sheet behind him, and bit her leg.

"How dare you, you little imp." She leaned down, smacked him hard across the face, and stalked out of the house.

Nathaniel didn't cry. He just sat under the table feeling his cheek, as if he didn't really believe what had happened.

"You lied," said Sarah, scratching her back with her whip. She was smiling.

"But I lied to keep your grandmother from beating you up," Laura said.

"Still. You lied."

"Only because I didn't want you to be punished."

"Don't you believe in punishment?"

"No, certainly not."

"Of course not," said Bess. "Laura has tenure. She would never have gotten tenure if she believed in punishment."

"She can still send us up to the Thinking Room."

"Oh, she wouldn't ever do *that*. I'm sure she wouldn't. When she's here, I feel happy, much too happy to want to think."

"I hope you weren't upset by what your grandmother said," Laura told them.

"Oh, she's just an old fogey."

"I don't want you to become ashamed of your bodies just because of what she said."

"Never!" said Sarah, throwing off her sheet. She put her hands in the air and began to dance around the room. "I have a beautiful body," she said, caressing Grosvenor's back with the whip. "And when I develop, it will be even more beautiful."

Laura wasn't used to being around naked people so she bent down to pick up the soiled clothes, shoes, sheets, and broken bits of glass. While she mopped the floor, the girls returned to their game of Catch the Dog. But not with the same spontaneity as before, Laura noticed.

Finally she sat them in front of the television, uncovered it for the first time since her arrival, and let them watch *Million Dollar Movie.* They were thrilled by this: they said they never had the chance to see much trash.

The movie was about the RAF during the Second World War. Laura was surprised to discover that they had never heard of it. They were fascinated by the shots of small planes flying over Germany in formation, dropping bombs, crashing into cliffs on their homebound journey, but bored with the romantic heroine. They said she had funny hair and wore ugly dresses. They knew exactly what the hero was going to do to her when he closed her bedroom door and kissed her. Didn't Laura know? Hadn't Laura ever done it? They described sexual intercourse to her in clinical detail, stopping only when there was another bombing mission, another series of explosions.

The first thing Kay did when she arrived home with Bob and Martin was to switch off the television. She countered the children's displeasure with warm hugs, crying, "Oh, my little chickadees, you don't know how I missed you!"

Martin came galloping into the living room, growling and making monster faces. The children howled and ran into his arms, shouting, "Me first! Me first!" He twirled each of them once and then tried to twirl Laura as a joke. But she was too heavy for him. When he dropped her, she hit the floor so hard that the whole room shook. Everyone thought this was very funny, except for Laura, even though she was now accustomed to Martin treating her like an eight-year-old.

"Hey," said Kay when she stopped laughing, "why don't you girls go up and run your bath? And Laura, we're going to discuss what happened this afternoon at dinner tonight. I feel you should be here to discuss it with us. After all, you're a member of the family now, and we'll need to know how you feel about almost everything."

While Martin continued to twirl Nathaniel around in the air, Kay and Laura went into the kitchen to prepare dinner. Bob was walking back and forth with the telephone on his shoulder, praising someone or other for his invaluable efforts and saying that when it came to the crunch, it was probably going to make all the difference. The girls shouted down the stairs that the bath was ready, and Bob told the person on the other end of the line that he had to run. He went upstairs with a resigned expression.

"How about chicken? Are you in a chicken mood?" Kay said, taking a tray of half-eaten chicken pieces and halved sweet potatoes out of the refrigerator. She put the tray into the oven, then, whis-

—— 40 ——

tling cheerfully, she melted some butter in a pan and poured in a can of mixed nuts. "And some protein," she said, "to tide us over."

Shrieks of laughter floated down the stairs. Bob was roaring like a wild animal. "Should I eat this arm, or this arm?" he was saying. "No, I'll have this leg! I had arms yesterday!"

Soon they came downstairs, glowing and wet. Bob Pyle went immediately to the phone and the girls helped Laura set the table. The bath that Kay then had with Nathaniel was much quieter. When they came downstairs a few minutes later, Kay was explaining where cocoa beans came from and why dogs barked. Nathaniel was naked and shivering and he never took his eyes off his mother.

At dinner the conversation centered on Lieutenant Calley until Bess mentioned Grandma's visit.

"Oh, did she?" asked Bob, playing with his food. He didn't seem to like the chicken or the nuts any more than Laura did.

"Yes, Bob," Kay said, "and she called me while she was here." She winked at him and smiled.

"Well, I feel I hate her," Bess said.

"Why, dear?" Kay asked.

"Because she was mad at us, and that was bad."

"Why was she mad at you, chickadee?"

"Because we were playing Catch the Dog."

"Was that all you were doing?"

"Yes," said Bess.

"Perhaps she felt you were being cruel to Grosvenor."

"No," said Sarah. "I told you. She felt we were naked."

"Well, were you?" Kay asked.

"Of course."

"Sarah," said Bob, looking at his daughter without enthusiasm, "do you remember when we discussed being naked in front of strangers?"

"Yes."

"And what did we decide?"

"That some people don't understand why clothes aren't important, so we were supposed to wear clothes if other people were in the house."

Kay put her arm through the baby rubber plant in the middle of the table to squeeze Laura's arm. "Of course *Laura* doesn't mind. She's one of the family now."

"But why does Grandma mind?"

Bob sighed. "She's from a different world, Sarah. You've got to understand that she has different ideas than we do. In her time the world was black and white . . ."

"It *was?*" Bess and Sarah cried at the same time.

". . . the world was black and white and people saw things as good and bad. You understand that I'm speaking metaphorically," he said, pausing to look at the girls.

"I bet Grandma was in the Second World War," Sarah said, "wasn't she?"

"As a matter of fact, yes. She was a nurse. Why did you want to know?"

"Because I thought I saw her today on television, kissing the enemies."

"Grandma's a good woman. You shouldn't say that."

"No, she's black and white! Black and white! You should never have allowed her to get into color. Never!"

"Now, now," said Kay. "I feel you are all getting a bit too excited. Off you go downstairs to get ready for Mommy to read you a story."

She herded them to the stairs and waved good-bye. Then she returned to the table. She rested her face on her hand and looked earnestly at Laura.

"How do you feel about all this?" she asked. "Are you pro or con?"

"What do you mean?"

"Pro or con clothes, I mean."

Bob and Martin, who had been discussing a rumor that My Lai was not the worst massacre to have gone down in Vietnam during the past few years, stopped talking and looked at Laura with appreciative smiles.

"I suppose clothes have their uses," Laura said. "They conceal ugly bodies, for example."

They all looked at her quizzically, as if she had just admitted a sympathy for the John Birch Society. It was a long time before Kay could muster up a smile.

"Hey," she said, "that's a wacky way of looking at it."

"It sure is." Bob and Martin laughed. But Laura felt they were less than sincere.

Laura felt uneasy. She always tried to see the best in people, but behind this humanitarian facade was a second voice. And now the second voice told her that she was sitting with a group of idiots who were playing a game they didn't understand, just as it had told her, during the most romantic hour of her life, when Stavros pledged his undying love after years of silence, that she was sitting with an idiot who had horrible eyebrows and a pedestrian mind. She smothered this thought as soon as it surfaced, and vowed never to think that way again.

"But for future reference," Kay said, still smiling, "I want you to know that we disapprove of television unless there is an educational program on. And I am so gratified that you were able to handle Bob's mother this afternoon, but in the future, please try not to cope with the situation by telling a lie."

For a moment Laura's long-dormant temper flared. She felt the blood rising to her cheeks. She felt like getting up from the table and saying something very rude and then slamming the door on them forever. What right did they have to tell her what to do? But then she remembered they had every right to tell her what to do, and she remembered how gloomy it would be in her dorm, and how lonely she had been until coming to this house.

"I'm sorry," Laura said, meaning more than Kay could possibly imagine. "I still have so much to learn."

"Oh, don't feel bad about it. Bob and Martin and I have so much to learn from you, too. It's going to be so refreshing, isn't it, Bob, to have a new point of view around the house."

"I want you to feel that you're part of the family," Bob said solemnly. "I want you to feel that you can share all your thoughts, even bad ones, with us. The more we know about human nature, the more honesty there is in everyday life, the better it will be for all of us."

"I trust your instincts," Kay said.

Laura reached through the rubber plant and squeezed Kay's arm, perhaps·a bit more roughly than she had intended.

5

It was obvious that Sarah did not want her father to go away. Her first ploy on Sunday afternoon was to announce that she no longer felt comfortable having open shelves for walls. She wanted real ones, the kind that went from the floor to the ceiling. A door could wait, but she wanted the walls right away, which meant that her father would have to give up his project in Washington and stay home until they were up.

A tight schedule had been arranged for the afternoon. According to the list on the bulletin board, they were already running late. Lunch had taken half an hour longer than expected because Nathaniel's strawberry omelet had spilled all over the stove, nearly causing a fire. And even though the twenty minutes allotted to Fun and Tickling Games had been canceled, Bob Pyle and Martin had less time than they needed to complete a proposal Bob was going to have to present in Washington the following day. With Sunday Sermon scheduled for half past four, the children were pressed for time, too. They would probably not be able to complete the portraits Kay had suggested they draw for their father. Departure was set for five fifteen because it was imperative that Bob make the seven o'clock shuttle. Laura could see that Bob Pyle's hands were shaking as he took notes on what Martin was saying. He was probably, Laura decided, nervous about flying.

Or was it the noise? The easels Kay had set up around the kitchen table screeched horribly every time one of the children moved. Nathaniel kept on dropping his paint set on the floor. Bess and Sarah were having an argument. Whereas Sarah was in a position to draw her father's full face, Bess could only see his profile. She had never been taught to do profiles. The nose kept going wrong. In the end she threw all her paper on the floor and burst into tears. One of the kittens was crying, too. It had badly singed one of its claws and run off to nurse its wounds among the plants on the kitchen table. In so doing, it had knocked over a vase, drenching a thick file entitled "Interim Report." Too much noise for clear thinking, definitely—even Kay's singing as she threw together the ingredients for a fruit-and-nut pound cake showed signs of strain.

It was natural in the circumstances that no one paid much attention to Sarah when she first brought up the subject of her walls. She had to scream before they heard her.

"I just told you something!" she yelled, pounding her fist on her easel, "and you didn't listen! What do you care more about, huh? Your daughter or that stupid thing you're reading?"

Bob Pyle didn't look up. He was busy crossing out a paragraph and writing a new one between the lines.

"Answer my question!"

"What question?" her father mumbled, crossing out the paragraph he had just written between the lines.

"What do you care more about, me or that piece of paper?"

He crumpled up the piece of paper and said, "You, of course."

"I feel you're lying."

"And I feel I'm telling you the truth. Now please let me think. I have a lot of work to do."

"You know," said Kay, cracking an egg into the mixing bowl, "I think Sarah had a valid question there. Why did you decide it wasn't worth answering in depth?"

"You're right, Kay," he said. Grimacing, he turned his head slowly, as if his neck were stiff. "And Sarah, I owe you an apology. Why don't you come over here and sit on my lap and tell me what's on your mind."

"I've decided that you're not going to Washington," Sarah said firmly. "You're staying here and building my walls."

"I'm afraid that's impossible."

"What do you mean, impossible?"

"I'm sorry to say I have obligations I can't back down on. You can't imagine how much more I'd enjoy making you a wall, but at the moment it is just not possible."

"Why not?"

"I just explained, my dear. You must learn to listen. Obligations. I have obligations."

"Obligations to who?"

"Obligations to little girls like you whose mommies and daddies don't have enough money to feed them. Don't you feel I should try and help them?"

"I feel you never help anybody. I feel you're just being mean. You don't want me to have privacy, that's all."

"I feel you're being hasty with your judgments, Sarah. You know I always do my best to help you."

"I bet that if Bess asked you to make her some walls you'd stay and make them."

"Bess," he said, putting his hands over his eyes, "ask me if I will make you some walls."

"Will you make me some walls?" Bess sobbed.

"You can't imagine how much I'd like to, Bess, although I tend to think you are still a little young to need privacy. However, I'm sorry to say that there is no way I can get out of my obligations, so we'll have to discuss the whole issue in depth when I have some more free time."

"You were nicer to Bess," Sarah hissed.

"No, I was equally nice to both of you. And I promise I'll make walls for both of you as soon as I can."

"But I don't want any!" Bess said, breaking into tears.

"You see? You see how wrong you are?" Sarah shouted.

"Please, please."

"And you know what? If the world were still black and white you would be black. So black that the Ku Klux Klan would kill you."

"There's nothing wrong with being black, Sarah."

"Huh, that's just what *you* say."

"There is . . . nothing . . . wrong . . . with being . . . black."

"Huh!" She climbed down from her easel and stalked toward the door to Children's Paradise.

"Sarah, don't walk away. This is very important."

"Fuck you!"

Kay stopped mixing. Bob stood up. For a few moments they stared at each other. Kay pursed her lips. Bob scratched his hair. "I guess I'd better go down and talk to her," he said.

"You do that, darling. Laura and I will take care of the packing."

He hadn't even reached the bottom of the stairs when Bess broke down. "Now he's gone," she said. "Now I won't even be able to do this drawing."

"Nonsense," Martin told her. "You don't need him sitting here to finish this off. Just use your imagination."

"I don't have any," she said.

"Of course you do, silly! Everyone does."

"Everybody but me."

"Why don't you draw a nice big face of your daddy smiling? Don't you think he'd like that?"

"I can't," she said. "I can't remember how he looks when he smiles."

Upstairs in the bedroom Kay asked Laura if the children had been watching any more trash on television or if Laura might have been swearing—by mistake, of course—in their presence. Laura said no. "I didn't think so," Kay sighed, emptying a drawer of underwear and socks into the suitcase. "But golly, it hurts me, after all the years Bob and I have devoted to civil rights, to hear one of my children harboring prejudice."

"I think it was all a misunderstanding," Laura said.

"Misunderstandings are dangerous things, Laura. Later in life they can make good-hearted people do monstrous things." She threw open the wardrobe and took out three worn-looking suits, seven shirts, and two ties. Laura pointed out that the jackets were all blue and the suit pants black and brown, but Kay said it didn't matter. She seemed very upset. When Bob appeared at the bedroom door, she ran across the room and threw herself into his arms.

"Oh, Bob," she whispered.

"She wouldn't say much, I'm afraid."

"Well, we've *got* to do something."

"Scolding is not the best way," Bob said, nuzzling her shoulder. "I've tried."

"Well, I'll try to think up a more positive approach."

"I was thinking . . ." Bob said, rubbing his nose into her neck.

"Yes?"

"Louella mentioned that her girl doesn't have any friends."

"Right you are. I'll call her up this week."

"The sooner the better, Kay."

"And what now?" she asked, standing back to look into his eyes.

"I don't think we can have Sunday Sermon at all today. It's going on five."

"You're right, of course. I guess we'll have to put the whole thing off until next weekend."

"No, no, no," Bob said. "You just go ahead as planned."

"But I did want you to explain to them first."

"You and Martin can tell them just as capably as I."

"What if they react negatively?"

"I doubt they will. Not if you present it as something natural."

"It is natural, though, isn't it, Bob?"

"Of course. Of course."

"Maybe we should wait. Think about it a little more."

"What's done is done, Kay. It's merely a question of coming out into the open."

"Oh, Bob, you aren't having second thoughts?"

"I've thought it over more than twice, Kay, and I have progressed far beyond my initial anger. To tie you down would be unjust. To pretend would be cruel."

"Oh," Kay cried, "I'll miss you so!"

"I'll miss you, too, and don't you forget it!" There was a sudden roughness in his voice that Laura had never heard before. It embarrassed her, as did the animal growls that followed and the twang of bedsprings that told Laura that they had fallen onto the bed. She knelt over the suitcase and buried her face in its contents so as not to see what was happening, but even so the growls and the giggles grew too much for her. Slowly, quietly, she crawled toward the door. "Oh, Laura," said Kay, sitting up, "is that you?"

"I'm just leaving."

"What are you doing on all fours?"

"I didn't want to intrude."

"Oh, you silly billy," she said. "Hey, if you're going downstairs, do tell them we'll be right down."

Downstairs things were quiet except for the static, the bedsprings, the heavy breathing, the occasional moan on the intercom. Martin was reading record jackets, a look of total concentration on his face. The children were back at their easels. When Bob and Kay came downstairs a quarter of an hour later, Kay's hair was disheveled and her cheeks bright red. "Time to say good-bye to Daddy," she announced.

"He can't go yet," Sarah said. "He can't go to Washington until I've finished my portrait."

"But darling, he has a plane to catch."

"You can catch another one, can't you?"

"I'm afraid not, Sarah. I have a meeting scheduled at nine thirty and to be there on time I'll have to catch this plane."

"Well, I hope it crashes!" she screamed, and ran upstairs.

"Oh, well," Kay sighed, "you can pick it up next weekend. Bess, Nathaniel, do you have your paintings ready?"

"Can't let your daddy go without *something*," Martin said, nudging Bess, whose head was between her arms. He gently pulled her drawing out from under her. "Let's see what we have here. Hey, not bad!" He waved the drawing in the air. In the middle of the paper was a tiny head with wiry hair and an inverted nose, and around it were five sets of lips, one upturned, one downturned, one round, one square, and one large set shaped like an amoeba with tiny lacelike teeth drawn along the inner edges. All of them had been crossed out. "Wow, abstract!" Martin said, handing the drawing to Bob. "Just think how much cozier that hotel room will be with this masterpiece hanging over the bed."

"It's terrible," Bess said.

"Nonsense. And what have we here?" Martin boomed, moving over to Nathaniel's easel. He was still drawing and babbling to himself. "Hey, Nathaniel, where did you pick up all these new tricks?"

"On trash," said Nathaniel.

"What are those things. Spiders?"

"No, stupid!" he squeaked, "they're bomber planes."

"And those squiggly thingamajigs over here?"

"Explosions. These used to be houses but then the bomber planes dropped bombs on them and now there's nothing there and this is a man falling out of the bomber plane and he's screaming because when he hits the ground he's going to die."

"Two down, one to go," Martin said, handing the drawing to Bob. Kay pursed her lips and Bob scratched his left ear. For a few seconds they stared at each other.

"Can't win 'em all," Martin murmured. Bob turned around, opened his mouth to say something, then closed it again. He stared at Martin. His face got very red and for a moment Laura thought he was going to hit someone. Then he left without saying good-bye. "Do you have your toothbrush?" Kay shouted after him. Laura couldn't hear him answer.

The fruit-and-nut pound cake was ready. In fact it had burned slightly. Kay decided that it and some frozen peas would be enough for dinner. While Laura was setting the table, Kay asked her what the movie the children had seen on trash had been about and Laura told her World War Two. "I thought so," said Kay. "I suppose it was silly of me ever to think I could shield them from the concept of war forever. I *am* silly sometimes. Whatever must you think of me."

"I was never interested in war," said Laura. "I always thought that that was the main difference between boys and girls."

"You know, you have a point there. And sometimes it makes me wonder. If we'd had women presidents instead of men presidents all these years I kind of doubt we'd be in Vietnam. Don't you think so, Martin?" He had just brought Sarah downstairs on his back. "Don't you feel women have a better understanding of peace?"

"When women smile," he said, dropping Sarah to the floor, "the whole world smiles with them."

Sarah would not come to the table. She insisted on having her food brought to her at her easel. She had gone to the Thinking Room of her own accord after her father had left and now had decided to finish her sketch. It was a tremendously good sketch for a ten-year-old: the hair and the eyes looked almost real, and although she had shadowed the face so heavily that it was almost all black, she had succeeded in capturing her father's tired, haunted expression. Kay praised the drawing highly before sitting down to eat.

"If you finish it this evening, we'll just put it in an envelope and send it down. Won't Daddy be pleased."

"Don't be so sure," Sarah whimpered. She wiped the last tears from her cheeks and continued working. She was calmer, but her mood had not improved: Laura could tell from the thinness of her lips. Bess didn't look very cheerful either, but Kay's steady smile was contagious and as the dinner progressed, and Martin went through his repertoire of kangaroo jokes (Laura had heard them all before, as Polack jokes) Bess began to smile. And when Martin told the one about the kangaroo who always carried a bucket of spaghetti over one shoulder because two heads were better than one, even Sarah could not help giggling.

"That's better," Martin said, throwing her a pea. "That's the way I like to see you." The pea bounced against the back of the easel and Sarah giggled again. She reached for the red paint on Bess's easel.

"Well! Now that you're all feeling better, Martin and I have something to tell you," said Kay. She reached out clumsily and pulled Martin's head to her shoulder. "Martin and I are planning to sleep together tonight."

"Oh, really?" Bess said, playing with her hair. "In the same bed?"

"Yeah, that's right," said Martin, a bit too loud.

"And what are you going to do in it?" Bess continued. She picked up one of her curls and wound it, very carefully, around her finger.

"Hey, dummy, what do you think I'm going to do? What do *you* do when you're sleeping with your mom?" said Martin.

"I put my arms around her neck. If I feel like it."

"Then I guess that's what I'm going to do."

"I bet you do a lot more than that," said Bess.

"Hey!" He reached across the table and rubbed her hair affectionately. Her head bobbed back and forth.

"Stop doing that. It gives me a headache."

Sarah was still intent on her painting. Nathaniel was busy playing bomber plane with his peas. Kay looked at them nervously, then turned to Martin.

"I feel we owe them a full explanation, don't you?"

"They're your kids, Kay. You do what you like."

She squeezed his hand and, looking at no one in particular, cleared her throat. "Children, when Martin and I go upstairs to the bedroom tonight, we plan to make love."

There was a silence, broken only by a snigger from Sarah. Laura felt uncomfortable, almost as uncomfortable as she had felt upstairs when Kay and Bob had fallen on the bed.

"Does that mean that you're canceling Fairy Tale Hour?" Bess asked finally.

"Of course not, Bess. Of course not! You've read my thoughts, as a matter of fact. I was just going to suggest that we have Fairy Tale Hour right now. You don't mind, do you, Martin? It's something the kids look forward to all week."

"He can read the man parts," Bess said. They all rushed upstairs, even Sarah, who was screaming at the top of her lungs that whoever was last was a rotten egg. Laura got up to clear the table and it was then that she saw what Sarah had done to her painting. There was a dagger—an unfinished dagger—sticking into her father's deeply shaded neck, and little drops of blood dripping out of the left-hand corner of his mouth.

Laura knew from experience how dangerous it was to criticize a child's painting. At Sarah's age she had considered herself a great artist, and the walls of her room had been covered with abstract trees, scenes from ballets she had never seen, sketches of Mediterranean villages, portraits, large murals of shipwrecked sailors riding the waves of a stormy sea. Her last work had been an oil painting in six stages about the passage of a child from her coffin to the gates of heaven. She had seen something like it in a museum in Italy—or was it Spain?—and although her parents had always taken pains to point out that when you died, there were no gates of heaven waiting to receive you, nor was there a soul waiting to be released from your body—although they had always been adamantly opposed to the concept of eternal life, they praised the painting highly. An artist friend of the family called it a masterpiece and it was on his recommendation that she decided to show it off at school.

Perhaps she had presented the oil painting in too self-important a manner; perhaps she shouldn't have told her classmates how good it was before asking for their opinions, but nothing, not even false modesty, would have prepared her for the brutal comments and the laughter. Didn't she realize that wings were attached to an angel's back and not her arms? Hadn't she ever heard that God's beard was white? Why did all the hands look like mittens? Why didn't the legs bend at the knees? That evening Laura took all her paintings off her walls to examine them for defects, and she found defects everywhere. And after that she didn't draw another thing for years and years.

Sarah had often said she wanted to be an artist when she grew up. Although she had also decided to become a professor, an acrobat, a veterinarian, a farmer, and an astronaut, Laura did not want to be the one to disillusion her. She remembered—very vaguely—what it was like to believe that when you grew up, you could be as many things as you liked. And she remembered her terrible disappointment when she realized she would never be a great artist. How one by one the options had faded away: the dreams of becoming an actress, a ballerina, a horsewoman, a member of a royal family. Laura slowly came to see that she was only a normal human being, that in all probability she would become nothing.

Perhaps she could take Sarah aside and explain to her gently that it was mean to stick a dagger into your father's neck, even if it was only a painting. It hurt other people's feelings, created misunderstandings. Nothing good would come of it. If only there was a way to say things without making her think that her painting was bad.

They sounded so happy upstairs in the master bedroom. The intercom crackled with laughter as Kay began to read them their fairy tale. "Once upon a time there was a king with three daughters. They lived in a sumptuous palace in a city where the streets were paved with gold and the hands of the clock on the watchtower were made of diamonds . . ."

If they came downstairs and saw Sarah's picture, the magic atmosphere would be destroyed. Kay would think her daughter was full of hate. It would ruin her day.

Kay would blame herself. She would wonder where she had gone wrong. When she hadn't gone wrong. Nor had Sarah. Sarah was just playing a game. How many times had Laura played that same game as a child? How many times had she painted red spots on her mother's hand while her mother was napping to convince her she was suffering from a mysterious disease? How many times had she put pins in her father's cushion and imitation frogs in his drink? Those were the things you did when you had temper tantrums. It was part of the game to say sorry just in time. The pin was never in the cushion by the time her father sat down with his newspaper, the imitation frog no longer in his drink. Laura had never carried through with any of her revenge plans.

She understood Sarah, but Kay was another question. For no matter how hard she tried, she could not imagine what she saw in this graduate student. He had nothing to commend him by normal standards: There was nothing romantic about his close-set eyes, his ragged blond hair, his way of putting his feet on the table, his chubby white hands. Laura had an aversion for work boots, especially orange ones, and she did not think that overalls were terribly attractive. When Martin wore them he looked like a pear. Of course Laura realized that she was prejudiced. There was nothing wrong with orange work boots, and overalls were so functional. She had spent too many years in Europe among people who gave great importance to what they wore. And when she swept aside her prejudices, when she considered Martin as an idea rather than a person, she could sympathize with Kay, and that, she hoped, was the first step toward understanding her.

Laura had been back in America long enough to know that women had been chained too long to their kitchens. Many women had been pushed into marriage before they had had time to discover themselves, and now they were rebelling against the conventions that had tied them down. That was what Kay was doing. She had a right to find out about herself after all those years of housework and bringing up children.

And Laura did not want her to have any more worries than she already had, so when she had finished clearing the table, and watered the plants, changed the cat litter, stacked the dishes in the dishwasher, she picked up Sarah's painting and threw it into the fire.

6

There was the expected commotion on Monday about the disappearance of the painting. Sarah searched under all the beds and in all the cabinets. She went through the files where Kay kept the children's most promising work but could not find a trace of it until she went through the ashes in the fireplace, which she claimed had the same feel as her painting. When she accused Laura of having thrown it away, Kay suggested that she was letting her imagination run away with her.

"Don't you remember the first day Laura came to play?" Kay said to her, "and even though we didn't give her any instructions about what to throw away and what to keep, she didn't throw a single thing away? She's not a throw-away-type person, Sarah." Sarah was finally forced to agree.

Kay suggested she do another painting just like it, but Sarah didn't seem to want to. So Laura suggested a new plan. Why didn't they do all kinds of paintings for their father, and when he came home for the weekend, he could choose the ones he liked best? Portraits were too easy, Laura told them. They should try something more ambitious. She arranged some plants on the table so that they could do still life; suggested scenes from fairy tales that they could do from their imagination; showed them how to do compositions with squares, circles, and triangles. No matter what they drew, even when Bess drew a crowd of Chinese children none of whom had arms, she praised each painting highly.

Nathaniel was harder to direct than the girls: he was fixated on bomber planes and explosions. When she tried to suggest more peaceful topics like cars and trains, he had them crashing into each other and falling off cliffs. Bess did beautiful work although she rarely finished it: her figures were tiny and crunched together at the bottom of the paper, and her hand always got tired before she finished filling in the sky. But with Sarah there was no problem. She never gave up, never faltered. She had a style of her own and a penchant for vivid colors. Whenever Bess was out of the room, Laura told her that she was the best of all. She had professional talent, Laura told her: a genius that was not to be wasted. Sarah agreed readily. She said she had always known she was something special.

By Thursday Sarah had become a new person. It was a trance Laura remembered well from her own childhood. It was as if— Laura could tell from the hazy, superior look in her eyes—as if Sarah were a fairy godmother preparing to grant other, less fortunate beings' wishes. She was always ready with a kind word for her sister, and when Nathaniel cried because he missed his mother, she would rock him in her arms. She walked about the house as if in a dream.

From the moment Jingle stepped into the house, it was clear that Sarah intended to extend her full mercy.

Jingle was Louella's daughter, the one Bob Pyle had mentioned as having no friends. She was black, with large brown eyes set far apart and a loose Afro the color of mahogany. She was seven years old, the age when children are so perfectly proportioned that they look like dolls. She had only just moved into her mother's apartment in the only apartment house in the neighborhood. For the past two years she had been living with her father in California. Louella had been awarded custody of Jingle, but the father had kidnapped her soon after the divorce.

Louella was the secretary at the Political Science Department. Laura knew her vaguely from the times she had come by to pick up the extra work she did for Bob, now that he was officially on leave from the department. She was nervous, pretty, eager to please. She dressed well but not flamboyantly, and spoke carefully, as if she had once taken elocution lessons. She seemed overawed by the Pyle household. She was always more interested in talking to Kay than Kay was in talking to her. (Her main topics of conversation were film stars and household products and all the other things Kay tended not to discuss.)

When Louella brought her daughter to the Pyles' that Thursday, she was especially nervous. She took Laura aside and told her that she was leaving an extra set of underwear next to Jingle's coat, as Jingle often wet her pants when she got overexcited.

Jingle had brought with her a sackful of toys which she handed out as gifts as soon as she was sure her mother was out of sight. A toy television, a radio, a talking doll, a gold paper crown, another crown studded with glass that looked like diamonds, and a squirt gun.

"You can keep these presents forever as long as you're nice to me," she said.

Bess and Sarah answered that before they were nice to anyone, they had to put them through a series of tests to see if they were really alive.

"I'm alive," said Jingle. "You'll see."

They took her down to Children's Paradise where they made her lie on the billiard table. They then tested her chest with their stethoscope, delved into her ears, examined her eyes with a cracked magnifying glass, moved her legs up and down to make sure that the muscles were in working order. While Bess counted Jingle's pulse, Sarah held her hand over Jingle's heart to make sure it was beating. Throughout the examination Jingle was an ideal patient, except for one moment toward the end when Sarah decided to operate on her brain with a pair of knitting needles "to see what size her brain is." The knitting needles tickled, and Jingle screamed. Fortunately Laura was present when this happened. Although Kay had asked her only to observe and not to intervene, Laura decided that this brain operation was going too far, so she told them that she had already seen an X ray of Jingle's brain and that it was enormous.

"Oh," said Sarah. "Then she passes the examination. Now it's her turn to examine us."

"Ask us any question," Bess told her.

Jingle thought for a while, then asked them if they had any dolls. Bess said yes, and Jingle asked her how many. Bess thought for a long time, and by the time she had decided she couldn't remember how many, Sarah had lost her patience.

"Is that all you care about? Dolls?"

"Of course not," Jingle said.

"Then what do you care about besides dolls."

"Lots of things."

"What do you care about more than anything else?"

"TV," she said. They could hardly believe her. They listened, breathless, to her tales of cowboys and cartoons, Sesame Street and Mr. Rogers. (Mr. Rogers was her uncle, she claimed; never once had he forgotten to greet Jingle personally at the end of his show.) They listened to her tell the story of Lassie, and the Flintstones, and the Three Stooges. When Jingle was sure of her audience, she went on to talk about the enormous television her father had in California. It could close like a cabinet, she said, and if you turned a certain knob you could make the people's faces change from pink to orange to green. It was a huge house, she told them, so huge that all her friends were jealous. They would gather at her door every morning and fight for the privilege of watching cartoons with Jingle. She would choose three friends, a different three each day, and then when the cartoons were over and her father locked her out of the house she would play "Queen for a Day" in the enormous backyard all afternoon. Even though she urged her friends to be "Queen," they always wanted her to be "Queen" because they enjoyed being her "servants."

"What are the rules of the game?" Bess asked.

"One person is Queen, and everybody else has to obey all her orders."

"Well, I hope you know that if we play it in this house, we'll have to take turns being Queen. In this house we're democratic."

"Well, I'll have to be Queen today at least, or you won't know how to play." They agreed with this so they pinned the crown Jingle had brought to her hair and put blankets over the chair they decided would be her throne. Jingle filled the squirt gun with water and showed Nathaniel how to use it. He was to be the guard. Grosvenor was her royal horse and the toilet was the prison.

For the next hour Bess and Sarah crawled back and forth across the room pretending to be a crowd of thousands bearing gifts to the Queen. The game grew tedious as Jingle's regal orders disintegrated into hysterical screams. "This is not a jewel!" she would shriek when they bowed down before her, in their hands a pillow with a sock on it, "this is not a jewel, it's a sock! Go get me a jewel before sundown or I'll chop your head off!"

Nathaniel soon got bored. He started shouting that there were bomber planes at the edge of the sky, and when no one paid him any attention he started squirting water into Grosvenor's eyes.

Grosvenor went crazy. He tried to pull the blankets off the throne. Jingle hit him with her wand and he tried to tear off the tattered robe that was supposed to be her gown. Jingle fell on top of the dog. Nathaniel, who had been clinging to Grosvenor's tail, fell on top of her. The crown fell under the dog, and by the time

Jingle recovered it, it was dented. "You're fired!" Jingle screamed. "What kind of guard do you think you are? You'll pay for this! You'll pay for every single jewel in my crown. Servants, take him away. Throw him into prison."

"But it was just an accident," Bess protested.

"You heard me! I'm the Queen and you're my servants! You have to obey me or I'll have your heads chopped off."

"That's not democratic," Bess told her.

"It's the rules of the game. I told you that at the beginning and . . . ouch!" Nathaniel had bitten her leg. She screamed and started hopping around the room.

"Nathaniel! Shame on you. Why did you do that to our new friend?"

"Because. I feel I hate her."

"That's a terrible thing to say. Maybe you should go to prison after all."

"Nathaniel's not going to prison," he said firmly. "It stinks in there."

"Well, if you don't go in there then I'm taking you to the Thinking Room."

"No," he whimpered.

"Yes," Bess said. When she took his hand, he did not offer any resistance, but halfway up the stairs he put his other hand in his mouth and started to moan. Laura couldn't stand to see his eyes so full of fear. So after Bess had returned and Jingle had reestablished herself on the throne and the other two had resumed their ritual crawling across the floor with gifts for the Queen, and after Jingle shrieked, "That's not a jewel, that's a doll's leg!", Laura went upstairs to find Nathaniel.

The Thinking Room was a closet. It was the only room in the house without an intercom. It had been fitted out with blankets and furry cushions and, although there was no lock on the door (only some grooves for a padlock), it was difficult to open and close. When Laura finally managed to open it, she found Nathaniel huddled in the corner, his thumb in his mouth. "Why don't you come downstairs and I'll make you some hot chocolate?" she said. He didn't answer. He just stared. "Well, if you want to stay in there, it's up to you. Wouldn't you like the light on? It's a bit dark in here." She fumbled for the switch and when she found it, no light went on. Looking up, she saw that the bulb, if there ever had been one, had been removed from the socket. Nathaniel whimpered and buried his face in the cushions. She left the door ajar but, going down the stairs, she heard it slam shut.

Kay was in the kitchen. She was walking around with the telephone receiver wedged between her shoulder and her ear, watering the plants. "Hello!" she cried, putting her hand over the receiver. "How are Jingle and the girls faring?"

"They're all right. Nathaniel's in the Thinking Room. He got bored with their game because it was a girl's game so he started acting up."

"That's silly of them. But how about the girls? Have they been showing any signs of prejudice?"

"Not really," Laura said.

"That's wonderful. How do you feel about her yourself?"

Laura thought before answering. She was going to say that she found Jingle immature but then she realized that that would sound prejudiced so instead she said that Jingle was a wonderful person who needed friends.

"Good. I trust your instincts. How about if I arrange for her to come and play on a semipermanent basis?"

"It's fine with me."

Sighing, Kay put down the phone and dialed again. There was no answer on the other end. "Can you imagine?" she told Laura, "some of my data doesn't fit in with my central thesis. I can't imagine what I'm going to do." She smiled and gave Laura a big wink and started to say something else but Laura couldn't hear her because Jingle had started to scream.

"That's not myrrh! That's a plastic cup!"

MOTHER'S HELPER

Kay's eyes were bloodshot with rings underneath that were so dark that they almost looked like bruises.

And when Jingle acted up during Queen for a Day the following afternoon, Laura controlled her temper by telling herself about Jingle's underprivileged background. According to Kay, Jingle's father had locked her out of the house every afternoon, and her mother slapped her at the slightest provocation. She had done so in front of the Pyle children the evening before when Jingle refused to put on her coat and go home. "And if you don't come right this minute, you'll get no dessert!" she had said. Jingle obviously had very few friends. That was why she found it difficult to cooperate and take turns. She loved playing Queen but refused to take orders as a servant.

Granted, some of Sarah's orders were ridiculous. Jingle could not have been expected to stand on her head for an hour or train Grosvenor to do somersaults, and certainly Sarah's suggestion that she unbutton her dress so that they could see what color her nipples were was offensive. Laura got them upstairs for their afternoon hot chocolate just in time. Sarah was still officially Queen—she was wearing a pink chiffon nightgown and Jingle's crown—but she agreed not to give any more orders until Jingle had calmed down.

Instead they talked about careers. Bess said she was going to be a nurse. Jingle said she was going to be a dancer. After much coaxing, Sarah confessed that she was going to be an artist.

"But anybody can do that," Jingle said.

"Not things like I can do."

"Anybody can draw. We draw all the time in school and there is just nothing to it."

"Nonsense," said Sarah, "you haven't ever seen what a genius can do. And I'm a genius."

"That's a lie," said Jingle.

"Oh no it isn't."

"Well, I don't believe you. You have to prove it before I'll believe you."

"No problem." Laughing haughtily, Sarah went to the drawer under the telephone table and pulled out the paintings she had done for the competition. "This, for example," she said, waving her "Still Life" in the air.

"That's just a bunch of plants," Jingle said.

"That's what you think. And this!" she shouted, showing Jingle her composition of geometrical shapes. "Artists all over the world have tried to do things like this, and I'm the first one to do it perfectly."

"You haven't finished painting it," Jingle said. "Look, there are loads of little white spots near the edges. When I do a drawing, I color everything in and when I'm finished, there isn't a single white spot."

"They're there on purpose!" Sarah shouted.

"It's dumb. It isn't a picture of anything."

"You're just ignorant. I bet you don't even know how to read," Sarah sneered.

"I bet *you* don't!" Jingle shouted.

"If you don't like my paintings you can leave the house."

"That's fine with me! I hate this house anyway! It's dumb! It doesn't even have a color TV!"

"Your house is underprivileged!" Sarah said.

"Sarah!" Bess said, "Mommy said that we weren't supposed to tell her that. She's not supposed to know!"

"I don't care what Mommy told us," Sarah said, sticking her chin in the air.

"And *I'm* going to tell *my* mother that I hate you!" Jingle sobbed.

"You know, Sarah," Bess said, "I feel you're being very mean. Jingle is supposed to come here on a semipermanent basis. All the time, that means. Don't you remember? Mommy told us this morning."

"She's not the only one in the family who has a vote! Wait until I tell Daddy about how horrible Jingle is. Then she'll never be allowed to come back!" Sarah picked up all her drawings, put them back into the drawer, and went downstairs.

"My father's stronger than your father!" Jingle screamed. She pounded her fists on the table.

"Oh, Jingle, don't cry," Bess said, stroking Jingle's hair. "Sarah has a bad temper, so don't you pay any attention to her. Anyway I'm the one you're supposed to be friends with. We're both the same age." She motioned to Laura to leave the room. Laura was glad for the opportunity to go downstairs and comfort Sarah.

She expected to find her crying or at least upset about the criticism of her paintings, but instead Sarah was reading on her bed, humming to herself as if nothing had happened.

"I hope you're not disturbed," Laura said.

"Of course not. Jingle's an idiot."

"I want you to know that I consider you a genius. So please don't give up."

"I know I'm a genius. I don't need you to tell me."

"But I think your father won't agree to banish Jingle. He'll probably ask you to bear with her."

"If I'm a genius," Sarah said, giving Laura her snakiest smile—and Laura could see that she still had that hazy, superior look in her eyes—"if I'm a genius, I don't have to bear with anybody if I don't want to. And that includes you."

Laura's feelings were very hurt. After all the things I've done for her, she said to herself. All Friday night, at the parties; all Saturday, at the hockey game that she did not understand; all Saturday night, which she spent riding around on a motorcycle with a boy from a neighboring dorm whom she hardly knew, she thought about how no one understood her. She had tried to help Sarah, but Sarah didn't care. Sarah had thrown a book at her as one would throw a stick at a barking dog. "Get out of my room," she had shouted. It was hard to believe.

Weekends were hard to live through if you stayed in the dorm, especially if you were depressed. And of all the meals of the week Sunday brunch was the worst. All those ugly people in their bathrobes, discussing Kant as if he were a next-door neighbor; the social habits of apes; the article on page forty-two of the Sunday *Times.* "And what do *you* think, Laura? You've been very quiet today." There was always one person at each table who played the professor. And then the food: this week it was green eggs and ham for the fourth Sunday in a row. The eggs were made from some sort of powder and if you didn't eat them right away they turned green at the edges.

She was still in low spirits when she went to the Pyles' in the middle of the afternoon.

There were two new announcements on the bulletin board: "I vow not to even look at my thesis until Bob leaves for Washington, and to devote my whole afternoon to fun and games. Signed, Kay" and, in the father's handwriting, "After a deep discussion with the family I now understand that Jingle is a good person inside and I must try to be as friendly as possible when she comes to play. Signed, Sarah."

Martin's slippers and pajamas were still where they had been all week, lying in a heap at the foot of the bed in the master bedroom. The father's suitcase was in his study and next to the sofa, which had been slept in, was an empty bottle of whiskey and a glass. Laura wondered if the father resented being deprived of his own bed. But when she looked out the window at the backyard where they all were, she saw no signs of discontent. Bess and Nathaniel were on the swings, and Sarah was pushing them. Martin, Kay, and Bob were standing among the icy mounds that had once been snowmen, holding hands. Their cheeks were rosy and they were all smiling.

They came inside just as Laura was getting ready to mop the

kitchen floor, so she had to take all the chairs off the table again and throw away the water in the bucket. "Oh, you shouldn't have done that," Kay told her. "You could have used that water later."

"Waste not, want not," Martin said. She felt like hitting him with the mop, but instead she put it outside on the porch. Then she made a gigantic pot of steaming tea as Kay had requested.

Sarah was sitting on her father's lap. They were going through a catalog to choose a paint color for her walls. Martin, Kay, and Bess were sitting at the other end of the table playing Snakes and Ladders. When Kay invited Laura to sit down and pour herself a cup of tea, she sat down next to Martin, so that she was as far away from Sarah as she could be.

"We'll probably have to hire a carpenter," Bob Pyle was saying, "if you want your walls right away."

"I want you to do them," Sarah said.

"Well, it's conceivable that I might be able to, Sarah. We'll have to wait and see how Washington shapes up."

"I want to have them as soon as possible. Like the end of the week."

Bob Pyle laughed. "Even if I stayed here all week, which is out of the question, I doubt if they'd be done by then. We have to find the right kind of plywood, and the paint, and the material for the door. Rome wasn't built in a day."

"What's Rome, Daddy?"

"Oh, it was the capital of a great empire. The first republic, as a matter of fact."

"What's a capital?"

"You should know that. A capital is the center of a government. Like Washington. Of course there are many differences between Rome and Washington. For example, although Rome started out with an elected executive, they ended up having emperors instead. So it wasn't really a democracy as we understand the term."

"You know," said Kay, shaking the dice, "come to think of it, Washington is getting more like Rome every day."

"Kay!" Bob almost shouted, and his face turned red. When he spoke again it was in a lower voice. "I would like you to take that back."

"No offense to you, darling. I was only thinking aloud."

"Well, let me tell you, it isn't easy to work for a government you don't approve of, but in my opinion our country needs good men down there more than ever before. To check their baser drives, to make sure . . ."

"Oh, Bob, I was just *teasing.*" She got up and went over to hug him. "Try and relax, darling. This new project has gotten you all jumpy. More tea?" she said, going to the stove. She looked out of the window. "Oh, dear," she said. "This pane is cracked."

"Jingle did that," Bess explained. "She didn't mean to. We were playing catch and the ball hit the window."

"Oh, dear. Oh, dear."

"I still hate Jingle," Sarah said. "And to tell you the truth I don't know how I'm going to be able to keep that vow."

"Why do you hate her, Sarah?" Bob Pyle asked. "Because she's black?"

"Of course not. Anyway she's brown. I hate Jingle because she's stupid."

"You've known her for less than a week. How can you be so terribly sure she's as bad as you say?"

"I can tell."

"Well, I'll tell you one thing, Sarah, and that is, I expect you to keep your word and be nice to her."

"And what will you do to me if I'm mean?"

"I'll be very disappointed in you," Bob Pyle said.

"All right. Maybe I'll try to be nice to that girl. And maybe I won't. Does that satisfy you?"

"All I can say is that I hope you keep to your vow. For your own peace of mind, if nothing else."

"Artists don't need to have peace of mind. Not great ones like me, anyway."

"Who told you that?"

"Laura."

"Laura, did you say that?"

Laura had only said that about Rembrandt and a few other painters but before she could explain, Sarah said, "So you see? I know what I'm talking about."

"I don't know about that," Bob Pyle said. "I have the feeling that even great artists would be miserable all the time if they made vows and failed to live up to them."

"How would you know?" Sarah said. "You're not a great artist."

"That's true, certainly."

"Do you think I'm a great artist?" Sarah asked.

"I feel you do wonderful work, if that's what you mean."

"Well then, why haven't you asked to see the things I did this week?"

"Oh, my goodness, yes!" Kay cried, jumping to her feet. "How could I forget? Bob, she's been doing the most wonderful things this week and she wants you to look at them and choose one for your hotel room." She took the paintings out of the drawer. "I've had them here ever since you got back on Friday, but somehow it just slipped my mind."

"What vivid colors," Bob said over and over again as he leafed through the paintings. "Splendid. Sensational. Hmmm. Just wonderful. Sensational. I'm very proud of you, Sarah." His face didn't show the slightest enthusiasm.

"Then choose one," Sarah said.

"It's almost impossible to honor one of these wonderful paintings over another. Why don't you help me choose?"

"No."

"Then how about this beautiful one of the plants on the kitchen table?" Kay suggested. "Wouldn't it do wonders to that grim hotel room, don't you think?"

"You're right, Kay, it would. Yes. This is the one I'd like to take down with me, Sarah, if it's all right with you."

"Is it your favorite?"

"I think it is," Bob Pyle said, nodding solemnly.

"You're absolutely sure?"

"Absolutely. I am surer every minute."

"Good," she said, and standing up, she ripped the painting in two. Then she ripped each half into three pieces, and each of these she ripped in half, and soon the painting was nothing more than a pile of flakes.

Kay gasped. "Sarah, whatever possessed you to . . . ?"

"That's enough, Kay," said the father grimly. "I'll handle this. Sarah, I want you to look at me. Why did you ruin your painting?"

"Because!" she shrieked, "I *felt* like it!" Laughing hysterically, she picked up the little bits of paper and threw them into the air, like confetti.

"It wasn't very kind," said her father, "to me."

"Are you angry?" Sarah asked.

Bob Pyle's face was a mask. His sad brown eyes rolled back and forth, like puppet eyes. "Of course not, Sarah. I'm just a bit surprised."

"So what are you going to do about it?"

"There is nothing I *can* do, is there?"

"I bet you want to hit me."

"No, Sarah, I don't. As you know I am against all forms of violence."

"Still?" she said, kicking the bits of paper around the floor.

"Well, I might as well admit it," he said, sighing heavily. "Yes, Sarah, I am a bit hurt. But whatever happens I want you to know I won't hold it against you. You are angry about something. But it will pass. I understand your anger, Sarah, I honestly do."

"How could you?" she screamed. "How could you?" Bob Pyle sighed and left the kitchen. Martin suggested that it might be a good idea if they moved their game of Snakes and Ladders to the living room, so that Laura could get back to her mopping. Bess and Kay picked up the board and the cards and the little plastic men and followed Martin out. When there was no one left in the room but Laura—and what did she matter, Laura said to herself, she might as well have been invisible—Sarah knelt down on the floor and tried to put the pieces of her painting together. When she realized she couldn't, she began to cry.

7

Bess was going through a feminine stage. She said she didn't know why. Ever since Jingle had been coming to play on a semipermanent basis, she had developed a great interest in dancing. She wanted to be a ballerina. Kay didn't quite approve. She seemed to think it was a bad sign. When Bess asked if she could join Jingle's Saturday morning ballet class, Kay suggested other, more rewarding activities: horseriding, swimming, judo. Even karate would be more relevant, despite its slightly warlike character. But when Bess found out what karate was, she said she didn't want to be relevant, just pretty.

It was Laura who had suggested it was just a stage and Kay who had refined the term. Bess was in the room at the time and she liked the sound of it. Feminine stage. She was going through a feminine stage. Over the next few days she used this as an excuse for almost everything: her crying fits, her fear of heights, her sudden and very premature desire for a training bra, her aversion for uncooked vegetables and her refusal to do any arithmetic at school. Kay was frankly alarmed. She had often said that children should be allowed to pursue whatever course they wanted, so long as it did not cause anyone any harm, but she also felt she had a duty to protect her children from damaging influences. Not that ballet was a damaging influence, she explained to Laura. As an art it allowed women more freedom of expression than any other. Especially modern ballet. But Bess was interested in ballet for the wrong reasons, Kay felt. She was interested in the glamor, the costumes, the fairy-tale aspect of ballet. And since Bess was falling into the stereotype of the woman as a delicate, mindless weakling, Kay wanted to keep her away from anything that might reinforce this stereotype. At least for the time being.

Kay confessed that she had always found something frivolous about a career in dancing. She had never wanted to study dance herself. If she had, her parents, being puritan in outlook, would certainly have objected. There were so many other more important things in life, and when it came to sports, Kay had always been a tomboy. She was sure that all girls were tomboys at heart.

This business with dolls and dollhouses and cookery lessons was just a hoax to make girls feel different from boys: inherently inferior. "I'm sure Laura was a tomboy," Kay said when Bess confessed that she wasn't. Actually, Laura had also wanted to be a ballerina when she was Bess's age. (Her dreams of romance and glory were abruptly terminated halfway through her fifth lesson, when the ballet mistress asked her to kindly leave the building— her mother had forgotten to pay the fees.) And she had never had the courage to be a tomboy: she had never done a flip on a trampoline, had given up climbing trees when her mother told her about a distant relation who had broken her arm that way, had once walked down a four-mile ski slope after panicking near the top and sending the skis down on their own. After twelve years of trying, she was still not able to stand on her head. But she went along with Kay and pretended that, deep inside, she was a tomboy.

"You see, Bess?" Kay said. "And I'm sure Laura never wanted to become a ballerina either."

Bess pouted. "Yes, she did."

"But she changed her mind, didn't she? Otherwise she'd never have gotten into college. Do you realize that if you become a professional ballerina, you won't ever be able to go to college?"

"I'm not sure I want to," Bess said.

"But of course you do, darling. You'll have to, if you want to have a fully developed mind."

"I'm not sure I want to have a fully developed mind."

"But of course you do. How can you expect to cope in the world of today if you don't develop your mind to the fullest?"

"To tell you the truth," Bess said, "I'm not so sure I have a mind."

"Whatever made you think that?"

"Sarah told me."

"Dear me. What exactly did she say?"

"It's not what she said, it's what she did. She took a picture of my brain with her camera and there was nothing there."

"Dear me, that was inconsiderate of her. Of course you realize that it was all a game."

"It wasn't a game. It was true."

"You can't take pictures of brains with that Brownie camera. I hope you know that."

"Oh yes you can. Laura said so. Laura even saw a picture of Jingle's brain and she said it was enormous."

"Oh, did you, Laura?" Kay turned around and tried to smile. "When was this?" Every story Laura told had a way of getting back to her. Kay usually dismissed them by saying that Laura's imagination had run away with her again. "My, what a vivid imagination you have," she would say. But some things were more difficult to explain away than others.

Laura had told the children the lie about the X ray of Jingle's brain because she didn't want Sarah to operate on Jingle's brain

— 76 —

with knitting needles. But to bring this episode up now would only complicate matters. Kay would wonder why it was that Sarah wanted to operate on Jingle's brain and draw all sorts of conclusions about Sarah's latent racist tendencies. It was easier, as usual, to tell another lie.

"Oh, it was an X ray," Laura told Kay, "an X ray of Jingle's teeth."

Kay was satisfied by this explanation, but Bess was puzzled. Later, when Kay had left for her office, Laura had to make the lie more elaborate.

"You know how you can tell a horse's age from his teeth?" she said. "Well, with humans you can tell a lot more."

"No, you can't," Bess said. "You can only tell how many cavities he has."

"Yes, but the cavities tell a story. By looking at the cavities, you can find out how many brain cells the human has. And you can find out all about his life, just like you can tell about his future from the palms of his hands."

That night, when Kay came home from her office, Bess asked her if she could read her cavities and tell her her future. The whole fabrication about teeth and the things you could learn from them came out into the open. Kay gave Laura a very strange look. She tried to explain that it was impossible to divine someone's future from her cavities, but when Bess began to cry, she reluctantly peered into her daughter's mouth. "I see a long life with a rewarding career," she said slowly. "Not a career as a ballerina. Something more serious, more rewarding. A job in which you help many helpless children. Hey, maybe this means UNESCO. How exciting that would be, don't you think?"

Bess often told Jingle that her mother had one wrinkle on her forehead for every starving child in India. Nineteen and a half at the last count, she would say: ten girls, nine boys, and one cripple. After Kay's cavity reading, Bess's story became more elaborate. When Bess grew up and Sarah was studying to become a monster in the university, her mother was going to take her to India. The two of them would help the starving children there. Kay would sing. She would sing until all the children were happy and fat and there were no more wrinkles on her forehead. And Bess would dance. The kindest ballerina in the world: she would dance on every stage in the country and, when she finally found that cripple, she would adopt it. That was Bess's future. It was written on the silver in her teeth that she would become the most serious, most rewarding ballerina that had ever worked in India for UNESCO.

Jingle listened to Bess's UNESCO fantasies with an awe verging on horror, her mouth wide open, her large brown eyes almost popping out of her head. Then she would tell her own stories. Despite the obvious exaggerations and her preoccupation with the number "thousand" (her mother had a thousand dresses, her father had a thousand cars, wherever she lived she had a thousand friends) Jingle's stories had a pathetic ring of truth. Because it was so obvious that she had spent most of her life alone.

But when she danced, you could not feel sorry for her, because she was magnificent. There was nothing pathetic about the way she twirled, leaped, swayed, and used her hands to express the curves and rhythms of the symphonies, violin solos, and folk music that Laura would play for them on the stereo. When Jingle danced, she took command.

She told Laura that she had only been taking ballet lessons since the beginning of the year, a few days after her mother had appeared in front of her house in California in a big black car and taken her to Massachusetts. She had been very scared when her mother appeared because she had almost forgotten what she looked like. Her mother didn't even let her say good-bye. She had been in the backyard at the time. The sun was going down, which meant that her father would unlock the back door at any moment, but her mother wouldn't wait. She just took her away, and for the first few days Jingle thought her mother was a monster. Then one day her mother came home with a pair of ballet shoes and a tutu. "Baby, you have natural rhythm just like me," she had told Jingle, "so you're going to have lessons."

Of course Jingle had the advantage with her beautiful leather ballet shoes, her leotards, her tutu. Bess had to dance in her underwear, and no matter how hard she tried, she could not duplicate Jingle's grace. When she held her arms over her head her fists were clenched; of the ten basic positions she could only do three. Jingle was not an ideal teacher: she claimed that a true dancer could jump and land on her toes even if she was barefoot. Kay saw Bess try this one evening, and it was the sight of her daughter landing on her clenched toes, falling on her knees, and hitting her head on the bookcase that made her decide to allow Bess to go to a ballet lesson.

Laura's roommate Beryl had become even gloomier now that she had lost her virginity. She had not gotten around to taking any precautions so she blamed her continuing depression on the possibility that she was pregnant, although it also depressed her that all three of her sexual relationships to date had failed to develop into meaningful relationships. That weekend a boy she had dated on a Platonic level in high school was coming up for a visit, and after much pondering, Beryl decided that the whole thing would work out better if Laura kept out of the way.

Laura was glad to comply with Beryl's wishes. She had already spent one night in her room when Beryl had had a friend to visit. It was one of the times when a sexual relationship had failed to develop into a meaningful one. The sexual part of the friendship had been very loud, the grunts unbearable, the hours of futile conversation during which they tried to understand each other's hang-ups even worse. Mothers, fathers, sibling rivalries, dreams, repressed traumas, recurring nightmares, fantasies about sliding down banisters that were actually razors—they discussed everything, but despite the collective wisdom of Freud and Jung and Skinner and Erikson and Laing and Reich and all the other people

Laura was supposed to have read for her psychology course but hadn't, they were not able to reach an agreement. The misunderstanding persisted. All night Beryl fought off her friend's advances on the top bunk. "I've had enough, I've had enough," she kept saying, and he kept answering, "But I haven't." The friend was rather obese and every time he moved, Laura thought the top bunk was going to fall on top of her.

She was not eager to relive the experience. When Kay suggested that she spend Friday night in the Pyle house so that she and Martin could go to their respective meetings, she jumped at the opportunity. Bob Pyle called at the last minute to say that he would not be able to make it up that weekend. So Laura would be able to sleep on the couch in his study. Since she was the one who would be taking Bess to her ballet class early Saturday morning, it was all very convenient.

Bess was in tears at dinner because Kay had forgotten to buy her a leotard. She said she didn't want to go to her lesson in her underwear. Kay said not to worry. In the morning they would work something out. Nathaniel threw his food on the floor. He was angry at Martin although Laura could not tell why. Most of the argument had taken place upstairs during Bath Hour and the only thing Laura had heard was Nathaniel screaming that it was his turn. When he bit Martin at the dinner table, Kay took him onto her lap and told him she would try and work out some sort of compromise.

Of the three children, only Sarah was unperturbed. She had taken to reading books recently after years of ignoring them. Her teachers at the open school were apparently very pleased. In their note to Kay that was displayed on the bulletin board, they said that this proved how much better it was to wait for a child to develop at her own pace. A few months earlier she had been having difficulty with the most basic of first grade texts. Now she was reading horse books. *My Friend Flicka* was the book she was reading at the dinner table and it engrossed her completely. When Nathaniel threw his plate on the floor, she only looked up for a second, and her smile was the smile of a very superior, very disgusted onlooker.

Laura got them all to bed early by putting the clock four hours ahead. They thought it was midnight. She found a tape of Kay singing Christmas carols, which she played over the intercom when she had finished faking Kay's and Martin's footsteps. Then, when she was sure they were thoroughly convinced, she settled down in the living room to listen to a Cat Stevens record.

The songs were all about undeserved heartaches, faithful but abandoned lovers, sad ballads sung in a sad voice that tried not to crack but always did. During the three months that Stavros had failed to write to her following her confessional letter about the boy she had had a crush on who had rejected her, these songs had made her occasional fits of grief bearable. Her heartache was definitely deserved and, although she regarded herself as an abandoned lover, she had certainly not been a faithful one. Even so, she identified with Cat Stevens. Melancholy could be beautiful, as beautiful as it sounded. Sadness was just a part of life. Cat Stevens had hopes for the future and so did she: one day Stavros would forgive her and all would be well.

But that night as she lay among the pillows in the living room listening to the same heartrending songs, her emotions were complicated by the fact that he had finally forgiven her. When she read in his letter that things were finally back to normal—"Do not fear, we will meet in Paris this July as planned"—she found to her surprise that she was disappointed.

Earlier in the year his references to her as "my little jewel" and "the one precious thing in my life," the house they would buy in later life, the children she would bear, the wonderful Paris fashions she would wear—"We will go to the openings together"—all these things had pleased her, but now they seemed tasteless. Of course they had made these plans together, and Laura was not the type of person to go back on a promise. But when she reread the last sentence in the letter: "Do not worry, my little one, no matter what happens I shall always be at your side," she felt trapped. She found herself hoping that he would be involved in a car crash so that she could be free once again: free to be as sad as she wanted whenever she wanted, free to indulge herself, free to cry without feeling guilty, free to stay away from people who thought she was a jewel, a free woman totally responsible for every tragedy that befell her.

She realized how nasty it was of her to wish that Stavros would conveniently eliminate himself. After all, he had been kind to her. She took his photograph out of her pocket so as to conjure up some feelings of affection, but the eyes looked too closely set, the nose too large, the lips too thick, the hair too wiry, the pattern of his shirt too loud for comfort. How would she ever be able to face her friends if her children looked like him? When she went upstairs and climbed between the sheets on the couch in the father's study, she had a vision of the nursery: three cribs, three simian infants snoring in their sleep, their thick lips parted, their bushy eyebrows moist, their large ears pointed like the ears on the gnome dolls her parents had once brought her as presents from Germany.

She stared at the heavy volumes on the opposite wall and the darkened pictures of Bob Pyle standing on a mountain, Bob Pyle holding a fish, Bob Pyle reading in a tropical setting with his back to the sea, Bob Pyle shaking hands with African dignitaries, trying to smile and as usual not succeeding. She knew these pictures by heart, so instead of counting sheep, she supplied the pictures with the details that the faint light of the streetlamp could not provide.

Finally Kay and Martin came home. They crept up the stairs and when they got to the bedroom they began to laugh. Fortunately the intercom was not on, so their voices did not disturb her. All they did was lull her to sleep. She woke up several times during the night and was soothed by the sound of Martin snoring.

Then suddenly an alarm went off in the parents' bedroom. The intercom clicked on. "Calling Nathaniel. Calling Nathaniel," Kay announced in what Laura was sure she intended to be a soft voice.

"This is Mother. You can come up now if you wish. It's six o'clock."

For the next few minutes Laura listened to Kay's heavy breathing and Martin's amplified snores. She saw Nathaniel's small shape creep past her door and stop in front of the master bedroom. "Come in! Come in!" Kay cried. Laura could hear two voices, one melodious and real, the other husky, metallic, and very loud. "Come in, Nathaniel," said the two voices. "If you stand out there, I'm sure you'll get cold."

"Nathaniel doesn't think he wants to come in," said Nathaniel.

"No, Nathaniel, *I* don't want to."

"You come downstairs to my bed, Mommy."

"Why should I do that, my little chickadee?"

"You come down or else."

"Or else what?"

"Or else I'll bomb you."

"Nathaniel! What a mean thing to say."

"I feel angry," Nathaniel said.

"Why do you feel angry?"

"Because I want to sleep with you and I don't want to sleep with that lump there and I don't want you to sleep with that lump because I want to have the *whole bed* just for you and me."

"But darling, I feel you're being silly. Come in here and sleep with us. Martin's asleep and you can pretend he's not even here."

"Oh, no. If I stay here then Martin has to go sleep somewhere else."

"But why?"

"Because I want to have the whole bed just for you and me. You tell that lump to go away right now or I'll bomb you."

Martin rolled over and groaned. "Martin," Kay whispered, softly she thought, but the whisper echoed in every room. "Nathaniel is going through a bit of a crisis. He has suggested that you sleep somewhere else for the rest of the morning. Do you mind?"

"What?"

"Would you mind sleeping somewhere else for the rest of the morning? Nathaniel feels he wants to sleep with me alone for a change."

"Yes, goddammit," Martin said in a grumpy voice, "I *would* mind."

"He minds," Kay said cheerfully. "Well, Nathaniel, I guess that's that."

"Oh no it isn't. I'm going to bomb you."

"Nathaniel, please!"

"And shoot you!"

"Please!"

"And stab you with a knife!"

There was a silence, followed by a deep, reverberating sigh. "Martin, I'm afraid I'll have to insist on your leaving us for a while. Nathaniel's in a terrible state and I feel we should go along with him. Couldn't you go away for just an hour? Then you can come back and I'll take Nathaniel downstairs."

"Oh, Oedipus!" shouted Martin as he got out of bed. "Oh, Oedipus, I love you. You've done it again, boy, you've done it again."

"Hey," Kay said tenderly, "you've forgotten your slippers. They're over here."

"They're over there, are they? Well, how about that."

"I'll set the alarm for seven. All right?"

"Fine!" he shouted. He shuffled out of the bedroom and into the study where Laura was trying to sleep. Still grumbling to himself, he pulled off her covers and sat down on her back. Laura screamed.

"Jesus fucking Christ!" He was out of the room before she had time to collect her nerves and apologize.

"Kay calling. Kay calling," said the intercom. "Is everything all right?"

"Yes," said Laura. "It was just an accident."

"Were those Martin's feet going downstairs or were they yours?"

"His."

MOTHER'S HELPER

"Do you think he can hear me?"

"I don't know."

"Well, I'll say it anyway, just in case. This is Kay to Martin. Kay to Martin, saying many thanks and sweet dreams. And I've set the alarm for seven ten precisely so that Nathaniel gets his full hour."

"I want more than a full hour," said Nathaniel. The intercom clicked off. Their voices became muffled. Laura drifted off to sleep. When the alarm rang at seven ten, Laura woke up again. She heard Kay go downstairs with Nathaniel and then come up again. A few minutes later there was a loud yawn in the living room, some sleepy muttering as Martin made his way up the stairs, the sound of creaking springs as he fell onto the bed.

Outside the sky was growing light. A melancholy blue, that was the name of the color. The leafless branches outside the window looked like spiderwebs. Laura rose and went to the window. It was much too late to think of going back to sleep, much too empty in the streets below to feel happy. The parked station wagons, the rickety fence, the brown snow in the backyard that had slowly receded to reveal dead grass. If this were the whole world, Laura said to herself, I would feel like dying.

And while she sat looking at the sun rise between two houses and then disappear under a bank of clouds, they had a fight. Martin swore and Kay reproached him, and when their voices grew loud enough for Laura to hear what they were saying, she went downstairs to the kitchen. There was no butter and no bread for toast. She wasn't in the mood for eggs as they were too filling. Instead she ate a gallon of strawberry ice cream that she found in the freezer. She always ate to forget about suicidal thoughts. Food gave her a reason to keep on living. And the plans she made later, about how many breakfasts, lunches, and dinners she would have to skip so as not to get fat, provided her future with a definite structure. If you were in good health there was nothing to look forward to, but if you felt ill—and Laura felt very ill when she finished the ice cream—you could at least look forward to feeling better the next day.

Kay came downstairs with a pile of important-looking files. She looked haggard. The rings under her eyes were more like bruises than ever before. When Laura brought her a cup of instant coffee, she didn't even say thank you, and that was certainly out of character. When Nathaniel came up from Children's Paradise and climbed onto her lap, she moved her chair to make room but didn't look at him and didn't stop reading. "Did he punch you?" Nathaniel asked, holding her chin in his hands.

"No, dear, he didn't."

"Then why is it so black under your eyes?"

"I guess that's from working too hard," she said in an absent-minded voice.

"Are you working too hard, Mommy?"

"I suppose I am."

"Then today Nathaniel will take care of you and Nathaniel won't let you do any work. Okay?"

"I'm afraid that's impossible."

"Why?"

"I have too much work to do."

"Do you want me to make you a strawberry omelet?"

"No, darling. I'm not hungry."

"Why aren't you hungry?"

"I guess I'm too busy to think of food."

"Are you sure?" Nathaniel asked.

"I'm sure."

"Why are you so sure?"

Kay put her head on the table and sighed. She counted to ten. "Climb down, Nathaniel, would you please?" she said a few seconds after she had reached ten. "Perhaps Laura would like one of your delicious strawberry omelets."

Laura gagged. "There aren't any strawberries," she said.

"Then Nathaniel will make Laura a normal one," he said.

"There aren't any eggs," Laura said.

"Oh, really?" said Kay, putting a giant exclamation point next to the paragraph she was reading. "Yesterday there were half a dozen."

"Yes, I know. But Jingle broke them."

"Dear, oh dear. That Jingle's quite a menace."

Laura felt terrible. Jingle had not broken any eggs on Friday. She had broken five mugs but that was an accident. She had fallen down the stairs to Children's Paradise with a tray of refreshments. Later, when Sarah accused her of being as clumsy as a pickaninny (apparently she had picked up the word in one of her horse books), Jingle had crushed a doll's head, but even then it was her own doll.

Laura now felt she should confess this to Kay, but Kay obviously did not want to be disturbed. She was busy writing comments in margins and paid hardly any attention to her son, who had dragged a sleeping bag out of a closet and was writhing around the floor inside it. "Look, Mommy, I'm swimming," he said.

"Yes, I see," she answered without looking up.

"Look. I'm a salmon swimming down the river."

"Salmon swim up rivers, dear, not down."

"Okay, okay. I'll go in the other direction. I'll go up the river, but you'll have to look."

She put down her pen and watched him writhe across the floor. "Very good," she said. "That was wonderful. Now could you swim quietly for a while? I have a tremendous amount of work."

"But I'm not a salmon anymore!" he said.

"What have you become?" Kay yawned.

"I've become a . . . a . . . I've become a . . . testicle."

"No, Nathaniel, you are not a testicle."

"Yes, I am. Nathaniel's a testicle."

"Please try to speak correctly. *I* am a testicle."

"No, you're not!" Nathaniel cried.

"That's not what I meant. What I wanted to explain is that

you're not the testicle. You are the sperm. The sleeping bag is the testicle."

"I'm a sperm! I'm a sperm!" Nathaniel shrieked. He thought for a moment. "What do sperms do?"

"Oh, they swim up vaginal canals in search of an egg. You know that already."

"Where's the canal?"

"Let's see. It's from where you are now to the dishwasher."

"Okay," he said. Diving back into the sleeping bag, he struggled across the kitchen floor making engine noises. When he was halfway to the dishwasher, Martin came downstairs. He went over to Kay and kissed her. "I'm sorry, babes," he said, "I guess I lost my temper."

"That's all right, Martin. So did I."

"Who's that?" Nathaniel said from the confines of the sleeping bag.

"And *who's* that?" Martin knelt down and began to tickle the small shape at the bottom of the sleeping bag. "Is that Nathaniel?"

"No, it isn't!"

"Then who is it?"

"A sperm."

"A sperm, is it? I didn't know that sperms were ticklish." He unzipped the sleeping bag halfway and put in his hand.

"Stop! Stop!" Nathaniel screamed. "You can't come in. You can't come into my testicle, or I'll shoot you."

"*I* didn't know that sperms could shoot."

"Martin, please, don't encourage him," Kay whispered.

"Oh, come on, Kay. We're just playing around. And after all, this is the first gun-toting sperm I've ever met. How do you do, sperm? Glad to meet you."

"I'm not a sperm anymore," said Nathaniel, crawling onto the floor. "I'm Nathaniel. And I'm going to kill you. I'm going to get my gun and kill you, and that's that."

— 88 —

"But you don't have a gun," Martin shouted as Nathaniel ran to the stairs.

"That's what you think. But you're just a stupid lump."

When he was gone, Kay grabbed Martin's hand. "Oh, darling. I feel that something's gone wrong. Don't you?"

"Hey, the little fellow is just a bit confused. It's natural. It will take him a while to get used to me. What do you expect?"

"Anger is something I am capable of handling," Kay sighed. "But all this talk of weapons and killing . . ."

"Ever heard of an Oedipus complex?"

"Martin, I'm a grown woman."

"Well, there you are, that's the whole problem."

"But all this talk of guns."

"Hey, that's natural for a fellow his age. When I was a kid, I played at war, too."

"Things have changed," Kay said. "In those days there was no atom bomb."

"I'm not *that* old," Martin protested.

"We can't even let our children pretend to play war anymore. It's too dangerous."

"Do you see *me* throwing atom bombs all over the place? Now really, there's a limit."

"Please, please, don't be facetious. Help me think of a constructive way to cure Nathaniel."

"Time, baby, time," Martin said. "As soon as he gets used to seeing you hang around with Bob one day and me the next, he'll be fine."

Kay rubbed her eyes. "Then you think the duality of the situation disturbs him."

"Of course it does. It's natural."

"I do wish you would stop equating natural with desirable."

"Listen," Martin said, "stop worrying."

"I can't. I'll have to think up some more positive course of action. Perhaps I should suggest to Bob that he stop coming here for weekends."

"Kay, you surprise me. I thought this was supposed to be a friendly arrangement. Forget your marriage vows: Bob happens to be one of my closest friends. Not to mention my one and only mentor! That wouldn't be too friendly, would it, if you told the poor guy he couldn't even come into his own house!"

"You make it sound as if I didn't contribute to any of the mortgage payments."

"Oh, Jesus," Martin said, falling into a chair, "why did I ever wake up?"

"Oh, dear. I didn't mean to be unkind. I'm just trying to think of a positive course of action for Nathaniel. Perhaps you could talk to him. The two of you alone. Play around with him and try to make friends."

"What do you think I've been doing all these months?"

"Just for me," she pleaded. After a few moments of weighing his head clownishly to either side, he agreed. "Oh, thank you!" she cried, jumping onto his lap. The chair groaned. While they were embracing, Nathaniel came back into the kitchen. He walked slowly to the table, his hands behind his back.

"Okay, you two. Stick 'em up!" He held out Jingle's squirt gun and sprayed them both. "Bang!" he said. "Fall down. You're dead."

Kay started crying. "I try so hard," she said, "I try so hard to please everybody." Martin wrenched the squirt gun out of Nathaniel's hand. By shaking him violently and threatening to knock his head off, Martin was able to get Nathaniel to say that it was Jingle's squirt gun and Jingle who had taught him to say "Stick 'em up."

"That does it," Martin said, throwing Nathaniel his coat and boots. "Put those on over your pajamas and then we're going out for a walk."

"I don't want to!"

"Oh yes you do!" Martin growled. "You and I are going to have a man-to-man talk." He grabbed Nathaniel by the waist and pushed him out the door. "It's time some sense was knocked into your head."

Laura watched them walk together down the path. Before they even reached the gate, Martin changed his manner. He said something so funny that Nathaniel fell on the ground laughing. Kay was blowing her nose so she didn't see. "Oh my, I hope they're not too rough about it."

"I don't think there's any danger of that," Laura said.

"I suppose you're right." She laughed painfully. "Men are so funny sometimes, aren't they?" Without waiting for an answer she got up and went to the refrigerator. "You know, I'm suddenly hungry. How about you? Oh, look," she said. "Here are the eggs. How strange."

"Oh, I forgot. Jingle's mother replaced them," Laura lied.

"Did she? How unnecessary. Gee, I wish she'd be as careful about her love life as she is about things like this."

"What do you mean?"

"I thought you knew," Kay sobbed. "She's constantly being duped by men. And now there's a fellow she thinks she's engaged to, someone she met through us during the summer school program. I haven't mustered up the courage to tell her that he married someone else last week. It's not the first time. I suppose that's why her daughter is so . . . so . . ." She rested her head on the swinging refrigerator door and started crying again. "It was . . . it was . . . Jingle's gun, wasn't it?"

"I guess so," Laura said.

"She's been such a terrible influence on the children, hasn't she," Kay sobbed. Tears rolled down her face.

"Well, I think that with time . . ." Laura said, but then Kay blew her nose.

"You know, I hate to say this, but sometimes I wish that Jingle wasn't black. But since she is, I can't bring myself to ban her. I would never forgive myself for not having given her a second chance." She hobbled back to the table, leaving the refrigerator door open. "Things have gotten so *complicated.* I just don't know what to do. I hope Martin isn't being rough with Nathaniel. It will only make matters worse. It's gotten to the point where I don't know where to turn. And I try so hard to please everyone. I try so hard." She wiped her eyes and blew her nose. Laura closed the refrigerator door.

"Mommy?" Bess shouted over the intercom.

"Yes, dear?"

"I'm ready for my lesson."

"Oh, are you?" Kay said. "How wonderful."

"I've decided not to wear my underwear."

"That's fine with me, dear."

"I'm wearing something fancier."

"Come upstairs so we can see."

Bess ran up the stairs and twirled into the kitchen, her arms curved above her head. She was wearing an evening gown of the postwar period. It was pink, and she had cut the gauze skirt short to make it look like a tutu. But it sagged: the waist hung around her knees, making it difficult for her to walk. In her hair was an assortment of ribbons salvaged from old Christmas presents, and on her feet was a pair of airline slippers that flapped in the air as she bounded across the floor. When she paused to bow she very nearly tripped and fell. "How do I look?" she said breathlessly.

Kay seemed to think she looked fine. But then again she wasn't really looking. It was Laura who insisted that Bess go downstairs and change back into her underwear. Bess was furious. She said she had promised Jingle that she was going to wear the most beautiful ballet dress in the world. In the end they had to make a compromise: a pullover and tights underneath and the postwar evening gown over it. She agreed to take the evening gown off as soon as Jingle had finished admiring it.

MOTHER'S HELPER

The ballet class was being held in the public school down the road. It was supposed to be a very good public school, and Laura had often wondered why Kay, who championed the public school system in letters and telephone conversations (and in the excerpts of her thesis that Laura had glanced at), sent her children to a distant private school instead. From what she had overheard Bess and Sarah say to each other when they watched the hordes of children pour out of the building every day at three fifteen, she gathered that they thought the children who went to the public school were monsters, who beat you up for no reason, and were so mad for riches that they even pried the silver out of your teeth. Halfway to the public school, Bess had an attack of nerves. She was trembling when they went through the swinging doors.

When she saw the cluster of girls in their neat little leotards standing in the middle of the auditorium, she grabbed Laura's hand and said she wanted to go home. But the teacher had already seen them. While she welcomed Bess and tried unsuccessfully to convince her to take off her coat, the cluster of girls started to giggle and point at the frayed pink gauze that dangled around Bess's ankles.

The ballet teacher had a soft, round face and a bun so tight that it made her eyes look slanted. She had the patronizing laugh of a first grade teacher, a melodious tinkle that Laura did not find quite appropriate when Jingle claimed never to have seen Bess before in her life.

"She looks weird," Jingle said, looking anxiously at her classmates for approval, "and I never make friends with any-one who looks weird. The Bess I told you about was someone else."

"Well, I think she looks fine," said the teacher, taking a reluctant Bess to the bar. "And I'm so glad she's come to join our class. And I also think her dress is just the prettiest thing I have ever seen. Wherever did you get it?"

Bess didn't answer. She put her thumb in her mouth.

"If you ask me, though," the teacher continued, "you'll have to take it off to give your legs room to move around in. Don't you think that would be a good idea?"

Bess shook her head. Two of her ribbons fell to the ground. She looked at the girls behind her, all huddled together and snorting, their hands on their mouths. She sank to the floor and the teacher got down on all fours.

"My, you're shy, aren't you? Maybe your friend Jingle can convince you that we're not the monsters you think we are. Jingle? Come over here and help your friend get up."

"She's not my friend," Jingle said.

"I'm not so sure about that myself," said the teacher with a saccharine smile. "And even if she isn't, I think you should come over here and help her." Jingle shook her head. The teacher practically had to drag her over. By now Bess was trembling, but when Jingle finally put her hand out to help Bess up, Bess took the thumb out of her mouth and started to get up. At that point Jingle noticed that the cluster of girls behind her was laughing. So instead of being helpful as Laura was sure she had intended, she kicked Bess in the shins.

Laura gave Jingle a stern lecture before they left. She said that she was very disappointed in her and didn't know how anyone who thought herself a Queen could act so low. She felt she had to say something, for Bess's sake. So that Bess would understand that it was Jingle who had done something wrong, and not think herself abnormal.

Bess didn't say much on the way home. She sucked her thumb and listened to Laura with disbelief as Laura went on and on about similar things that had happened to her as a child. When they got back to the house, she curled up on the living room couch with Nathaniel, who had returned from his walk. Kay was working in the study, unable to give her daughter the sympathy she needed, so Laura decided to postpone her long overdue trip to the library and stay with Bess.

She sat in front of the couch and told her and Nathaniel about every humiliation she had ever experienced in her whole life. But it was like talking to a wall, because neither Bess nor Nathaniel said a thing. They just stared at her.

Bess was regressing, or withdrawing, Laura said to herself. So she illustrated her accounts of humiliating experiences with dramatic gestures, hoping to make them laugh. She began to feel very silly. "I bet you think that everyone hates you," Laura said in a desperate attempt to elicit some response. Bess nodded, her thumb still in her mouth. "Well, that's what I used to think, too, when I was your age. But then when I grew older, I found it wasn't true. It was all in my imagination," Laura said, avoiding their blank gazes. "You see, Bess, it's not only you. I went through a feminine stage, too."

The phone rang. It was Louella, Jingle's mother, calling to apologize for Jingle's "reprehensible" behavior at the ballet class. "I'm making her write a formal apology to poor Bess as soon as we can find a card that's pretty enough," she said, "but if you could let me speak to Kay, I'd like to make my apologies, too."

Laura went upstairs to get Kay to pick up her extension. When she returned to the living room, she found that Nathaniel had crawled onto the floor and was feeling Bess between her legs, which were wide open. Laura didn't want to make them feel guilty but she didn't feel this behavior was completely right, so she tried to distract them with suggestions of exciting games, wonderful stories, and finally, a pink elephant she claimed to see walking down the road in front of the house. Bess and Nathaniel gave each other knowing looks.

"I think we'd better go downstairs, don't you?" Bess said to her brother.

He nodded, his eyes suddenly the eyes of a grown man.

Laura tried to follow them down but when she got to the door to Children's Paradise, she found that they had closed it behind them. She wandered around the kitchen uncertainly, and when she heard Kay coming down the stairs, she started picking up dirty dishes so that it would look like she had something to do.

Kay's eyes were still bloodshot. She stood at the doorway, her hands clasped. "I've just talked to Louella," she said sternly. "She was quite surprised when I thanked her for the eggs."

2
SPRING

8

Over Easter vacation Jingle introduced the children to a terrible new game. It was called Trying to Get Men's Pants Off. Martin was their first victim and although he suffered a few bruises and a black eye in the resulting skirmish, he took the whole thing as a joke. All they were after was attention, he told Laura, and you had to make allowances for Jingle, who was probably going through a crisis stage. It wasn't every day of the week your mother had a nervous breakdown, and it wasn't ever fun.

Kay was not so sure it was a good idea, however, so she launched a campaign against the game. "Trying to Get Men's Pants Off is SILLY" proclaimed the poster she put on the bulletin board, "and it can be DANGEROUS too! Did you know that too much punching in the penis area paralyzes most men?"

Her warnings did not have the desired effect. Martin continued to be attacked. There were several embarrassments: the head of Bob Pyle's department, one of his colleagues from Washington, the postman. The day Dennis was due to start work on Sarah's walls, Kay sat down with the girls for a serious talk.

"Remember Edith?" she said, stroking both her daughters' heads, "that nice student from the Equal Admissions Committee who came with us when we presented the dean with that petition? Well, this fellow who's coming over today is her man friend. Now Edith's a pretty funky lady, but I don't think she'll be happy if she thinks that all you want to do is take his pants off."

"Why not?" Bess asked.

"Well, let's put it this way. I haven't confronted her with this, of course, but she's from way below the Mason-Dixon line and I have the feeling she's a teeny bit conservative."

"You mean . . . you mean she doesn't believe in people being naked?"

"Not really, darlings. I'm sure she enjoys being naked when they're alone. It's just that she doesn't believe in sharing their nakedness with everyone else in the whole wide world."

"If they don't want to share their nakedness," Sarah said, "that means they're selfish."

"Not really, my little chickadee. It just means that they're going through a monogamous stage."

"What's a monogamous stage?"

"It's when you think you can spend your whole life with one man, like Daddy and I used to think we could."

"When do people think that?"

"Oh," said Kay, winking at Laura, "they usually think that when they're in college, or just after, when they're having their first mature relationship. Sometimes they go on thinking so for a long time, too."

"How long?"

"Well, Daddy and I thought so for almost ten years."

"And now what do you think?"

"We think that we love each other very much, but we think that we will love each other even more if we are emotionally and sexually involved with other people at the same time. Like Martin," she said, lifting Bess onto her lap.

"Is that why we can pull Martin's pants down but we are not supposed to pull down this other guy's pants?"

"Oh, my little chickadee! I heartily wish you wouldn't pull down *his* pants either!"

By the time Dennis arrived, they were thoroughly prejudiced against him. He was monogamous and therefore dull. When he asked Sarah if she had any suggestions for her walls, she wouldn't answer him. Laura, on the other hand, took to him immediately. She had a long history of finding "monogamous" people attractive: even Stavros, when she met him, had been in love with someone else.

It was Saturday afternoon. Nathaniel was away being tested by a friend of the family who was doing experiments of aggression displacement for her thesis in child psychology. The object of the experiments was to discourage violent behavior, and Kay had volunteered Nathaniel as a test subject, hoping that this might help him lose interest in bomber planes and guns. According to the schedule on the bulletin board, Laura and the girls were supposed to spend the afternoon washing children's fingerprints off the living room walls. But Laura, who usually enjoyed this type of chore, could not keep her mind on her work. She was relieved when Sarah asked her mother if Louella suffered from hemophilia and Kay decided to take the girls with her when it came time to go change Louella's bandages, so that they could see with their own eyes that the slits on Louella's wrists had indeed clotted. As soon as they were out the door, Laura went down to Children's Paradise to watch Dennis work.

Dennis was Louella's next-door neighbor. It was he who had discovered her bleeding to death in her bathtub and taken her to the hospital. He was tall and fair, wore work boots and overalls. On the back of his jean jacket was a clenched fist in careful red embroidery. He had piercing blue eyes, the kind Laura associated with ranch hands and mountaineers. His gaze was so steady, so unfearing, that even after a morning of dragging plywood from one end of Children's Paradise to the other, he looked as if he had spent his entire life outside fighting the elements. He had a tilted smile. He talked about wood as if it were an idea, something as elusive and changeable as Truth or Beauty, and Laura was not at all surprised to discover that he had a degree in anthropology.

"I have a theory," he told her, "and that is that a house can be one hundred percent functional and intensely personal at the same time. You know what I mean, the total environment. Take these walls I'm putting up. Okay, we all know *why* they're going up, so the kid can get some privacy. So that's the functional part taken care of right there. But what about the personal part? Unless she can *feel* something for those walls, unless she has some sort of emotional or creative involvement with them, she's going to resent them. She's going to see these walls as an *ex*cluding as opposed to an *in*cluding factor. So we've got to think of something to make these walls personal. And *I* thought, since the kid draws, why not paint picture frames on these two sides for the kid to fill in whatever way she likes?"

Dennis had a way of talking eye to eye. No matter how he stood or what he was saying, whether he was leaning against the wall or sitting on the billiard table or crouching on the floor. At first Laura tried not to look back. She tried desperately to concentrate on the little green balls of fuzz on the billiard table and the wrinkles on her hands, the pattern of his shirt and the shape of his collar, but his gaze was as inescapable as a television in a dark room. Soon she lost all shame and stared straight back into his piercing blue eyes, and they told her more than words could ever tell.

When he described his childhood in upstate New York, she could see the house he had lived in. She could see the leaves on the trees in his backyard slowly turning red and yellow and the black water of the lake beyond. When he talked about his college days, she saw him tramping through snowdrifts and playing Frisbee in the quad, studying in the library, adjusting his headband on the steps of an occupied building, bicycling to the Social Sciences Quadrangle, waving absentmindedly to friends.

Dennis had almost as much to say about his girl friend Edith as he did about himself. She was, as he put it, a total woman. She modeled herself on Kay, whom she had met two years previously when Kay was the graduate student delegate from the Social Sciences at a university symposium against the war, and Edith was the undergraduate delegate from the Humanities. Since then they had worked together in a large number of volunteer programs. Dennis told Laura that he and Edith had the perfect relationship. When he described her accomplishments on the campus newspaper, in prisons, at the Rape Center and the Suicide Prevention League, in the Far Eastern Languages Department, on the women's squash team, a thin film covered his eyes. That was when Laura's imagination failed. She just could not see Dennis with another girl.

The Edith in Laura's mental tableaux was faceless and stayed in the background: she was too frail to tramp through snow drifts and too busy to play Frisbee in the quad. The more Dennis talked about her, the less significant she became, and by the time he got around to describing the trip they were going to take to India after Edith's graduation in June, Laura had banished her from the scene altogether. When he described their tentative itinerary, it was Laura she saw picking grapes with him in France—not Edith—and it was Laura shivering under his blanket in a Cretan cave; Laura helping him hitchhike out of Tehran; Laura leaning against his shoulder on the Afghan border; Laura keeping him company in the hospital when, after two exhilarating weeks of exploring Calcutta, he came down with malaria.

The walls of Children's Paradise whirled around and around and were replaced by foreign landscapes. Laura didn't even hear the front door open. Even when Jingle, Bess, and Sarah came rushing down the stairs, their laughter sounded miles away. After such a long period of eye-to-eye contact Laura's eyes were out of focus. It took several seconds before she realized that there was a girl stroking Dennis's hands and that this girl was probably Edith.

Far from being faceless, the real Edith had large blue eyes, a tiny pug nose, and the kind of disheveled blond hair that a hairdresser would need four hours to recreate. It was halfway between bushy and wavy and formed a halo around her perfectly formed face. She was small and thin and seemed lost inside her oversized man's shirt and faded overalls. She had a large, almost childish smile and a breezy manner that made Laura feel like a ton of lead. When Dennis introduced her to Laura, she waved her right hand and mouthed the word "Hi," then turned back to Dennis and told him that Louella had eaten a hamburger.

"Isn't that incredible?" she went on. Her voice was folksy. There was only a trace of a southern accent. "Kay and I just couldn't believe our eyes. She even asked if we had any dessert."

"Hey, that's really great," Dennis said.

"So listen. I'm going to the supermarket to get her a whole load of ice cream, and then I'm taking the four-to-eight shift at Suicide Prevention. Kay's gone to reprocess some data at the Computer Center, so Martin is going to take the afternoon shift with Louella. But he has to return some reserve books by seven thirty, so I said *you* would take the evening shift with Louella, which means you should get there by seven. Okay?"

"Sure," Dennis nodded, "sure."

"Great," Edith said with a radiant smile. "The squash tournament has been postponed until next week so I'll be home for supper unless Jake hasn't gotten back from his *Newsweek* interview and I have to take the night shift in the press room. Okay?"

Dennis nodded. Edith went over to the children, who were crouching at the foot of the stairs, and picked up Jingle. "Now are you going to be a good girl for Auntie Edith?" she said in a loud, indulgent voice. "Kay says that you and your two friends here have been playing a very naughty game! She says Martin has bruises *all over* because you've been trying to take his pants off! Now you're not going to do that to Uncle Dennis here, are you?"

Jingle put her thumb in her mouth and shrugged her shoulders.

"I wouldn't touch that guy with a ten-foot pole," Sarah shouted. Jingle took her thumb out of her mouth and asked why not.

"Because," Sarah said, pushing her hair back with great disgust, "he's going through a monogamous stage."

Edith laughed uneasily. "Now who told you that?"

"Mommy said that's why we can't pull down his pants," Bess explained.

Edith paused, then clicked her fingers. "Oh, I get it. Your ma told you not to pull down Dennis's pants because we guys are monogamous. Hey, that's pretty good. I'll have to remember that."

Bess stared at Edith accusingly. "Why don't you believe in sharing?"

"But I *do* believe in sharing," Edith answered. "I don't know where you got the idea, or Kay got the idea . . ."

"Why don't you want Dennis to make love to anyone else?"

"Hey, hey, hey," Edith laughed. "Let's not get so personal, shall we?" There was an edge to her voice that made her cheerful smile seem forced. "And just for the record, you guys," she said when she reached the top of the stairs, "I *do* believe in sharing. Dennis can do what he wants, and so," she paused to take a breath, "can I." She pointed her finger at Laura, rather in the manner cowgirls on televisions pointed pistols, and said, "Hey, you and I have got to get together for a rap one of these days."

Then she was gone, but she had ruined all the magic. Dennis no longer looked at her the same way. Of course the children made civilized conversation almost impossible. Jingle couldn't seem to understand what a monogamous stage was, and every time Bess or Sarah whispered something into her ear she shouted, "Huh? You talking about *him?*"

Dennis went back to work on the plywood he had abandoned many hours before. Even when he looked up, he avoided her side of the room. It was as if the children made him uncomfortable. When Bess said to Jingle in a very loud voice, "It means he doesn't believe in being naked with anyone but *her,*" his face turned scarlet.

"Will you kids cut it out?" he said, throwing down his saw. That only made the girls laugh louder. "See," Bess said, "I told you. Dumb monogos are afraid of people even *talking* about being naked."

"*Him?*" Jingle screamed, "*him* afraid of being naked? *He's* not a dumb monogo. I mean, he's dumb, but he's not a dumb *monogo.* You know what he did to my mother?"

Dennis threw down his hammer. "Okay, Jingle, that's enough. Upstairs. And you too." The three girls scrambled up the stairs, laughing wildly, while Dennis watched from the bottom step, his hands on his hips. "And Jingle," he said sternly, "get this one thing straight. I have *not* been climbing through the window in and out of your mother's bedroom. Edith and I are your mother's very good friends and when we want to see her we come in *and leave* through the front door."

"Well, let's see if the shock technique works," he said when the door at the top of the stairs slammed shut. He wiped the perspiration from his forehead. "That kid is real sick. I mean sick. The trouble is, she's had a mixed-up childhood, so I guess it isn't her fault. I mean, she thinks I sleep with Louella. Well, I guess she's seen her mother make it with some other guys or something, but it sure wasn't me. And leaving through the bedroom window? Not on your life. That apartment's on the second floor. I'd have to be pretty worried about my reputation to risk my neck like that. I mean, even if I had been balling Louella, which I wasn't. Anyway Edith and I are too close to let that sort of thing upset us. I mean, she was sort of annoyed when she found Louella sitting on my lap half-naked the other day, but as soon as I got a chance to explain things, she understood." He paused for a breath. "I mean, we're not going to let our relationship get bogged down by a load of antiquated taboos."

"What were you doing naked with Louella on your lap?" Laura asked.

"She was the one who was semidressed, not me. I had more layers of clothing on than you could count. It's just that Louella's one of those preliberation ladies who are obsessed by their bodies. Like, she doesn't even know she has a mind. The only way she has ever been able to relate to her environment is through her body. So she's grateful to me for all the support I've given her lately. She wants to thank me. There's only one way she knows how to thank people. And that's by jumping on their laps and making love to them. Now I don't go for that kind of scene, as I try to explain to her. But she breaks down and says I probably am turned off because she's just another ugly nigger. So I tell her, first of all, nigger's not a word in my vocabulary. Second of all I tell her she's a beautiful person with a beautiful mind and a beautiful body, that she probably has a beautiful cunt even though it's not the time and the place for me to find out, and I tell her she has beautiful tits, which I can see with my own eyes, because the first thing she does when she gets on my lap is to pull off her nightgown. Edith understood perfectly when I got a chance to explain. She even understood about my sucking her tit. I mean, I wasn't doing that when she came in, but I told her anyway. Edith and I tell each other everything. She knows as well as I do that I couldn't reject Louella out and out, not after all the things we'd said to her about how we cared for her. Anyway, it was all for the best, because we had a long talk when we got back to our apartment and we decided that we were becoming too possessive. Sort of slipping into the traditional roles without knowing it. Well, the next day Edith got sort of drunk at a party at the newspaper and she let someone give her a finger job. So I guess we're even. And, if anything, the whole incident has made Edith feel even closer to Louella, like, she feels she has a deeper understanding of Louella's psyche and the reason why she slit her wrists in the first place."

He went on to tell the whole story of the suicide attempt, from the emergency room in the hospital where the doctor, a white male, had been criminally offhand, to the therapy that he and Edith and Kay and Martin had been conducting ever since. The point of the therapy was to convince Louella of her worth as a person. Dennis went into great detail about how wonderful Martin had been throughout. "No one can make Louella laugh like Martin," he said, shaking his head. "It must be that year he spent working at McLean's." He embarked on a long explanation of how tricky it was to tell jokes to the mentally disturbed, but Laura could barely hear him.

Instead she stared longingly at his nose and the beginnings of a mustache below and thought about how unfair it was that he was going through a monogamous stage with someone else. Laura would have been so perfect for him. If only they could both start all over again, Laura thought to herself. If only she had never promised to marry Stavros. If only Edith died or did not exist. It was tragic. When Bess came downstairs and shouted, "If you two love each other so much why don't you kiss?" Laura suddenly realized how even this simple act of affection could ruin their lives. Maybe not his life, but for Laura it was too late. She had already condemned herself to Stavros, and if she kept up this disturbing practice of kissing other men she would end up hurting Stavros's feelings. When Sarah came down and screamed, "Why don't you two just get it over with and go make out?" Laura felt tears collecting in her eyes. She rushed upstairs and locked herself in the bathroom.

She stared at her blotched face in the mirror, and washed her face five times, until the rash she always got from crying disappeared. Then she practiced breathing normally. Ten minutes had passed before she was normal enough to return to Children's Paradise. When she got there, she found Dennis lying helpless on the floor with the three girls on top of him.

Jingle was sitting on his chest and punching his forehead, while the other two sat on his thighs and struggled with his belt. "Hurry! Hurry!" Jingle was screaming. Dennis grabbed her by the waist and tried to throw her off but then let go when she kicked him in the eyes. Grosvenor was running around them, barking frantically. He put his mouth around Dennis's shoe. Quickly Laura pulled Bess off Dennis's leg and then grabbed Sarah, giving Dennis just enough time to get back on his feet.

"What in God's name do you think you're doing?" Laura asked.

"Trying to get his pants off," Sarah gasped.

"But why?" Laura screamed, and then, realizing how Kay would deal with a similar situation, she added in a softer, more controlled voice, "why don't you explain to me what you hoped to achieve."

Bess giggled. "We wanted to see what it looked like."

"*I* don't have to see how it looks," Jingle said, sticking her nose into the air. "I already know."

"Now listen, Jingle," Dennis said, adjusting his belt. "Let's get one thing straight. You have never seen me with my pants off."

"Oh yes I have!"

"Oh no you haven't!"

"You mean you forgot already?" Jingle squealed.

"Forgotten what?"

"Last night and last last night and last last last night and . . ." Bess and Sarah joined in. Dennis looked at them rolling on the floor and scratched his head, as if he were surprised that anyone, even a child, could be so silly.

"They're lunatics," he finally said to Laura. "I'm so surprised. Kay made her children sound so mature."

"I'm no lunatic," Jingle screamed, "and I saw it with my own two eyes. It was pink and wrinkled!"

"Come off it, Jingle."

"But I saw you. You thought I was asleep! But I was peeking at you! I was peeking at you through the door and then I made a barking noise like a dog, just to see what would happen, and you put a robe on and sneaked out of the window!"

Hammer in hand, Dennis approached them. The girls ran upstairs, screaming that Dennis was going to smash their brains open. Dennis stared at the doorway for a few seconds, then shook his head. "I think Kay might be right," he said slowly. "Love and care must just not be enough for that kid. Professional help might be the only thing."

"Didn't she ever try to take your pants off at her house?" Laura asked.

He shook his head. "She hardly says a thing at home. She just sits in front of that tube all day long. Hey, that's another thing. TV. I mean, wow."

"The Pyles lock their TV up in a black furry bag," Laura said. "They only keep it in case there's something educational."

Dennis nodded approvingly. "Right. I mean, like, every once in a while TV is okay. But when Edith and I have kids, man, and I catch them spending their afternoons inside watching those racist cartoons, that TV set is going out the window with the Superman comics."

"You and Edith are planning to have kids?" Laura asked weakly.

"Sure. I love kids. So does Edith. Edith wants to have a family something along the lines of this family. You know, with the mother's family life and professional life balancing out harmoniously. I mean, we believe that our kids will only be happy if *we* are happy and *both* of us are fulfilling our emotional and intellectual needs. What we want to avoid, of course, is a situation like Louella's."

He sighed. "I don't want to put down Louella or anything. I mean, in a lot of ways she's pretty cool. It's not her fault she's the way she is. It's the goddamned system. Louella is the classic case of the unfulfilled woman. No education to talk about, inability to take pride in a routine job, sees herself only in relation to the man in her life. Gets married, has a kid, really throws herself into the housewife role, and then the guy leaves her high and dry, and then he comes back and kidnaps the kid in the bargain. Wow. So she goes back to work. She's lonely. She sleeps around. She's not too careful, and the kid sees her with a lot of different guys and this really messes up her mind, I mean the kid's mind. And then, bang, she meets a man who takes her seriously, and they've been sleeping together for about three weeks when he proposes, and she feels like a new person. But all along the bastard is engaged to someone else. And one day he takes a plane down to Baltimore and gets married to this other woman. Wow, what a shit. Kay said it really blew her mind when she found out. An old college friend of hers, if you can believe it. Kay's the one who got them together in the first place. I mean, if Kay hadn't knocked on our door the day she broke the news and asked us to keep an eye out, Louella would be six feet under."

In the ensuing silence Laura heard metallic breathing and some muffled laughter, then a theatrical scream. The intercom was on. "What's wrong?" Laura asked.

"There's an animal in the Thinking Room," Sarah shouted over the intercom, "and it just bit Jingle. I think she's going to faint."

Dennis rushed upstairs. Laura followed. Lying on the floor outside the Thinking Room with her mouth wide open was Jingle. Dennis jumped right over her and plunged into the closet. Laura followed. Together they searched under the foam rubber and the pillows. "Did it have a tail?" Dennis asked.

"It sure did," Sarah said, "a really long and thin one, like a snake, except it wasn't a snake, it was a tail."

"Sounds like a rat," he said firmly. "I bet it's hiding in this here hole." He crawled toward the back of the closet, and suddenly the door slammed shut, leaving Dennis and Laura in what seemed like

—— III ——

total darkness. Outside the closet the children screamed with laughter. "We've locked it! We've locked it!" Bess screamed.

"It doesn't have a lock, stupids," Laura said.

"Now it does! It has a padlock! So you're stuck in there. Ha ha ha."

Laura pushed at the door but it wouldn't budge. As she tried to push it open she felt blood rushing to her head. "If you idiots don't let us out right now," she screamed, "I'll . . ." She felt a warm hand on her shoulder and a deep voice—much deeper than she remembered Dennis's voice being—telling her that hysteria would get them nowhere.

But reason didn't get them anywhere either. When Dennis told them they were acting childish, they told them that of course they were. They were children, weren't they? When he told them that their mother would get angry, they said that this was impossible. Kay never got angry. She didn't believe in punishment either. "We can do anything we want in the whole wide world just as long as we think it through," Sarah said, "and we're not letting you out of there until you do it."

"Do what?" Dennis asked.

"It! *It!*" Jingle screamed. "What you did to my mother."

"We'll be out here listening," Sarah added.

"Wow," Dennis mumbled. From the back of the closet where Laura had taken refuge under some cushions, she could just make out a nodding head. "Wow. They're really sick." Through the door Laura could hear Bess giggling, "He thinks we're sick."

The only light in the closet was the thin yellow line between the door hinges, but Laura's eyes had adjusted to the darkness just enough to see a large gray shape approaching her on all fours. Outside she could hear the children twittering. "He's getting ready. Then he's going to do it." She closed her eyes and then she felt something hit her between the legs, and she screamed, louder than she ever had before.

Four hours was a long time to spend in a closet. If it hadn't been

for Dennis's phosphorescent watch, she would have thoug\
longer. He wanted to, as he put it, get to the bottom of her \
scream, and after an initial period of embarrassment Laura f\
herself telling him the story of her life and her deepest secrets. \
listened quietly as she told him about her parents and their inability
to act like adults, her roommate, who had not washed her sheets
since the beginning of the year, and her fiancé, who she now wished
was dead.

Dennis had wedged his flashlight between his knees, and the
strange red glow it cast on his features made Laura feel as if she
were talking to a statue. Perhaps that was why she told him everything, even her most private thoughts. She confessed that she
had no idea what career she should go into anymore, that she
wasn't even sure she wanted a career at all because she didn't
think she could handle it, that sometimes she felt she was nothing
more than a leaf riding the waves in a storm, controlled by events
and completely unable to fight back. No matter how hard she
tried, she could not understand the meaning of life. Sometimes
she even wondered if it had any meaning at all. She didn't understand what it meant to be an American, and even after half a year
in Massachusetts, she could not get over her deep distrust of
American men.

"What do you think the reason is for that?" he asked. She didn't
know. "Do you think it might be true that you mistrust men in
general?" She didn't think so. It was just that she had had only one
real boyfriend in her entire life. At least only one boyfriend who
had been nice to her. Everyone else had always thought of her as
a freak. Since coming to college, she had almost gone all the way
with four or five people, but then in the end she had remained true
to Stavros, at least in her heart, even though she sometimes wished
he were dead. He was the only one who had ever been nice to her,
and really she had remained true to him in her body, too, because
none of the four or five people she had almost gone all the way with
had excited her in the least. Actually Stavros didn't excite her very

much either. She was one of those people who could not have orgasms.

With this admission Dennis lost his clinical composure. "Who told you that?" he almost shouted. She explained that she was just one of those people. One of those people who had never had an orgasm and who never would. She could become excited, of course, but never to the point of what her psychology textbook called release. She described the diagram she had seen in Masters and Johnson. It looked like a plateau, a plateau that never managed to rise above the dotted line.

Dennis put his chin on his flashlight. "You realize that's all cowshit," he said slowly. "Everyone can have orgasms. The only reason you can't is because you are afraid of your body."

"You think so?" Laura said.

"Yeah. It's pretty clear to me that you're sexually and emotionally repressed. You're hiding from reality and you're trying to protect yourself from your own emotions. But your body is beautiful. You should learn how to touch it, to respond to it. Your body is your friend, not your enemy. It can give you great pleasure."

No one had ever said that to her before. She stared at his translucent chin and the dark mysterious grooves hiding his eyes, and her heart began to pound wildly. "Do you really think my body is beautiful?"

Dennis rubbed his chin back and forth on the flashlight. "Sure," he said.

"You really do?"

There was a long pause. "Yeah, I really do," he said finally. "I really think you're beautiful."

"You don't think I'm frigid?"

"No," he said slowly, "I don't think you're frigid. Like I said, all you have to do is open up and treat yourself right."

They listened to each other breathing. "How?" she whispered.

"There's lots of ways."

"Can you show me one?"

He hunched over his flashlight, tapping it lightly with his fingers. Then he let the flashlight roll onto the cushions. "Sure."

He put his arm around her shoulder and pulled her over next to him. As he unzipped her jeans, she let her head slide down his chest to his lap. "Are you sure Edith won't mind?"

"Edith won't mind," he said softly. He brushed the hair off her forehead and kissed it lightly.

In the beginning his fingers scratched her but then as he whispered to her and told her to open herself up, her muscles and her mind relaxed. She found herself opening her legs wider and wider and pushing herself against his hand. Watching the small ring of light that the flashlight cast on the door, she saw herself on the Masters and Johnson chart, climbing faster and faster toward the dotted line, and then above it. And then she came, and for a few seconds nothing mattered except pleasure.

She sat up. She leaned against his shoulder, breathless and very surprised.

"You see how easy it is if you just let yourself go?" Dennis said, stroking the inside of her leg. "You've just got to stop hiding from yourself. The world is so much more beautiful when you free yourself of your hang-ups. You know what I think you should try and do?"

"What?"

"When something happens to you, don't rationalize. Just ask yourself, how do I *really* feel about what just happened? How did I *really* react? Don't feel ashamed. Try to answer honestly. You understand what I mean?"

He rubbed his moist fingers against her cheek. She looked into his eyes, which she could barely see, and nodded. Then she asked herself what she really felt about what had happened. At first she could not accept the answer, but then she opened up and accepted it. It was so easy, once you accepted the truth. For the first time in months Laura felt completely free. She put her arms around Dennis's neck and said, "I love you."

Dennis didn't say a thing. He just shook his head and slowly zipped up her jeans. Downstairs they could hear the front door opening, running footsteps, and two frantic voices—Edith's and Kay's—shouting "Anybody home?" Dennis tried to disentangle himself from Laura's arms.

"Please don't take that the wrong way," Laura said. "I'm not asking you to make any commitment. I'm just telling you the truth. I really do love you, from the bottom of my heart."

Dennis shook his head and said, "You don't know what love is."

9

When Edith had let herself into Louella's apartment that evening at a quarter past eight, she had found Louella lying on the kitchen floor with her head in the oven. Fortunately the gas hadn't been on long, and Louella was still semiconscious. Still, it was a close call, and Edith was badly shaken. As soon as she had aired out the apartment, she had called up the Pyles to find out what had happened to Dennis, only to be told by a hysterical Bess that both he and Laura were in the Thinking Room and probably dead. Apparently Laura's scream had frightened them.

Now, while Edith cooked up some instant Armenian pilaf for their dinner and Laura halfheartedly tidied up the kitchen, the girls were acting uncharacteristically meek. While Kay conducted a cryptic phone conversation with Martin, who had canceled his plans for the evening so as to be with Louella, they didn't say a thing. To cheer them up, Kay read them "Rapunzel" while they ate their dinner, but when she got to the part about the mother exchanging her baby for a cabbage from the wizard's garden, Jingle started sobbing. They toyed with their food.

Only Nathaniel was in high spirits, or rather, hyperactive. He kept babbling about the guns he had been given in the psychology lab. They screamed like Sarah every time he tried to shoot them. And sometimes they made *him* scream too, and he felt funny and shaky all over, like the time the plug wouldn't come all the way out of the socket and he had tried to take it out with his bare hands.

"It was a real gun," he told his mother. "I don't like real guns. They hurt. And I don't like it when they scream."

"Oh, you poor little chickadee," Kay said, lifting him onto her lap. "I guess you won't ever want to shoot again, will you?"

"Not if they scream," Nathaniel said. At which point Jingle told him that real guns never screamed. "My dad had a real gun and he even shot it at my mom once, so I should know." Before she could go into any more detail, Kay packed the children off to bed.

Laura was too exhausted and confused to join in the after-dinner conversation. While Edith, Kay, and Dennis analyzed Louella, she tidied up the kitchen yet once more and cleaned the refrigerator. Kay hadn't heard the story about Louella's play for Dennis, and she listened to Edith's version with solemn interest, interrupting only occasionally to point out that Louella was a product of her environment and to suggest alternative methods of therapy.

Edith was on the defensive. She did everything she could to convince Kay that she was not jealous. "I mean, I guess you thought we were pretty conservative or something, but really, the fact that Dennis actually got turned on by her tits and stuff really doesn't bother me at all," she insisted. "It's Louella I'm worried about. I really want her to make a complete recovery. If she continues to encourage men to exploit her, she'll *never* learn to respect herself."

"I wonder if it wouldn't be best to have someone confront her directly over this issue," Kay said. "I'll see what Martin thinks."

"If anyone confronts her I guess it should be Martin," Dennis said.

"I think you're right there," Kay agreed. "Martin seems to be getting through to her better than the rest of us."

"Well, I've tried to get through to her, too," Edith said. "But at this stage she isn't used to confiding in another woman. I mean, she's got it into her head that I'm jealous about that lap scene. I've tried to explain to her that Dennis and I have a very open relationship."

"Hey, that's interesting," Kay said. "I was under the misguided impression that you two had virtually cut off any sexual interaction with the outside world."

"Not at all!" Edith protested. She squinted at the ceiling as she tried to find the right words. "I mean, like, spiritually speaking, Dennis is the only one. But you can't cut yourself off completely from the community. I mean, I love Dennis, but I don't own him. And he doesn't own me, and just because I give a close friend a blowjob doesn't mean I won't continue to have a full relationship with Dennis."

Dennis flushed. "When did you do that?"

Edith gave him a coy smile. "Nosy!" She flicked her finger gently against his nose.

"You're going to continue to live together, though, after graduation?" Kay asked.

"It really depends on what's happening with my career. I mean, Dennis isn't too crazy about the prospect of living in New York City." She went on to describe the options open to her: the job prospects at two prestigious women's magazines and an internship at a large publishing house. Earlier that year she had shown some of her work to Anaïs Nin, who had advised her to devote herself exclusively to poetry and fiction. Then sometimes she played with the idea of taking a year off and going with Dennis to India, and then doing something more meaningful, like going to law school and becoming a Legal Aid lawyer specializing in women's problems. Of course she sometimes had daydreams of doing something that was both fun *and* meaningful, like starting a magazine for professional women.

"Actually that's been one of my pet projects, too," Kay said. They started talking about what the ideal magazine would be like: small, personal, not slick like the one Steinem was putting together, with feature articles on accomplished women, woman-oriented book reviews, a watchdog column for sexist practices in the professional and academic worlds, a "Gripes" column, Letters from Washington and London, a job-finding service. "You realize that if you and I and a couple of other gals got together, we could put together a dummy along those lines by the end of the summer," Kay said. They started drawing up lists of other people they knew who might be interested enough to sacrifice a few months of their time without pay. "Oh, wouldn't it be wonderful if it all worked out!" Edith cried. She lunged across the table and took hold of Dennis's arms. She looked radiant. "Then I wouldn't have to commute down to New York. I could work from home." Dennis looked lovingly into her eyes. "That would be great," he said.

They were a charming couple, Laura told herself. Why was it that she couldn't be playful and self-assured like Edith? Never in a million years would she be able to rock back and forth on someone's lap and chew his ear in public. Why not? Why was she the only person she knew in the world who didn't know what love was or what life meant and didn't even understand her own body?

"Laura! You look so glum!" Kay said. "Why don't you whip yourself up some coffee and join our silly bull session here?" But Laura was too depressed to be able to bear the company of happy people. She wanted answers, not sympathy. So she went upstairs to the bathroom and read a book on love.

The Art of Loving. It had been on the bathroom bookshelf all along, sandwiched between *Sexual Politics* and *The Bell Jar,* but Laura had never had any reason to look beyond its covers. Even now she did not read the whole thing, as love of God did not concern her, but the chapters she did read had a shattering effect.

She discovered among other things that her boyfriend Stavros had unhealthy sadistic tendencies. She hadn't imagined this possible before because he had never hit her, but it was now clear that his possessiveness, his jealousy, and the careful way he had shaped her character over the years so as to make her acceptable to his friends—he often compared himself to Professor Higgins—were signs of a hidden sadism. A painful discovery after years of thinking his love was pure.

For the next few hours, while the three adults continued their bull session downstairs, Laura lay on the couch in Bob Pyle's study and thought about her relationship with Stavros from their first meeting at a ski resort five years before to his most recent letter. She made mental notes of even the most insignificant of his sins. Seen in the light of the book on love, he was an unbelievable monster, and when Laura finally took his photograph out of her pocket, she became physically ill.

Edith and Dennis left well after midnight. Kay poked her head in the door before turning in.

"Dennis tells me you had your first orgasm today," she said cheerfully. Laura nodded. She felt the blood rising to her cheeks. "Hey, I think that's really great. They're pretty funky things, aren't they?" Laura nodded again, then tried to free herself from Kay's warm, almost hypnotic gaze. She was determined not to talk about it. She had exposed enough of her soul for one day.

"That Edith is pretty funky too, don't you think?" Kay continued. "When I first met her two years ago she was a fairly unnerving combination of radical and grass-roots southern. But she sure has come into her own. Dennis too. They're a groovy couple." Laura tried very hard to smile. Kay blew a kiss and closed a door. Then she opened it again. "There's some butter pecan ice cream in the freezer if you find your appetite somewhere. And hey—before I forget—if you and Dennis ever feel the hots for each other again, please feel free to use my bedroom."

Martin was sitting up with Louella so Kay was sleeping alone. She had some sort of nightmare. Laura could hear her moan. Laura did not bother to turn off the light. She had too much to think about. She read the book on love again, and toward dawn she wrote Stavros a letter.

Every paragraph began with a quote from the book and ended with a reproachful question. Didn't he realize how terrible it was of him to have ever called her a "precious jewel"? Why didn't he love her for what she was instead of considering her as an attractive package of marketable value? Laura's parents had never cared much for Stavros. They wanted her to marry someone creative. Someone like Dennis, someone who lived in the world of ideas, even if all he did was build walls. Whereas Stavros was planning to enter his father's business. Her parents told her that if she stayed with Stavros, she would spend her whole life at tea parties playing cards. Although she never admitted it, this prospect haunted her. Her upbringing had been relatively free of prejudice, but there had been a definite bias against people who devoted their lives to making money. Businessmen were ogres. He was one of them. She ended the letter by reproaching him for being businesslike even in his heart. "I am not a marketable commodity," she wrote, "so it follows that our love is false. Why continue? We have both been deluding ourselves. I don't think we should meet this summer as planned."

She put the letter into an envelope and went outside into the empty street. The still-bare branches rustled against the blue-white sky. On the way to the mailbox she passed the apartment house where Louella and Jingle and Edith and Dennis all lived. There was an open window on the second floor and as Laura passed, she heard laughter. A man and a woman. It was probably Dennis and Edith. Whoever they were, they were having a good time. If it was Dennis and Edith, they were probably laughing about her orgasm, shaking their heads about the awkward way she had told Dennis the truth. What right do they have to laugh at me? Laura asked herself angrily as she turned onto the highway. I *was* telling Dennis the truth. If that's what happened to people when they tell the truth, then she would rather lie. She remembered that Stavros had never laughed at her, not even when she was fifteen and her nickname was Freak. By the time she reached the mailbox she had decided to throw the letter away.

He wouldn't have understood what she was talking about, she said to herself on her way back. The letter would have hurt his feelings. There was no real reason why she shouldn't have her summer in Paris. She had worked hard and deserved a vacation. The only friends she had in Paris were his friends: she didn't like the idea of eating in restaurants alone. Even if he was a sadist, he certainly knew how to live. She couldn't deny that, nor could she get rid of an uncomfortable feeling, an inner voice that disliked her almost as much as it disliked her family and her friends, that told her she might be sadistic, too.

Or even worse, masochistic. "Our true emotions are very simple," Dennis had told her in the Thinking Room, "but we weave elaborate webs to hide them from ourselves." Thinking back on her letter, she realized that it too was an elaborate web, hiding yet another simple emotion.

She had spent too much of her life lying to herself. She had to start afresh, even if it meant giving up her summer vacation and all her dreams. When she got back to Bob Pyle's study she sat down and wrote Stavros a shorter letter. All it said was: "I hate you. I have always hated you without knowing it. I never want to see you again." She went right out and sent it before she could have second thoughts.

10

For years Laura had assumed that she was destined to become a bored housewife, the mother of several children whom she saw only once a day, when the nurse brought them into her bedroom after breakfast, because they looked like monkeys. A terrible fate, but reassuring, because if you were enslaved by circumstance you did not have to exhaust yourself by living up to your ideals. A horrifying prospect, to be obliged to spend your life with a man you only pretended to love, but the fact that you didn't really love him gave you a certain license: you could do whatever you liked behind his back.

Nothing was your fault if you were oppressed, but now Laura was free. If she didn't have a good, clean, full, happy, and highly successful life, she would only have herself to blame. The burden of freedom terrified her. She began to worry that her life would be a failure. She longed for someone to cling to, but Dennis said it was time she learned to stand on her own two feet. He told her that if she continued to rely on him for finger jobs she would be establishing an unhealthy dependence.

Dennis was very helpful during those first days of Laura's independence. He helped her weather the dizzy spells and rapid heartbeat that she suffered whenever he came upstairs for a coffee break and their eyes met. "What you're going through is an infatuation," he told her. "Infatuation is a cheap thrill. It means that you're projecting your ego-image on people, instead of trying to see those people for what they really are."

Dennis advised Laura to strip her conversation of all the reactionary defense mechanisms that turned well-meaning conversations into battles of wit. But Laura was so conditioned after a childhood spent with bohemian pseudo-intellectual misanthropes who wasted their energies lashing each other with cruel words in a futile fight for dominance (at the time she had found them witty), that bad conversations came to her as naturally as sleep and hunger. Despite her sincere efforts to edit all unkind and counterproductive tendencies from her train of thought, she still managed to ridicule her environment without meaning to. That was what happened when Edith and Kay had their first meeting with the three other women who were going to help them found their magazine. After serving them lunch, Laura went downstairs to visit Dennis in Children's Paradise, and in a misguided effort to amuse him she described each of the newcomers in less than ten words.

She hadn't meant any harm. But Dennis was totally disgusted. When would she stop seeing people as caricatures? he asked. So what if Rachel had thick hips and walked like an elephant? What did it matter if Melissa had the beginnings of a mustache? And how was Laura so sure that the marks on Gail's right arm were from heroin injections and not insulin? A whole was more than a sum of its parts, and you couldn't tell a book by its cover. Ugly people could have beautiful souls. Dennis had a way with platitudes. He made you understand why people said them so often—because they were true.

He told Laura she should sincerely try to understand these people. As active and committed feminists, they probably had a lot to teach her. And Laura, who from kindergarten through high school had been the kind of student teachers said were "a delight to teach"—her essays were always "delightful," her manners "impeccable," and her treatment of fellow classmates "considerate beyond the call of duty"—obeyed her new mentor's instructions to the letter. She made a point of cutting her late morning classes so that she could sit in on their daily meetings, and when she had finished serving them lunch she would sit down with them at the table and try to find out just exactly where they were at.

Kay called them her Minerva group, because the tentative name of the magazine was *Minerva*. They hoped to be able to put a dummy issue together by the end of August. Kay was the editor in chief, mainly because she had more time on her hands than the others, who were all involved in various graduate and undergraduate programs. With very little ado and exactly on schedule, Kay had submitted her thesis to the Sociology Department. Now all she had to do was get ready to defend it. If all went well, she would receive her degree in June. With the girls in school until the middle of June and Nathaniel participating in the experimental all-day program, Kay said she had masses of time to devote to the Minerva project, "and a lifetime if it manages to work out."

First they had to work out the magazine's general stance, and here the group was of two opinions. Kay thought that the tone should be professional, loving, and as politically detached as the underlying morality of the women's movement permitted. Edith agreed with her one hundred percent, and so did Rachel for the first few days, although Rachel could not help pointing out that she didn't see how a magazine could be loving.

Rachel was the oldest woman in the group and the easiest to accept as a person. She had a B.A. in philosophy (she described herself as an Aristotelian housewife who had been liberated by Wittgenstein), and now she was studying for her Masters in the education school. For years she and her husband had run a poetry bookstore in Provincetown, but now it was a shoe store and her husband was dead. She had short gray hair, brown eyes that popped slightly, and a warm, slow smile. She was sarcastic, but it was the kind of sarcasm that made people laugh instead of cry.

Except for Melissa, of course. Melissa was the leader of what Kay jokingly referred to as "the enemy camp." She was deadly serious about her views. Not once during that first week did Laura see her smile. She had a long, pinched face and a nervous bush of wiry black hair. She had a way of sucking in her lips when she was thinking, and the resulting absence of lips, together with her large goat-like eyes, gave her the lost, belligerent expression of a bully who has been sent to bed without supper. Kay said that a traumatic experience in medical school had ended Melissa's lifelong dream to become a doctor. Although she was now enrolled in a public health program, she was a broken woman. Only by trying to imagine this trauma, could Laura could feel any sympathy for Melissa. She had a harsh, loud voice that made Laura's ears sting and spoke invariably in slogans. She believed that a potentially radical woman's magazine should not allow itself to be swallowed up by bourgeois liberalism, that *Minerva* should be uncompromisingly opposed to everything the Establishment stood for, from war to the nuclear family. Since the Establishment regarded lesbians as perverts, lesbians like herself had no choice but to destroy the Establishment.

All this put Gail into a strange position. As Melissa's lover she felt obligated to take Melissa's side, and she did so every time an issue came to a vote. But in all honesty, she had come into the group as an arts consultant and had no idea what the magazine should or should not stand for. She was neither for nor against families and the same applied to lesbians. She told Laura she wasn't even sure if she *was* a lesbian. Until very recently Gail had been exclusively into men. Her cohabitation with Melissa was in the way of an experiment, she said in her thin, tired voice. As far as the

Establishment was concerned, she certainly found many faults in the American system, but a year spent studying in Rome and Berlin had convinced her that other countries didn't have it any better. She just couldn't make up her mind. That had been her problem ever since graduating from Reed, and now, as a special student in the school of architecture, the problem persisted.

Indecision, and of course ill health. Gail was a Korean orphan. When she had been adopted by a Methodist family in Ohio at the age of four, she had been suffering from malnutrition, and even now she was painfully thin. Although of course she turned her frailness into an asset with her dramatic scarves and see-through blouses. With her white complexion and her almond-shaped eyes, she reminded Laura of a brush painting.

Kay did not want to do any serious work on the dummy until all five founders came to a compromise that satisfied them. But by Friday of the first week, they still had made no progress. Kay was lighthearted about the deadlock when they broke for lunch. She suggested that they all reconsider their positions seriously over the weekend. But the others were on edge. They were obviously tired of covering the same ground over and over again. Even the ever-smiling Edith looked discouraged.

Contrary to Dennis's predictions, Laura did not feel as if she had learned anything at all by sitting in on these meetings. She was tired of their faces, which could not stand up to close scrutiny. The bags and the nervous tics depressed her. After a week of model behavior, she was tired of watching those around her break the rules. She felt weighed down by her good intentions. She could hear them clanking like a coat of armor every time she looked around her or tried to say something or walked across the floor under their gaze.

Worst of all, Laura felt left out. She had been secretly hoping that they might invite her to become the sixth cofounder. They didn't. They rarely even asked her opinion, leaving her to sit in silence at the end of the table, fighting migraine headaches as she tried desperately not to think unkind thoughts about the women in front of her. Objectivity: Dennis had said she lacked objectivity. She would concentrate on the coffee mugs and wonder what factory they came from, where the factory workers lived, whether they were still alive, how much they had been paid, how old they were, what they looked like. She did the same for the pencils, the tables, the telephone, the paper, the clothes they were all wearing, the dishwasher motor, the windowpanes, the flowerpots. But this game of objectivity became depressing too, as the number of factory workers who had slaved away on assembly lines to create the Pyle kitchen swelled into thousands and tens of thousands. And then there were the forests that had been demolished, the rivers that had been polluted, the minerals that had been mined, the waterpower that had been harnessed, the middlemen, the construction companies, the consumer watchdog agencies, the banks, the real estate agents, the legislation, the paper work, the postal workers. Was the end result worth it? Kind thoughts were not enough to keep Laura afloat: the terrible implications of objectivity depressed her. She despaired of ever becoming an adult in this fashion.

And why did she have to confine herself to constructive thoughts, when Melissa had so many negative ones? Melissa was always attacking something. And, this Friday lunchtime, it was Kay's sentimental attachment to the reactionary family ethic. Kay listened with a pained smile. When Melissa ran out of nasty things to say, she got up and walked to the bay window.

"In any normal committee situation," Kay said turning slowly, "I would now suggest that you, Melissa, and I cannot collaborate successfully in any endeavor. We would go our separate ways and achieve our goals with others who shared our respective points of view. This, however, is an extraordinary situation. Although Edith and I do, as initiators of this project, have the technical right to ask you to leave, we feel that it would not be just to do so. We have in mind a women's magazine that encompasses all the views and needs of professional feminists, and certainly the lesbian and radical voices should be heard as well as the viewpoints of widows and mothers and minority groups. And let me add that I feel you are a good person and I do sincerely believe that we can come to some sort of an understanding.

"That said, I would like to suggest that the basis of our misunderstanding can be found in our widely divergent conceptions of the word 'family.'

"You, I believe, are referring to the traditional nuclear family, which is, in a certain sense, exclusive and reactionary, as you say. I, on the other hand, am referring to the modern *extended* family. For I most sincerely believe that society will only succeed in achieving true peace when every member of society is well loved and well cared for. And the most efficient unit for ensuring this love and care is, in my opinion, the family. The *extended* family, with a nuclear family at the core to provide a certain stability that I have found lacking in most communes. An extended family that is structured to absorb friends as well as blood relatives, homosexuals as well as heterosexuals, blacks as well as whites; grandparents, parents, and children; mother's helpers, carpenters; representatives from all three generations, all walks of life, and all races. For surely we have much to learn from one another, and where better to do so than in our very homes."

Kay's lips were trembling. She had a sweet, dreamy look in her eyes. "Those are the rules we live by in this crazy household, anyway," she said, turning to Melissa with a hopeful smile. "And need I add that we would welcome you into it with open arms?"

"I hate to say this," Melissa answered, her head bobbing nervously, "but I still think our differences are political. Your concept of the extended family just oozes with bourgeois liberal assumptions. For example, who's going to pay for all these gigantic families . . . ?"

"But I don't see how it is a liberal concept at all!" Kay protested. "What could be more radical than a society of large, loving, peaceful families that are free of sexual taboos? And as far as financing is concerned, if we could rechannel the money that is at present being poured into the war machine . . ."

"It's not radical, it's impossible. An impossible dream. And it's fascist to assume that everyone wants to be under the control of a large, smothering patriarchy."

"How about a matriarchy?" Kay suggested, smiling.

"Patriarchy, matriarchy, it all boils down to control. Some people like privacy. Like me. Anyway, I hate kids. They drive me nuts."

"But children are our saving grace!" Kay cried.

"They are also a fucking pain in the neck," Melissa said, and she swallowed her lips.

"Oh, oh, oh," Kay gasped. She slumped into a chair as if someone had stabbed her in the heart. "If only you could see with your own eyes how large groups can love and interact harmoniously. And discover the added insight into the human soul that cohabitation with children brings." She buried her face in her hands and breathed deeply. Edith went over and stroked her back. The others rose to leave. But just as Melissa was about to go, Kay stood and took her by the hand. A cold spring wind blew all the papers off the kitchen table.

"Melissa, I want you to know that it's not the magazine I'm worried about," she said as Laura picked up the papers from around their feet. "I am absolutely positive that we'll work something out. What I am worried about is you, Melissa. I want you to be able to love men and children and little old ladies as fully as you now love Gail. And I would very much like you to become friends with my children and everyone else in this crazy family. It's my middle child's birthday tomorrow, and as good a time as any for making friends. Bess will be overjoyed to have you come to her party. I've told her so much about you. Why don't you come?"

Stepping back, she smiled at her Minerva group with glittering eyes. "Why not come, all of you? We'll make it a double celebration. The birth of a magazine and the birthday of a child."

11

Things did not go well the following morning. For a while it looked as if there was going to be no celebration at all. Bess was very upset when she discovered that three strange grown-ups were coming to her party. "It's my party and it's my birthday and I should be the one who says who's coming. And you didn't even ask me," she sobbed.

She was also upset because the presents that Kay and Edith and Laura gave her at breakfast all had to do with her well-publicized passion for ballet: some black-leather ballet slippers, a bright blue leotard, and a beautiful white tutu. But Bess wasn't interested in ballet anymore. As a matter of fact she hated it. Of course she had forgotten to tell anyone about her change of heart, and it was too late now, but what she really wanted was baby dolls. "You know why?" she said. "Because the only thing I want to be when I grow up is a mother."

When Kay was out of earshot, Sarah told her that she could

never be a mother in a million years, because unlike Sarah, who was a perfectly normal child, Bess had been conceived in a test tube. This meant that Bess didn't have a real birthday—people who began in test tubes were never really *born*, they just *grew*—and since they had not yet perfected the technique of growing babies in test tubes, Sarah told her, Bess had been born without her reproductive system. "So you can never have babies," she concluded. "You're an experiment that didn't work."

"That's not true!" Bess squealed, and although Laura assured her that the story was a malicious fabrication, she broke away from Laura's arms and took refuge in the Thinking Room, where Nathaniel was also hiding.

Nathaniel had a stomachache. After the aggression-displacement experiment, Nathaniel had lost interest in games with guns. But he had started sucking his thumb. Kay had been trying to discourage him but with no success. So Sarah decided to try her own brand of aversion therapy on him. She smeared a combination of lipstick and dishwasher detergent all over his thumb. Now his face was red and he felt terrible. But as Kay said when she gave him the stomach medicine and put him back to bed, you couldn't really blame Sarah. Sarah was recovering from a snake stage.

Dennis had carried out his original plans with Sarah's walls and painted picture frames on the inner walls, but since Sarah was going through a brief snake stage when she colored them in, the frames were filled with nightmarish visions instead of the happy children's drawings Dennis had visualized. There were snakes eating babies, snakes strangling grown men, snakes coiled around tree branches, and snakes digesting trucks, all painted in violent blues, oranges, and reds.

After a few nights in her room Sarah had begun to have nightmares, so she had moved her bed out into the central playing area. Even when Dennis had covered the offending paintings with three coats of white paint, Sarah still claimed to see snakes. This morning

Kay had finally found herself obliged to ask Dennis to take the walls down.

Dennis was appalled. He had put a lot of creative effort into those walls, and the thought of having to undo so much careful work sent him into a rage. Laura found this difficult to reconcile with his peaceful philosophy. "Is the same thing going to happen to all my other projects?" he wheezed when Kay had gone back upstairs. "Am I going to have to take down the tree house as soon as I get it up? And what about the ferris-wheel bookshelves for the bedroom, and Kay's loft, and the tool shed, and the work bench, and the cat closet?" He was so angry that he punched a hole through the plywood. Then he sat down in the middle of Sarah's empty room and stared angrily at the ceiling, his fists clenched. Laura went over and stroked his hair, just as she had seen Edith do one day when he got angry at her because he was unbelievably hungry. "Don't worry, dear," Laura said timidly, "everything will be all right." But her small gesture of affection made his face go even redder and the vessels in his neck stand out. "Leave . . . me . . . alone," he snarled. "Leave me alone or I'll break every bone in your body."

His cruel words sent Laura into a deep depression. Edith had to take time out from her cake-making to calm her down. She held her tight and massaged her back, then gazed into Laura's eyes with embarrassing sincerity. "Did he tell you that nonsense about breaking every bone in your body?" Edith asked softly. "Honestly!" she said, when Laura told her he had. "Sometimes I think all men are just nuts. They can't seem to curb that aggressive instinct. Next time I see it coming I'll send him outside so he can take it out on that nice football I got him for Christmas."

After she had dried Laura's tears, she went to the door to Children's Paradise and shouted, "Dennis! Next time I'm going to lock you out of the house and you're going to have to take it out on your football!" That made Laura feel better. It restored her confidence to see how willing Edith was to gang up on Dennis. For the first time Laura thought of Edith as a true friend.

She felt well enough to help Kay prepare the place mats for the twenty-odd classmates Bess had invited to her party. "Where's the guest list you and I made out last week?" Kay asked Bess, who had finally emerged from the Thinking Room. Bess didn't know. "Run along downstairs and see if it isn't still in your bookbag."

Two minutes later Bess reappeared in the kitchen, her mouth wide open with agony. She was too appalled to cry out loud. Opening up her tattered blue bookbag, she showed her mother the twenty-odd invitations that she had forgotten to hand out to her classmates.

It was her birthday, but none of her school friends knew about it, and none of them cared, and the only people who were coming to her party were some stupid grown-ups. She spent the rest of the morning crying about her wicked fate.

But by the time the guests arrived, Bess had calmed down. She was courteous and friendly to the four strange children Edith had recruited from her apartment building to replace the uninvited classmates. When Martin and Louella's present turned out to be yet another tutu, she pretended to be delighted. After Jingle and Sarah had sung "Happy Birthday" and she had blown out the candles on Edith's organic cake, Bess stood up to recite the poem that her mother had helped her write so as to convince her that life was still worth living.

A morning of anguish had somehow succeeded in making her look even prettier. She did not seem to notice Sarah's scowl when she adjusted her wreath of paper roses. Jingle was silently seething, jealous of Bess's presents. She claimed that both tutus had been stolen from her toychest. She was having difficulty breathing in the mask and snorkel Martin had given her as a booby prize and the two small girls sitting next to her looked equally uncomfortable under their party hats. They were much too big: the brims dangled between their noses and their mouths. Sitting next to them were two chubby fair-haired girls about Sarah's age. They were the daughters of a visiting professor from an unspecified European university, and the only reason Edith knew them was because their mother complained frequently about the loudness of Edith's stereo. After an embarrassing attempt to draw them out, Edith had been unable to get them to divulge their names. So she had introduced them as the "Fulbright sisters." Whenever there was a lull in the conversation, Laura could hear them making snide comments about the company in French.

"The name of my poem is 'Reasons Why I Am Glad,' " Bess announced in a shaky voice. She paused, and Kay smiled nervously at Rachel, Gail, and Melissa, who were huddled around the dishwasher like girls at a junior high school dance. Since their arrival they had been ill at ease—shocked by the amount of noise Sarah and Jingle could make when they talked at the same time, puzzled by Louella's coquettishness and Martin's antics, disapproving of the grandmother's disapproving stare, unappreciative of Edith's dandelion wine, disturbed by the fact that Bess didn't know the names of four of her party guests. Kay's loud and positive comments seemed to embarrass them even further.

"Reasons Why I Am Glad," Bess repeated. Downstairs there was a crash as Dennis knocked down one of Sarah's walls, and muffled oaths as he kicked it across the floor.

"Oh, good," Kay said. "I'm so glad he's finally done it." Rachel looked at her as if she were possibly mad. Bess wavered. She put her thumb in her mouth. Her grandmother bent over and pulled it out again.

"Go on," she said, waving her walking stick, "we can hear you loud and clear."

"But I'm too embarrassed," Bess said.

"Silly girl!" Kay said fondly, "you recited it so beautifully this morning. Come on, now. We'll say it together. Ready, set, go. Reasons Why I Am Glad."

"I am glad," Bess continued on her own, "because today I am seven. I am glad, because today Sarah told me a very funny joke about a test tube. I am glad, because Laura is going to be our mother's helper all summer long . . ."

"And we hope forever," Kay added.

"And we hope forever," Bess repeated. She scratched her head. "I don't remember that part. Now I'm lost."

"I am glad," Kay reminded her softly, "because Daddy came all the way from Washington to come to my party."

"But he didn't," Bess protested.

"Silly billy! I'm sure he'll be here any minute," Kay chided. "Go on."

"I am glad, because Mommy finished her thesis and today she got a telephone call from the man and they said it was very good and they wanted to make it into a real book."

There was a general "ah" and Louella ran across the kitchen to congratulate Kay. Louella looked very well. She was wearing long silver earrings and a bright blue turban that matched the blue in her dress, and if it weren't for the bandages that poked out of her sleeves whenever she lifted her arms, Laura would never have believed she was the same woman whom Dennis described as a twisted sex object, Edith found to be emotionally crippled, and Kay saw as the product of a sick urban environment.

To Laura she seem to be a normal woman, a bit overdressed, perhaps, for a gathering of people who did not believe in the importance of clothes and therefore dressed like farmhands, but her jewelry and brightly colored clothes were a refreshing change.

It was her first day out since her second suicide attempt, and Laura was sure that much of her nervousness came from her awareness that she was on trial. From the moment she had walked through the door, Kay had been going to great lengths to prove to her Minerva group that Louella was a full-fledged member of the extended Pyle family, that she provided invaluable insights into current black attitudes, that her daughter Jingle was thriving in the open environment of the Pyle household after a disturbing early childhood in a California ghetto.

Louella was not the only subject of Kay's continuous whispered commentary. She also went into great detail about Martin's success in his dual role of lover and foster father, and explained how the grandmother's iron morality provided the children with a sense of heritage and generational continuity. But Louella was sitting near enough to hear her, whereas Martin and the grandmother were not. Louella was also conscious of Melissa's hostile stare and Gail's dry-heaving when she rushed past her to congratulate Kay on her thesis. The reason Gail was dry-heaving was because she was allergic to perfume, but Louella misunderstood her. After she had kissed Kay on both cheeks, she laughed nervously and said, "Don't worry, you guys, I'm not a dirty dyke. That's just the way people congratulate each other in Europe."

Melissa's jaw dropped but before she could say anything, Kay motioned for Bess to continue her poem.

"I am glad," Bess said, looking at the ceiling, "because Dennis is going to make us a tree house starting tomorrow. I am glad, because Jingle gave me a beautiful ashtray that she made herself. I am glad, because Edith made me a nourishing cake that has . . . that has . . ." She looked helplessly at her mother. "A nourishing cake that has . . ."

"That has all sorts of lovely ingredients, like bee honey and golden sunflower oil and whole wheat flour that has none of the goodness taken out of it, and fresh brown eggs and lovely granola instead of frosting . . ."

Jingle pulled the snorkel out of her mouth. "Yuck. That sounds terrible."

Louella leaned over and slapped her. "You mind your manners, girl." Jingle opened her mouth wide to cry, only to be slapped again. Her teeth closed around the mouthpiece of the snorkel. Through the fog on the mask Laura could see Jingle's eyes fill with tears.

"Which ones are left?" Bess asked. "I'm getting hungry."

"Let's see," Kay said. "There's Martin, and Minerva, and Grandma, and Louella, and all your lovely little friends here . . ."

"I am glad," Bess continued, "because Minerva is born. I am glad, because Martin has a funny face that makes me laugh. I am glad, because Louella's cuts . . . because Louella isn't . . . didn't . . ."

"Because Louella looks so lovely in her blue-and-green dress," Kay said quickly, "and felt happy enough to come to my party."

Louella laughed and wiped some tears from her eyes.

"And I am glad," Bess concluded, "because my new friends from Edith's apartment house and my two new friends from across the ocean could come to my party even though I forgot to make them invitations because I didn't know them until Edith invited them while I was crying. Can we eat now? I'm starving."

"You left out Grandma," Sarah said.

"No, I didn't. We didn't write any line for Grandma so how could I leave her out?" Bess said.

"We didn't know she could make it in time," Kay interjected, "but I for one am very glad she did. And I'm sure she's just starving after that rally."

"What rally was that?" Melissa asked.

"The Daughters of the American Revolution," the grandmother told her. "I'm the head of our chapter. We've been active for generations. We can trace our ancestry back to the fifth English boat that ever . . ."

"What do you say about cutting open that cake?" Kay said in a loud voice. "I for one am just dying to have a taste."

"Right," said Edith, and she began to hand out pieces of the cake, along with the frozen strawberry yogurt that had never quite managed to freeze. Sarah took the first piece but after one bite she pushed away her plate and grimaced. The Fulbright sisters did the same. Bess and the two five-year-olds from Edith's apartment house plowed slowly through their servings, trying desperately to smile. When she thought no one was looking, one of them spat out a mouthful.

Everyone was looking. The girl was so embarrassed that she hid her face behind her hat and slid under the table. Jingle didn't even bother to try. Sobbing, she spooned little bits of melting frozen yogurt over the cake and watched them dribble down the sides. When her mother told her to cheer up, she said how could she, it was all so unfair. "Why did Bess have to steal all those tutus from my toy chest when her daddy's so rich?" she moaned.

"You know that's not true. And anyway, you ungrateful girl, you haven't even thanked Martin for that mask."

"But I didn't want a mask," she moaned.

"Nonsense, girl. Think how much fun it will be when the Pyles take you to the pool in the summer."

"But Sarah says I can't go. She says that pickaninnies never can learn how to swim."

"Who told you you were a pickaninny?" Louella asked sharply.

"Sarah told me I was a pickaninny." There was an embarrassing silence. Kay glared at Sarah and Sarah glared back. "Now I don't believe a word you say is true, and I think you are being a very ungracious guest," Louella said, "making up all those malicious stories. Shame on you. Everyone has been so nice to you here, and the least you could do is eat your friend Edith's cake."

"Why should I be the only one who eats it," Jingle whimpered, "when nobody else is?"

Edith laughed. "Well, I guess these kids don't think much of organic goodness."

"I can't see why," Louella said.

"Then I shall tell you," said the larger of the Fulbright sisters, "because it is not goodness."

The grandmother gasped, but before she could say anything, Kay said, "I am sure they make things differently in France. Especially cakes. Cakes in France are really yum."

"We are not from France," the younger sister said scornfully. "We are from Brussels."

"Cakes in Brussels are *really* yum," Kay said.

"It does not matter. We do not think that we children should be obliged to eat this cake. We think that possibly it is poison."

"If my mother saw it," the older sister added, "I am sure she would throw it out the window for the dogs."

No one knew quite what to say to that. Fortunately Martin was able to come to the rescue with a joke. "Did you kids ever hear the one about the dog in the Chinese restaurant?" While he amused the children by acting out the way dogs used chopsticks and devoured fortune cookies, Kay tried to patch things up by telling her Minerva group how it usually took a year or two for her children's foreign friends to overcome their cultural snobberies. "Despite the dangers involved in exposing children to prejudice, I still encourage intercultural contact," Kay told Rachel. Rachel started to point out that Bess didn't seem to know these particular foreign friends, but her voice was drowned out by Martin's barks as he continued with the one about the poodle in a china shop and the other about the first German shepherd on the moon. He rolled, whimpered, and panted until everyone, even Melissa and the grandmother, was laughing. His grand finale was to pick up a plate of cake from the table with his teeth and deliver it to Louella's lap.

"Oh, Martin," Louella giggled, "I don't think I've never met anyone who makes me laugh so much as you do."

"Martin's wonderful with children," Kay agreed, smiling at him indulgently as he rubbed his nose back and forth on Louella's leg. "I actually don't know how I could have gotten my thesis finished if it hadn't been for Martin."

"Now that you *have* finished," the grandmother said in her high, quavering voice, "I assume you will have more time to spend with the children."

"Well, as I explained to you already, I'll be primarily involved with this magazine. But the time commitment will be flexible, so there will be plenty of time for family fun."

"That's good to hear," the grandmother said. "I know my son feels just as strongly as I do about your staying closer to home."

"Actually," Kay said with an anxious smile and her voice low enough so that only the Minerva group and Laura could hear her, "my husband has been incredibly supportive of my efforts to establish a career. And the girls, too."

"And the girls too what?" Sarah asked.

"Oh, I was just telling your new friend Rachel here how glad you were that your silly old mother was trying to start a magazine."

"But I'm not," Sarah told her.

"Sarah!"

"I hate magazines. I think they're stupid. You know what I think about magazines?" Sarah said, surveying her audience with pleasure. "I think they're . . . frivolous."

"Ah," Kay said with great relief. "Now I get you. You're thinking about those normal, pointless magazines. Ours won't be like that. Our magazine will have a purpose."

"The reason *we* want to start a magazine," Edith explained, "is to make life easier for women who are lawyers and doctors and journalists and professors, so that by the time *you* go to college and choose a career, you will be able to develop to the fullest without any of the trouble *we* have had with sexists."

"I'm not going to college," Bess said softly.

"Oh," said Kay, rubbing her hair roughly, "I think you will."

"But I don't have to. Mothers don't have to go to college."

"*This* mother went to college," Kay reminded her. Bess looked at her suspiciously. "Hey, hey, don't look so sad. I think it's really funky that you want to have lots and lots of children, and I'll be the happiest grandma in the whole wide world if you do. But don't you have the desire to do something else too? Something different? Something daring?"

Bess shook her head. "I'm sure your friends do," Kay said. But on questioning the other children, it turned out that they all wanted to be mothers, except for one of the Fulbright sisters, who wanted to be a nurse. And Jingle, who started to cry again inside the mask when the topic of careers came up.

"I bet Jingle here is going to be the exception," Edith said, trying gently to remove the mask from Jingle's head. "What are *you* going to be? A pilot? An astronaut? An underwater fisherwoman?"

"I can't," Jingle sobbed.

"What do you mean, you can't?"

"It's not fair," she wailed. "I don't want to have to pick cotton balls all day long for my whole life!"

"Now whoever told you you had to do that?"

"Sarah told me! She even showed me the picture in one of her horse books, but I don't think it's fair. Do you? And I don't think it's fair for Bess's mother to steal all my tutus just because I have to be Sarah's slave."

There was an uncomfortable silence. Martin was just about to come to the rescue with another joke when a very haggard Bob Pyle appeared at the kitchen door. "Daddy!" Bess cried. She threw open the door and jumped into his arms. While he squeezed her against his chest and wished her a happy birthday, the older Fulbright sister turned to Sarah and said, "Why do you have two fathers?"

"I don't," she answered.

"Then who is this man?"

"My father."

"I thought the man who rolled on the floor like a dog was your father."

"No," Sarah explained, "that's Martin."

"Why does Martin kiss your mother if he is not your father?"

"Because Martin is her lover," Bess explained.

"Shut up," Sarah said. "You know you're not supposed to say that in front of strangers." The Fulbright sisters exchanged disapproving looks. "I do not know about your father," the older one said, "but if my mother kissed another man, my father, who is very strong, would beat her."

"Girls, girls, girls," Kay said, sweeping across the room into Bob's arms, "this is no way to welcome back our favorite knight in shining armor after a hard week in Washington." She kissed his forehead. "Come on over and let me introduce you to the latest additions to our crazy household."

"Additions?" Bob said, faintly alarmed. Kay led him firmly across the room. "This is the groovy fellow I was telling you about," she said to her Minerva group. "That hopeless optimist who's trying to inject some morality into the Nixon administration."

Bob Pyle cleared his throat. "Not anymore, I'm afraid." Kay wheeled around with drama and stared into his eyes.

"I'm afraid I've been fired."

"Oh, darling!" She buried her head into his bony chest and held him tight. "Darling, darling, darling. I don't know whether to laugh or cry."

"The order came straight from the Oval Office," Bob said with a crack in his voice. "Get that Bob Pyle out or else."

"Oh, oh, oh. After all that time and effort."

"Don't worry," said the grandmother, her eyes blinking back the tears, "there will be other administrations. Your time will come, Bobby darling, I'm sure of it."

"Did you bring all your things with you?" Kay asked, stepping back to look him straight in the eyes. "Are you back for good or will you have to return to attend to loose ends?"

"There are no loose ends. He's hatcheted the whole program. I'm back for good all right. Dirty laundry and all."

"Then I'll get Laura to make the bed in your study," Kay murmured. "And in the meantime let's see what we can do about that dirty laundry."

Arm in arm, they moved out to the hallway, and while they divided the contents of his two suitcases into whites and coloreds and talked to each other in low, shocked tones, the older Fulbright sister turned to Bess and said, "You have a very strange mother. All she does is kiss, kiss, kiss."

"That's not true!" Bess cried. "She also has a mind!"

"And she dresses like a gypsy," the Fulbright sister continued in a spiteful voice, "and I think she forgot to brush her hair."

"My sister and I think we want to go home now," said the other. "We have not enjoyed this party. Please, would you call for our mother."

Bess began to cry. "They hate my party," she whimpered. "Everyone in the whole world hates me."

The grandmother had had quite enough. She went over to the Fulbright sisters and said, "You two are the rudest children I have ever met in my entire life. I want you to apologize for your inexcusable rudeness to my granddaughter here, or else . . ."

"Please," Kay said, coming back into the kitchen, "no threats. You know we disapprove of the use of threats in this household."

"I'm tired of the spineless methods you use to bring up my son's children!" the grandmother raged. "I've had enough! Ten years I've been enduring your half-baked theories and I've had enough. Bobby, I just don't understand how you can let her tramp all over you the way she does. And if it's true what the children have been saying about this young man here . . ."

"If you are referring to Martin, Mother, he is a man of the highest integrity and a close personal friend," Bob Pyle said in a dull, unconvincing voice, "and I assure you that he would not be Kay's lover if I had not convinced them both that it would not harm our friendship."

"You're courting disaster, Bobby. You can't stand for it. If I were you I'd . . ."

"Mother," Bob said between clenched teeth, "I am not an eighteen-year-old boy."

"I would just like to try and knock some common sense . . ."

"I am a grown man, Mother, and if there is any common sense

to be knocked into my head, *I* will do the knocking." He glared at his mother with barely concealed hatred. Without saying another word, she grabbed her coat and left, slamming the door.

"Well," said Kay, "I'm glad *that's* over. I must say that my constitution can only take very small doses of Grandmother. Not that I don't recognize her value as a part of the family," she added when Rachel cleared her throat. "I think that her firm traditionalism helps the children put our own beliefs more into perspective."

"Sure," said Rachel.

"Well then," Kay said, "who'd like more of that scrumptious dandelion wine? It's time we all sat back and relaxed and enjoyed each other's company. And when we all have our wine in hand, I'd like to propose a toast to the man who dared to brave the wrath of Nixon."

"How could you ever compromise yourself to work for that crook?" Melissa asked, leaning forward. But before Bob could answer, Martin reminded him about the present he had forgotten to give to Bess. "Right you are," Bob said, jumping out of his seat. Confrontation was avoided.

Bob's present to Bess was yet another tutu, this one pink. Bess was hardly able to hide her disappointment. And Jingle went mad. "You thief!" she screamed. "You stole all three of my tutus and it's not fair! It's not fair, and I hate you Mr. Pyle! I don't want my mother to be your cook when you move into that big white house and I don't want to pick your cotton balls!" Louella rushed over to the table and was about the slap her when Martin caught her hand.

"Be easy on the kid, Lou. Let me talk to her." He picked up Jingle and placed her on his lap. "Now let's get to the bottom of this, shall we?" While Jingle patiently sucked her thumb, he explained to her that in his opinion Jingle was making up a lot of fairy tales about thieves and cotton balls, for the very simple reason that she was jealous. If Jingle came clean and admitted that she was jealous of the pretty tutus Bess had gotten for her birthday, then maybe they could do something about it. After a bit of coaxing, Jingle took her thumb out of her mouth and admitted she was jealous. She had been making up stories. There weren't any tutus in her toy chest and there weren't any thieves. Martin suggested that Jingle be given a reward for coming clean, and Bess offered one of her tutus.

"See, Jingle?" Martin said when she had put on her tutu, "it just doesn't pay to tell lies. See how nice people are to you if you tell the truth?" Jingle nodded. "Then let's hear you say it. 'From now on, I, Jingle, daughter of Louella, promise to tell the truth forever and ever, in sunshine and moonshine, no matter what the weather.' "

"I Jingle daughter of Louella promise to tell the truth in sunshine and moonshine forever in the weather."

To celebrate her new leaf Jingle did a ballet dance to a Joan Baez song. Laura had never seen her so open and happy. She laughed and twirled and jumped and curtsied so beautifully that no one noticed how jealous the Fulbright sisters looked. Until the older one reached out and tore a great clump of gauze from her tutu.

The Fulbright sisters didn't seem to think anyone should get so many rewards merely for admitting to a lie. Edith put their coats on and hustled them out of the house before they could expand on this theme.

Jingle was in hysterics. While Martin took her back into his arms and tried once again to calm her down, Kay turned to Laura and said, "What a pity we didn't get to screen those children." Her eyes glowered with the injustice of it all. "I'm afraid that after witnessing this afternoon, you must think that we're all totally mad!" she said, turning to Gail, Rachel, and Melissa. "I assure you that normally we are a very quiet, peace-loving group of people."

"That I'll believe when I see it," Rachel said.

"I guess a certain amount of conflict is inevitable in a large group. It's your ability to make peace that counts. Your flexibility in dealing with the real situations of everyday life," Kay ventured.

"I was never one for letting reality ruin my pet theories," Rachel said.

"Shall we all make a vow to be peaceful and loving for the rest of the afternoon?" Kay said in a loud voice.

Martin lifted the sobbing Jingle in the air. "What do you say to that?" he said. "Kay seems to think we should stop crying and start loving. Are you game?"

Jingle nodded. She put her head on Martin's shoulders and her hands around his neck. "I love you," she said.

And Martin said, "I love you, too."

"And you know what?" Jingle went on, "I'm glad that Bess's daddy has come back to live here forever. You know why? Because that means you can come and live in our house forever."

"Is that what you'd like?" he said, tickling her stomach.

"Yes. And then you can get married to my mother and I'll be the maid-in-waiting and then you'll never have to climb out of the bedroom window ever again when you hear me coming down the hallway, in sunshine or moonshine or any kind of weather."

Martin went a deep red. "I thought you promised not to tell any more stories."

"But it's the truth!" Jingle protested. "I saw you doing it with my own eyes. You thought I was sleeping but I was peeking through the door and then I made a noise, so you put on your pants and went out the window. And I was so scared. I thought you were going to fall and hurt yourself." Jingle paused, suddenly aware of Martin's embarrassed frown. She put her thumb in her mouth, but then Louella started giggling.

Her bracelets clanged and her turban shook as the giggling turned into laughter and the laughter into hysterical screams. "Oh, Kay," she gasped, but she couldn't finish. Jingle started to laugh with her mother, but then she looked up and saw Kay's lips twitching in a very uncharacteristic way. Her eyes glistened with a thousand emotions. She had been betrayed.

After a week of telling her Minerva group how wonderful families were, her children, her husband, her relatives, and now her lover had betrayed her. She had described a model family, and despite monumental efforts to keep her vision and the birthday party under control, the extended Pyle family had shown itself to be normal, argumentative, even subaverage.

In the course of the afternoon Kay's apologetic asides to her Minerva group had annoyed Laura. But now Laura saw that they were heroic efforts to present the people she had sacrificed her life for in a true perspective. Kay was a hero. At a time when Laura would have tried very hard to sink below the floor, Kay suddenly rose. She took the helplessly giggling Louella by the hand and said, "Don't be embarrassed. I understand." She said it with a compassion that Laura was sure was genuine.

Then Bob Pyle began to laugh. Kay let go of Louella's hand and turned around. She tried to smile but her eyes burned like coals. Her trembling lips became thinner and thinner.

Laura did not think it was fair for Bob to laugh so hard. She did not see what was so funny about Jingle's ill-timed decision to tell nothing but the truth. But there was no stopping him once he had started, and there was no telling Jingle that Bob Pyle's laughter, though hollow, did not make the situation certifiably funny. She rolled on the floor, delighted by the mirth she had so inadvertently caused.

That was the way Laura came to remember her, a small, round-faced, beautiful child in a half-torn tutu, kicking her feet with childish joy and looking toward Bob Pyle for approval, the purple ribbons in her hair half undone and her patent-leather shoes unbuckled, because that was the last time Laura ever saw her, and no matter what happens to a child in real life, in your mind's eye she never grows older.

— *12* —

At an emergency meeting of Family Council the next day, Kay announced that Jingle was to be banned for a minimum period of six months. Bob Pyle was going to arrange for her to spend the summer at a psychiatrist friend's farm, where she could play all day with the ducks and the cows and the pigs and also receive the therapy she needed in order to get well.

Laura had not expected such ruthless measures but even in her position as interim secretary, she had no voice in Family Council, and her opinion was not sought. She was shocked, and even more so when the children accepted without question that Jingle had been a bad influence who needed fresh air and professional help.

Bob Pyle acted almost sheepishly. When he pressed for questions, and Sarah asked why all black people were mentally disturbed, Bob went into a long explanation of how it was not the color of your skin but inadequate housing and broken families that caused mental illness. The children seemed satisfied by the graphs

ver the portable blackboard to prove his point. What
n't understand was why Martin had disappeared. Kay
d that he was getting ready to go on a long trip to Mexico,
at didn't make any sense to them. If he was going away for
ong time, why hadn't he said good-bye before he left?

Kay looked tired. She was wearing dark round sunglasses and
her hair was coming out of her ponytail. The morning light made
her look as if she had a halo. She didn't seem eager to answer the
children's questions. When Bess asked her for the third time why
Martin had left so abruptly, she sighed and pursed her lips. After
a long pause she said, "Because we felt that it was time he had a
good think." Although her voice was just as cheerful as ever, she
could not bring herself to smile.

"A good think about what, Mommy?"

"A good think about his feelings toward the family."

"Are you angry because he wants to marry Louella?"

"Let me stress two things," Kay said in her most matter-of-fact
voice. "First of all, neither Daddy nor I are *angry* at Martin.
Martin is a dear, dear friend of the family. And he didn't do
anything wrong. He certainly never asked Louella to marry him,
Bess. That was just the figment of the imagination of a very disturbed child."

"If he didn't ask Louella to marry him, then what did he do?"

Kay sighed and brushed some strands of hair off her forehead.
She turned to her husband, who was standing at the head of the
kitchen table, his head cocked thoughtfully, his back to the window. "Bob?" she said weakly. He cleared his throat.

"As you know, Martin has been spending a lot of time with
Jingle's mother lately, after her attempt to end her life. You see,
we wanted her to realize that there were people in the world who
loved her . . . people who would be very unhappy if she left this
world. It's what you call therapy. It's what you do for sick people
to make them well again, just like that psychiatrist is going to cure
Jingle. Well, Martin took his therapy a few steps too far. Instead

of merely establishing a friendship, he also establishe
a sexual relationship with her. Do you follow me so fa
peering at his children. "Sarah? Bess? Nathaniel? How a
Nathaniel? Between you and me, you look a little lost." Nat
put his thumb in his mouth and gave his father a blank stare.

"Martin and Louella made love," Bob ventured. "Now do you
understand?" Nathaniel shook his head.

"I think he's regressing," Kay said in a loud whisper.

"Hey, Nathaniel," Bob Pyle said, picking him up and removing the thumb from Nathaniel's mouth, "we've been through this hundreds of times before. What do cats and dogs do when they want babies?"

"They mate," Nathaniel said.

"Well. Then that's what Martin and Louella did," Bob said, a bit too joyously. "They mated. Martin took his penis and put it into Louella's vagina, just like our cats."

"Bob, please," Kay whispered.

"Is that all they did?" Bess asked, kicking her feet back and forth.

"As far as we know, yes," Bob said.

"Well, what's so bad that Martin has to move out of the house? I thought you said to me that making love to people was good."

"Of course it is. But making love is a very serious thing. People shouldn't make love by accident. You see, Martin had made a commitment to Kay and he should have consulted her beforehand."

"What's a commitment?"

"It's promising to do certain things for certain people."

"So what did Martin promise?" Bess asked.

"He promised to become a responsible member of our family."

"And you see," Kay added, her teeth flashing ominously under the dark round sunglasses, "if he were going to make love with Louella in a healthy way, then he would have to make a commitment to her, too."

"And if he promised to become a responsible member of her family, why, he wouldn't have enough time left to fulfill his commitment to Kay."

"So now he has to rethink his commitment," Kay added quickly, "and while he's thinking it over, Daddy is moving back into my bed."

Bess looked at him, puzzled. "What's wrong with your study?" she asked. Her father chuckled sadly. He sat down next to Bess and took her hand in his.

"Let me see if I can explain. Now first of all, who is your Daddy, Martin or me?"

"You."

"And who paid for this house?" Kay opened her mouth to speak but Bob silenced her. "Don't think I'm trying to put down your thirty-seven percent, dear. I was just trying to make a point."

"But we don't want them to get the wrong . . ."

"All right. All right," he said in a tired voice. "Who paid for sixty-three percent of this house, and who," his voice suddenly shrill, "pays for you to go to school, and to eat, and to go on vacations?"

Bess thought for a long time. Finally she said she didn't know.

"Well, I do," he said dully.

"Oh."

"Of course this won't always be so," Kay added. She took off her glasses. Her eyes were puffed up but they still glittered. "As soon as I get my degree, and as a matter of fact if this Minerva idea gets rolling, even before I get my degree . . ."

"Kay, I was only asking Bess . . ."

"But I didn't want you to give them the impression that fathers are the only ones who ever . . ."

"Would you kindly let me finish!" Bob hissed through gritted teeth. "Now that I'm back in my own house, I'll be damned if I can't have my say!" For two seconds his face was convulsed with anger, but then as he turned toward his daughter the mask of serenity reappeared. "The long and the short of it, Bess, is that since I'm your father and I earn the money and this is after all my house, I should have the right to sleep wherever I choose."

"And since Martin decided that the time was ripe for him to rethink his commitment to this family," Kay added brightly, "everything has worked out for the very best."

"What will happen when Martin comes back?" Sarah asked.

"I'm not certain he will," Bob said.

"Please," Kay said, "try not to prejudge the case."

"Well, let's be honest about this, Kay. I goddamn well hope he's not."

"Do you hate him?" Bess asked.

"No, dear, I just feel tired of other people taking over our house. I feel much happier when it's just the five of us in the house."

Kay winked at Laura. "Plus Laura, of course," she said playfully.

"Of course," he said, "plus Laura."

"And Dennis."

"And Dennis," Bob Pyle agreed.

"And Edith when she wants to come and play."

"And Edith when she wants to come and play." He stood up, defeated, and moved toward the stairs.

"I have just one question before you go up," Sarah shouted. "And boy! Are you out of practice! How do you think you are going to leave the room if we haven't even adjourned?"

Bob Pyle turned. "What's your question?"

"How can you say that you pay for everything when you've just been fired and you can't earn any money at all?"

"*Bravo!*" Kay said.

"I will continue as planned," Bob Pyle said softly. "Washington was just an experiment, an experiment that did not work. I have a book to write, and as you know, I will be returning to the university in September. We will talk about all of that some other time. But for the moment, Sarah, I request that the meeting be adjourned. And please try to be quiet. I have a headache."

Without waiting for anyone to second the motion, he turned his back to the kitchen and plodded up the stairs. Kay gazed for a few seconds at the cabinets above the telephone table, then jumped out of her seat and bounded up the stairs after him. When she caught up with him in the washing machine alcove there was a loud kiss. "Oh, darling, I didn't mean to hurt your feelings, if that's what's bothering you. But *do* you have to be such a patriarch?"

The intercom in the washing machine alcove was on, so when he threw her against the drier it sounded in the kitchen like a truck unloading a large load of rocks. The intercom magnified the noise greatly, Laura decided, because there were no screams when Kay picked herself up, just a long, loud, metallic sigh. "I suppose you can live without freshly laundered shirts until Dennis has a chance to try and fix it," she said.

"I suppose I'll have to."

Laura felt empty for the rest of the day. She couldn't understand how Bob Pyle could become so violent without even raising his voice or losing his temper. And the reasoning during the Family Council meeting disturbed her.

Kay had often told Laura that she was a full-fledged member of the family, and encouraged her to say what she felt at all times. But Kay was not her mother; she was her employer. And employers could get rid of you if you didn't behave as they thought fit. Which was why Laura had always tried to act more politely than she had in her own home, and had stopped having temper tantrums altogether, and hesitated to criticize Kay, even when Kay invited her to, even when she thought Kay might be wrong.

"Why the long face?" Kay asked when they were stacking the lunch dishes in the dishwasher.

"I'm worried about Jingle," Laura said.

And Kay said, "Golly, so am I."

Downstairs in Children's Paradise, Dennis assured her that Jingle was better off in the hands of professionals. When you were that disturbed, he told her, amateurish love and care only made things worse. He and Edith would make sure nothing drastic happened to Louella. "And as far as the other thing is concerned," he said, "it's pretty obvious that you regard Bob and Kay as father and mother figures. That's why you get upset when they have a fight and descend to the level of ordinary humans."

Maybe Dennis was right. He certainly knew more than she did about the human mind. But there was something else that disturbed her. While she leafed through Sarah's horse books in search of racist illustrations (to be on the safe side Kay had asked her to double-check), she tried to translate her uneasiness into words, but she couldn't.

13

Just when Laura was getting over her infatuation stage and coming to accept Dennis as an older brother, he decided it was time for them to make love. It was the same day Edith announced to the Minerva group that she was feeling bruised and exhausted on account of having been picked up by a townie. Laura could not help wondering if that had something to do with his decision. There had to be other considerations, Laura said to herself, when he threw down his tools and led her down the hall from the washing machine alcove to the master bedroom. Dennis was much too mature to be governed by jealousy alone.

Kay had arranged for Bob Pyle to attend that day's Minerva meeting as a special consultant, so for the first afternoon since he had returned from Washington, he was out of his pajamas and the master bedroom was free. The sheets were all wrinkled and the furry bedspread was half on the floor, but when Laura instinctively tried to make the bed Dennis lunged over and tried to pull off her

"Stop acting like a housewife," he said gruffly, "we have to this spontaneous or else there's no point."

That made Laura feel insulted, and although she had been longing to make love with him, she froze up inside. They had an argument. First of all, Laura told him, she wasn't going to make love with him unless he assured her that Edith didn't mind. Edith was her friend now, and she didn't want to hurt her feelings. Dennis assured her that Edith didn't mind. Second of all, Laura told him, she wasn't going to make love with him if he treated her like a sex object. She resented his reference to housewives and she didn't want him tearing off her clothes. Her jeans were slightly ripped already. Dennis apologized. He was suddenly very meek.

"And there's one more thing," she said as she took off her clothes. "Do you want to make love to me just because you happen to be horny, or do you want to make love to me personally?" He told her what she wanted to hear. He wanted to make love to her personally. He covered her face with kisses and climbed on top of her, already breathless.

Laura was very proud of herself. She had asked all the right questions. She had asserted herself in a very liberated way. She had proved to herself that she was no longer passive. Now she could relax and enjoy the unexpected luxury of making love with the person she loved more than anyone else in the world. Even though she was almost over her infatuation stage, she still loved him. And she was sure she would always love him, if only eventually as an older brother. When he had kissed her in the washing machine alcove, her heart had been pounding so fast that she had almost fainted.

The trouble was that she was no longer aroused. The question-and-answer period had killed all her romantic illusions. She was glad he did not think of her as a sex object, but the answers he had given to her formula-questions had been so devoid of passion that she no longer felt any passion either.

She wondered if she should stop him and explain that she was no longer excited. But Dennis was very worked up and by the time he had managed to enter her, his face was red and he huffed and puffed like a man halfway up a mountain. Laura could feel nothing except for a faint itch in her vagina and a soreness where a bedspring rubbed against her bottom, and the same soothing sensation of weight on her stomach that she had enjoyed as a child when her friends had buried her alive on a beach in Lebanon. The last thing she wanted to do was to make Dennis any more frustrated than he was (she was sure that was why he had called her a housewife), so she looked at his narrow white bottom in the mirror on the ceiling and tried to excite herself by thinking of other people's fantasies. Years of repressive sexual behavior had prevented her from developing her own. Waves pounding against rocks, galloping horses, chariots, spaceships, crowds, obelisks, whips—nothing she could think of made her heart beat faster, and when she closed her eyes all she saw were furry white lambs leaping over a fence.

She thought of all the hours she had spent clinging to her pillow, longing for a chance to make love with Dennis, and to feel his naked body against hers. And suddenly she felt happy that she could put her arms around him and rub her nose against his neck. But Dennis's neck kept bobbing up and down and happiness soon turned into boredom, and boredom soon brought on despair and despair's attendant unanswerable questions. She was sorry to note that excitement had done nothing for Dennis's appearance. He had lost his air of superiority that Laura had found so attractive. The pupils of his eyes had all but disappeared under his eyelids. They bobbed wildly among the lashes and the great expanse of white below them made him look more like an idiot than a college graduate. His nostrils were distended and Laura could see every little hair inside them.

Was this all sex was? Laura asked herself as she averted her eyes to look instead at the depressing way the afternoon sunshine highlighted the dust on the wooden floor. Was this the reason why Louella was no longer welcome in the Pyle house, and why Martin had to go all the way to Mexico to think things over, and what Kay had wanted to do with Martin so badly that Bob Pyle had had to spend his weekends on the couch in his study? Was this all Jingle had seen when she peeked through the keyhole? Laura longed for the pushing and heaving to come to an end. As she had done so often on long boat journeys, when the world seemed to be an endless sea of small gray waves and the boat's constant bobbing deprived her life of any possible meaning, Laura closed her eyes and imagined she was in her own bed at home reading a mystery story, a tray of toast and tea on her bedside table.

Then Dennis stopped pushing back and forth and asked her, "Have you come yet?" She told him no. "Well, listen, I can't wait all day."

"There's no need for you to wait all day," Laura said. "Come whenever you want. I don't think I'll be able to come today, but it doesn't matter."

"What do you mean, it doesn't matter? Of course it matters. It matters a fucking great deal. I mean, if you can't come, I might as well jerk myself off. Why don't you try and move around a little? For the last half hour you've just been lying there like a rock."

So Laura tried to move around a little. She was not quite sure what Dennis intended her to move, and since her torso was firmly pinned under his, she waved her legs around and tickled his bottom lightly with her fingers. She had very little experience in lovemaking, and the few times she had made love with Stavros he had very firmly told her *not* to move. That was why she was now in a quandary, but she was too embarrassed to explain this to Dennis. And since it seemed as if he was about to come, she did not want to interrupt him. In a halfhearted attempt to make up for her stupidity when he told her not to tickle his bottom, she started to give him a love bite, but she wasn't quite sure how to do that either, and while she clamped her lips on the side of his neck, trying to get up enough courage to sink her teeth in, Dennis slowly lost his erection. Swearing, he climbed off the bed.

"You didn't give me a chance," Laura said. "I was just about to get excited."

"Come off it," he said. "I don't know if you've always been this way or if someone has fucked you up, but in your present condition you have about as much libido as a fucking Barbie doll."

"That's not fair!" Laura shouted in an effort to appear assertive, but secretly she was ashamed of herself for not being excited and not knowing how to move. Dennis stalked across the floor, and Laura noted with disappointment that he looked very silly with nothing else on but his white socks. When he had retrieved his cutoffs and his T-shirt and left the room, slamming the door behind him, Laura curled up in a little ball at the foot of the bed and tried sadly to remember Dennis as a superior being, the way she had thought of him before finding out about the socks and the hairs in his nose and all the other disappointing details that romance and infatuation and dark closets eliminated.

And while she was wondering if she was one of those people who only had orgasms if other people gave them finger jobs, Edith crept into the room. Laura was only half dressed, so she covered herself with the bedspread, but Edith pulled it off. "There's no need to be modest in front of me," she said. "We're both sisters."

She had come upstairs to find out how things had gone. She sat cross-legged on the floor gazing thoughtfully into Laura's eyes as Laura explained how Dennis had blown up at her because she had failed to become excited. She asked Edith if there was something wrong with her, and Edith assured her there wasn't.

"Honestly," she said, "men are so self-centered sometimes. Sometimes they think that the sight of their hairy chests is enough to melt us with sexual desire. But Dennis is usually pretty good about these things as long as you remind him. Next time just make sure he sucks you or something before penetration."

Laura was astonished by Edith's generous hints and clinical detachment when discussing someone she had lived with for three and a half years. She seemed completely free of that sickness called jealousy as well as all other inhibitions. When she suggested that they go downstairs for lunch and Laura got up to finish dressing, Edith neither stared at her breasts or made any effort to ignore them. She just accepted them as part of the environment, a completely natural addition to the bedroom decor.

Downstairs Bob and Melissa were deeply involved in an argument about alternative working hours for professional mothers. It had been decided a few days earlier that *Minerva* should strive to present a "rainbow of opinion" instead of a predetermined stance. Instead of editorials there would be a ten-page forum in which the editors would discuss a single topic from many different points of view. For the dummy they had chosen the innocuous topic of working hours for professional mothers (they didn't want to scare off any prospective backers by appearing too radical) but since they all seemed to agree about the importance of alternative working hours for professional mothers, they were having a hard time making it into a controversy worthy of the forum format.

So Bob had been brought in as "the voice of the other half" and devil's advocate. By introducing Bob into the meeting, Kay had hoped to bolster up his badly bruised ego as well as provide her Minerva group with a springboard for ideas, but by the time Edith and Laura arrived in the kitchen, the bull session had disintegrated into a fight. Bob was saying that in a democratic society it would not be fair to grant alternative working hours to women unless they were also offered to men, and Melissa was accusing him of being a bureaucratic rapist.

There was a sign on the refrigerator. "Could anyone (male, female, cat, dog, carpenter, person?) who has a free moment to toss together some tuna salad please feel free to do so? And how about some yummy fruitcake to go with it? Gee, thanks, Kay." Laura knew from experience that this was Kay's way of asking Laura to make lunch, so while Bob told Melissa that he had not come down to be abused by a rabid lesbian and Melissa told him that she had always known he would turn out to be a sexist, Laura cut up the onions for the tuna fish salad and searched in vain among the six-month-old apples and hardened strands of bacon on the bottom rung of the refrigerator for a stalk of celery.

Kay was trying desperately to restore the peace. "Oh, can't you try to treat my husband as a person instead of dealing with him as a stereotype? Can't you understand that he is not a male chauvinist but a good and sensitive man who is *on our side?*"

"He's not on *my* side," said Melissa. "He's the type who would do anything in his power to ruin my life."

"Oh, why oh why must you take things so personally, Melissa!"

"How can I *not* take things personally," Melissa retorted, "when for the last two hours he has hardly ever taken his eyes off Gail's tits?"

"Oh, come, come. Such unfounded jealousy will get us nowhere," Kay said. But then Bob must have looked at Gail's breasts, because Melissa jumped up and said, "See? He just can't get over the fact that someone as tiny and delicate as Gail would prefer me to a gorilla like him."

"My Bob hardly has the physique of a gorilla," Kay said in a jokey voice, but instead of relieving the tension, her remark made Bob jump up from the table and march upstairs.

"And just for the record," Gail said in her thin, bored whine, "he *hasn't* been able to take his eyes off me for the last hour. I guess maybe this has something to do with this Indian blouse I'm wearing. But honestly, I really think that in this day and age I should be able to wear whatever I want without being stared at like a sex object or something. I really am offended, well, not offended really, I mean I'm not against being admired, it's just that I don't like to be lusted after . . ."

"So much for jealousy being unfounded," Melissa said. "Ask Gail. He's been secretly lusting after her ever since the day they met."

"Well, I mean, if I were still into men," Gail continued, "I'd probably be *complimented* by all the attention he's been giving me.

— 163 —

But the thing is it's really hard to get my head together about my bisexuality when he's constantly . . ."

"But I had no idea!" Kay said. She was balancing Sarah on one knee and Bess on the other. Laura could not tell whether her pained expression was caused by Nathaniel's attempt to climb on her head or Gail's confession.

"We didn't want to hurt your feelings by telling you what your husband's been doing behind your back," Melissa said.

"No need for such delicacy," Kay assured her. "Bob and I granted each other complete sexual freedom months ago. But in a way of apology to you, Gail," she added in a deeper voice, "I feel I should tell you that Bob and my sexual relationship is not at the present time very rosy, and since he seems to have no other established outlet it is very possible that this interest in you is due to severe sexual frustration. But don't worry. I'll talk to him about it tonight."

"He's probably one of those assholes with an Oriental fetish," Melissa moaned. "They're such a goddamned pain in the ass, so assured of their own importance. When will they realize they're superfluous? Why can't the world just let us live in peace?"

"That's the motto of the extended family," Kay reminded her in a gentle voice, "and in the same breath let me say that it is one that *this* family takes with a grain of salt. We have an additional creed: 'Thou art not an island. Seek happiness among your spouse and children, but do not lose consciousness of affection among a larger community.' "

Laura looked up from her tuna fish salad to see if there was any irony in Kay's expression, any hint that her tongue might be in her cheek, but instead she saw the usual loving smile and eyes glistening with sincerity. Nathaniel was pounding her head with a rubber hammer, but Kay was paying no attention to the popping sound the hammer made or Nathaniel's constant chatter. "Don't stick that thing in me ever again," he was saying, "you bastard! Don't you ever stick that in me again, or I'll take this hammer, and I'll . . ."

"How can you believe this love-and-peace hogwash?" Melissa said, drowning out Nathaniel's pip-squeak voice. "The fact is that men are threatened by the fact that women are not dependent on them for orgasm. Even if they don't think they are, men are out to destroy us."

"Not true," Kay said evenly. She took Nathaniel's hands and removed the rubber hammer from his grasp. "Not in this house at any rate. We're here to love you and help you and accept you as you are."

Kay smiled sweetly as Laura brought the tuna salad sandwiches to the table. As soon as she had taken her place next to Edith, Dennis came slinking through the kitchen, in his hand a tool box. "Your drier's fixed," he said to Kay.

"Oh, wonderful. Now I wonder if you'd mind finding out where that penny in the dishwasher motor has got to, while you still have that tool box in hand." He nodded heavily.

"Hey, cowboy! Catch!" Edith shouted, throwing Dennis a sandwich. Half the filling fell on the floor before he could catch it. "Serves you right for skipping foreplay, cowboy." She winked and gave him a radiant smile. Dennis quickly sank down below the counter to deal with the dishwasher motor.

Melissa was pacing the floor, chewing her sandwich thoughtfully. "I wonder," she said, stopping at the bay window. "You're always talking about love and freedom of choice, but what if your daughter became a lesbian? Or Nathaniel started fooling around with boys? Would you be so ready to say we're healthy influences then?"

Kay cocked her head thoughtfully. There were murmurings among the group.

Nathaniel took a piece of Kay's tuna sandwich and tried to stick it on her forehead, and Kay waved it away as if it were a fly. "You know, Melissa," she said, "in a way you're right. I've thought it over and yes, I admit that I would be a mite upset if Bess here came home one day and told me she had decided she was a lesbian. I would learn to accept it, of course, especially if it seemed that the relationship in question was productive. But given the unspoken preconceptions of a mother, my first reaction would probably be one of dismay."

Bess squirmed and said, "What are you talking about?"

Kay let out a concerned sigh. "We were just discussing how I would feel if you became a lesbian, dear."

"What's a lesbian?"

"It's a woman who loves other women instead of men."

Sarah covered her mouth and giggled.

Melissa swallowed her lips. Rachel sighed. Gail gave the bay window an inscrutable look and ran her pale white fingers through her hair, very slowly.

"No dear," Kay said sternly. "It is not a joke. It happens all the time."

"Like when?" Sarah asked.

"Gail and Melissa love each other, for example."

"Oh," Sarah said, "you mean that's why they're always smooching and holding hands, because they love each other? I thought it was because they were queer."

"Please, Sarah, try not to use that cruel word. There's nothing wrong with women who love other women."

"Do *you* love other women?" Sarah asked her.

"Oh, I love *lots* of other women very much, Sarah, but so far only platonically."

"What does that mean?"

"It means that I have never made love with another woman."

"Made *love?*" Bess laughed. "You mean Gail and Melissa make love? How can they do that if they have no penises?"

Kay frowned. She seemed hesitant to go into details. Finally she said, "Well, there are many ways to excite the human body and cause orgasm without the use of a penis."

"But they can't have babies," Bess pointed out.

"That's true," Kay agreed.

"I thought people made love so they could have babies."

"Not always, my little chickadee. Sometimes they make love for self-fulfillment and pleasure. And it just so happens that whereas some women derive self-fulfillment and pleasure from making love with men, other women derive self-fulfillment and pleasure from making love with other women."

"Well," said Sarah, making a face, "I don't think I'm going to become a lesbian, so you don't have to worry."

"Why not?"

"Because they're ugly."

"Oh, you silly billy," Kay said. *"That's* not a very good reason."

"At least, Gail and Melissa are ugly," Sarah said, watching them squirm uncomfortably in their chairs. "I can't understand how they can even love each other."

"Sarah, my little chickadee!" Kay exclaimed. "How many times have I told you that it is not the skin that counts but the heart underneath?"

"Then why aren't *you* a lesbian?"

"Gee, I don't know. That's a very good question. I guess it is because of societal pressures from when I was young. Everything's different now, though. I just haven't had time to catch up with the times."

"Is Laura a lesbian?"

"Gee, you know what? I've never asked her. Or Edith for that matter. How do you two feel about it?" Kay asked. "Do you swing both ways or are you boring old heterosexuals like me?"

Edith was trying to comb her bushy blond hair into a bun. "I've always meant to try it," she said between bobby pins. "Of course, sexually speaking, I'm just coming out of hibernation. The closest thing I've ever had to a lesbian relationship was with my freshman roommate."

"With Miriam? You never told me that," Dennis said, rising from behind the kitchen counter.

"Well, there's really not much to it. More mental than physical, if you know what I mean." Dennis didn't. He looked at Edith with incredulity as she drew up her chair behind Laura's.

"Did anyone ever tell you you have beautiful hair?" Edith murmured. "I just love the color. It's what I call natural henna." She brushed out the half-formed tangles and then began to comb Laura's hair with her fingers. "I guess I'll get around to it sooner or later," she continued, "it's not that I'm in any great rush."

"I've more or less decided to give it a try myself if ever a Mrs. Right happens to wander into my life," Kay said. Bess gave her mother a very sad look. Nathaniel was trying to tear great clumps of hair from Kay's head. He was threatening to burn her into little pieces if she ever tried to stick it in again, so Kay decided to take him up to his bath earlier than usual. He could probably use that afternoon nap.

While the others spread out through the house, Edith continued her games with Laura's hair. Buns, braids, curls, dramatic twirls —the constant brushing made Laura's skull tingle. She relaxed completely, possibly because she was fairly certain that Edith's soothing fingers would not stray from her head. At the other end of the house, she heard Melissa say, "I should never have allowed you to wear that blouse. It's practically transparent." Melissa was a caricature of the jealous husband, Laura said to herself. She felt vastly superior to her. It was so much better to be friends with people than to be their lovers. Because their friendship was a union of minds rather than bodies, she and Edith would be friends forever, forever above jealousy. They were sisters, and sisters never blew up at each other or hurt each other's feelings or had temper tantrums like Dennis. And the pleasure she derived from Edith's brushing was so much easier, so relaxing and so free from risk, Laura thought.

3
SUMMER

14

Summer came slowly. On the first warm day, which wasn't until the middle of May, the dormitories on Laura's quadrangle organized a celebration. The dining halls made picnic lunches and everyone went outside to sit on the grass and listen to a band called Jagger Clapton. Laura spent the afternoon on her window ledge working her way through a box of chocolate cookies and staring at the sea of blue jeans and red bandannas and painfully white flesh below her.

As in any crowd there were exceptions—the small group playing Frisbee near the library, the people reading on tree branches, the black militants who, in accordance with their policy of being very visible and very separate, had occupied the small hill to the left of Laura's window. But the rest were as indistinguishable as soldiers on parade. They all lay on their backs with their knees in the air and their arms beneath their heads, staring at the sky while Jagger Clapton pounded out one psychedelic instrumental after another.

When a big black cloud appeared in the sky, they quietly gathered their belongings and went inside, only to reappear as the first drops were falling. Hands high, mouths open to receive the rain, they ran around the quadrangle in joyful disarray. What started out as a celebration ended up as a mudsliding contest. When a police car appeared a few minutes later at the north gate, the two fastest mudsliders sped through the puddles shouting "Power to the people!" One of them gave the police car the finger and the other gave it the revolutionary fist. As if responding to a single will, the crowds on the sidelines shouted "Pigs!" Patiently, blankly, Laura waited for spring fever to turn into the revolution that was going to make them cancel exams. But the police did not react as the upperclassmen on Laura's floor had led her to believe they would. No tear gas, no troopers, no tanks, no smoke bombs. After a few tense moments the police car turned around and went off in the opposite direction. For the first time in years the revolution did not happen.

That night Laura panicked. She had three days to learn German, five days to study five thousand years of Chinese history, and one weekend in which to read all of Shakespeare's comedies. The Pyles had not left her with much free time for schoolwork: although Kay tried hard not to interfere with Laura's academic commitments, there had been any number of last-minute emergencies, and so Laura had ended up skipping more than half her classes that term.

Kay was very understanding when Laura called up to explain. "Don't you worry about us," she said. "You just go ahead and study for those horrid exams. And anyway, Melissa and Gail are moving into my study while they look for another apartment, so there won't be any lack of mother's helpers while you're gone." She had a special voice for emergencies, soft and ultracalm. "And hey," she said before hanging up, "the kids will miss you."

Laura managed to get through the first two exams without much trouble. She had always been good at languages and the main text for her Chinese history course had excellent summaries. It was

Shakespeare who undid her. Halfway through the ninth comedy she came down with what she was sure was a fever. It was five in the morning, only four hours until the exam started. The nurse on duty had her hands full with other, more serious problems such as suicides and overdoses, so she refused to admit Laura and sent her away with a bottle of aspirins.

Somehow Laura managed to write her way through that exam, too, but the experience scarred her. That night she had a nightmare about a wedding ceremony that never ended. Several times she woke up in a sweat and then, when she closed her eyes, she saw it again: the same procession of maidens with roses in their hair and men who looked like Greek statues, the same white-haired parents limping behind them, the disturbingly familiar court jesters and the donkeys that brayed whenever the lute music stopped. They went around and around, pausing only to make speeches. Their voices sounded like seawater. The land below them swayed like a raft in a storm.

Then she had a week, a whole week, to write a paper for her anthropology course. It was a course she had enrolled in at the last moment, when she decided to drop her psychology course after reading about an experiment in which a psychologist chopped off a monkey's hands to find out about its tactile perception.

It was quiet in the dormitory. Laura's roommate spent most of her time asleep because she had to write a paper for her course on dreams and she hadn't had any dreams yet since the beginning of the year. Laura was too lazy to go to the library so she decided to write her anthropology paper on the one book she had bought for the course. Little did she know that its radical theories about society and human thought would paralyze her. For five days she sat on her bed unable to write a thing.

Years earlier Laura had gone through a brief religious stage and then, for a while, she had been a nihilist. But to walk around all day reminding yourself that nothing had any meaning was like trying to sleep while a fly kept landing on your nose. Eventually she had come to the unsatisfactory conclusion that there was something somewhere called God or Good or Truth or Heaven that made life worth living. Now this book deprived her of even this uncertain comfort.

She was ignorant of even the most basic tenets of anthropological theory, as she had attended only five of the lectures and slept through three of them. Consequently, she had read the book out of context, and its radical theories were just out of reach. But only just. Desperately she tried to formulate the truth she almost understood in her own words. But the only thing she was able to think while her roommate moaned about the F she was going to get in her dream course because of her inability to dream, the only thing she could say to the yellowing posters that surrounded her—the naked foot, the brilliant sunsets, the Desiderata gravestone—was that the only truth was that there was no truth and that society was a box.

Society was a box. Nothing had any meaning outside the box. Outside the box was the unknown. Laughter was just another way of dealing with the unknown. Inside the box, everything was ordered. "Dirty" just meant "out of place." "God" was just another relative concept. He only existed in your mind, and there wasn't anything anywhere called Good either, or Truth, or Heaven, that gave life meaning. Life had no meaning. Life was just what went on in that box. And there couldn't be any freedom either, not if you were imprisoned in that box. Laura had been fooling herself when she thought she was free.

Her mind reeling with inaccurate generalizations, and still unable to write, Laura drove herself to hysterical laughter, but every time she laughed she was reminded of what laughter really was and ultimately of the fact that society was a box. This made her laugh even more. Even though she gave up on the sixth day and went to the library to write a paper on the customs of Navahos, she was still in terrible shape the following afternoon when she moved out of her dorm room, which, after she had put her books and winter clothes away into boxes, also looked like a box. As she dragged her suitcases over to the Pyle house, she wished she could turn off her mind and never have to think again.

She was going to spend her entire summer vacation at the Pyles', even though her parents had made a gesture of unprecedented generosity and offered to pay her way home. "We miss you," they had written, "and we won't let a few hundred dollars keep us separated." For a few days in May when the weather was terrible, Laura was on the verge of accepting, but Kay and the children were so upset when she mentioned she might take a few weeks off to go see her parents that she decided against it. Her parents were acting selfishly, she decided. They had to realize sooner or later that they could no longer monopolize her time. And besides, the Pyles needed her. Kay even called her indispensable. She had no choice but to stay.

"Welcome!" said the note she found waiting for her on the kitchen table. "Rachel and I have gone down to New York to drum up some support for *Minerva*. Would you believe Margaret Mead?!! Hey, you must be tired after all those exams. Why not take it easy. I hope you don't mind camping out in Bob's study for the time being. See you! Peace, Kay." Next to her signature was the smiling face that had almost become her trademark.

During the two weeks that Laura had been absent from the Pyle house, the trees in the backyard had filled out, and although she could hear the children's laughter in the backyard she could not see them through the bay window. Just the occasional splash of color between the green leaves as they ran back and forth. It was oppressively humid and Laura could not find the energy to go outside and greet them. It was only with the greatest effort that she made it up to Bob Pyle's study. Opening both windows to catch any breeze that might happen to wander by, she stretched out on the sofa and tried, unsuccessfully, to go to sleep.

The floor was covered with pieces of paper that rustled slightly with every stray gust of wind. Discarded pages from

Bob Pyle's book, or was it an article? Some were crumpled up, others folded. Most had only a few sentences written on them. "The power struggle at the upper echelons of HEW is indicative of . . ."; "The increased politicization of what should rightfully be a nonaligned . . ."; "How can a man—or a woman—of conscience hope to . . ."; "There is only one conclusion a man —or indeed a woman—of conscience can come to when confronted with a situation in which the good of the nation is being deliberately sacrificed for . . ."; "When faced with the terrible insouciance with which the present government approaches the problems of the poor and infirm, a man, or a woman of conscience . . ."; "At this point, a man—or indeed a woman . . ." Then, on the end of the couch, were several drafts of an unfinished letter.

Dear Ted, We're all just thrilled about your suggestion that the Pyle clan get together this Christmas, and Saint Croix sounds like just the place for the big bash. Gee, I don't think I've been back to old Saint Croix in a full ten years! I've discussed the idea with Kay and she is just as enthusiastic as . . .

Dear Ted, That Saint Croix reunion you suggested is just what the doctor ordered. Gee, I don't think I've been down there for a full eight or nine years. As a matter of fact, I was running out to buy our tickets when Kay reminded me that . . .

Dear Ted, I'm afraid we won't be able to make it to the reunion, much as we would love to. First of all, I have a lot of work left to do on *The Road to Legitimacy* before it goes to press some time this year, and Kay has gotten all wrapped up in a new magazine idea . . .

Dear Ted, We're all just thrilled at the prospect of Saint Croix this Christmas. Frankly, I think it is just what the doctor ordered. I could use a sunny vacation after the Washington debacle, and poor Kay is working herself to the bone over some ridiculous women's magazine. You'd think there were enough of them on the stands already! How on earth will the market absorb another, especially if it turns out to be as highbrow as she plans? Oh well, you know Kay! She's as stubborn as ever! Nonetheless, I will do my utmost to convince her that she needs a vacation, although the crew of misfits she is working with will probably say I am using this vacation as an excuse to exert my God-given . . .

Dear Ted, If it weren't for the fact that liberated women never take vacations . . .

Dear Ted, If it weren't for the fact that I have a book to finish that is already two years overdue and that I will be a dead man in the profession if I don't get it done very soon, we would certainly be joining you in Saint Croix. Kay especially is pining away for a good vacation. She's been overextending herself as usual and says that if she weren't so worried about my career, she would jump at the . . .

Dear Ted, What a grand idea to get together! But to be perfectly frank, I don't think it is the right time for me to go traipsing around the Caribbean. I have been suffering from a crisis of confidence as a result of the Washington upset, and between you and me, my work has suffered too. You know what they say! Publish or . . .

Laura was too tired to read the others. She was tired of words and tired of people, especially unhappy people. Propping herself up on some cushions she looked out the window and tried to find peace of mind among the large green leaves of the oak tree. Just beyond them, standing on the top branches of another oak tree, was Dennis, his straight blond hair tied back into a ponytail. He was working on Children's Retreat, the third and highest level of the famous tree house. Looking below him, Laura saw that the other two levels, Children's Escape Pad and Children's Observation Deck, were already finished.

She remembered the fights they had had thinking up those names. In the beginning each child was going to have his own private level—Sarah was going to call her level Horseback Heaven, Bess was going to call hers the Pink Palace, and Nathaniel was going to call his Bomber Plane. Kay had been disturbed by the sudden reemergence of the word bomber in Nathaniel's vocabulary. When it became apparent that he was not going to switch to another, Kay decided against private ownership of tree-house levels. Days of squabbling followed. Then the children lost interest in the naming of the tree house, leaving Kay with the task of thinking up suitable names.

Just below the tree house was Melissa. She was running around the lawn with a hose, and the children were running ahead of her, screaming with delight as they jumped in the spray. At first Laura did not recognize her. She looked strangely vulnerable in her bright blue two-piece bathing suit. Her skin was as white as marble, her arms as thin as sticks. A tire of fat wobbled uncomfortably around her middle and her thighs were the thighs of a woman who has not exercised in ten years. But the main difference was in her expression. Kay had succeeded. Something had loosened in Melissa's face during the two weeks she had spent in the Pyle house. She and the children had made friends.

Melissa had rediscovered the magic of childhood and the children were taking advantage of it. They screamed out directions. "Now let's play water jump-rope!" "Now make it come out in waves!" "Make it come out in little waves!" "Now let's play water jump-rope again!" "Faster!" "Slower!" "Now it's your turn!" Melissa tried frantically to keep up with their directions. Every once in a while she sprayed Gail by mistake. Gail was lying on a blanket at the far end of the lawn. She was reading in the sun and wearing enormous blue sunglasses that made her look more like a Kabuki doll than ever. Whenever Melissa sprayed her, she would whine and ask her to come off it.

After a brief pang of jealousy (the children could play happily with someone other than herself), Laura felt glad that the children were someone else's responsibility for a change. She noticed with some pleasure that they were hysterical and that they were going to get worse. She saw all the danger signs: that extra little bit of shrillness in Sarah's commands; the way Nathaniel was babbling and slapping his face; the way Bess was jumping up and down with her hands between her legs, as if she had to go to the bathroom, except, as Laura knew, she didn't; the frantic dog. If it had been Laura down there, she would have turned off the hose and sent them inside to take a rest before anything unpleasant happened. But Melissa was not used to being with children. Or else she wouldn't have said, "Ho! Ho! Ho! Very funny!" when they tricked her into thinking that the hose wasn't working and spurted water in her eyes when she bent down to look. She wouldn't have let Sarah throw mud in her face when she lost her breath and sat down for a rest. From the way she seemed willing for the children to walk all over her, Laura could see how desperate she was for them to like her. She wanted to show them that she was a good sport. But as Laura knew, and she congratulated herself for being so wise, children took advantage of you if they sensed you were desperate.

She watched the water games disintegrate along the usual lines. First there was the dog chase. Sarah chased Bess and Nathaniel with the hose and soon Grosvenor was sopping wet. Then, after Bess had fallen into a mud puddle, there was the mud fight. Then all three children tore off their bathing suits and went after Grosvenor. Sarah began to wrestle with him. Melissa tried to pull her off but in so doing, she stepped on one of Grosvenor's legs. Grosvenor yelped with pain and scrambled to his feet, only to be hosed down again by Bess. Running sideways away from the hose, Grosvenor walked right over Gail's face. "My eyes! My eyes!" Gail squealed. Her sunglasses were crushed in the middle of her forehead. Melissa rushed over to her side, wrapped her up in the mud-splashed blanket, and took a whimpering Gail into the house. Sarah was furious that the games were over. "You come back here!" she screamed, when they had disappeared under the branches. "You know what I'll do if you don't come back here right now and hold the hose?" She paused for effect, and then stamped her foot, screaming, "I'll tell Mommy that you are an unhealthy influence, and you'll never be able to come here again!"

And all the while Dennis worked away on his tree house, whistling softly, totally oblivious to the scene below. It was as if, Laura said to herself before the leaves outside the window turned into blurred green patches and she was finally able to doze off, it was as if he thought that wood and a bit of hammering could solve all the problems in the world.

She slept fitfully. Several times she woke up to hear Melissa consoling Gail in the bathtub and the children giggling outside the bathroom door. Then there was a big commotion when Melissa discovered them and chased them away from the keyhole. The bath went on for a very long time, but then there were footsteps and slamming doors and silence. Except for Grosvenor's whimpering in the backyard. He was lying despondently next to a badly chewed paperback that Gail had forgotten to take in with her.

It was early evening by now. The grass and the leaves were so green that they were almost yellow. This was what her parents had called the lemon hour, except that here there was no terrace from which to enjoy the view, no mountains changing color, no Mediterranean. Just lawns and trees and hedges and station wagons, the purr of a lawn mower down the road, and the smell of wet grass.

Melissa had a motorcycle. Laura watched the two of them fasten their helmets and zoom off down the road. In the wake of the exhaust she saw the first firefly. Somewhere in the depths of Children's Paradise, a child was crying. They were probably hungry, but Laura forgot about them as the fireflies multiplied. Soon there were hundreds of them, perhaps thousands. Why so many? What was the point of so much beauty if society was nothing more than a box and God was just another relative rationalization and the only thing you could ever hope to achieve in life was death? Laura stared at the hundreds and thousands of fireflies as the sky grew darker and suddenly she had an epiphany.

The point of it all was nature. Nature for nature's sake. Her heart filled with joy as she looked at the beauty around her. She could hardly hear Nathaniel's hungry screams. On Bob Pyle's desk was a cocktail shaker. She caught a firefly in her hands and put it into the cocktail shaker, and then she watched the beautiful little light flit about inside between the recipes for martinis and Manhattans and authentic whiskey sours. That was a good enough reason to continue living, Laura said to herself: to observe nature. Then she dozed off again. When she woke up the first thing she noticed was that the firefly in the cocktail shaker was dead.

"Ah. Just the person I wanted to see." It was Bob Pyle. He was standing over her. What looked like a fatherly smile in the half-darkness looked more like a leer when he turned on the desk lamp. Laura sat up. "Exams over?" Laura nodded. "Well, that's what I call good news. What do you say to a long, tall gin and tonic to celebrate your return?"

Without waiting for an answer, he took a bottle of tonic out of the refrigerator beneath his desk. "We even have bitters," he said as he measured out the drinks. "Now that's what I call lucky. You know what the secret to a good gin and tonic is? A drop of Angostura bitters right over the ice cubes."

"Cheers." He pulled his desk chair close to the sofa and stared into her eyes with an overappreciative smile. She had never had the opportunity to examine his face from such close range before. He looked worn and years older than usual, although of course the half-light accentuated the purple shadows under his eyes and the wrinkles on his forehead. "Well," he said, leaning forward a little bit too eagerly. To avoid his eyes she looked down at her glass, which had all the *Kama Sutra* positions painted on it in little black boxes. "Well, well, well." He cleared his throat and was just about to say something when Sarah threw open the door.

"Laura!" Bess cried. "What are you doing here?"

"She's just moved in," her father explained.

"But what are you doing up here then?"

"She and I are having an adult conversation."

"Why?"

"Because there are a number of issues I would appreciate having a second opinion on," Bob said.

"What are you drinking?"

"We are drinking gin and tonics."

"What's that?"

"That is an adult drink," he said between his teeth.

"What is an adult drink?"

"Look," he said abruptly. "Why don't you two girls go take your bath?"

"Because we're hungry," Sarah whined.

"As you both know, I have a roast beef in the oven which we will eat all together when it is sufficiently baked."

"All together? You mean even Mommy?"

"No, I do not mean even Mommy. Mommy is in New York."

"Why is Mommy in New York?"

"Mommy is in New York to look for backing for her magazine. Backing means money."

"Why does she have to go to New York to find money? You could have given her the money, couldn't you?"

"Not that kind of money."

"What kind of money?"

"The . . . kind . . . of . . . money . . . needed . . . to . . . bring . . . out . . . a . . . new . . . publication. Sarah, Bess, please leave me alone. Go take your bath, and then we'll eat."

"What's so secret that you have to talk about that we can't listen to it too?" Bess whimpered.

"Adult subjects. Now let's go and get this bath on the road, shall we?"

"I know why you really want us to go away," Bess sobbed. "Because you want to do it."

"Bess, be reasonable! You know that's not true!"

"Oh yes it is!" she cried. "Whenever you want to do it, you tell us to go take a bath or go to sleep or go away. Every time Mommy wants to do it we have to go somewhere else. Well, I'm tired of people who tell me to go away just because they want to do it," she wailed, "and I don't want *you* to do it or *Mommy* to do it or *Laura* to do it ever again!"

"Bess! Bess!" Bob Pyle picked her up. He held her in his arms lovingly, but the expression on his face was one of annoyance. "Now I think that you are getting upset about nothing."

He took his two daughters into the bathroom and turned on the tap. "Look," he said, his deep voice carrying above the sound of the water, "I will leave this door open and I will leave my study door open, so you can be sure Laura and I are not doing anything you would not like us to do."

The first thing he did when he got back into the study was to shut the door. Pulling his chair closer to the desk, he turned on the intercom and listened to the girls settling into their bath. There was a small quarrel about whose bath toys were whose, but then Sarah turned on the shower and in no time they were screaming and splashing and sliding from one end of the bathtub to the other. "Kids," Bob chuckled as he turned off the intercom, "they're all the same. They'll do anything to keep out of the bath, but once they're in there . . ." He shook his head. "What time did you get here?"

"About three," Laura told him.

"Hmm." He drained his glass and got up to make a second round of drinks. "Then I take it you know about Gail and Melissa."

"What about them?"

"Well, they're living in Kay's study."

"And what happened?"

"Nothing specifically," Bob said with an embarrassed smile. "I was only wondering if you knew."

"Knew what?"

He handed her her second drink. "Cheers." They clinked glasses. Bob sighed and grinned broadly. "Yes, I think it was the first day you didn't come to work that Kay invited them to move in."

"So they've been here about two weeks," Laura suggested.

"Two weeks. That's about right. What do you think of them?"

"Oh, I guess they're all right."

"You think they're all right," Bob murmured.

"Well, Melissa's a bit of a loudmouth sometimes."

"That's one thing I'll back you on."

"And the other one's a bit of a crank. But they seem to be pretty happy together, so I guess it doesn't matter."

Bob nodded. "They certainly make no bones about their being sexual deviants."

"Oh, of course not!" Laura said. "That doesn't shock me at all. Most of my parents' friends were very open about it too, and it was much better that way, and anyway in that part of the world they're so much more tolerant of that sort of thing. The closet cases always did disturbing things."

"Gee, that's interesting," Bob said with a fixed smile.

"What's interesting?"

"I hadn't realized that your folks were, ah, gay. I think that's the word we're supposed to use now, isn't it?"

"They aren't gay. It was just their friends."

"It was just their friends," Bob repeated, with a smile that indicated that he disapproved but was prevented by his open-mindedness to be open about his disapproval.

"Most expatriates tend to be homosexual," Laura tried to explain. "I mean, most Americans in that part of the world. Not

— 184 —

most, but many. That's why they left in the first place, and stayed so long."

"I see," Bob Pyle said, the same smile still fixed on his face. He cleared his throat. "How old were you when you went to Europe?"

"Three."

"Ah. Tell me. Did you ever cohabit with any of these people?"

"No," Laura said. "They just came to the parties."

"They just came to the parties," Bob Pyle repeated. He scratched his head. "Tell me, at these parties . . . did you ever see anything . . . graphic?" He cleared his throat. "Interaction."

"Oh, no," Laura said. "Never."

"Ah," he said, apparently relieved. "Well, that's where the difference lies, then. You see, Melissa and Gail are very . . . open. Very . . . graphic, as it were. And I was wondering whether it was a good idea to expose the girls to this type of deviancy at a time when their sexual identities are not one hundred percent established. Kay seems to think that the danger period ends at five years of age, but I was just reading an article the other day that maintained this was not so." He looked up, slightly embarrassed.

"What do you mean by graphic?" Laura asked.

"Ah, open displays," he said, making nervous gestures with his free arm. "You know, kissing and things like that."

"Oh, kissing," Laura said, very dizzy now from her second drink. "I thought you meant going all the way. At those parties they were always kissing, but that never bothered me."

"They were always kissing," Bob Pyle repeated, chuckling uneasily. "I see. And from what I gather you don't seem to think that this influenced or damaged your sexual . . ."

The intercom clicked on. "Daddy!" Sarah shouted. "Come in and play with us."

"No, dear," he said sternly into the intercom. "Not today."

"Why not?"

"Because Laura and I are just finishing up our adult conversation and are going downstairs to get dinner on the table."

"But we want to play marshmallow! You haven't played marshmallow with us for ages!"

"Well, it will just have to wait one more day." Bob Pyle moved his face closer to the intercom. "Why don't you play with your rubber ducks instead?" Then he turned it off and took Laura's glass for a refill. "Marshmallow is a sponge game," he told her almost apologetically as he dashed angostura bitters over her ice cubes.

"Oh."

When they sat down with the third drink, Bob Pyle chuckled again and said, "So I take it you side with Kay on this issue."

"Yes."

He bowed his head and stared into his drink.

To break the silence, Laura asked, "How is she?"

"Oh, she's fine, she's fine," he said, knocking back his drink. "Just as dynamic as ever. I'm not too worried. I have always known that there were more pitfalls on your way down a mountain than there are on your way up, and before you know it we'll be at sea level again."

He was slurring his words. Laura wondered if he had been drinking all afternoon, if that was why he was referring to mountains. But when he got up and walked to the window he was quite steady, and when he spoke again he sounded sober, sober to the point of sadness. "It's funny how things change," he said. "You know, I'm not even sure I love her anymore."

He looked at Laura with longing. Perhaps he expected her to come over and pat him on the back and tell him that he was just imagining things, that everything would work out. But at an age when people who were twenty-five seemed ancient, the idea that someone who was old enough to have wrinkles was in need of her help struck Laura as slightly obscene. And the idea that Kay's husband might not love Kay was terrifying.

Laura said nothing. The moment passed and then she was sorry she hadn't said something to make him feel better.

He was smiling again as he moved to the door. "Now what do

you say to some prime beef?" Laura got up. He opened the door. "I know I'm not supposed to say this, but ladies first."

Laura was very dizzy. When she looked down the hall into the bathroom and saw Bess and Sarah kissing, her first thought was how pretty they looked. The water streaming down their faces and their hair made them look like marble statues. Sarah was rubbing Bess between the legs with a sponge. Then, while Laura stood there admiring the beautiful way their skin glistened under the sheet of water, Sarah knelt down and licked Bess's stomach. Bess opened her mouth wide but Laura could not hear her voice above the magic hush of running water. Bess pulled the sponge up to her own chest, and then, as Sarah let her tongue slip down between her legs, Bess shook the sponge over Sarah's head, chanting something that Laura could only just hear as she made her way down the hallway. A nursery rhyme. It was a song about marshmallows.

"Good God!" Bob Pyle pushed Laura aside and went careening into the bathroom. "Stop!" he screamed in a hysterical voice. "Stop!"

Sarah was so surprised that she fell backward and hit her head against the side of the tub. She screamed, but her father made no motion to help her out of the water. With shaking hands he turned off the shower.

"How many times have I told you not to play that unless . . ." He didn't finish his sentence. He just stood there staring at the green bathwater as Bess bent over and took her sister into her arms. "My head! My head!" Sarah cried. Her father watched her, his hands and his mouth trembling. Slowly they stopped trembling. When he finally spoke his voice was calm.

"I'm sorry, girls. I'm afraid I lost my temper."

But they looked at him as if he had committed a murder.

15

The fight Bob and Kay had later that night after Kay had returned from New York started out as a friendly discussion. From the couch in Bob's study Laura could only hear the occasional comment about behavior models, viable alternatives, and stimulus reassessment. Their voices were soft, matter-of-fact, professional. A stranger would have thought they were discussing the trajectory of a spaceship or the unexpected demise of a hamster in a control group.

Then, just as she was falling asleep, the discussion turned to bourgeois morality and they began to shout at each other. Bob accused Kay of deliberately confusing the children's sexual attitudes and Kay accused him of overreacting. "They were only showing affection for each other!" she protested. "Well, it didn't look like that to me," Bob retorted. "And what if I did overreact? I don't want this behavior to be encouraged, by you or by me. Or by your two friends."

"You're trying to make people ashamed of loving one another!" Kay cried. "It's hard enough for people to love each other already without you interfering. You've probably traumatized them for life shouting at them like that!" "Well, my word stands," Bob said. "Either those two perverts leave this house, or I do."

"They're two very harmless and very funky ladies!" Kay sobbed, "and for the first time in their adult lives they were learning to trust people with other life-styles than their own. They were getting along with the children so well, and now you have to ruin the whole thing." "I'm sorry!" Bob shouted, "but I don't want my children to turn into perverts. I want them to become upright men and women." "Why oh why do you have to divide humanity into those hateful categories," Kay wailed. "Why can't you think of our children as *people?* Why are we forced to wear our sex and sexual preferences around like yellow Stars of David?"

"I'm sorry," he said, knocking something over, "but I'm not going to fall for this latest fad of yours. I'm not going to let anyone try and convince me that I'm not a man just because I am a person. And I'm not going to let my children be unduly confused by close contact with sexual deviants."

"You call yourself a man!" Kay cried. "But how can you be a man if two women who love each other make you so insecure about yourself?"

They went on and on until finally Laura stopped her ears with the cotton from a jar of aspirin she found in the medicine cabinet. Arguments between adults disturbed her almost as much as earthquakes: you couldn't even depend on the earth to stay in one place. The added knowledge that Bob and Kay probably did not love each other made it even worse.

She prepared herself for the worst. So she was not prepared for the jovial displays of affection in the kitchen the next morning, the kisses and spontaneous embraces as Kay whipped up some banana bread for her Minerva group luncheon, and Bob made his special vinaigrette for her green-bean-and-creamed-corn salad.

Kay and Rachel had been unable to meet with Margaret Mead as they had hoped, but they had met with executives from two prominent corporations who had expressed an interest in *Minerva* and would seriously consider backing the magazine if the dummy lived up to their expectations. Melissa was getting some friends at an underground newspaper to check out the background of the two corporations to make sure that their investment portfolios were ethical. But this was just a formality, as both had excellent reputations.

So the luncheon on Dennis's new picnic table in the backyard was a lighthearted affair. From the way Bob and Melissa bantered with each other, you would never have known that a few hours earlier he had dismissed her as a pervert. Only the little red marks under Kay's eyes hinted at the night of argument. And Bess's hysteria when she spilled some milk on her blouse and Sarah tried to wash it off with the hose. And the way Nathaniel pushed the cat's face into his salad when the cat wouldn't eat it. And the way Sarah was speaking to herself. She was pretending to ride a horse called Flicka. On the left side of her forehead was a large blue bump.

Kay was pouring out Bob's specially perked coffee when Melissa turned to Sarah and asked her how she had gotten that bump.

"I'm not allowed to tell you," Sarah told her.

"Why ever not?"

"Because if I tell you Mommy says your feelings will be hurt."

"Hey, come off it," Melissa said with a good-natured smile. "Now how could a bump on *your* forehead hurt *my* feelings?"

"Don't ask *me*. *I'm* not going to tell you. *I'm* not going to be the one who makes you start hating families again."

"I don't get it. Who told you I hated families?"

"Mommy told us."

"But why?" Melissa asked, looking very hurt.

"We can't tell you," Bess explained.

"But why not?"

"Because Mommy doesn't want you to know that Daddy doesn't trust you."

"What in God's name is this all about?" Melissa shouted. Kay and Bob cleared their throats at the same time. Kay looked sadly into Bob's eyes and Bob started coughing.

"Well, Bob," Kay said, "we don't have any choice now, do we? The cat's out of the bag." Bob cleared his throat again and nodded. "Well, darling, would you like to explain this to poor Melissa here," she said, "or shall I?"

"I found Bess and Sarah fondling in the bathtub," Bob Pyle said dully. "I came to the preliminary, and, according to Kay, unfounded conclusion that your presence in this house was somehow related to their activities."

"It was just a misunderstanding," Kay added.

Sarah snorted. "Misunderstanding? You were shouting at each other all night."

Melissa stood up. She was trembling and on the verge of tears. "If you think we're so idiotic, if you're so paranoid that you think we've been giving sex lessons to your kids, then we might as well end this stupidity right . . ."

"Melissa, please!" Kay cried, lunging across the table to catch her by the hand. "Do believe me when I say that, whatever the misgivings of my poor old-fashioned husband, myself and the children do indeed cherish you dearly. Please, please, don't take this little upset to heart." She looked passionately into Melissa's tear-filled eyes. "The truth is often a heavy burden to bear, Melissa. But in the end, I believe it to be the best path we can take."

Rachel muttered something under her breath about mixed metaphors. Gail ran her fingers through her hair, and then, examining the purple nail polish on her fingernails, said, "Well, it's true we took a bath together yesterday, I mean, we don't always take baths together because usually I'm into privacy when it comes to taking baths, but that dog Grosvenor whatever-his-name-is just about gave me a heart attack stepping on my face like that." She rubbed her eyes and looked vaguely in the direction of the house. "I guess it's because for some reason I prefer my bathwater really scalding and other people prefer it sort of lukewarm. It's funny, well, I guess it's not *funny* really, but just sort of, you know . . ." Her voice trailed off.

"You said you came to a preliminary conclusion," Melissa said to Bob. She was still trembling. "Have you come to any conclusion that's definite?"

"I don't know, Melissa, I really don't know."

"Don't know what?" she shouted.

"I don't know whether you are a good influence or a bad influence."

"You bigot! You goddamned bigot!" Melissa screamed. "For Kay's sake I've tried to get along with you. But you're just as evil and insidious as all the others!"

"I am *not* a bigot," Bob said between his teeth.

"You're worse! You're a turncoat! Anyone who has so little pride that they can actually work for that bastard in Washington . . ." Bob got up and raised his hand as if to hit her. Kay caught it just in time. Turning sadly toward her Minerva group, she said, "What are we to do with this man? What indeed?"

"Draw him and quarter him and burn him at the stake," Rachel snapped. "That's what we used to do to sexists in *my* neighborhood." Everyone laughed, even Bob, who hung his head and chuckled ruefully. Rachel had a certain way of relieving tension, Kay always said.

"Hey, you people drive me crazy sometimes," Rachel said. "Why don't we cut the postmortems and get back to work. Give this guy here some time to think things over before we pass final judgment. Melissa, you go call those cronies of yours and see if it's permissible for us to permit those nice young executives to back our little project here. We've been running around in circles too long. It's getting pretty boring. I'd like to get going on some real work one of these days."

After Melissa had gone inside, Bob sighed and got up to take in the dishes. Kay grabbed his hand. "Oh, darling, don't feel bad. I think we did the right thing bringing our hostilities out into the open. And listen. We were going to spend this afternoon drawing up a sort of manifesto for the dummy. Sort of a centerfold stating our general beliefs about the aims of the women's movement. And I for one would be overjoyed if you could stay put and tell us what you think about its feasibility." She turned to Rachel, Gail, and Edith. "Would you be terribly put out if Bob sat with us this afternoon? Oh, wonderful," she said without waiting for an answer. "It's about time we took full advantage of a male viewpoint."

"Why do you need that?" Sarah asked.

"Because men have a different outlook."

"But you said that was wrong."

"Sarah, please," Kay pleaded.

"But you told me it was bad to think like a man."

"No, no, no. All I said was that it would be better if we all thought like *people* instead of like men or like women."

Laura went inside to do the dishes. Dennis had not been able to find the coin in the dishwasher that was making all that trouble, so the sink was piled high with dishes. When she turned on the water, the Minerva group was laughing, but when she turned it off to do the drying, Melissa was shouting again. As far as Laura could gather, Melissa's friends had discovered that one of the corporations had a plant in South Africa and the other owned an Israeli hotel. Rachel was furious. She couldn't understand what was wrong about a corporation owning property in Israel. And even if it was wrong, she said, it was impossible to launch a magazine in a capitalist society without accepting the capitalist facts of life. When Laura came outside again, Melissa was denouncing Rachel as a petty bourgeois pawn.

The children were playing a strange game under the tree house. They were chasing three of the younger cats with paper bags. When they caught them they would run around the tree trunk three times while the captive cats yowled and scratched and tried to fight their way out. Then they would turn the bags upside down and drop the cats, shouting, "The cat's out of the bag! The cat's out of the bag!"

Laura tried to stop them, without success. Finally Kay had to come over and threaten them with the Thinking Room. "We're having a very serious discussion," she explained, stroking Nathaniel's head to stop his teeth from chattering. "Why don't you play some sort of word game with Laura?"

While Bob Pyle tried to explain why he believed that ethical projects could, in certain circumstances, justify unethical investors, and Melissa accused him of being an instrument of repression, Laura tried to get the children interested in a game of My Grandmother's Trunk. That was too boring. She couldn't get them to go beyond "d." Sarah invented a word game of her own called "Mate."

"What happens when a donkey mates a horse?" she asked.

"A mule!"

"What happens when a fish mates a plant?"

"A plish!"

"What happens when a brother mates a sister?"

"A brister!"

They rolled around the grass in hysterics. "What happens when a cat mates a dog?" Sarah asked. And Bess and Nathaniel screamed, "A dat!"

"Let's make a dat!" Nathaniel cried.

"No," said Laura, "let's not make a dat." It was too late. Sarah had grabbed the dog, and Nathaniel, a cat. He threw the cat onto the dog's back. Howling, the cat scrambled off Grosvenor's back and raced up the side of the oak tree, way above the highest tree house. Sarah shouted for it to come down, but it wouldn't.

"Someone come and get this cat down!" Sarah shouted, but Laura could not climb trees, Dennis was filling in for Edith at Suicide Prevention, Bob was explaining that it was immoral for ethical people to avoid taking positions of importance in an unethical administration, Melissa was listening furiously, Rachel looked disgusted, Edith was busy combing Gail's hair, and Kay was busy holding everyone's hands and listening to the argument with an anxious frown. No one made a move to get the cat.

"Daddy, come right now and get this cat down!"

"Daddy's busy right now, dear," Kay said.

"But this is an emergency! The cat's in danger! Daddy, come right now and help me get the cat down the tree."

Bob Pyle didn't hear her. "I do not find this vituperation to be at all productive," he was saying to Melissa.

"Why won't Daddy come and help me?" Sarah cried.

"You men are all the same!" Melissa shouted.

Kay suggested that Sarah find someone else to get the cat down the tree, but Sarah stamped her foot. "I want Daddy to do it. Why won't you do it, Daddy?"

"Do what, Sarah?" Bob asked.

"What do you mean, do what? Aren't you strong enough or something? Aren't you a man?" Sarah screeched.

"Now, now, Sarah," Kay said with a playful grin, "let's not hit below the belt. You know as well as I do that Daddy doesn't have to act like a man unless he wants to."

"That does it!" Bob growled, slamming his fist down on the table. He stalked over to the tree and began to climb up the rope ladder. "You know what you are?" he shouted when he reached Children's Observation Deck. He shook his fist at the picnic table and swung up the ladder. "You think you can walk all over me!" he yelled from Children's Escape Pad, "but I'm a man and you can't do anything about it! And you know what, you bitches?" he shouted as he scrambled onto Children's Retreat, "I'm proud of it! To hell with all of you bitches!" he roared. He gave his audience an insane smile, then reached up into the branches and grabbed hold of the cat. Just then one of the planks in the tree house came loose. He lost his balance. The cat howled, tried to cling to his left arm, and then went flying into the air. Bob lunged for a tree branch as he fell over backwards. That was when Laura closed her eyes. Before he hit the ground, she could hear the change falling out of his pockets.

Just as the two ambulance attendants were maneuvering Bob Pyle onto the stretcher, the cat rolled over and died. It had landed on its back and then been hit by one of the loose boards from Children's Retreat. No amount of nursing, nursery rhymes, or cold milk could reverse its passage from life. While Kay calmly supervised the transfer of her husband's broken body from the grass to the stretcher and the others tried to revive Gail (Gail had fainted when she saw the bone sticking out of Bob Pyle's shoulder), Laura sat under the oak tree with the children and tried to concentrate on the cat, now frozen in mid-spasm. Its legs were stiff and red foam was coming out of its mouth, but its eyes were still open. It wasn't until Kay and Edith had followed the stretcher into the ambulance that Sarah realized it was dead.

When alive, the cat had had no name, but now as Sarah pressed it against her chest she called it Flicka. Gazing at the white summer sky, she asked Flicka why it hadn't listened to her warnings about the loose boards, why it had climbed so high when the people who loved it were so low, why it had been so afraid of playing with the dog. Laura was no good in emergencies. By the time she remembered that it was dangerous to fondle dead animals, Sarah was trying to give the cat mouth to mouth resuscitation. The foam from the cat's mouth was smeared across Sarah's cheek.

Suddenly aware of all the deadly microbes that the foam almost certainly contained, Laura jumped up screaming and tried to pull her away. "It's diseased!" she shouted, but Sarah was too furious to listen. She punched and kicked and dug her fingernails into Laura's arms. While they fought, Nathaniel grabbed Flicka by the tail and dragged it across the yard. "My cat was just about to be alive again!" Sarah shouted. "And now you ruined it!" Laura tried to explain that when animals, or for that matter, people, died they were dead forever. She tried to explain that you couldn't bring them back, but this made Sarah cry even more. After a while Bess joined in. While Nathaniel dragged Flicka around the yard, making motor noises, and Rachel tried halfheartedly to distract him, while Melissa contorted her face into a lipless grimace and Gail leaned against the tree trunk, gasping dramatically for breath, Sarah and Bess rolled around the grass crying "Flicka! Flicka! Come back, come back, wherever you are!" Laura had never been so glad to see the grandmother.

Sensible in her gardening outfit, her hair wrapped up in a red bandanna, she strode purposefully into the middle of the lawn and took Nathaniel by the hand. "Now what do you think you're doing to that poor cat," she said. "Don't you realize you could damage it permanently?"

"It's not a cat, it's a tank and the tank is broken and I'm taking it to the gas station," Nathaniel informed her.

Then she realized that the cat was dead. She knelt down next to it and for a few seconds, while Nathaniel explained to her that he was no longer Nathaniel but a tow truck, her eyes filled with tears.

One deep breath and she was on her feet again. "You, you, you," she said, pointing at Rachel, Gail, and Melissa, "I'm afraid I'll have to ask you to leave. Laura, see to it that they take all their belongings with them. Sarah, come here so that I can blow your nose. When *will* your mother remember to give you handkerchiefs. No use crying over spilt milk, Bess, that's what they say. Run along into the house and fetch a shoe box for this poor little creature."

Within minutes the cat was lying on the side porch in a shoe box, ready for burial. The lawn was cleared of toys and people and coffee cups and books. Melissa and Gail had been dispatched to the movies "or whatever else catches your fancy" with clear instructions not to return to their lodgings in Kay's study until after the children's bedtime. The contents of Bob Pyle's pocket were neatly arranged on the telephone table. There was a roast in the oven and a tumbler full of pink lemonade on the kitchen table. The grandmother had brought an easy chair in from the living room. The children were perched on the armrests and she was reading them fairy tales.

Laura sat on the other side of the table peeling the vegetables that had been assigned her and listened to the stories she had almost forgotten. "Little Red Riding Hood." "The Princess and the Pea." "The Frog Prince." And then the ones she almost knew by heart from having read them to the children so many times: "Sleeping Beauty," "Rapunzel," "Rumpelstiltskin." "Rapunzel" was Bess's favorite, and once it had once been Laura's favorite, too. She remembered the nights she had spent as a child with her hair trailing out the window, cursing her mother for having exchanged her for a cabbage, and waiting for the prince to come to the rescue. Laura found the grandmother's voice strangely soothing. She liked the way it deepened for kings and squeaked for animals and dwarfs. She was comforted by the way the grandmother let her reading glasses slide to the end of her nose before she pushed them back up again, the way she wet her finger before turning the page, the slightest hint of disapproval in her eyes when she answered Nathaniel's questions about where the princes hid their air forces and why the pictures didn't show any gas stations.

Under her spell Laura tried to forget her recent past and convince herself that she was four years old again. While the grandmother explained time and time again that horse-and-carriages did not need oil or gasoline, Laura looked into Nathaniel's wide, unbelieving eyes and remembered that at his age she had believed in giants. She looked out the window and tried to remember what trees and leaves had looked like to her when the world was still magic, before it became real. But something—was it Nathaniel's insistence that fairy godmothers who flew had to be equipped with outboard motors?—something ruined the spell.

The telephone rang. After a brief conversation of monosyllables, the grandmother returned to her easy chair and told the children in a brave but cracking voice that their father was still sleeping.

"What will happen if he doesn't wake up?" Bess asked.

"Oh, he'll wake up soon enough. There's no doubt about that. He's very lucky to have gotten away with a few broken bones."

"But what if he doesn't?" Bess insisted. "Where will he go?" At first the grandmother didn't know what to say, but after clearing her throat a few times, she said Heaven.

Heaven. The most beautiful place in the universe. Laura knew that Kay would not have approved of this subject and she sensed that this was why the grandmother got carried away with her descriptions of the music, the peace, the beauty of the angels. Every time she mentioned God she glanced over her shoulder, as if she expected to see Kay frowning behind her.

"If Daddy goes to Heaven, will we be able to go and visit him there?" Bess asked.

"I'm afraid not. Not until you go there for good yourself. But don't worry. God makes sure that families stay together in Heaven, just like He keeps them together here on earth."

"Can animals go to Heaven?"

"I'm afraid not."

"Then you mean I'll never be able to see Flicka again?" Sarah wailed. "Not even when I die?" She buried her head in her grandmother's bony shoulder.

"Calm, girl, calm. The good Lord takes care of all his creatures." She gazed fervently at the furry black television cover. Her eyes filled with tears and her nostrils distended. "Haven't you ever heard of Happy Hunting Grounds?"

Happy Hunting Grounds. She told them it was the second most beautiful place in the universe, and much better suited for animals. A vast green field where the sun always shone and there was no limit to the number of mice and birds the cats could hunt. At first Sarah was skeptical. But then she relented when the grandmother explained away a score of logical contradictions by saying that the good Lord would provide.

"How do I make sure Flicka gets there?" she asked.

"Just put the poor creature into a good grave," the grandmother told her. "The good Lord will take care of the rest."

Sarah was in no mood to leave things to God when they lowered the cat into its shoe-box-sized grave the next morning. She decided they would all have to stay next to the grave until God came to pick Flicka up. Or else how could they be sure Flicka had gotten to Happy Hunting Grounds? It pained Laura to see them squinting so eagerly at the tree tops. She wondered whether she should tell them the truth, that God didn't exist, and that all that was going to happen was that the cat's body would decompose.

In the end she decided not to disappoint them. To speed things up she told them God was invisible. How were they so sure He hadn't come and gone already? Because they hadn't seen the cat leave the grave yet, they told her. Laura told them that cats became invisible too when they died. This they refused to believe. How could a cat expect to go hunting in Happy Hunting Grounds if it was invisible? Because they traveled so fast, Laura told them, so fast that all you saw was a flash of color.

How fast was fast? Faster than the speed of sound? If cats on their way to Happy Hunting Grounds traveled faster than the speed of sound, then there would have to be a supersonic boom, Sarah informed her. So they couldn't be sure Flicka was on its way until they heard a boom. Exasperated, Laura suggested that they sing some songs to attract God's attention. Something sad, she suggested. They walked slowly around the grave singing "She'll Be Comin' Round the Mountain When She Comes" as if it were the saddest song in the world. Unfortunately they knew all the verses. Nathaniel soon got bored. He picked up the hose and started watering the popsicle stick that marked the grave.

"How dare you?" Sarah screeched. She grabbed him by the collar and was apparently about to strangle him, when Laura said that God would have an easier time getting the cat out of the grave if the ground was wet. "See?" Laura cried when no one was looking at the popsicle. "There it goes now." She pretended to have seen a yellow streak and when the others looked up into the sky they thought they saw it too. A distant motorcycle backfired, thus providing the supersonic boom. Sarah pointed out the faint trail of yellow smoke that Flicka had left in its wake.

"Just think how happy Flicka is now," Laura said to them as they went inside for lunch. She felt uncomfortable about all her lies, but decided that it really wasn't her fault. After all, Happy Hunting Grounds hadn't been her idea, it had been the grandmother's. It was a beautiful idea, one that Laura herself would have been delighted to believe in. Conveniently forgetting her own misadventure with religion—the sleepless nights she had spent as a child searching the skies for the man in the white beard that her father had told her did not exist—Laura assumed that this Flicka nonsense would soon be forgotten.

16

The children did not think much of their father when he came home from the hospital. Even after Kay had covered him up with a silk Japanese bedspread and surrounded his sofa with fans and flowers and Get Well cards, Nathaniel still insisted that he looked like a car crash. Bess couldn't look at him without laughing. She said that the cast around his neck made him look like a turtle. In addition to breaking his collarbone, his left wrist, and his right arm, and dislocating a hip, Bob Pyle also had broken his jaw. Now it was wired—healing nicely, Kay said—but Sarah was infuriated by his helpless grimace.

Kay had hoped that the children would assist her in making his convalescence a rewarding one. She had even gone so far as to assign chores. But Bess wouldn't go near the chamber pot that first evening, and when Sarah finally agreed to feed her father his liquid meal, the first two offerings dribbled down his chin. Instead of wiping his face with the napkin Kay gave her, she threw the rest of the meal on the floor. She said it wasn't fair. It wasn't her fault that he couldn't talk or swallow. She said that the reason he couldn't eat or pee or change position without Kay's help was that he was a Mongolian idiot. He had always been a Mongolian idiot. This father nonsense was just a disguise.

All night Bob Pyle cried. From her new bed in the central playing area of Children's Paradise, Laura could hear his broken sobs over the intercom and Kay's soothing words when she went into his study at regular intervals to blow his nose. In a voice normally reserved for educational chats with Nathaniel, she told him not to worry. Sarah was still grappling with the terrible discovery that fathers were not infallible. Bess was going through that stage when children laugh at everything abnormal. Nathaniel called almost everything a car crash these days. He never played with guns anymore but was still enthralled by the destructibility of powerful machines. Although his general attitude left much to be desired, the fact that he often pretended to be a tow truck was a positive sign. By expressing a willingness to pull wrecked cars to the "gas station," Nathaniel was exhibiting a new concern for the consequences of destruction.

"If he keeps on trying to put Humpty Dumpty together again," Kay said to Bob, the intercom, and everyone in the house, "maybe one day he'll realize it's impossible." Kay was going to do everything in her power, she said, to reinforce this constructive approach to car crashes, accidents, war, and violence in general. It was all part of a program to match Nathaniel's yin with his yang. In the meantime she urged Bob to try and understand how traumatic it was for a four-year-old to see his father half embalmed in plaster.

She assured him that the children would soon grow accustomed to his new appearance. And even if they didn't, he would be shedding casts soon enough. If his jaw wasn't as straight as it had been, he could always grow a beard. And of course, they could sue. And he was going to get A-1 care.

Edith had agreed to take over the publicity campaign that Kay had initiated in order to find ethical sponsors for *Minerva,* and Melissa and Rachel were to take over the bulk of her editorial responsibilities. This meant that she would be able to give him top priority until the end of August, maybe even mid-September. He was going to have to prepare himself for massive doses of loving care. She didn't mind sacrificing her summer one bit. This *Minerva* business had made her somewhat flighty of late, and the one good thing this tragedy had done was to bring her down to earth. The children were good eggs. She was sure they would be exhibiting charity and understanding by the end of the week, and without any prodding from her. There was no reason for him to cry so, she told him, but when his sobs turned into what sounded like an attack of asthma, she said that if the unguarded reactions of three young children bothered him that much, she would try and think up a positive course of action to ensure that they saw as little of their father as possible.

By now it was four o'clock in the morning, or maybe five. To Laura's relief, Kay decided to sleep on it. From her bed in Children's Paradise, she listened to the crackle of Kay's slippers on the parquet floor, the squeak of bedsprings, a few more sobs from Bob Pyle's study, and then silence, a few bars of a French ballad from Kay's bedside and then heavy breathing, the occasional whimper, a recurring nightmare.

When all the channels of communication were open, Laura felt as if she were sleeping in an airport lounge. Of course the discussions interested her. She had become something of an eavesdropper. And when everyone else in the house was asleep, the amplified breathing and snoring and bedsprings and animal noises were as hypnotic as the sound of waves in the Mediterranean. Laura thought herself to sleep that night, thinking of all the places she could have been at that very moment if she had gone home for the summer: the whitewashed villages, the cities, the simple fish restaurants, the moonlit chapel on the island in the middle of the harbor.

"We are so disappointed to hear you're not coming," Laura's

mother had written. "We had so many plans. Your father actually cried when he read your letter. Who are these Pyle people anyway? And why are you letting them run your life for you?" Listening to the snores and heavy breathing, thinking of her father crying on a whitewashed balcony in a whitewashed village, brushing away his tears in a simple restaurant on the waterfront, Laura asked herself the same questions. Who were these people? Why did she let them run her life? She couldn't think of any answers. She fell asleep wishing she were home.

The next morning, while Laura helped Nathaniel make his scrambled eggs (or, as he called them, his crashed omelets), Kay pinned a large multicolored poster to the bulletin board. "Who wants to spend summer inside anyway?" it said. "If *I* didn't have to work on crazy magazine dummies and take care of silly fathers who fall out of trees, *I* would pack all sorts of goodies in my lunch box and make someone (someone, please!) take me on picnics to all four corners of Massachusetts (and maybe even New Hampshire!)."

When breakfast was over, Kay got the children to draw up a list of all the beaches and forests and parks within a fifty-mile radius that they had never seen. All the museums, zoos, and quarries they would like to revisit. After they had numbered these in order of preference, Kay suggested that they figure out some way to link all these outings together. It would be so much more rewarding, so much more exciting, if there was a quest. Like a search for hidden pirate's treasure. Or a collection of shells and rocks and leaves that they could catalogue on rainy days. Or some sort of hobby, like birdwatching or finding berries for natural dyes. "What kind of things would *you* like to spend the summer looking for?" she asked. Sarah answered without hesitation. There were exactly four things: the road to Heaven, the city where the most angels came from, the Star of Bethlehem, and the funnel.

Kay frowned. What funnel? she asked. The funnel to Happy Hunting Grounds, Sarah explained. Apparently it was the main entrance for mammals. Who had told her that? Kay inquired. Well, Grandma had told her about Happy Hunting Grounds, Sarah explained, and the three other things she had thought up at Sunday School.

Kay rose abruptly. She looked deeply shocked. For a few very long and silent moments she stared out the bay window. She stared at her fingernails as if they were juvenile delinquents who had betrayed her trust. Then she strode to the telephone table. She picked up the phone, then put it down again. She caught her breath. She turned around. She smiled. "Sunday School?" she asked in an ultracalm voice, "when did you go there?"

Although her mother was smiling, Sarah seemed to realize that she had broken an unspoken rule. When she answered, her voice was full of defiance. "When Grandma was taking care of us," she said, "for three Sundays in a row. While you were in the hospital taking care of Mr. Fart."

Over the intercom they could hear Bob Pyle trying to breathe through a stuffed-up nose. Kay gave the intercom a quick look, and her eyes filled with tears. "Sarah, Sarah, how many times must I ask you not to use such cruel nicknames?"

"Why shouldn't I?" Sarah asked.

"Because he's listening, stupid," Bess told her. "You're not supposed to say things like that when he's listening."

"I don't care if he's listening," Sarah said. She shrugged her shoulders. Upstairs Bob gave out a long deathlike moan.

"Now he's crying again," Bess said. "And it's all your fault. You'd better say sorry to him."

"Oh, Sarah, do," Kay pleaded.

"Why should I say sorry to him?" Sarah asked.

"Because he's a cripple," Bess explained.

"All right, all right. I just can't stand all this nagging. I'll say sorry so crybaby feels better." She walked over to the intercom and shouted, "Sorry, Mr. Fart!"

Kay lunged across the kitchen and flicked off the intercom. "Oh, if only that wretched woman would only try and teach you children Christian values like compassion and charity instead of jamming nonsense down your throats about angels and the road to Heaven."

"It's not nonsense," Sarah said. "It's the truth!"

"Oh, my little chickadee!" Kay said, "it's only *half* the truth!" She draped her arms around her daughter's shoulders, and Sarah bit her. They had a fight. Or rather, Sarah had a fight. She thrashed and wriggled in her mother's embrace and accused her of not wanting her daughter to believe in God, of wanting her to be left out of Heaven.

"I have a human right to go to Sunday School, and I don't care if you hate Grandma, and I don't care if you lock me up in the closet just because you hate Sunday School. And even if you lock me up in the closet so I don't go, I'll get a hand drill and drill a hole through the door and go there, and if you're too mad to see me again if I go to Sunday School, that's okay with me! I'll buy a farm and you'll never ever, never ever see me again!" While she screamed and kicked and dug her fingernails into Kay's arms, Kay stood behind her. Sad but serene. There was just a hint of condescension in her smile as she gazed at her daughter's head below her and waited for her to stop overreacting.

"Why do you think I hate Sunday School?" she said when Sarah ran out of things to say.

"Because Grandma said so."

"Do you think it is a good idea to take Grandma's word for it when you have every opportunity in the world to ask me directly? You know for a fact that she tends to be a bit hysterical when it comes to her beliefs."

"You just hate her, that's all," Sarah said.

"Why do you think I hate her?"

"Because you said so yourself."

"All I said was that she was wretched, and although I now feel it was said in a rash moment, Sarah, I do honestly feel that she has been the tiniest bit subversive in her efforts to get you kids hooked on Sunday School."

"Well, why can't we go?"

"I never said that, did I? I just feel we shouldn't have jumped into this situation without sitting down together and really figuring out the whys and wherefores of the whole idea. But why don't we do that right now? Let me give Laura my laundry, and then we can sit down and talk the whole thing over." Laura went dutifully upstairs to do the laundry and by the time she returned Kay and the children had come to a compromise.

They put it into writing. The children could go to Sunday School so long as they agreed to keep their minds open and bore in mind the fact that the Bible was an allegory and that Christianity, especially the Episcopalian variety, did not provide all the answers.

It was not that she was an atheist, Kay explained to Laura. It was just that she had an open and fairly abstract conception of God. In her opinion, organized religion tended to oversimplify what she persisted in calling "the whole issue." It was too narrow and authoritative in its teachings; it tended to stifle creative thought about the meaning of life. "I don't want the kids to be told whom and what to believe in. I want them to be able to decide for themselves." She urged Laura to steer the children toward a more creative and comprehensive attitude to God, the afterlife, and religion in general, if ever they expressed an interest in such topics in her presence.

. This was hardly necessary, for Sarah's attitude to religion during those first summer excursions was so creative that it verged on violence. Wherever they went—to the seaside, to the aquarium, to the riverside, to the hills above the university to fly kites, to the battlefields of the American revolution, to the natural history museum, to the *Mayflower*—Sarah scratched the ground and the stones and the sand and the surface of the water with a makeshift geiger counter in search of angel deposits, the road to Heaven, the funnel to Happy Hunting Grounds. No outing was complete without a discovery—a dinosaur bone, a million-year-old penny, an Egyptian parchment scorched by the fierce radiation of the first Star of Bethlehem. Bottle caps became meteors from Outer Heaven, discarded cans were once containers for frankincense and myrrh. Dawn was the reflection of the sun on the Golden Gates of Heaven. Sunsets were red when God was angry. Clouds were warnings that Heaven's bathwater was on its way. Fireflies were spies from the Right Hand of God.

Laura was never sure if Sarah believed her wild claims, but it was clear that Bess believed everything her sister told her. It was clear from the way she looked at waves after Sarah told her that foam was really the tips of angel wings; the patience with which she awaited God's commandments on dune tops; her fascination with the fossil of a dinosaur footprint that Sarah told her was the hand of Jesus; and the gold-and-orange tropical fish that Sarah claimed was the original Son of God.

Kay needn't have worried about her daughter getting brainwashed by Christianity. She had already done a detailed study project on evolution in school. She was responsive to the Greek and Celtic and Chinese and Aztec and Indian myths that Kay now read to them during Fairy Tale Hour. She spent rainy days devouring the *Child's Treasurebook of World Civilizations, Everyday Life in Ancient Egypt,* and *Ancient Rome,* romances about Babylonian princesses, Arabian slave girls, deepest Africa. One night when they got up in the middle of the night to look for the Star of Bethlehem, Sarah told her sister her version of the beginning of the world. In the beginning there was only God, a big red-and-yellow ball of fire so large that you would almost think it was infinite. Then one day he lost his balance and exploded into a million and one pieces. God decided to become invisible so he could travel around in one piece. He built a house in Heaven and spent the day inspecting his million and one sons. He traveled on the Milky Way. One day when he was passing his favorite son, he noticed his son was crying. Cold wet tears. One of them was half dry and that one was Earth. The son was crying because he was so bored. So God gave him a pet amoeba and told him to put it on the Earth and see if he could do anything constructive with it. The son fell in love with that amoeba and did everything he could to develop it to its fullest. And so, after a period of millions of years, the amoeba turned into a fish and the fish turned into a reptile, and the reptile turned into a monkey who turned, after millions of years, into Adam, whose rib turned into Eve. The son was so happy to see Adam and Eve that he gave them a garden, but the apple they ate made them forget about their Father. For years and years the children and grandchildren of Adam and Eve thought that the Earth was the center of the universe, until one day an Italian called Galileo saw Heaven through a primitive telescope. Jesus was the first one to get to Heaven. Zeus used to guard the only road. Now there were several—a Buddhist road somewhere in the Himalayas, a Moslem one in Mecca, and a pagan one in the Yucatán. And of course the Tower of Babel. If you went to Heaven, you became an angel for ever and ever, so of course there were people who preferred to stay on Earth in one shape or another until they felt they were ready for the experience of Heaven. These people were called Hindus. Between lives they rested up in a place called Hades. The main part of Hades was underground, but at the very back was a fence from which you could see a part of Happy Hunting Grounds. The entrance to Hades was under a pile of sticks next to a river so clear that it had never been polluted. Since Massachusetts was one of the places where people used biodegradable detergents, Sarah was fairly sure it was in Massachusetts. She wanted to find it. People who discovered the entrance to Hades could come and go as they pleased, but they couldn't turn back or else they were condemned to Hades forever. There was only one other danger and that was the piranha fish—but only if the piranha fish happened to be going through a hunger frenzy.

On the outskirts of the city was a graveyard, an overgrown graveyard with wildflowers and blueberry bushes and gigantic weeds, and where the gravestones ended was a lopsided iron fence. On the other side of the fence, behind a jungle of brambles, was an abandoned arsenal. A concrete shell of a building, with iron staircases leading nowhere. Weeds grew between the cracks in the floor and, even when you whispered, your voice echoed. Behind the arsenal was a stream, and because of the thick bushes, it seemed to flow right into the arsenal, or under it. That was what gave Sarah the idea that the entrance to Hades was in the vicinity. This was the river: now all they had to do was find the sticks. From then on they gave up on beautiful beaches and museums and historic monuments and took their picnics to the arsenal.

Laura was not at all sure Sarah really expected to find Hades when they set off every morning in search of the river sticks. She didn't really think it was possible for an eight-year-old to believe in the supernatural. Or was it? What was clear was the pleasure Sarah derived from the power she wielded over her sister. Sarah was the priestess; Bess was the dupe. Bess was the one who had to test the water for piranha fish. Bess was the one who had to risk her life by looking over her shoulder when they waded across the stream. "You're just lucky that wasn't Hades," Sarah would tell her when Bess's teeth started chattering. Bess was the one who always got frightened, and although Laura noticed how Sarah capitalized on this fear, she did not intervene.

For what was adventure without fear? Fear and Sarah's wild imagination had turned a dull suburban stream bed into a Garden of Eden. The shrubs concealed the ruins of the Tower of Babel and the leftovers of Noah's Ark. The water in the stream had special powers. If you rubbed it on your eyelids in a special way you could see your future, and if you recited a special set of numbers your echo traveled through the walls of the arsenal to Happy Hunting Grounds, to Flicka. Allah lived on the edge of the horizon; Poseidon lived under the arsenal floor. If you looked very carefully at your reflection in the stream, you could see Narcissus. Lightning was a warning that Zeus was on his way, thunder was the sound of angels' wings as they rushed back to Heaven, and when the sky was blue, you could almost make out the shape of Mount Olympus, the abode of the President of the Gods.

When Laura was a child, she had read a book about four children who could enter a supernatural world through their wardrobe. They would stay in that other world for years and years but then one day they would say the wrong thing in the wrong place and find themselves back in that wardrobe. It was terrible, after all those adventures with kings and queens and witches and noble animals, to find themselves inside a dusty wooden wardrobe, in an old house in the English countryside, ten miles away from the nearest railroad station, in the middle of World War II. After a glorious adulthood in Narnia, to be children once again. To have to obey their parents. To have to go to school.

That was how Laura felt when she would return from the arsenal in the late afternoon. There were HUSH! signs on the door. The house was deadly quiet except for the rattle of Kay's electric typewriter, the telephone, the metallic ticking of a disembodied clock, Bob's buzzer, Kay's soft welcome over the intercom.

"Could you bring up five coffees—three black and two with milk and sugar?" Kay's study was not big enough for five people. They would be sprawled on the floor and the sofa, haggard, with lips pursed, or making conspiratorial comments to each other in unnaturally low voices. Laura stayed away from Bob's study, but more often than not, she would bump into him as he dragged himself to and from the bathroom. In the beginning he had moaned quite a bit, but Laura guessed he grew tired of being unintelligible. Now he didn't even try to say hello. His face was yellow and terribly thin and his eyes looked dead. His arm soon lost its cast and so did his wrist, but contrary to Kay's bulletin announcements, he did not look happy about it. "Only six more days until Daddy's arm cast comes off!" "Yippee! Only five!" "Only one!" "Only one more afternoon!" "By the time you kids go back to school, Daddy will be as good as new!" Kay had asked Laura to talk their father up if they asked about him, "appearances notwithstanding," but there was no need. They never asked after him. He might as well have not existed.

When Flicka was alive he had had no wife, but now that he was dead, Sarah had assigned one to him. Toward the end of August she gave birth to four gray kittens and one white one. The children were very excited and there was talk of an elaborate christening at Flicka's graveside. There was also talk of getting Flicka to come back for the occasion, but no amount of messages to Happy Hunting Grounds could bring an answer.

Then one day Sarah flashed a message to Heaven with a mirror. She told her sister she had received an answer with detailed instructions but would not tell Laura what it was. The next day they began to gather leaves and stones and berries for the ceremony. It was while they were away on one of these prop-gathering excursions that Dennis first came to visit the arsenal.

Dennis had been busy working on a two-room tool shack all summer, and higher, deeper open shelves for Children's Paradise. Dennis and Laura had been avoiding each other, even though Edith had advised against it. Dennis had felt that he needed time by himself to think through his problems, and now, after two months of almost total solitude, he finally felt that he had come to terms with the human predicament. "You see," he said to Laura when they had settled down on the top landing of one of the iron staircases, "the basic problem was that I was jealous of Edith's sexual independence, and so instead of relating to you as a person, I used you sort of as a tool to get back at her sometimes. You know, sort of a competition. I'm really sorry if I fucked up your mind, but thinking it over, I also decided that it was partly your fault.

You're too passive. Edith says you're pretty hip to bad vibrations, and you know, you should have confronted me then and there. I mean, all that stuff you told me about being a leaf in a storm. Well, that boils down to having a basically nonassertive attitude to the world, and man, you've got to assert yourself if you're going to get where you're going."

"It's not that I'm not asserting myself," Laura said. "It's just that I don't know where I'm going. That's the main problem, not my attitude." Dennis agreed. That was his problem too. He was all for being against the Establishment, but if you really were true to your principles, the only thing you could do besides grow your own vegetables was be a lazy bum. He was considering architectural school—the logical extension of his interest in carpentry—but that would have to wait until the following year. In the meantime the most important thing to do was to sort himself out and try to discover where he was at. Generally speaking, he felt as if he was a much saner and better-balanced person than he had been at the beginning of the summer. For example, he could even visualize Edith making love with someone else without feeling the slightest pang of jealousy. And that was good, because that meant that if he came home one day and found her in bed with someone else, he could handle it. Because these days when she picked up guys who lived out of the neighborhood, she was bringing them home.

He looked earnestly into her eyes for approval. She took his hand and squeezed it just as she had seen Edith squeeze it hundreds of times before. At the back of the landing where they were sitting cross-legged, there was an opening in the arsenal wall, through which they could see the stream and the trees and the overgrown weeds and the small form of Nathaniel, who was playing by himself on a slab of stone.

Nathaniel had been left to his own devices all summer. He played his own games. Sometimes he made believe he was a motor-cycle rider. Other times he played at being a car, a dog, a captain, a fireman, a tow truck. Today he was a gas station attendant. He was filling a Coke bottle with water from the stream and pouring it into a blueberry bush, wiping the brambles with an imaginary cloth, checking the oil with a stick. They sat there watching his game for a few minutes in silence, and then, very suddenly, Dennis drew her close to him and they began to kiss.

There was none of the foreplay that Edith had described to her on so many occasions and in such detail, but his warm hands sent electric currents through her body that no amount of foreplay could have ever caused, and the passion with which they tore off each other's clothes and the way he seemed to be kissing her bare skin in a thousand places at the same time made her forget about the coldness of the metal landing, and she didn't care about the echoes in the arsenal as they wrestled their way toward orgasm, as they bounded from plateau to plateau to heights no chart had ever charted. They both came—not at the same time, but almost, and then they held each other very tight until Laura could no longer feel his heart beating.

Dennis sat up, very abruptly. While Laura lay there naked, he put on his socks and his pants and his sneakers. Then with averted eyes he apologized for his behavior. "I really didn't mean to," he said. "I don't know what came over me."

"What are you apologizing for?" Laura asked. "I came more than I have ever come in my whole life."

"You did?" he said. He scratched his head, relieved. As a matter of fact, he told her, it was the most amazing total orgasm he had had in a long time. Of course he had been incredibly horny. That was because he had more or less given up sex for the summer in order to have a clear enough head to think things over. He hadn't even masturbated. That would have been the cheap way out. When Laura had put all her clothes back on, they went down to sit next to the stream bed, where they tried to analyze why it was that they had had such a totally and unexpectedly satisfactory sexual encounter. There were many possible factors, they decided: the unfamiliar setting, the fact that they were probably both horny, the fact that they had not had a good talk for almost two months, personal magnetism, a simple desire for physical contact between two people who respected each other. Laura wondered if Edith's absence had anything to do with it, but she didn't mention this possibility. They concluded that sex was always best when it was natural, when two people who respected each other as human beings acted on impulse.

When they came to their conclusion, Laura felt the empty glow of disappointment after pleasure. She still felt as if she were floating when they kissed again. But at the same time it upset her that such pleasure could be pinned down so easily and in so few words, just as she had never been able to enjoy adventure stories and thrillers as much after her teacher had explained to her that the theme of all adventure stories was the triumph of man over his environment through the use of his mind and body, and been unable to laugh at jokes for weeks after discovering that laughter was just another way of dealing with the unknown.

They went out to sit by the stream. While they watched the water flow through their toes, Nathaniel walked back and forth between the stream and the bushes, until every single bush in the area had been filled with imaginary gasoline. He then came over and told Dennis he was a truck. "And I think you need a lot of diesel," he said. "And Laura is a minibus and she needs lots of gas. High octane or low octane?" "Low octane," Laura told him, and Nathaniel poured a Coke bottle full of water over her head.

It was funny the first time and funny the second and the third, but when Nathaniel poured the fourth bottle of water over Dennis's head, Laura told him that they had enough diesel and low-octane gas for the moment.

"Why don't you fill up those cars on the other side of the arsenal?" she said, pointing at the bushes behind the Pyles' dark green station wagon.

"Okay," he said. He filled his Coke bottle with water from the stream and toddled away. As he shuttled back and forth between the distant bushes, Laura and Dennis agreed it was a pity that grown people couldn't have such vivid imaginations as children, although they both understood what would happen if they did. They both deplored the way adults were imprisoned by their personalities. They agreed that the only way for adults to transcend their identities was through sex. Not any sex. Good sex. That was the only time you were at one with the universe. Laura and Dennis both confessed they felt nostalgic for the world view of a child. Laura described how trees had looked to her when she was four, and Dennis said that that was how they looked on mescaline. Trees looked really cool when you were on mescaline. You could spend hours and hours in absolute raptures about a perfectly ordinary tree. In a certain way, childhood was one long mescaline trip, Dennis suggested. "You can get high on life then, I mean, literally." But after childhood, sex, and in certain ways yoga, were the only ways you could transcend reality without using artificial stimulants. And of course mental illness. As they discussed the similarity between drugged states and mental illness, Nathaniel poured several bottles of water into the gas tank of the station wagon. When Dennis turned on the engine later that afternoon, it wouldn't start. It started to but then died abruptly.

It was the children's last day at the arsenal. They had to hitch-hike home.

Kay dealt with the mishap with her customary good humor. She took Nathaniel aside and explained why you couldn't mix water with gasoline, what it was about gasoline that made engines work, where gasoline came from, what happened if you added salt, what happened if you drank it, how human stomachs differed from car engines and why. She always kept a gallon of gasoline on the porch for emergencies, and when Nathaniel refused to believe that it turned into caramel if you added sugar to the tank of a car, she poured a bit of gasoline into a cupful of sugar so that he could see how thick and sticky it became. "Now you wouldn't want that to happen to the gas in *your* car, would you?"

"Are you mad at me?" Nathaniel asked.

"Of course not, my little chickadee. I just thought it was as good a time as any to tell you exactly what gasoline was and how to treat it. But now that you know, maybe it would be a good idea if you didn't play at being a gas station attendant for a while. Hey! I have a good idea! Why don't you spend the day being a nice little peace-loving four-year-old boy?"

Sarah had other plans. She was furious at Nathaniel because they had not had time to gather all the necessary props for the christening of the kittens. Now they could not go back to the arsenal to find them. "You're going to pay for this," she told him when Kay was out of earshot. "You've committed a mortal sin. You're going to have to do everything I tell you tomorrow at the ceremony or else I'll get them to turn you into a frog."

"I'm not a frog today," Nathaniel said, "I'm a boy."

"Well, you won't be for long, not if you don't obey me at the christening."

Laura was helping Dennis paint the higher, deeper open shelves in the tool shed in the garden when the children came out for the christening the following morning. Sarah was dressed in a blue negligee from the dress-up chest and on her head was Jingle's gold paper crown. In her right hand was an open shoe box with the kittens in it, and in her left hand was the wand Jingle had forgotten to take home before she was banned. Sarah was chanting "America the Beautiful" in a deep and solemn voice. Behind her was Bess. She had one tutu around her neck and one around her waist and was carrying a large plastic bag full of flowers and stones. Behind Bess was Nathaniel. He was wearing a pillow case over his upper torso. It had arm holes and eye holes and mouth holes and two little nostril holes but they weren't all in the right places, so he was having difficulty walking. He tripped three times before they reached the popsicle that marked Flicka's grave under the elm tree.

"Bodyguard! Stand to attention!"

While Nathaniel stood to attention and tried to adjust the pillowcase so that the eyeholes matched his eyes, Bess and Sarah arranged the flowers and stones and shells in an elaborate pattern around the popsicle stick. When they were done, they dug a small hole next to it and sprinkled earth over it.

"Bodyguard! Take this!"

Sarah pressed a small pink object into his hand. "What is it?" Nathaniel asked.

"The water machine for the baptism."

"What water machine?" Nathaniel asked.

Bess pulled up the mouth hole so that Nathaniel could see. "It used to be Jingle's squirt gun," Bess explained. Nathaniel screamed and threw the squirt gun on the ground.

"Don't hurt me! Don't hurt me!" he cried when they tried to put the squirt gun back into his hand.

"Come on, you can't act like such a scaredy-cat! You're a body-guard!" Sarah cried. She threatened to turn him into a frog if he didn't obey her. "And I'll get them to turn you into a frog for a hundred years, and when you become human again you'll be so old and wrinkled that you'll want to die."

But still he wouldn't take the squirt gun, so she did abracadabra with her wand and told him she had reincarnated him into Achilles. Achilles, in other words, the bravest man in the whole world. He just had to hold that gun and squirt it at the right times, or else the whole ceremony would be in vain. Still, Nathaniel refused.

"If you don't take this gun right now I'll kick your heel, and you know what will happen then?" Bess took his legs. Sarah took his arms. They pinned him on the grass and then Sarah pressed the squirt gun into his hand. He screamed and kicked for a few moments. Then suddenly he stopped. He sat up and looked at his sisters. "It doesn't hurt," he said, looking at the gun in his hand with surprise.

"Of course it doesn't. Now you stand up and stay right next to the cat box, and when we tell you to you squirt three times over each kitten's head."

"What am I now?" Nathaniel asked.

"You can be anything you want so long as you keep quiet during the ceremony and do what we tell you."

"Then I'll be a cowboy."

"Okay, you be a cowboy."

"And the kittens are broncos."

"Okay, the kittens are broncos."

"Except that white one, that white one is a cattle thief and if I don't shoot it right now it will take away all my broncos! Oh, no! I have to shoot him before it's too late. Bang bang bang bang bang." He squirted all the kittens in the cat box. Even from the other side of the lawn you could hear the kittens' tiny meows.

"You idiot!" Sarah screeched. "I could kill you! You've ruined the whole thing! Now we'll never be able to do it." Nathaniel squirmed out of the pillowcase and got away from his sisters as fast as he could. Sarah went after him, her arm upraised. She was holding something sparkling in her hand, but Laura could not see what it was until Sarah had caught up with him in front of the tool shed and knocked him over. It was a penknife.

Dennis saw it at the same time. He jumped out of the tool shed, grabbed both of Sarah's hands, and wrenched the penknife from her fingers.

"You idiots!" Sarah shouted. "Now the whole thing's ruined! Now Flicka won't ever even know he has kittens and it's all your fault!"

During the commotion the cat box had tipped over and the tiny kittens had spilled onto the lawn. By the time Laura got to them, four of them were trapped inside the strange geometrical patterns of rocks and flowers and the white runt had fallen into the hole they had dug next to Flicka's grave. "Since when do you chase your brother around with a penknife?" she said to Sarah. "And what were you doing out here with a knife in the first place?"

"None of your business," Sarah said.

"And what's this hole for anyway?"

"None of your business."

"Well, I don't care if it's my business or not," Laura said, "but I'm going to take these kittens back to their mother. And if I were you, I'd go to the Thinking Room and think this whole outrageous situation over."

"You can't make me go to the Thinking Room," Sarah said, but after a few minutes of whimpering in the kitchen and gnawing at her fist, she went up to the Thinking Room of her own accord. Even after an hour of solitude, when she came down for lunch, she was still angry at Laura, and when no one was looking, she stuck out her tongue.

17

It was a gloomy group at the lunch table. Edith was fretting over her failure to find enough potential subscribers willing to commit funds to *Minerva* sight unseen. Gail was worried that the layout format she had been working on for the past five weeks was not "clean" enough for modern standards. Melissa was telling the latest installment in her battle with the neighbors—three physical-fitness freaks who gave frequent beer bashes—and Rachel was thinking out loud about the advisability of working your heart out on a magazine that seemed doomed never to find a single backer and doomed to remain forever in embryo form due to the objections raised by a certain so-called radical founder, whose hysterical and narrow-minded opinions on "sexist capitalism" were merely disguises for her basic laziness. "Here we are after two months of hard work with nothing to show for it," Rachel said.

"You know that's hardly true," Kay said to her. "That general survey of where we stand in the professions has been ready for weeks."

"Yeah, but look how much got past the censors. Three lines, or does my memory fail me, and is it four?"

"Well," Kay said. She had food in her mouth but still managed to sound fairly businesslike. "I'm sure we could figure out some way to override our critics."

"You just try," said Melissa, pointing her fork at Rachel.

It was all Kay could do to keep the peace. Every time Bob's buzzer went off and she went up to find out what was wrong, Melissa and Rachel were at each other's throats by the time she got back to the kitchen. "Gee, you all look so gloomy," she said after she came back from her fourth trip. "I hope we all look happier and more productive by the time Martin gets here, or else I can't think *what* he'll think of us."

"Martin?" Melissa said. "Who's he?"

"You remember him, I'm sure. My lover. He's been in the Yucatán this summer, trying to choose among several paths for his future. If his postcards are trustworthy, he should be flying in some time today."

"Your ex-lover," Sarah corrected her.

"Well, we're still very dear friends." Bob's buzzer went off again.

"Why does Daddy keep ringing that buzzer?" Sarah asked when Kay came downstairs again.

"Well, I guess he's the tiniest bit jealous that Martin's coming over to visit. Although that's very silly of him." She smiled at the intercom. "Very silly indeed."

"Is Martin going to sleep in your bed tonight?" Nathaniel asked.

"I don't think so, my little chickadee. But if we do, I promise to let you know."

"Well, you know what?" Nathaniel said.

"What, dear?"

"You know what I'll do to him if he decides to sleep in your bed? I'll shoot him. I'll shoot him three times in the stomach, like this."

He took Jingle's squirt gun out of his pocket and sprayed the bay window. "Pow pow! Pow pow! Pow pow!"

Kay's face crumpled when she saw the gun. "Oh, Nathaniel!" she cried. "I thought you had given up playing with guns forever."

"But I like to play with guns. They don't hurt anymore."

"Whatever made you suddenly think of playing with guns again?"

"Sarah gave it to me."

"Sarah?" Kay said, looking at her daughter.

"Nathaniel's a liar," Sarah said. "He just has a warped mind. I didn't give it to him as a gun, I gave it to him as a water machine. He's just going through an unhealthy stage. I think he met a bad influence last week at Sunday School. You know what he did? He crawled under the tables when the teacher was reading us a story and bit her leg."

"Nathaniel! Whyever did you bite your teacher's leg?"

"Because I was a dog," he informed her.

"Why can't you play a peaceful dog, instead of a biting one?"

"Well, I'm not a dog anymore."

"Then what are you?"

"A cowboy."

"Oh!" Kay sighed painfully. "Gee, Nathaniel," she said after a long pause. "Wouldn't it be possible to be a peace-loving cowboy, and never have to carry a gun or shoot at anything?"

"Cowboys have to shoot bad guys or else all the broncos get stolen."

"Then why don't you play at being someone more peace-loving? Like a construction worker or a train conductor, or just a plain old four-year-old boy like I said yesterday?"

"Well, maybe tomorrow. First I have to shoot Martin."

"Oh, why oh why must you say such things? And Martin loves you so. Why, he's practically your second father!"

Bob's buzzer went off. "Oh, that man, he's just impossible," Kay said under her breath. Leaning over to the intercom, she said,

"Coming, dear!" She looked at her watch. "Gee, I'd be awfully grateful if one of you could clean up the kitchen a little bit so it looks nice for Martin. Especially the table," she said, winking at Laura.

"You know what?" Melissa said when Kay had left the room. "I have a theory."

"No kidding," said Rachel.

"I think this stuff about penis envy is all bullshit. It's really the opposite. I mean, instead of penis envy, castration compensation. It explains why they all have such a fascination for substitutes like guns."

"Oh, Melissa!" Rachel said. "You never fail to astound me. I have never in my whole life met someone with such an amazing ability to never utter a thought that hasn't already been uttered by about ten thousand other people first."

For a moment Laura thought Melissa was going to throw her coffee in Rachel's face, but then she caught herself. She swallowed her lips. She looked as if she were about to cry. Gail didn't seem to notice anything was wrong. When Melissa buried her head in her hands, Gail asked her in a very annoyed voice if she would mind removing her elbows from the table. "It's really incredible how clumsy you are sometimes. Well, not clumsy really, but if you keep getting in the way with your elbows and legs and everything I can't see how you expect me to get this done, I mean really."

That did it.

"What a load of crybabies you people are," Sarah said.

"Now don't you make fun of Melissa just because she's express-ing her emotions," Edith chided. She knelt at the foot of Melissa's chair and stared with great concern at the hands that hid Melissa's face. Sighing, she got up and began to massage her back. There was silence, except for the intercom. Bob was desperately trying to say something to Kay, although the meaning was lost in transmission, and Kay's voice was raised. "No, I have *not* been meeting with him secretly. I told you. He didn't get back until this morning . . . No,

I am *not* planning to move him back into the bedroom and disturb your sleep . . . No, I am *not* trying to pull the wool over your eyes. Nor am I planning to abandon you or the children or anything of the sort . . . Oh! If only you people would leave me alone for just five minutes a day, so I could think! Why do all men think that all we women think about is sex? Can't you understand that all I want is a career? Is that so objectionable?"

It was at this point that Laura saw Martin's face pressed against the screen door. He was smiling, and very bronzed. His hair was longer and more bushlike than ever, and in the sunlight it looked almost white. "I never thought I'd have to tell you this, Bob, but this summer has turned you into a sexist." A door slammed on the intercom. Kay came running down the stairs.

"Martin! Oh! How wonderful! How marvelous and healthy you look! Oh, what a wonderful surprise!" She threw open the screen door and threw herself into his arms. "Sarah! Bess! Nathaniel! Everyone! Look who's here!" The children looked at the hugging couple with suspicion.

"Hey, hey, hey!" Martin said. "What's all this silence and sobriety? Cat bit your tongue?" He swaggered over to Nathaniel and picked him up. "Is that what happened? Is that why you're so glum? Eh? Is that what's wrong, you silly little sperm, you?"

"I'm not a sperm," Nathaniel said.

"Then what are you?"

"A cowboy."

"That's interesting," Martin said, "and I'm an Indian. You and I should make a pretty good pair."

"And you know what I'll do if I catch you sleeping in Mommy's bed?" Nathaniel continued. "I'll shoot you."

"Oh, you will, will you? And what if I wear a bulletproof vest under my peejays? Then I can sleep all night without even worrying, and all the bullets will bounce off."

"In any event," Melissa interjected, "it's not for you to decide."

"I guess you're right," Martin said sheepishly. He glanced at

Kay and she smiled at him fondly. "Well, well, well, it sure is great to see you guys again." He sat Nathaniel down on the side of the table.

"I hope you realize you're fucking up Gail's layout," Melissa said.

"Oh, sorry." He lifted Nathaniel to a chair.

"You can't wear a bulletproof vest all over your body," Nathaniel said to Martin. "So you know what? I'm going to shoot you in the mouth and then the bullets will go down your esophagus and then they will go to your stomach and then you'll explode like Humpty Dumpty, and Mommy and I will try to put the pieces together again but you'll be all exploded so we can't put you back together again and then you'll be yuck and Mommy will be all mine."

"Is that so?" Martin said. He let Nathaniel put his squirt gun in his mouth. Nathaniel squirted. He squirted again, but nothing happened. Nathaniel looked at his gun with surprise. "Doesn't seem to work on me," Martin said, winking at Laura. "Maybe it only works on eggheads."

"Maybe something's wrong with this gun," Nathaniel said. He tested it in the air. A great arc of water shot out of the gun, all over Gail's layout, blurring all the ink.

"Five weeks of work!" Gail wailed.

"That does it." Melissa bounded across the room, grabbing the gun out of his hand, and shook it in front of his face. "You know what this is, you little idiot? This is a penis substitute! A penis substitute! And do you know what's going to happen if I catch you playing with this penis substitute one more time . . . ?"

"Melissa, please," Kay said, "let me handle this."

"But that's five weeks of work wasted!"

"I'd appreciate it if you would let me be the judge of that," Kay said in a soft but stern voice. She took the gun out of Melissa's hand.

"You don't understand, Melissa," Rachel said. "Your threats

are too crude. Kay here believes in bringing up kids by trial and error. Nathaniel here might like to play with guns now. But one of these years he'll give it up of his own free will. Maybe not this year, but next year certainly. As a matter of fact, if you bring up kids on the trial-and-error method, the whole upbringing process takes about eighty years."

"Rachel! How could you?" Kay reeled around as if the wind had been knocked out of her. Nathaniel got down from his chair and ran toward Rachel. "Pow pow! I got you!" He ran out of the house.

"Oh, girls," Kay said to Bess and Sarah, "you're going to have to help me steer your brother away from all this violence. You're just going to have to help me. I can't go it alone. The three of us are going to have to do everything in our power to discourage him.

"Anything you can do," she said, squeezing their hands as they got up to go play in the garden. The Minerva group had returned to work, and now that the kitchen was relatively quiet, you could hear Bob Pyle's irregular breathing.

Something was smelling up the cupboard over the sink, Kay told Laura. Would she mind taking the afternoon to wash it and then rearrange the contents in a more reasonable fashion? "Martin and I will be outside enjoying the last of the summer sun," she said with a haggard smile. The two of them went out and sat on the swings, where they had an earnest conversation, far away from the intercom, they thought. But the window next to the stove was open, and when the breeze was blowing the right way, Laura could hear what they were saying.

Kay was telling Martin about her problems with *Minerva*. She had decided it was not a professional group. Edith was wonderful, but Gail just did not have the necessary technical expertise when it came to putting together a professional-looking dummy. Melissa, though brilliant, was crippled by her emotional problems. And Rachel had turned out to be quite a monster, as Martin had probably seen with his own eyes. From the way Rachel approached

things, you would have thought they were putting together a bro-
chure for the Pillsbury BakeOff, Kay said.

In the meantime she had run into an old classmate who was now
one of the top producers for Channel 2. She was putting together
a program, a sort of serious women's talk show, and she wanted
Kay to be the moderator. She said Kay had the right kind of voice
and compassionate face, as well as the right kind of background.
Wife, mother, homemaker, accomplished sociologist, aspiring
journalist, civil rights activist, and liberated woman all at the same
time: she would appeal to all the groups they were aiming to reach.
And then of course she had the right kind of charisma. It was an
incredible opportunity. And, personal ambition aside, if her mission was to reach the maximum number of women, then she could
reach so many more on a television program than she could ever
hope to reach via a rinky-dink magazine.

She had talked it over with Edith, and Edith was gung-ho
about being Kay's assistant. She said it was much more down her
line. The problem was how to break the news to the others. The
person they were most worried about was Melissa. They were
worried that if they told her the magazine project was over, she
would go into a downward spiral. It would only foster her paranoia. She and Edith felt a nurselike responsibility toward Melissa,
and they were perfectly willing to sugar the pill and have her
come in on the television thing as a volunteer researcher. But
what to do with Gail? She just wasn't professional enough. Between herself and Martin, Gail wasn't really right for Melissa
anyway. Kay happened to know that Gail had initiated a sexual
relationship with a next-door neighbor, and Kay didn't know
whether it was better to wait and let Melissa find out on her own
or break it to her gently. Gail had never struck Kay as a very
committed partner in the first place. When she and Edith had
first discussed the television possibility, Kay had felt very guilty
about the prospect of letting Rachel down. But after this afternoon it was obvious to Kay that she owed her nothing. She had

mentioned the television show to Bob, and that was the other problem.

Bob. Laura had thought that Kay almost enjoyed taking care of him during the summer. But now she discovered that he had made her life hell: his jealousy, his pathological dependence on her, his resentment of her career, his psychosomatic headaches, his refusal to do even an hour's worth of constructive work on *The Road to Legitimacy*—"Frankly, I wouldn't be surprised if they don't give him tenure," Kay said—the terrible demands he had made on her sexually, only vaguely alluded to, the way he insulted her when she tried to help him, the cruel things he had said when she told him about the television job. He had told her she was shirking her duties as a mother.

"That was the last straw, when he insinuated that as a wife and mother it was wrong for me to work full-time, as if it were one of the ten commandments that a mother's place is in the home," Kay told Martin. He had even threatened separation if she took the job, and Kay was so angry that she thought she might just take him up on it. She was going to think it over for a few days and then make a final decision when he got his jaw unwired. That would be next week. She didn't feel it was right to make a decision until then. She knew it sounded ridiculous, but that cast around his neck and that wired jaw made her feel as if she had an unfair advantage.

The cupboard was sparkling clean by now, and Laura had re-arranged its contents in a more reasonable manner. The guilty party had been a plastic bag of rotten fruit, which Laura had now sent down the Disposall. She looked out the window.

Kay and Martin had gotten up from the swings. They were holding hands and looking earnestly into each other's eyes, as if on the verge of a momentous decision. On the other side of the garden were the children. Nathaniel was tied to the oak tree, and gagged. The girls were walking around a rectangular carpet of flowers and stones, chanting "America the Beautiful." In Bess's hands was a cushion. On the cushion was Jingle's squirt gun. In Sarah's hand was a knife, and when Bess stopped in front of Flicka's grave, Sarah picked up the squirt gun and sawed at it. Finally she snapped off the plastic barrel. She dropped both halves into the hole next to Flicka's grave, and then, with Bess's help, she began to shovel dirt into the hole.

They were following their mother's directions and doing everything in their power to discourage their brother from playing violent games. They were burying his gun.

"I think you should try a trial separation," Martin was saying as they came across the lawn toward the house. "Not for my sake, but for yours and for his."

"You may be right," Kay said. She was looking at the ground intently but her thoughts must have been far away, because she walked right through the elaborate carpet of stones and flowers that Sarah and Bess had laid out for the funeral. Her work boots scattered the stones and crushed the flowers. And she didn't even know it.

18

The next week was for clearing up old business. On Monday, Kay called an emergency meeting of her Minerva group and announced that she was abandoning the magazine to go work on a women's talk show. She then told Gail and Rachel that their services were no longer needed. Rachel was outraged to be dismissed in such an arbitrary manner, and left without saying good-bye to anyone. Gail was indifferent, but even so, Melissa was uneasy when Kay and Edith asked her to stay on as Special Volunteer Researcher. She said her first responsibility was to Gail, and asked for some time to think it over.

And then, the Friday before Labor Day, Bob Pyle's jaw was finally unwired. Bob did not seem overjoyed to have his powers of speech restored to him, but Kay thought it was wonderful. She said that since Bob's commitments at the university did not begin in earnest until Registration on Tuesday, that gave them a full weekend to discuss their future.

On Saturday Laura took the car to the garage for repairs and the children to Sears Roebuck to buy school clothes. On Sunday she moved her belongings back to the dorm. This year she had a single room on the top floor, and she planned to decorate it lavishly with some of the money she had saved over the summer. She had decided to live a different life this year—take courses that would be useful to her in later life; never skip any classes; spend more time alone in her luxurious room reading and listening to classical music (she knew nothing about classical music); spend less time at the Pyles'; be firmer with Kay when Kay asked her to skip morning classes or put off evening visits to the library so that she "could be sure the children were in trustworthy hands."

But even that first Sunday things started going wrong. When Laura arranged her books on her handsome new bookshelves, they took up only a bookshelf and a half. The books reminded her of courses she had lost interest in after three weeks and courses she had had nightmares about, and of all the things she had failed to accomplish and failed to learn. She tried other arrangements, separating the books she had read from the books she had not read, the books she had enjoyed from the books that had disturbed her, but even when she had spaced them evenly over all six shelves, there was still too much blank space. The blank space reminded her of all the things she did not know and could not do, would never be able to do. It was the first omen that her plans for a new life were doomed.

On Labor Day, Bob and Kay formally announced their decision to separate. Since they had left the intercom on for most of the weekend, Laura already knew they had decided to separate to opposite sides of the house instead of endeavoring to set up a second household.

What surprised her was the reason they gave, or rather the reason Kay gave, at the "Ratificatory Meeting."

Bob said nothing at that meeting, although Laura knew from what she had overheard on the intercom that the concept of "limited-space separation" was just as much his brainchild as it was Kay's. He just stood there at the head of the table with his arms hanging at his sides and stared at the rubber plants. When Kay announced that they were separating to opposite sides of the house for the children's sake and the children's sake only, he had a coughing fit. And Laura remembered how Kay's work boots had scattered all those flowers.

In accordance with the separation contract that they signed at the Ratificatory Meeting in full view of all concerned, Bob got the living room, the green bathroom, the front staircase, and his study. Kay got the master bedroom, the blue bathroom, her study, and the back stairs. They agreed to share the kitchen. Kay had priority in the mornings, Bob had priority in the afternoons, and the evenings were flexible. Whoever presided over the bath-supper-story routine got first choice of evening hours.

The idea, as put forth in the concluding paragraph of the contract, was to eliminate all possibility of physical contact between the parents while providing the children with unlimited access to both the mother and the father. Hence the separate telephone line that Bob was planning to have installed in his study, and the separate intercom system that would enable Bob to get in touch with the kitchen and Children's Paradise without disturbing Kay, and the new doorbell Kay had Dennis install above the old one when, after three or four embarrassing confrontations earlier that day, she decided they should receive their guests through separate doors. The new doorbell made a chirping sound instead of the traditional buzz. Above it Kay scrawled a message in purple Magic Marker: "Hello, friend(s)! Would you mind stepping around to the back door after ringing this bell? Love and chirps, Kay Carpenter." Carpenter was Kay's maiden name. The separation contract stipulated that she could use it instead of her married name if she so wished.

"We hereby pledge to safeguard the cheer and harmony of household life," the contract began. "Professional commitments notwithstanding, we resolve to do everything in our power to ensure that the continuity of the children's growing-up process is not jeopardized by this experiment in limited-space separation." To this end, the contract called for a myriad of charts through which Kay and Bob would be able to communicate "child-related information in a scientific and nonemotive fashion." A superficial glance at the large new bulletin board would make you think they had anticipated and solved in advance every possible type of crisis. But Laura knew better.

She knew from the very beginning what was going to happen to all those weekly planning sheets, bedtime story coordination charts, the coded bimonthly child assessments, abnormal behavior and record of remedial therapy sheets, monthly excursion hour-allotment charts, chore rotation sheets, feedback reports, interparental warning systems, and single-parent Family Council meeting decision-records. Like all the other programs and resolutions that Kay had drafted during the eight months Laura had worked at the Pyle house, these charts would be half filled and then forgotten, but would hang there for months, like bad consciences, or become covered with Sarah's hieroglyphics, like the TOMORROW IS ANOTHER DAY posters.

Or be covered with telephone numbers and dentist appointment reminders, like the posters Kay had drawn up one rainy day during the summer before more pressing questions made her forget about Sarah's religious problem altogether:

"Did you know that thousands of years ago people thought of trees and rocks as gods? . . . The Greeks believed in a whole lot of gods (and goddesses!). God number one was a nifty little fellow called Zeus. He and his wife Hera lived on a mountain called Olympus . . . The Moslems believe in an all-powerful fellow called Allah . . . Did you know that the Hindus believe that you can be born again as a horse? A frog? A Nathaniel? A Sarah? A Bess? If *you* were going to be reincarnated (REE-in-CAR-nate-ed) what would *you* like to be?"

Laura told Dennis he had made the new bulletin board in vain.

—4—
FALL

19

Toward the end of September the girls came down with chicken pox. They were accustomed to a certain amount of freedom when they were ill: Kay allowed them to set up makeshift beds wherever they liked, and if they didn't have a fever, they could play quiet games or make cookies. They didn't have to wear slippers unless they wanted to, and since the house was well-insulated, they didn't have to wear robes either, not unless they felt more comfortable in them. But this time it was Melissa who was in charge, and she had different ideas.

Her intentions were excellent—even Laura knew that. Ever since Gail had left her, Melissa had become the children's most devoted servant. It was the way they had acted on that first day. Laura remembered the scene well: Melissa sitting next to the window in the darkened living room, a mountain of used tissues beside her, staring at the candlelit cake the children brought in from the kitchen. While Sarah and Nathaniel sang "My Bonny Lies Over the Ocean," Bess gave her their presents. A half-used tube of glue from Nathaniel (for her heart, as he explained), a blue clay ashtray from Bess, and from Sarah a poem entitled "We Think You're Neat." (The title was in Kay's handwriting and the rest was in hieroglyphics.) At first Melissa couldn't find her voice. Then, as the last candle burned into the cake, she burst into tears. She opened her arms and tried to hug them all at once, knocking their heads together without meaning to, gasping, "Thank you, thank you."

From then on the children could do no wrong. Encouraged by this breakthrough, Kay asked her if she would mind acting as Auxiliary Mother's Helper when her duties as Special Volunteer Researcher for the television show were not too demanding. Melissa was more than happy to oblige. Like Laura before her, she relegated her studies to second place, and although she often let her temper and her slogans get the better of her, she tried to treat the children as Kay would have treated them. She tried to count to ten instead of shouting, tried to say "I think" and "I feel" instead of giving orders. She even took books on child psychology out of the library.

But as Kay pointed out privately, "Breeding will out in a crisis situation." Melissa came from an Italian family that obviously did not take illness lightly. When Sarah and Bess came down with chicken pox she wouldn't let them out of bed except to go to the bathroom, and if they went to the bathroom without their slippers and robes, she had a fit. She wouldn't let them read because the concentration might ruin their eyes. She changed their sheets every three hours, even when their fevers subsided. She checked their scabs constantly to make sure they weren't scratching them, and when she found one on Sarah's arm that she suspected Sarah might have scratched, she tried to force Sarah to wear mittens.

That was the last straw. "Will you tell this moron to get off my back?" Sarah said to Laura, who was also in the room at the time. (Kay had asked Laura to keep tabs on Melissa, and observe her interaction with the children without actually interfering, and to counter her occasional hostile outburst with massive doses of love.) "What does she think I am anyway, a three-year-old or something? I don't care if she's an emotional cripple. I'm not going to put up with her anymore."

Laura knew what it felt like to be rejected by Sarah after days, weeks, months of devotion. Although she was not overfond of Melissa and resented the way she had been slowly usurping her position in the family, Laura did her best to cheer Melissa up when she locked herself in the bathroom to cry. She left coffee for her at the door, and cookies. Through the keyhole she told her she was sure no one had told Sarah she was an emotional cripple—Sarah had probably made it up on the spur of the moment. Melissa didn't answer. She only sobbed. It wasn't until the evening of rage that Laura discovered that Melissa held her personally responsible.

In a way the evening of rage was Sarah's doing, too.

It was dinnertime. The children were better, though not well enough to go back to school. Bess looked radiant in her crown and her negligee (she was going through a princess stage). Sarah was wearing a bathing suit, just to spite Melissa. Now it was Kay who looked ill. Her face was pale and she was wearing dark glasses.

While Laura was clearing away the plates, Kay mentioned in passing that Bob had initiated a relationship with Louella. "I thought you should know," she said, "before he brings her here tomorrow." Laura wondered if that was the reason for the dark glasses.

Melissa was outraged. She was putting Bob down for going after a "blatant powder puff of a brood mare" just because his ego happened to have been challenged by a woman who happened to be his emotional superior and his intellectual equal, when Sarah interrupted her.

"Yes," she said smugly, "but do you know what will happen to him? He's going to end up in Hell."

Kay had trouble concealing her distress. Who had taught her that cruel, cruel word? Sarah wouldn't tell her, but Kay thought she had a fair idea who it was, and when the children had gone to bed she called up the grandmother.

As far as Laura could gather, the grandmother denied filling the children's heads with fire and brimstone. Nonetheless, Kay canceled the Sunday School experiment and threatened to give serious thought to the advisability of the grandmother spending any time alone with the children in the future. She told the grandmother that Hell was a concept that had gone out with the Middle Ages. She couldn't imagine what kind of Sunday School teacher the grandmother's church had. "Hell, if it exists at all, is this miserable life we live on Earth." The grandmother shouted something, and Kay slammed down the phone.

"Do you know what that woman said to me?" she gasped. "She said she had never met a woman who was more bent on destroying her children than myself!" She collapsed into a chair. She tried to laugh it off, but there were tears in her eyes.

Edith tried to get her to admit that she was angry. Kay said it was impossible for her to be angry. She understood the grandmother's motivations too well to be angry at her. The grandmother was a prisoner of her own prejudices. Kay found it all very sad, almost inevitable when you considered the grandmother's background. She cited her age, the norms and standards of her generation, the Oedipal question, which in Kay's opinion had never really been resolved, her deep jealousy of Kay, her deep involvement in a Protestant sect that Kay considered to be truly reactionary . . . she went on and on. But when she had run out of rationalizations, Kay was still frowning.

"You're right," she finally said to Edith. "There's a deep reservoir of anger in me that I can't seem to explain away." It was at this point that Edith suggested they devote the evening to rage. There was no reason why a group of women in twentieth-century America had to suffer silently on account of pent-up emotions.

They had to get this anger out of their systems. Then they could begin again.

They pushed the plants to one end of the kitchen table and pulled their chairs to the other. Laura and Melissa were on one side of the table, facing Kay and Edith. It was decided that Laura should direct her rage at Edith, that Edith should direct her rage at Melissa, that Melissa should direct her rage at Kay, and that Kay should direct her rage at Laura. They drew straws. Kay went first.

Laura had never attended an evening of rage before and she was not accustomed to sitting back silently while someone abused her for things she had never even dreamed of, or dreamed of doing. She was unnerved by Kay's accusations. Why did she, Laura, have to take the blame for Bob's mistakes? When Kay asked her why she didn't realize how it hurt her when they "did it like a dog," Laura didn't know where to look. She didn't want to know the intimate details of Kay's sex life. She didn't want to take the blame for it either. She didn't want to know how deeply Kay had resented Bob's dependence on her after the accident, or how helpless she had felt when Sarah's birth had forced her to abandon her studies *in medias res.*

"You knew how much I hankered after that doctorate, so why didn't you take precautions? You wanted a family, but why then? *Why then?* You were worried that we might not be able to have children, weren't you? But couldn't you have waited one more year before filling me nightly with potent sperm?"

She was looking at Laura in a new and very disturbing way. Her lips were twisted into a baby smile, her eyes coy and inviting. She looked weak instead of strong, and Laura liked to think of her as strong, unfearing, forever in the right. It was as if she were trying to coax Laura to change her mind. But about what, and if she did, would it matter? Laura was confused. As was usual whenever she was embarrassed in a public place, she had trouble figuring out what to do with her mouth, where to look, when to smile, whether to answer back or run away.

Then Kay discarded her beseeching look. The baby smile disappeared. Her lips trembled with undisguised anger.

"Don't you remember what I said to you that last day, how I hoped you would go for a total woman, a woman who would help you develop where you failed to develop with me? Don't you remember? You promised you would try, and now here you are shacked up with the easiest lay in town, you dirty coward! You want to make sure you don't end up with a woman who could challenge you, don't you?" She paused, as if shocked at her own ugly thoughts, then backed down slightly. "I don't understand how you can expect to have a rewarding relationship with someone as backward as Louella. What do all you men see in her? She's all wrong for you, Bob, can't you see? I think she's a very fine person in her own right, but for you, Bob, at this stage in the game . . ."

"Tell Bob what you really think of her," Edith interrupted.

Kay lurched forward as if to vomit and said, "I hate her!" Laura felt so uncomfortable that she laughed.

Dagger-looks from Edith and Melissa, who had stretched across the table to hold Kay's hands. "Now why don't you tell Bob how you feel, how you *really* feel about him?"

Kay withdrew her hands. Clutching her stomach, staring at the table like a sick, bewildered child, she said, "I hate you."

"Say it again."

"I hate you. I hate you, I hate you, I hate you!" She was screaming now and staring into Laura's eyes, and dripping from her own eyes was a venom that contradicted all the sweet things she had ever said to Laura and all her many kindnesses. "I resent you!" She spoke haltingly but with unusual violence, as if she had landed on her back in a deep canyon and was calling for help. "Oh! How you have oppressed me! You . . . you . . . you bastard! You . . . *son of a bitch!*" Edith and Melissa reached out and took her hands. Swinging back and forth to the rhythm of her words, her eyes on the ceiling, she whispered, "Bastard, son of a bitch, you bastard, you son of a bitch, you sexist son of a bitch, you dirty fucking, fucking, fucking bastard son of a bitch!" Then suddenly she pulled Melissa halfway across the table, knocking over a plant. "History shaped me!" she screamed. "Oh, how I wish I could break down my heterosexual barriers! Oh, oh, when will I be relieved of this poisonous anger?"

"Take it out on Bob."

She took it out on Laura. For the next ten minutes, wherever Laura looked she saw angry eyes, gnashing teeth, pounding fists, tottering plants. She couldn't focus on Kay's words. They didn't matter. The message was clear. The message was hate, and Laura felt it all around her.

Then it was Melissa's turn. Laura sat back, exhausted, and listened to the familiar story: a Brooklyn childhood spent primarily in the company of the first television in the neighborhood, an early interest in medicine, her seduction by a chemistry teacher at Bronx Science, the grocer who had thrown a tomato at her because she was holding hands with her Negro lover in the street, the cop who had threatened to book her for possession of marijuana if he couldn't have her, the injuries other policemen had inflicted on her during peace marches, City College, then med school, her nervous breakdown after watching a team of brain surgeons decide that their patient was dead and pull the tubes out of his head as if the patient were a transistor radio, the long recuperation period, the ill-fated decision to go into publishing, her humiliating six weeks as a receptionist at *Cosmopolitan,* the compromise—the Public Health Program. But she had ruined her chances of ever becoming a doctor. She listed the lovers who had abandoned her—Farley, Joan, Margo, Pat, Ariana . . . it was when she reached Gail's name that she started to scream at Kay. Kay was still shivering from her own rage. Laura didn't think she even heard what Melissa was accusing her of: frigidity, fear of taking risks, fickleness, her inability to hide her disgust for Melissa's straightforward passion. When she had run out of things to say to Kay she turned against herself.

She cursed herself for having such a belligerent attitude to the world. She talked of her failure to make friends with the children. She loved those children, yet they looked down on her. She was jealous of Edith because Edith could charm them so easily. It really hurt her sometimes to realize how perfect Edith was. Edith couldn't be blamed for being perfect. It was Laura who had prejudiced the children against her.

"I did no such thing!" Laura shouted, but Edith held out her hand to silence Laura. It was Laura who had told them she was an emotional cripple, Melissa continued. Laura was reactionary. She tried to impose her own ideas on the children, and one day she would end up destroying them.

Laura was not prepared for Melissa's attack. She wanted to laugh but she knew she couldn't. By the time it was Edith's turn, she felt as if there were a steel band around her head which someone was screwing tighter and tighter.

Facing Melissa, Edith told the story Dennis had already told Laura so many times: her first meeting with Dennis at the volunteer center, the first time they made love, the second, the third, their LSD trips together, her decision to move out of the dorm, the vacations, the campus revolution, the way she had saved Dennis's hand from getting crushed by a policeman's nightstick, the effects of Edith's recent liberation on their relationship.

Dennis's version had stressed Edith's heroism, Edith's wit, her accomplishments, her long, white neck and the way the Bermuda sun, the Vermont sun, the San Francisco sun, the Colorado sun, shone on her golden white hair. Edith's version was more clinical. She listed Dennis's deficiencies and tallied them with his redeeming virtues, contrasted early hopes to later disappointments, attacked him for being so possessive during the first two years of their relationship, gave a detailed appraisal of the first time they made love, the second, the third, the number of times they had made love over the past six months divided by the number of clitoral orgasms. She worked it out on the calculator Kay kept in the drawer of the telephone table. Dennis had satisfied her only seventeen percent of the time. She had never thought of it that way before. Putting their relationship into mathematical terms made her realize how futile things had become. "Dennis," she said to Melissa, "you know how I really feel about you deep down under? I hate you!"

Then, to Laura's surprise, she turned away from Melissa. "I hate you!" she screamed at Laura. Her nose was twitching and she had gathered her mouth to one side.

"Hey, listen," Laura said, "you're not supposed to be telling me that, you're supposed to be telling Melissa."

"SHUT UP! You stupid idiot, can't you ever shut up when I tell you? I hate you! You don't care if I have an orgasm or not, do you? All you care about is your own body and your own pleasure! You always come too early! You just think of me as a pleasure object! I hate you! I hate you! And you know what," she said, her lips curled, "you *bore* me. *She* bores me too. I couldn't care less whether you come together, or separate, or fucking *come at all!* You're just two very tedious people, and just the sight of you two talking together just oppresses me so much. I just fucking wish you two would GET OUT OF MY LIFE. I hate you! I hate you!" She went into hysterics, as Kay and Melissa had done before her.

Laura felt a pain to the left of her stomach. Somewhere in the area of her heart. Unless her heart was on the other side. She wasn't sure. She no longer remembered what she had been planning to tell the others she was angry about. She no longer wanted to share her inner thoughts with them. She didn't trust them. "You've used me!" Edith screamed. "You've used me for three whole years! You've treated me like an object!" Laura got up and bolted out the door. She had to spend ten minutes in the cold until someone came to let her in the dorm. She had forgotten her coat at the Pyles' and her key was in her coat pocket. Then she had to wait two hours outside her dorm room because the key to her room was also in her coat pocket, and the janitor with the spares was out at the movies.

While she sat staring at the scuff marks on the door to her room, she reviewed the situation from all the angles currently at her disposal: Sufi Poetry, Japanese Civilization, The Hemispheres of the Mind, Readings in Lévi-Strauss, Modern French Drama. She had just finished reading Sartre's *No Exit* for the French course. The professor had given one of those sketchy introductory lectures on existentialism for background. It was one of those lectures that condemned all those who neglected to pursue the subject in their own time to a lifelong misunderstanding of existentialism, just as Laura had already been condemned by other professors to a life-long misunderstanding of the Globe Theater, Taoism, and Einstein's theory of relativity. Yet it was her inadequate understanding of existentialism that gave her the strength to return to the Pyle house the following morning.

You must be involved. You must define yourself by action. Laura's job was to take care of the children. She had to become their active protector, a human shield against the hatred that Kay and Edith and Melissa had unleashed against each other. The children were her only friends. She had to help them before it was too late. She had to shield them from the facts of life and love and hate so that they could continue to be children for a little while longer.

Kay seemed to think that now that she had gotten her anger out into the open, it would go away. At breakfast she looked radiant. She told the children that she felt as if someone had done a spring-cleaning job on her insides. "From now on the Pyle-Carpenter household is going to be one big, joyful party."

But the girls' expressions said otherwise. And as Laura had written in the diary she kept three or four times a year, hate was not something you could wave away after you finished expressing it. Like clouds of exhaust in a windless city, it hovered in the air, it surrounded you, it poisoned you slowly and, in the long run, it killed you.

When Kay sat them down with their pancakes and bacon and

scrambled eggs, Sarah asked her what would have happened if her egg and her sperm had not met when they did, but after Kay had gotten her degree. Would she still have been Sarah? Well, by that time, Kay explained, it would have been another egg and another sperm. "As you know, dear, I produce between twelve and thirteen eggs a year. So that would have been eight or nine eggs later."

"You haven't answered my question," Sarah insisted. "Would the baby be me?"

"Actually, with that length of time difference, you would probably have been Bess," Kay said with a smile, "except I would have called you Sarah."

"You mean I wouldn't have existed," Sarah said.

"Gee, Sarah, it's hard to say. The whole question of identity is a very academic one at this stage in the game."

Then Bess asked her for the definition of "potent." The answer appeared to upset her, although of course she did not cry. Crying was strictly forbidden on weekends and holidays to members of Women of Paradise Council.

20

Women of Paradise Council was a secret club. Sarah was the president and chief rulemaker. Lately she had gotten into the habit of making rules up on the spur of the moment, either to annoy people or to have her own way. Usually it was Bess who bore the brunt of her arbitrary rulings. Today it was Melissa.

Melissa was a nervous wreck. The venting of rage had done her no good at all. To keep her occupied, so that Kay and Edith could do some serious work on the TV program, Kay suggested that she make a hot and nourishing lunch. Something Chinese, she suggested. It was about time someone made use of all those soya chunks that were cluttering up the freezer.

Melissa was not an inspired cook. For most of her adult life she had subsisted on fast foods, and ever since she had discovered what fast foods did to your system, she had been living primarily on raw vegetables and brown rice. When Sarah saw the soupy mess of bean sprouts, snow peas, baby corns, soya chunks, turnips, and cashews floating around in a dark brown sauce that no amount of brown rice could ever hope to absorb, she announced the beginning of a two-day fast. According to the bylaws of Women of Paradise Council, she informed Melissa, Fridays and Saturdays were for fasting. The only thing she and Bess were allowed to eat was strawberry ice cream.

Women of Paradise Council was for girls only, so Nathaniel was by definition not a member. But when his sisters turned down the Chinese stew, he did, too. Melissa had read in one of her child psychology books that it was harmful to force-feed children, but after ten minutes of trying to coax Nathaniel to feed himself, she lost her temper.

It was the worst tantrum Laura had ever seen. She kicked the walls and threw things on the floor. For a few seconds Nathaniel was paralyzed. Then he climbed off his chair, ran out of the kitchen, and came back with the yellow purse Edith had bought for him on the first day of school.

The purse was part of an all-out campaign to domesticate him —balance his yin with his yang, as Kay put it—but the purse had been a mistake. Nathaniel kept it filled with pebbles which he called grenades. Now he threw them one by one at the raging Melissa. When she turned around and started to go after him, he stuck out his finger and said, "You better watch out, or I'll kill you with my penis submarine!"

"That does it, that really does it." Folding her arms, she stomped upstairs.

Nathaniel still refused to eat the Chinese stew, despite Kay's assurances over the intercom that it was yummy. He told her it looked like number two. "The correct word is feces, darling, I do wish you would use the grown-up word." She directed Laura to make him his regular meal of one hot dog, "plus a little of something healthy on the side," but when Laura brought him his plate of hot dog, cut as usual into bite-size pieces, he said there was something funny-looking about the pieces. "I think the dog chewed them," he said.

Laura had a few standard tricks when it came to getting Nathaniel to eat. She told him that the fork was an airplane and his mouth was its hangar. She waved the fork around in the air, making motor noises, and when she announced that the plane was coming in for landing, he opened his mouth wide. The trick worked, even when it was a tomato instead of a hot dog. Laura was feeding him his last piece when Melissa came back into the kitchen.

"Do you really think that's ethical?" she snapped. "Poor Kay is trying to turn the kid off motors, and here you are pretending his food is a goddamned airplane. I don't think that's ethical at all."

"I don't care whether it's ethical or not," Laura said. "I'm more interested in seeing to it that he doesn't starve."

"Starve?" Melissa said. "An upper-middle-class kid with highly educated parents in a house that's absolutely overflowing with food? You must be out of your mind. Do you really think a kid could starve in this environment?"

"Yes," Laura told her.

"Then you're an idiot."

Laura was under strict instructions not to react to any of Melissa's provocations. But after an evening of undeserved abuse, Laura was in no mood to administer "massive doses of love." "You keep out of this," she said. "I'm the one who's taking care of Nathaniel, I'm the one who's getting him to eat, and I'm the one who will decide how to feed him."

"You act as if you were his mother or something."

"Well, I'm the one who takes care of him these days, and that's what counts," Laura said.

"You're not the only one who takes care of him."

"Oh, shut up," Laura said. On the intercom Kay cleared her throat.

"It really bugs me!" Melissa shouted, her face taut with frustration. "I mean, it kills me to see how you treat them. I mean, how is Nathaniel ever going to assert himself in the adult world if you keep on surrounding him with all these idiotic myths?"

"But he *already* asserts himself. Isn't that part of the problem? He threw those pebbles at you, didn't he?"

"Oh, you're insane!" Melissa cried. "I don't know how Kay permits you to stay with these kids at all! You're ruining him! You should be using mealtime as an opportunity for children to gain some control over their activities, but instead you use it as time to take control over the children."

"Oh, shut up," Laura said, very happy for the opportunity to abuse someone. She took the last piece of hot dog and told Nathaniel it was an airplane. She watched Melissa's face go into contortions as the fork with the hot dog on it looped its way very slowly into Nathaniel's mouth.

"You know what gets me more than anything else?" Melissa said, her lips quivering, "it's the tone of your voice, like you thought you ran the show or something. But basically you're in a zero power-position. You just *think* you're in charge because Kay thinks you'll act more responsible if . . ."

Kay cleared her throat over the intercom. "Hey, Melissa, let's not get carried away. I wonder if it wouldn't be a good idea to take a more humorous stance on the whole issue. I sort of have a gut feeling that our Laura has the best interests of the children at heart. And between you and me, I'll bet she's still touchy after last night. I know someone else who's touchy, and that's me!" Kay laughed. She did not sound touchy at all. "So, how about focusing all that famous aggression we were talking about onto something more constructive? Like a coffee cake for teatime, or a tea cake for coffee break, or some plain old all-purpose oatmeal cookies?"

Before Melissa could answer, the front door opened. There was the whiff of perfume, the flash of fur, the unfamiliar sight of a bare leg as Bob rushed Louella quickly up the stairs to his study. It was very tactful, as tactful as it could be in the circumstances, Laura thought. Especially in contrast to the loud, clownish entrances favored by Martin.

Although, of course, Martin came over so seldom these days. Kay said she was worried about depending on him too much, transferring her feelings about Bob to him, using him as a human warmth-substitute, so he only came over when they both admitted to a common sexual urge. Or so Kay claimed. She felt she needed a chance to see herself as a separate and self-sufficient entity and not first in terms of a man. Bob, on the other hand, was taking the coward's route: he had seemingly no interest in examining himself as a separate entity. He seemed to be seeking human warmth at any cost. At least that was what Kay had said the night before.

Laura did not know when to believe her anymore. The night before she had revealed shocking resentment with regard to Bob and his behavior since their separation, but now that all the rage had been drained out of her, she sounded almost conciliatory. Of course Laura could not see her face. She was still in her study. She was speaking over the intercom. Her voice was extra calm and ultrasoft:

"Hi there, Louella."

Louella, who must have been in the hallway outside Bob Pyle's study, gasped. "Why, hello there, Kay," she said after a long pause. "It's good to hear your voice again after all this while."

"And it's wonderful to hear yours. Gee, I'm sorry if my silence up until this point has caused you any discomfort. Please don't think it's out of any personal enmity. It's just that I've been outlandishly busy with this new women's talk show, as you can imagine. I can honestly say that I have only been home to get my statutory six hours' sleep."

"That's a lie," Sarah said, but Louella's voice drowned her out.

"Don't worry about me, Kay," she was saying. "I understand one hundred percent."

"Well," Kay said, "I must be keeping you stranded in the hallway."

"Oh, that doesn't matter one bit," Louella said in her professional office worker's voice, "but if it bothers *you,* I'd be happy to come over to your study. Why, it would be a joy to have a good talk with you. I mean, I've had my qualms about this arrangement and I've been worrying if there isn't some kind of misunderstanding on your part, and it would be just wonderful if I could iron things out with you . . ." Bob Pyle cleared his throat.

"Well, I see here that there's a barrier in the hallway," said Louella.

"Isn't it a beautiful color?" Kay said. "I must say we are extremely lucky to have such an accomplished and innovative carpenter-painter-inventor as Dennis on tap, don't you?"

"Hmmm, yes, it's a marvelous design."

"Do you see the trick window?"

"Hmmm, yes." Louella cleared her throat. "This here is a very exciting and innovative concept, Kay."

"It's for emergencies," Kay said softly.

"So I see, so I see. Well! I can run down these front stairs and reach you via the back stairs! If there's one thing I don't begrudge anyone, that's an excuse for exercise!"

"No need, no need," Kay said. "Edith and I are racing against a deadline. We're off to New York to do some interviews this evening—would you believe Margaret Mead?" Over the intercom Laura heard Edith's chuckle. "But please don't take this the wrong way," Kay continued. "I want you to know that I wish both you and Bob great happiness in your future relationship, however short or long that relationship may be."

"Honestly, Kay, please believe me when I say that I strongly resisted Bob's suggestion that we come home here. I mean to say, I said to him, there's always my place. But he'd say, 'why, I have a place, too. As a matter of fact I paid for sixty-seven percent of it, to be exact!' And I would ask him, 'but Bob, what about the kids?' "

"Don't worry about the children," Kay said. "I think it is better for them to see him this way."

"More natural," Louella ventured.

"Exactly," Kay said emphatically. "And speaking of children, they have a little surprise for you. At three o'clock. I've got the right time for it, don't I, children?"

"Yes!" Sarah shouted in the same voice Laura remembered using when her mother asked her if she had flushed the toilet or made her bed or thrown her cherry pits into the wastepaper basket.

"Three o'clock, then. In the living room."

"Why, thank you, Kay. I am looking forward to finding out what they have in store for us. I hope we can get together one of these days when you're not so busy, but until then, my hearty thanks for giving up the living room for the afternoon."

"I hope you enjoy it," Kay said softly.

"I'm sure we will."

"And gee. I'm sorry about Jingle."

"Oh, well! Girls will be girls! I'm hoping that she'll use this opportunity to catch up on her reading skills."

"The children have something for her, too."

"Why, that's very thoughtful of them. Dear me, won't that give Jingle a pleasant surprise."

The intercom clicked off. But Bob's intercom, which had lines to the kitchen and Children's Paradise, was on. As they clattered into his study, he was saying, "You didn't have to thank her for the living room. The living room's mine."

Kay had given Laura permission to control Bob's channels of communication if she felt they needed controlling, as Bob tended to be absentminded about such things. Laura turned the intercom off.

Melissa had now poured her uneaten Chinese stew into the Disposall, thus officially ending lunchtime. Kay called down briefly to remind the children that they had only two hours left until three o'clock. The children went downstairs, leaving Melissa and Laura to drink their coffees and glare at each other in silence.

Edith came down with a portable typewriter and fifteen thank-you letters for Melissa to type. When Melissa had finished telling her that she didn't know if she was in the mood to type fifteen thank-you letters, Edith came over to Laura's side of the table and placed her hands on her shoulders.

"Hey, I hope you didn't take what I said last night at face value, Laura. I was just getting my rocks off. I didn't mean any of it personally." Laura took one look at her large blue catlike eyes, her perfect smile, her perfectly freckled little nose, her amazing bush of natural curls, and threw the dregs of her coffee at all of them.

"Leave me alone!" she shouted. "I hate you!" She rushed for the door to Children's Paradise. She slammed it and then she sat, trembling, on the top step, and thought about how she had been betrayed by all of them, and how she hated all of them. Especially Edith. She would never trust any of them again. Her only friends were the children.

— *21* —

Below her, in the middle of the central playing area, was the Women of Paradise Council Club Cubicle. Its boundaries were defined by the low, shallow open shelves that had once defined the children's bed cubicles (these were now defined by the higher, deeper shelves that Laura had helped Dennis paint red). The entrance was blocked with a bulletin board, and the signs that were plastered all over the backs of the shelves proclaimed that the cubicle was for girls only and that trespassers, especially Nathaniel, would be persecuted.

The girls were crouching on one side of the bulletin board, whispering excitedly. Nathaniel stood disconsolately on the other. He wanted to join his sisters' club very badly and could not understand why they wouldn't let him in. He kept trying to sneak around the bulletin board, without success. When Sarah had thrown him out for the third time in a row, she asked Laura to come downstairs and keep him under control while they added the finishing touches to their play.

The play was Kay's idea. That morning after breakfast she had asked them to write, direct, and act in a short, cheerful piece of nonsense to put on for Bob and Louella at three in the afternoon. She thought that a play would help put Bob and Louella at ease and make them realize that, previous appearances notwithstanding, the Pyle-Carpenter household welcomed Louella in her new capacity as Bob's lover. She wanted the play to be ready by three because she was leaving on the six o'clock shuttle for New York and she wanted to be on hand in case there were any snags.

The children had spent the morning preparing Get Well cards for Jingle, who was at home with a broken leg after falling off a horse on the psychiatrist's farm. Now they were pinned to the bulletin board Sarah had blocked the entrance to the club cubicle with. The top one was a drawing of a rough version of Sarah sticking her tongue out at a rough version of a horse, and the caption said, "That horse sounds like a bad influence!" Below the stack of Get Well cards, in the center of the bulletin board, were the Ten Commandments for Members of Women of Paradise Council:

> You shalt not disobey Sarah the Priestess.
> You shalt not take the grave of Flicka in vain.
> You shalt not tell anyone about the ceremonies.
> You shalt not eat devil's food cake.
> You shalt not kill even a fly except for sacrifices.
> You shalt not commit adults to insane asylums.
> You shalt not forget to curl your hands around your ears
>   when you pray.
> You shalt not cry on weekends or holidays.
> You shalt not talk to people with black eyes.
> You shalt not let any boys in this club, especially not Nathan-
>   iel, never ever.

To the left of the Ten Commandments, on a piece of red construction paper that had been decorated liberally with skulls and bones, was a list of the things that could happen to you if you disobeyed the Ten Commandments:

> Ghosts will tickle you.
> Goblins will snatch you.
> Witches will grab your teeth and toenails and make potions out of them.
> Stepmothers will hide under the porch and grab your feet.
> Vultures will chew on you.
> Stepmothers will cut you up into thirty-nine pieces and put you into an envelope and send you to Happy Hunting Grounds, for dog meat.

When Nathaniel tried to storm the club cubicle for the fourth time, Sarah came out and read him this list of punishments.

"Do you really want all those things to happen to you?" she asked.

"What's a stepmother?" Nathaniel asked.

"It's a mother who hides under steps," Sarah explained.

"Why does she do that?"

"So she can grab your feet and pull you under and chop you up and . . ." Screaming, Nathaniel ran into his cubicle and hid under the crib.

The first act of the play was ready for rehearsal, Sarah announced. Laura was to be their trial audience. The play was a farce and its title was *Eggalina and Spermio*. Bess played Princess Eggalina and Sarah played Baron Spermio. There wasn't any curtain, so Sarah told Laura to shut her eyes while they arranged the props.

"Ready, set, open!"

When Laura opened her eyes she saw Bess standing in a cardboard box that reached to her waist. A sign on the front of the box said: "This is supposed to be a tower." Bess was dressed in the familiar blue negligee. On her head was the familiar paper crown. Under the crown was a long yellow nylon scarf that hid her own dark hair and flowed down her back. As Bess swayed back and forth Laura got a look at the message that was pinned to the end of the scarf: "This scarf is supposed to be hair."

"Spermio! Spermio!" Bess sighed, trying not to laugh. "Whither art thou, Spermio?"

Sarah leapt out of the club cubicle. She was dressed in red tights, Bess's black leotard, an alpine hat, and circa 1955 snowboots from the dress-up chest. They were gray with black fur linings and if you closed your eyes halfway, they looked like mice. She bowed.

"Why, hello, Eggalina, may I enter your tower?"

"Yes," Bess giggled. "I mean, why yes. Step right in."

Whereupon Sarah climbed into the cardboard box. They stared at each other, their faces red from trying not to laugh. "One two three, boing!" they shouted together. They quivered and shook and screamed and jumped until the box tipped over.

Laura told them it was a wonderful play (although the overtones vaguely disturbed her). Now they had to figure out the second act. Bess and Sarah retired to the club room, where they had a long conspiratorial talk in loud whispers. Nathaniel tried to sneak in again but Sarah pushed him out.

"Don't you remember what I told you about what will happen to you if you come in here?" Sarah shouted.

"I don't care," he said.

"Well, I don't care if you don't care. You can't come in and that's that."

"Why not?" Nathaniel asked.

"Because you're a boy, and this club is for *girls only.*"

"But I don't want to be a boy, I want to be a girl."

"Tough luck," Sarah told him.

The intercom clicked on. "This is Kay to kids, Kay to kids. How are you coming along?"

"She won't let me in the play," Nathaniel whined.

"Oh, Sarah, *do* try and find something for him to do." And then in a different voice, "You have forty minutes." The intercom clicked off, but then, a fraction of a second later, Laura thought she heard it click on again.

"Okay," Sarah said, "I'll make up a part for you, but in the meantime you better not come near the clubhouse, or else ghosts will . . ." Nathaniel put his thumb in his mouth and whimpered. "And goblins will . . ." He screamed. "And step-mothers will . . ." He got down on all fours and crawled into Bess's bed cubicle.

Laura chose a step halfway up the stairs and sat down. She listened to someone's almost negligible breathing, and Melissa in the kitchen. Melissa cleared her throat. She was drinking some-thing, rather noisily, Laura thought, although the intercom always exaggerated background noises. And the intercom was on top volume. When Melissa stopped slurping whatever it was and put it down on the table, it made a grating sound, like a motorcycle skidding or a distant car crash.

Then, somewhere else, was a loud bang, which Laura translated as a slamming door. This was followed by what sounded like cavalry coming down the stairs. Then sharp clicks down the hall-way to the kitchen: the unfamiliar sound of high heels on the parquet floor. It was Louella.

"Bob says he has kitchen priority in the afternoons," she said uncertainly.

"If that's a hint . . ." Melissa began.

"No, no! You just stay right where you are. I was only making sure Bob had it straight. Don't want to be stepping on anyone's toes!" Louella said in a singsong voice. "No, no," she continued, amid thunderous sounds of running water and the clatter of pots, "I'm just down here to make two cups of coffee, and then I'll be zip-zip-zipping upstairs again sooner than you can say Jack Flash."

Louella hummed nervously as she rummaged for cups and spoons, popped open the sugar canister, screwed open the coffee jar, retrieved the milk from the refrigerator, poured, put the milk back again.

"How long has this been going on?" Melissa asked abruptly.

"Pardon?"

"How long has this been going on?"

"Oh, the office! Oh yes, well, the office is fine. So much more cheerful with Bob back. You know, it was sort of gloomy with all those fogies last term and no Bob to cheer things up."

"Oh, forget it," Melissa said.

There was a silence. "And how is *your* work going?" Louella finally asked. "*Minerva,* wasn't that what it was called?"

"*Minerva*'s shit," Melissa said.

"Oh dear, oh dear. I'm sorry to hear that." There was a tremendous commotion as the water came to a boil. The whistle went off, piercing Laura's ears. Then the thunderous glug-glug-glug as Louella poured it.

"You see," Melissa said in a more cooperative voice, "Kay got this television job."

"So I hear, so I hear," Louella said amid a great clanging of spoons. "But I was under the impression that *Minerva* would continue along its merry way nevertheless."

"Well, it didn't."

"Dear me, I'm sorry to hear that. It sounded like a marvelous idea to me. Are you involved in this television thing to any degree?"

"I'm a Special Volunteer Researcher."

"That sounds mighty important to me."

"Well, it's really nothing more than a glorified secretary. I mean, look at all the fucking thank-you notes I have to do."

"Well, I wouldn't worry my head about it, Melissa. If you ask me, we secretaries are a vital part of the American system. Where this country would be without our nimble fingers I wouldn't know." She picked up the coffee mugs.

"Does he satisfy you sexually?" Melissa asked suddenly.

"Pardon?"

"I was just wondering," Melissa continued. "Kay said he was a lousy fuck."

Louella and somebody else gasped. Louella put down the coffee mugs, or rather, dropped them.

"Why, you piece of white trash," she said in a low and trembling voice, "how dare you ask me a question like that."

"Hold your horses, I was only asking, okay? I was only asking, okay? Maybe he's better with you." Louella picked up the coffee cups and Laura listened to her walk toward the door. She was almost out of the kitchen when Melissa added, "The white slavemaster, black slavegirl rape-fantasy, no doubt."

"Did I hear you right?" Louella said, clicking back into the middle of the kitchen. "Did I hear you denigrate my relationship with Bob, you malicious, despicable dyke, you?"

"Melissa," Kay said over the intercom. As far as Laura could tell she was speaking from her study. "Do you really have to . . ." There was a gong. When Bob's intercom came on it made a gong. Kay stopped in the middle of her sentence.

Melissa did not seem to have heard the gong. "Where's your liberated spirit?" she was saying. "Doesn't it rankle you at all that the females of your race have been used for hundreds of years as sexual toys of the white Establishment?"

"I'll thank you to leave my private . . ."

"Don't you care at all for the feelings of your sisters? Don't you realize that you and your sexist games are turning poor Kay into a nervous wreck?"

"You malicious liar! That's not true and you know it!" Louella shouted. "And let me tell you one thing, Miss Melissa. You may think I'm nothing but a good-natured secretary with not a brain in my head, but let me tell you, and don't you forget it. I'm black, and I'm proud, and I'm proud of being able to work for my living instead of sitting around working on useless magazines like the rest of you, and let me tell you this: I'm my own woman, and I'm proud of my man, and if you can't understand the difference between weakness and good manners and try to impose any more of your white trash . . ."

Bob interrupted her. "Melissa!" His voice was so deep it created an echo on the intercom system. "Would you kindly refrain from commenting on, or contributing to, my private life!" His jaw had been unwired for over a month now, but he still sounded as if he had to speak between his teeth. "You have ruined enough in this household already, Melissa. I would like you to take this as a warning *not to meddle in my private life* again *in any way,* and that includes Louella."

"What do you mean, I've ruined enough of this household?"

"If I didn't have my own sense of dignity to contend with," Louella said, "I'd have a mind to . . ."

"Honey, you come up here," Bob said in a stern voice. "She's not worth it. Let's have those coffees before they're cold."

"Are you really going to let him order you around like that?" Louella gasped.

"Melissa," Bob said, "I've warned you once and I'll warn you again. *Lay off!*"

Heavy footsteps as he walked away from the intercom, and then the house echoed with the thunder of running footsteps, the crash of slamming doors, sniffles, sobs, couch springs, creaking chairs. Over one intercom, Kay asking Melissa to come upstairs for a private chat. Over the other, Bob assuring Louella that Melissa wasn't worth it. The sound of a trunk being dragged from step to step as Melissa made her way up the back stairs. Then silence from Kay's intercom. The sound of wet lips parting, heavy sighs, ahs, couch springs, zippers, pops, and approving groans from Bob's intercom.

"Louella?" Kay called softly over the intercom.

"Whaa?" More couch springs as Louella jumped, apparently, to her feet.

"Hi, Louella, this is Kay to Louella. Gee, isn't this funny? Here we are talking to each other on totally separate systems. But we both have outlets in the kitchen and Children's Paradise, so I guess that's why we can hear each other so loud and clear."

Louella laughed uncertainly, as if she did not know whether it was better to be rude or polite. "Well! I certainly can hear *you!*"

There was a pause.

"Are you planning to make love?" Kay asked.

"Pardon?"

"Are you planning to make love? The reason I'm asking," Kay added quickly, "is not, I assure you, out of any prurient inclination. I only wanted to point out to you that you have left your intercom on." There was another pause. "I hope I don't sound like I'm handing out any directives. Please feel free to make love with the intercom on, if such is your wish. I just thought I would point it out because Bob," she cleared her throat, "usually preferred silence in such situations."

Another pause.

"So what I am asking you is this, Louella, could you possibly relay to Bob, from me, the information that the intercom is *on.* That whereas he is certainly free to *keep* it on however long he likes, he may feel that whatever it is he is about to embark on would benefit from a teeny bit more privacy. And if that is the case, could Bob please turn the intercom *off?*"

"Yes in*deed,*" Bob growled. Couch springs, screeching chairs, thunderous footsteps. "Yes indeed," he said, enunciating each word clearly, "Bob would be *delighted* to turn his intercom off!" There was a wrenching sound, a distant crash, and silence from Bob's intercom. No gong. A click, and total silence on Kay's intercom. Laura wondered if Bob had torn his intercom out of the wall.

Nathaniel emerged from Bess's cubicle wearing one of her sundresses. It was sleeveless and red polka dot, with a full skirt that dragged behind him like a bride's train. When he got closer Laura noticed he had it on back to front. He tried once again to get into the club cubicle, where the girls were still in conference, but it didn't work. Sarah barred the entrance. "Just because you have a dress on doesn't mean you're a girl, stupid!"

"But I want to be a girl," he protested. "I want to be in your club. And if you don't let me, you know what I'm going to do! I'm going to bomb you!"

"You know what will happen to you if you bomb our club?" Sarah said, "The goblins will . . ."

"No!" cried Nathaniel.

"And the witches will . . ."

Nathaniel ran into his cubicle and hid under his crib until Sarah dragged him out for the rehearsal of the second act of their play.

The second act took place a few years after the first act. Princess Eggalina had a baby by then and the castle had been under siege for over a year.

The girls had cast Nathaniel as the Enemy, but when he refused to take off Bess's sundress, they relented and made him Eggalina's baby's nurse. The baby was Nathaniel's boy doll. Kay had bought him the boy doll at the same time Edith had bought him the purse. But if you looked at the doll now you would hardly know it was less than a month old. In its short and violent life it had been bombed, bombarded with pebbles, battered with sticks, sat upon, viciously attacked by dogs, dragged over imaginary battlefields, and torpedoed by hundreds of penis submarines. An arm was loose, an eye was missing. There was a hole in its head, and its chin was an irregular black globule because Nathaniel had once thrown it onto the stove. As Nathaniel had pointed out a few days earlier, the doll looked very much like Daddy after he fell out of that tree.

After a brief discussion the girls decided to cast Grosvenor as the Enemy. Sarah had Laura close her eyes, then open them again when the stage was set. The second act began. Nathaniel wandered around the cardboard box with the boy doll in his arms, singing an approximation of "The Bear Went Over the Mountain."

"Spermio, Spermio, whither fart thou Spermio?" Bess said over and over again, giggling helplessly between deliveries.

Sarah hopped around, coaxing Grosvenor to her side and then chasing him away with her whip.

"Oh, Spermio!" Bess cried, rocking back and forth in her box, "why are they all after me? What do they see in me? I'm just a little secretary!"

When Sarah succeeded in chasing the frantic dog under Bess's bed, she grabbed the boy doll out of Nathaniel's arms (to Nathaniel's great distress) and gave it to Bess. Then she climbed into the box again, where they went through the boing-jiggle-and-jump routine that Laura had found so disturbing in the first act. "No one can boing like you, Eggalina!" "Oh, you sexist!" "No one can jiggle like you!" "Oh, jiggle jiggle!" The boy doll soon got in their way. They threw it at Nathaniel. "Here, nurse! Take this dumb baby!" "Hey, nurse! What are nurses for?" They continued their jumping and screaming until the box tipped over. They crawled out laughing and out of breath, and then they bowed.

"What do you think of it?" Sarah asked.

"Well, I think it's wonderful, but I don't know if it is quite right for the occasion," Laura said.

"Why not?"

"I think it might hurt Louella's feelings."

"It's a farce, stupid! Don't you know what a farce is? That means it's a joke. How can she get her feelings hurt from a joke? Stop acting so reactionary."

Laura felt a pain, like a heart attack. Someone had told the children she was a reactionary. It wasn't fair. Why wouldn't they leave her alone to take care of the children in her own way? She forgot about Louella's feelings. As she helped them take Grosvenor and the props up to the living room, she wondered who had been criticizing her behind her back. Since Melissa was the easiest target, the only adult who constantly offended Laura by telling her what she honestly thought of her to her face (it was harder to blame things on people who smiled at you and patted your back), Laura decided it was Melissa.

22

Three o'clock. The children were ready but there was no sign of Bob and Louella. Kay intercommed down to find out what the matter was. She asked Laura to try and contact Bob on the kitchen intercom, but when Laura pressed the button, nothing happened.

"Hmmm," Kay said. "Well then, I guess we'll have to send someone up to fetch them. Nathaniel? Could you run along upstairs and knock on Daddy's door?"

"I'll go up," Laura offered.

"No, Laura, thanks a lot, but I think Melissa here has a point. We've got to stop doing things for the children that the children can do for themselves."

Nathaniel had a hard time getting up the stairs. The boy doll and the billowing sundress kept getting in his way. Finally he made it up to the hallway. The intercom in the hallway picked up his tiny grunts. He knocked on Bob Pyle's study door. "Daddy!" His voice sounded like a meal whistle. "Come down now, Daddy! We're ready!"

The study door opened. The hallway receiver picked up Louella's gasp and then Bob must have punched the wall because on the intercom it sounded like a bomb and the whole house seemed to shake.

"CHRIST ALMIGHTY! I have had enough of this nonsense! This is CRIMINAL! And I'm not going to put up with it any longer. I'll sue the bitch. I just can't let this go on! I goddamn well won't put up with it one more day. Lou, I tell you I *have had it up to here!*"

"Bob, please don't act rashly!" Louella pleaded.

Bob came roaring down the stairs and into the living room. Laura had never seen him so mad, not even when he caught his daughters kissing or when he went after the cat in the tree. "Where is she?" he growled. He stormed into the kitchen and stopped in front of Melissa, who was sitting at the table nursing a cup of coffee.

"Melissa, I am giving you three minutes, no more, no less, to get out of my house. And if you ever try to come back here, you will be sorry you ever had a bone in your body, because I am going to break every single one of them."

Melissa looked genuinely surprised. "What are you talking about?"

"What am I *talking* about?" Bob threw back his head and laughed. "I am talking about my son, that's what I'm talking about. And I want you out of my house before you have a chance to play any more of your dirty tricks on him." He laughed again. "Or should I just call it a day and say *her?*"

"I have two comments," Melissa said in a shrill voice. "One: I don't know what the fuck you're talking about. Two: I am certainly not going to take orders from *you.* I am Kay's guest. I am definitely not leaving until *she* asks me to, and that's final."

Sarah and Bess watched, dumbfounded, from the hallway. Like

spectators at a tennis match, their eyes traveled from Bob to Melissa to Bob to Melissa. Bess was holding her paper crown in her hand. Laura noticed she had crumpled it. Her other hand was in her mouth. Sarah was holding Grosvenor by the collar. In her other hand was the whip.

"Get out of my kitchen!" Bob bellowed.

"It's not just *your* kitchen," Melissa said.

"It's my priority hours!" There was a hysterical note to Bob's voice.

"Who gives a shit?"

"*I* give a shit. And as a matter of fact I seem to be the *only* one who gives a shit around here, and by God I'm going to stop this nonsense here and now. I'll be damned if I'll let my only son be turned into a fag. What are you trying to prove by having him parade around in a dress with a doll in his arms? Are you trying to castrate him? Then why don't you cut out the Chinese water torture and give him a nice sharp knife to finish off the job? Or are you trying to make sure he turns into a sexual deviant? Well, you're doing a damn good job, Melissa, but if you come back to this house after today, it will be over my dead body."

"Save yourself the trouble. I'm not leaving."

"Do I have to chase you out?" Bob shrieked.

"Well, I'm not going to leave because you fucking asked me to. You're insane. You're paranoid. You see things that aren't there. You should get your head checked."

"Oh, I should, should I?" He grabbed the horse whip out of Sarah's hand.

"Bob, this is Kay to Bob, Kay to Bob, do you really feel you're basing your assumptions on reasonable . . ." Kay began, but it was too late. Bob cracked the whip against the floor. "OUT!" He took a step toward Melissa and cracked it against a chair. "OUT!" Melissa jumped out of her chair. Bob cracked the whip against the floor again and the very tip of it touched her boot. She screamed and ran to the dining room.

Growling like a lion tamer, Bob went after her. He chased her from the dining room into the front hallway, cracking the whip against the walls and the banister and the doorways, then through the living room to the back hallway, where Bess and Sarah were huddled among the coats on the coat rack. Through the kitchen once again, and again through the dining room to the front hallway, where Louella watched, aghast, from the foot of the stairs. Nathaniel was a few steps above her. He was crouching between the banister rails, his boy doll half concealed in the folds of Bess's sundress, sucking his thumb, a puzzled expression in his eyes, as if he couldn't understand what he had done to make his father so mad.

When Melissa came into the kitchen for the third time, the dog tried to attack her. She slid over the linoleum, screaming, "Help me! Help me!" as Grosvenor ripped at her. That was when the girls decided that the chase was a joke. Squealing with laughter, they chased after their father and Grosvenor.

When Nathaniel saw that the girls were running, too, he tried to run down the stairs and join them, but he tripped on the sundress and came rolling down instead. He hit his head on the base of the front door. Dropping his doll in the hallway, he shuffled after them, screaming, "I hurt my head! I hurt my head!"

Laura watched them come through the kitchen again. Melissa was screaming "Rape! Rape!"; Bob was cracking his whip and growling like a lion tamer. The girls were screaming "Get her! Get her!", and behind them was the overexcited Grosvenor. The boy doll was lying in their path. Melissa managed to leap over it, but Bob didn't see it in time. He tripped, went sprawling down the hallway, hitting his head against the base of the front door.

Screaming with joy, the girls climbed over him. Grosvenor closed his mouth around his leg. Bess pinned down Bob's arms, Sarah settled down on his back.

Over the intercom, they could hear Kay sigh. The intercom

clicked off. They heard her coming down the back stairs. She paused once or twice, as if to catch a thought. Then they heard her striding across the living room floor with true purpose.

After Kay had checked him thoroughly for bruises and broken bones, she sent the children, Melissa, and Laura into the kitchen to prepare for an emergency meeting of Family Council. She contacted Edith on the intercom and asked her to phone the film crew to tell them they would be taking the seven o'clock shuttle instead of the six o'clock shuttle. The film crew could go ahead or wait for them, as they pleased. She got Sarah to go fetch her first aid kit from the bathroom. While she checked his pulse and cleaned the cut on his scalp and lay him on the couch so she could check his blood pressure, she and Bob conversed in whispers. For once the intercom was not on, and Laura, who was sitting at the kitchen table with the others, could not catch what they were saying. They looked very stern, like people in pictures of cabinet meetings or international summits.

Bob had fallen on his bad hip. When Kay helped him into the kitchen he was wincing. His face reminded Laura of a sponge that had had the life squeezed out of it one too many times. He wouldn't look at the children, or at the plants, or even at Louella, who was poised against the refrigerator, stylish in a tailored suit, a scented handkerchief covering most of her face. He kept his eyes on the floor.

Kay called the meeting to order. She gave Laura a piece of paper from her yellow legal pad and asked her to stand in as secretary. Her eyes started watering. She put on her sunglasses and then turned to Bob with a smile.

"Bob?" she said.

Still staring at the floor, he cleared his throat. "I would like to take this opportunity to apologize to Melissa," he said wearily, "first of all for accusing her of something she had virtually no involvement in. I apologize profusely for failing to react to Nathaniel's appearance in a more rational and balanced manner. I apologize even more profusely for my completely unwarranted physical assault on Melissa. I accept full responsibility for any psychological damage I may have incurred." He sighed and put his face in his hands. "I apologize to the children for behaving in this despicable manner. I solemnly vow that this is the last time they will see me act in such a foolish way."

He stopped and sat back. Kay seemed to expect him to say something else. "Bob?" she said after a silence. "Are you going to explain the experimental basis of the contract or would you like me to?"

"Go ahead," he said.

"Well, children, as you all know, the separation contract we drew up last month was not only unofficial in that it would *probably* not stand up in court—and anyway it made no mention of division of property—but it was also *experimental* in nature and could be terminated if and when both parties came to an agreement that it should come to a vote in Family Council. And since . . ." She caught her breath. "Bob, I really think the statement about the spirit of the contract should come from you."

"Kay and I have both come to the agreement that I have broken the unofficial separation contract both in letter and spirit, and for this reason . . ."

His voice cracked. "Kay," he whispered, "I'm just going to have to ask you to handle this for me."

Kay removed her sunglasses. Tapping them against her yellow legal pad, she said, "We think it might be a good idea if Bob took an extended leave from this household to have a good think about his past actions and his resolutions for the future. We have discussed this in private and Bob has agreed that if the council vote goes against him, he will effect a move immediately." She looked at her watch. "I'd like a show of hands on this."

Bess looked confused. "What are we supposed to be voting about?"

"Whether you think that Daddy's behavior during the last few days, and particularly his vicious attack on Melissa, warrants a good, long, thorough think."

She glared at the children. They raised their hands. She counted with her pencil. "One, two, two and a half—make up your mind, Bess—three." She wrote something down on the legal pad.

"Well, that's four to nothing against you, Bob," she said, giving him a short, efficient glare. "I think it is in everyone's interest that we get this thing wrapped up as quickly as possible. I should be on my way to the airport in twenty minutes at the latest. Can you get your toothbrush and things together by then? Good," she said without waiting for an answer. "Laura, I seem to remember seeing a whole load of Bob's underwear sitting in the drier this morning. Is it still there?"

Laura went up to fold Bob's underwear. Kay went through the drawers in the bedroom and the kitchen for odds and ends she thought he might need. Bob waited on the living room couch while Louella cleared the bathroom shelves and put his suits, shoes, shirts, and ties into two large suitcases.

Bob said he had shooting pains. He could barely make it to the door. Kay sent Bess upstairs to find those crutches he had used during the summer. While they waited for her to bring them down, Kay apologized to Louella for dumping Bob on her with so little notice. Louella, meek now after her show of temper earlier in the afternoon, and apologetic as ever for being used, said it was a pleasure. Anytime.

The crutches arrived. While Bob arranged them under his arms, Kay told him she would be contacting him during the coming week vis-à-vis visiting rights, bank accounts, bills, and so on.

"If not me personally, at any rate, Brent." Brent was the family lawyer.

Bob tried to bend over to kiss the children good-bye, but halfway down he gave a loud cry of pain. He changed his mind. He went out the door without saying good-bye to anyone, and Louella followed him with the suitcases.

23

It took a few minutes for Bess to realize that her father had been banned.

Kay and Edith were rushing around the kitchen trying to find the list of vital New York telephone numbers that one of them had misplaced. Laura found it in the garbage can. Edith thanked her by kissing her on the nose and squeezing her hands. "Don't think I was offended by what happened," she told Laura. "I figure it was your turn to let off steam. I guess you could say that last night you really got the wrong end of the stick."

Laura said nothing. She wasn't as angry at Edith as she had been, but she still hated her, although it threw her off balance for Edith to be so forgiving. Laura preferred her enemies to be unremittingly evil, cruel, and hostile. That way you were never fooled by friendly smiles or confused by gentle fingers running through your hair and nothing in their demeanor could make you forget that they had betrayed you.

"One of these days I think we should let Laura have a go at us, don't you think?" Edith said to Kay.

Kay gave Edith and Laura a short and absentminded grin. She put on her vast orange parka and tied the hood very tight. She ran upstairs to make sure they hadn't forgotten anything. Edith went outside to start the car. It was when Kay was checking the drawers in the kitchen that Bess asked her why her father had left with his suitcases.

"Because he is moving into Louella's house for the time being," she explained.

"Why?"

"To have a good think."

"Why can't he think here?"

"Well, for one thing, he'd be too close to the situation to think objectively."

"You mean you banned him?"

"Not really, my little chickadee," she said, slamming the drawer closed. "He more or less banned himself. He was feeling pretty rotten about the way he acted this afternoon."

Bess put her hand in her mouth and began to hum. "What if he never comes back?" she asked, as her eyes filled with tears.

"Don't be a silly billy," Kay said, her voice curter than usual.

Nathaniel's boy doll's chest had been dented when Bob tripped on it. For ten minutes now, Nathaniel had been trying to straighten it out and now he lost his patience and started to bombard it with grenades. "Well," Melissa said, "now we know who *he* takes after."

"Nathaniel, please don't do that," Kay said absently.

"You're going to grow up to be exactly like your father," Melissa told him.

"No, I'm not," Nathaniel said.

"You're a very bad boy."

"No, I'm not. I'm a girl." Kay walked across the room and very gently put her hand on Melissa's mouth before she could say anything more to Nathaniel.

"Gee, Nathaniel, I think you're about the nicest boy I've ever run across. Especially when you play nice, peaceful games like Sarah and Bess. I *like* you as a boy. Why do you think you want to be a girl?"

"Because. I want to be in their club."

"Well, you can't," said Sarah.

"Well, you better let me in it," Nathaniel said, his small hands clenched. "If you don't let me in you know what I'll do? When I grow up I'll be just like Daddy."

Kay frowned. She glanced at her watch. Bess was humming louder than ever. Kay gathered the last of her papers, tightened her hood again, and bent down to kiss first Sarah, then Nathaniel, then Bess on their foreheads.

"You can't go," Bess said, "I have a stomachache."

"Oh, my poor little chickadee! Plenty of hot liquids and an early beddy-bye for you, then!" Outside Edith was warming up the car. She beeped twice.

"You can't go until I'm better."

"Oh, darling! Don't make me feel worse than I already feel! There is nothing in the world I would like more than to stay here with you. But gee, I have a film crew waiting at the airport. And all *sorts* of important people waiting to be interviewed. There's even one crazy fellow who's waiting to interview *me!*"

Bess started crying. When Sarah reminded her in a stage whisper what happened to Women of Paradise Council members who cried on weekends and holidays, she only cried more.

Edith beeped twice again. The door was wide open. A cold autumn draft swept into the house. "Bess! Bess! Will you look at me for a moment? What do you say to this? The minute I get back from New York, you and I will go out on a treat afternoon. School or no school. Just you and me, and we can go anywhere you like for however long. Okay?"

"I want you to stay here *now,*" Bess insisted. "I want you to read me a fairy tale and sing me songs to sleep."

"Listen, darling, I have to go. Laura, could you do everything in your power to cheer up this poor little chickadee?" Bess began to wail. Nathaniel dropped his doll and joined in, his mouth wide open, his eyes squeezed shut.

"Oh, golly gee, that man really knows how to stir a family up, doesn't he," Kay said.

"I don't know how you could have ever fallen for such a bastard," Melissa said.

Kay paused in the doorway. She stared at Melissa, her mouth firm, her eyes full of sorrow. "Let's not be grossly unfair about this, Melissa. I hope you believe me when I say that although I feel nothing but bitterness now, I did once entertain a very deep passion for that man."

She slammed the door. Melissa began to laugh in a nervous, indignant way. "I just don't know what I did to deserve that attack, I just don't know what I did to deserve that rotten attack. Is she nuts or something?" Melissa wasn't talking to anyone in particular. She was facing the rubber plants and waving her arms, in wild jerks, as if she was trying to justify herself to a large, skeptical audience. Outside a car door slammed. The car zoomed off down the road.

Then came Bess's hysteria, her "don't leave me here with these monsters!", her face pressed against the window, her dramatic collapse to the floor, her dry-heaving. Laura carried Bess to the living room couch. She brought her a plate of cookies, which she wouldn't eat. Then she remembered the fast that Sarah had called. She brought Bess a large dish of strawberry ice cream. She wouldn't eat that either. Laura took out the tattered book of fairy tales. It had been abandoned lately in favor of ethnic myths, but Kay still used it as a sedative in cases like this. She turned to "Rapunzel." It was Bess's favorite, and it had never failed to calm her down. She often claimed that Rapunzel was her middle name.

Sarah was reading a Nancy Drew mystery in one of the easy chairs, engrossed in the book but vaguely annoyed by all the noise Bess was making. When Laura started to read Bess "Rapunzel," Bess screamed for her mother to come back. "Why did you leave me, why did you leave me?" Her nose was running. Laura went into the kitchen to find some tissues.

Melissa was sitting at the kitchen table staring at Bess. She was calm now, but her face was full of pain, as if looking at Bess crying on the couch reminded her of many evenings she had spent doing the same. While Laura was searching for the tissues, she went into the living room and sat down next to Bess on the couch.

In a clumsy but well-meaning way she put her two hands around Bess's head and propped her up against the cushions. "Now calm down, Bess, and I'll tell you a story so funny that your sides will split open."

"But I don't want my sides to split open."

"You know what I mean. I mean you'll laugh a lot because the story is so funny."

"I don't want to hear a funny story," Bess said. She had stopped crying. She wiped the tears out of her eyes. Laura came across the room to give her the Kleenex. Melissa put out her hand as if to bar the way. "Just give me ten minutes, Laura, ten minutes is all I ask. Please don't interfere. All I ask is for you not to interfere. Just leave the two of us alone. I think this might work. Okay?"

Swallowing her lips, she waited until Laura had withdrawn to the other side of the room. Then she turned to Bess. "Now you know where the moon is, don't you?"

Bess looked at her sadly.

"You know," Melissa said, waving her hand impatiently at the window, "that thing out there. Well, this story takes place on the moon."

"I don't want to hear a story about the moon."

"What do you want to hear about then? Earth? Mars? Venus?

Saturn? The North Pole? Siberia? What's wrong with the moon? It's a very funny story. Why don't you want to hear it?"

"Because I want you to tell me 'Rapunzel.' "

"This thing here?" Melissa asked, pointing at the book of fairy tales. Bess nodded. Melissa wrinkled her nose. She picked up the book and leafed through the story. "Wow, you forget how reactionary these stories are, don't you?" she said to Laura. "Hmmm, yes," she said, swallowing her lips as she turned the page. "This one's a real zinger."

Bess waited, her hand in her mouth. "Hey, now what do you say to this," Melissa said, slamming the book closed. "How about if I told you the story of Rapunzel like if it happened in America today? This one here is unbelievably old-fashioned."

"You mean 'Rapunzel' could happen in America today?"

"Sure it could." That cheered Bess up. And Melissa proceeded to tell her the story of Rapunzel, born to a mother in a country where abortions were illegal, exchanged for food stamps at an early age, brought up in an ivory tower by a selfish sexist. Bess found the modern version of "Rapunzel" very funny, until Melissa got to the part when the prince should have been arriving every night and climbing up her hair. "After a few weeks of this nonsense," Melissa said, "Rapunzel said to herself: 'Why should I continue to let this guy use my body? I don't even know if he's a prince. He just *says* he's a prince. I'm tired of this passive role. Why should I sit here and wait for this jerk to climb up my hair every night? Why can't I use my hair to get out of this tower, instead of letting this guy use it to climb up to me?' " She smiled at Bess. She was flushed and looked very pleased, as if she had suddenly rediscovered her imaginative powers after years of disuse. " 'This pedestal nonsense is just the end.' And so that evening, an hour or so before the prince was expected, Rapunzel found some scissors and cut off her hair."

Bess shook her head and took her thumb out of her mouth. "No, she didn't."

"Anyway," Melissa continued, "having to comb all that long

hair every night was a real drag. When she saw it lying in a heap on the floor Rapunzel heaved a deep sigh of relief. What a load off her shoulders, literally. And then she got to work fashioning her hair into a good strong rope."

"That's not 'Rapunzel,' " Bess said, "that's 'Rumpelstiltskin.' "

"No, it isn't, you idiot," Sarah shouted across the room. "In 'Rumpelstiltskin' it's *hay,* not hair, and she doesn't turn it into a rope, she turns it into *gold.* "

"She fastened one end to her bedstead," Melissa said in a louder voice, to drown out Bess's objections and Sarah's retorts. She was so clumsy, Laura thought to herself, she never knew when to give in. She thought she knew best, but Laura knew better. Everyone thought they knew best when it came to children, Laura thought, without thinking of applying this maxim to herself.

"And she let the rest of her hair rope down the side of the tower," Melissa said in a loud voice.

Bess screamed, "That's not what happens!"

"When she finally climbed down the rope she was surprised at her own strength. She had been brought up to believe that girls didn't have any muscles, can you believe that? And she ran off to the city, where she found a friendly bank manager willing to give a single woman a mortgage, and she settled down to a rewarding career of making high-quality ropes. And she lived happily ever after, all alone."

"No," Bess cried. "She got married! She got married to a prince and lived happily ever after in a palace! You're lying to me. You told me the wrong story. That's not the way 'Rapunzel' ends!"

And Melissa said, "Well, it is now."

Bess was very quiet for the rest of the evening. She wandered around the house as if in shock and went to bed long before bedtime. When Laura cleaned her room the next morning, she found the remains of the tattered fairy tale book under her bed.

Some pages had been fashioned into rough doilies, others had been slashed with red and black Magic Marker. Hieroglyphics and stick figures decorated the blue skies in the illustrations of princes and princesses and fairy godmothers. The hieroglyphics were Sarah's and the stick figures were Bess's: Laura deduced that they had destroyed the book together. It had probably been Sarah's idea. As usual.

For the first time in a long time Bess did not wear her paper princess crown to breakfast. She was full of energy, bright-eyed, smiling, and she devoured her strawberry ice cream with enthusiasm. Kay had told Laura many times that this type of sudden energy burst meant that a child had resolved a conflict. It marked the end of one stage and the beginning of another. Laura wasn't sure. There was something about Bess's behavior that made her suspicious. It was all princesses one day and no princesses the next. Bess hadn't solved anything, Laura decided. She had destroyed a book. She had decided to forget about princesses, but Laura was sure she had only half forgotten. She hadn't solved their mystery, and one day they would return to haunt her, many unresolved stages, many misunderstandings later.

They had run out of strawberry ice cream. Laura got the children to put on warm clothes and jackets, and then they all went out into the windy autumn morning, that crisp, cold morning that is such a relief after a humid summer.

They made their way through the quiet tree-lined streets, past large, prosperous one-family homes, mansions that had been converted into university offices, smaller frame houses where untenured professors and graduate students lived, manicured lawns, lawns overgrown with weeds and littered with cardboard. In the streets were station wagons, a few VW vans and bugs, a sports car with a Florida license. The sidewalk buckled. There were potholes in the road, and everywhere you looked you saw bicycles—fastened to tree trunks and gates and parking meters and porches. A few neighborhood children were riding back and forth, a few students were speeding past on their ten-speeds. They were crouched low, their hair streaming behind them in a straight line, staring intently at the road ahead, going somewhere.

The children walked slowly, taking care not to step on any cracks, because their mother was still in New York and that was no place for her to break her back.

The ice cream store was on one of those dreadful American highways. It had four lanes with a concrete island in the middle. In the distance was a traffic circle, a shopping center, and behind a mass of unsymmetrical neon signs was the windowless brick monolith that housed Sears Roebuck. Across the street from the ice cream store, the buildings were one-story high and modern. There were stores, luncheonettes, Laundromats, a church shaped like a tent. On the ice cream store side, the buildings were seedier and housed small grocery stores, clothes shops with displays of matron dresses and girdles, second-hand typewriter shops, luncheonettes that were older and seedier than the ones across the road, card shops. The sidewalks were empty. On one side of the ice cream shop was a Dunkin' Donuts and on the other was a dark and dusty toy store run by a man so fat that his chin sagged halfway down his chest. "We have the new Halloween costumes," said the sign on the door. Halloween was still three weeks away, but Sarah wanted to look at the costumes. She knew what she wanted to be. She knew exactly what to look for. They weren't in any rush. They had a whole day to waste.

The Halloween costumes were at the front of the store. The clown outfits, witch dresses, space suits, and skeleton suits were hanging above the fat man's head. While Sarah and Bess examined them, Laura took Nathaniel on a tour of the rest of the store.

She had not been to a toy store for a long time and everything she saw brought back memories: the paint-yourself birds, the number paintings, the jigsaw puzzles, the blocks, the toy soldiers, the Silly Putty, the board games, the party favors; the children's typewriters, pianos, xylophones, drums, horns; the dollhouses, the doll furniture, the baby dolls; the doll who had a string in her back and could say twenty-three things and the one who had a string in her back and could say thirty-five things; the boy doll they had been making such a fuss about, called G.I. Joe. At the very back of the store were the miniature cars, fire engines, ambulances, pickup trucks, and cranes. When Nathaniel saw these he fell into a trance. He held Laura's hand very tight. His own small hand was moist.

Sitting on a display table was a tank the size of a large cat or a small dog. It was camouflage color and seemed, to Laura's inexperienced eye, to be a perfect replica of a real tank. The treads, the turret, the revolving gun, even the little man inside the cockpit, looked real to Laura. The box said it ran on batteries and could be turned on and off and made to go backwards, forwards, right, or left by remote control. "Just sit back with your remote control and watch Reddee Tank roll into action. Watch the gun go round and round while Reddee Tank moves through the battlefield of your choice. Reddee Tank comes with a five-minute repeating tape recording of authentic battle sounds, too!"

Nathaniel could not take his eyes or his hands off the tank. While his sisters lay doubled over with laughter in the aisle that the fat man couldn't see—they had taken a Barbie doll and a Ken doll out of their boxes and were laughing because the Ken doll had no penis —Nathaniel fingered the treads of the tank, the gun, the turret, the metal sides.

Later, while they stood in the ice cream store waiting to place their order for five gallons of strawberry ice cream, Laura thought how unfair it was for people to deprive children of dreams and toys just because they weren't educational or ethical. There was no reason why Bess couldn't be allowed to believe in fairy tales.

Fairy tales were harmless, and so were Nathaniel's war games. It made her furious to think how Kay and Edith and Melissa invaded the private world of the children's games. Laura had stood by and done nothing for long enough. From now on she had to act. She had to protect the children from their mother and their mother's friends. As Sartre said, she had to involve herself, implicate herself in the children's struggle against authority. If she didn't, she would be too low, too cowardly to deserve to exist.

Laura told the girls she was going back to the toy store to buy a present for Jingle. She went back to the toy store, but instead of a present for Jingle she bought Nathaniel the tank.

She waited until late afternoon to show it to him, until the girls were deep in conference in the club cubicle downstairs and Melissa had left for her Saturday seminar. Nathaniel was despondent after two hours of bombarding the club cubicle with a tennis ball. She told him not to worry. He had better things to do than try and join the girls' club. This afternoon she and Nathaniel were going to play a dangerous and exciting game called World War II.

It was a secret, she told him. He had to promise not to tell anybody.

She led him into the living room and when he saw the tank nestled beside the television bag, he squealed and tried to hide between her legs. Laura held him firmly by the hand and told him there was nothing to worry about. He approached the tank. After a few minutes he was touching it just as lovingly as he had touched it in the store.

Then Laura explained to him that the living room was Vichy, France. The couch was the beach at Normandy. The kitchen was Germany, and their destination was the refrigerator—Berlin. The hallway between the living room and the kitchen was the Ruhr Valley. That was where all the Enemy factories were, and when the tank passed through, they had to make sure to demolish all of them. She explained this simpleminded strategy several times. Nathaniel listened with a doubtful expression, his hand in his mouth. With great reluctance he acted out the landing of all the brave Allied soldiers on the beach of Normandy. He climbed onto the couch as Laura instructed, and then when she told him to, he climbed off it again.

"Now we're going to get into our tanks and set off for Berlin."

She brought the tank to his side at the foot of the couch and explained how to work it by remote control. "Do you want to try it the first time or should I?" Nathaniel just looked at her. He didn't say anything. Holding the remote control so that he could see what she was doing, Laura put the tank into motion.

Nathaniel watched with open mouth and eyes like saucers as the treads moved the tank slowly across the rug. The cockpit was bathed in red light, the human figure had his hands on the controls and followed the gun as it went around and around. There was a sound of an engine and a submachine gun. As it reached the television set, there was the sound of thunder and then a loud explosion. "That was Paris being liberated," Laura explained.

He looked at her as if she were a madwoman, but then as she turned the tank toward the kitchen, they heard hundreds of grenades whistling through the air. More submachine guns. Nathaniel whimpered and put his thumb in his mouth. A plane was flying far away and then suddenly it nose-dived. An explosion. An engine sputtering to a stop. The gun on the tank went around and around. Nathaniel buried half his head under a pillow. If Laura hadn't been watching his own war games for months and months, she would have thought he was scared.

"We're coming into the Ruhr Valley now." He sat up to watch the tank struggle up the half-step to the hallway. He was shivering. "Are you cold, Nathaniel?" He shook his head. "If you're cold I can nip into the Ruhr Valley and get you a sweater."

He whimpered. He put his thumb into his mouth. Laura reached out to pat him on the back but he scuttled away.

"Don't hurt me," he said.

The tank passed through the Ruhr Valley without incident and rolled on into the kitchen. Laura felt very foolish. Nathaniel was not enjoying the game. She played with the idea of bringing the tank back into the living room and starting a new game—Dunkerque, perhaps, or All Quiet on the Western Front, or The Battle of the Bulge. But her feelings were hurt. Nathaniel had not responded to her gesture as she had hoped. She decided to let the tank run its course to the refrigerator. Then she would put it away. Maybe she would give it to the boy who lived next door to her in the dorm. He was in the Big Brothers program. He would know someone who would appreciate it. She had never liked war games anyway. She had only done this for Nathaniel.

The tank rounded the corner and disappeared toward the refrigerator. Laura stared at Nathaniel and Nathaniel stared at her from the far end of the couch. They listened to the gunfire in the kitchen, the explosions, the grenades whistling through the air, the dive bombers, the bells, the death wails, the dying engines, the sirens, the authentic sounds of war.

24

There was a special Family Council meeting to discuss Halloween costumes. Sarah had been counting on being a devil, with Bess as her human pitchfork, but Kay used her executive veto on this proposal on the grounds that the concept of devils was unhealthy and counterproductive. Furthermore, she explained, the human pitchfork idea was laden with exploitative connotations. In response to her call for better and more relevant ideas, Edith suggested that the girls be Sacco and Vanzetti, but Kay objected to this too. She wanted Nathaniel to be in on the Halloween theme, and it didn't seem fair to dress him up as the Governor of Massachusetts, as Melissa had proposed in half-seriousness.

They then racked their brains for legendary threesomes: the Three Blind Mice, the Three Kings, the Three Men in a Tub, the Three Musketeers. Finally Sarah consented to the Three Little Pigs. Edith bought the pig masks, the coral-pink turtleneck T-shirts, the matching corduroy trousers. A few nights before Halloween, while Laura typed up a three-page paper on the Hemispheres of the Mind on Kay's electric typewriter, Edith settled among the brightly colored cushions on the divan in Kay's study. Using scraps of material from Kay's sewing kit, she made three pink tails, which she stuffed with cotton and pipe cleaners, fashioned into cork screws, and sewed to the seats of the three pairs of trousers.

Laura had long since forgiven Edith for the evening of rage. Now they were sisters and confidantes once again. The study was warm, partly because Laura had secretly turned the thermostat way up, partly because of the lazy, intimate way she and Edith talked about the small events of the day whenever Laura sat back and took a break from her paper. Kay and Martin were away at a seminar on the future of women in the social sciences. It was a three-day affair, and tonight they were drafting a resolution. They wouldn't be back until late. The children were asleep, Laura having played her clock trick on them while Edith was busy talking on the phone. It was Melissa's volunteer night at the hospital. Dennis was busy knocking down the barrier that Kay had had him put up between Bob's side of the top floor and Kay's side. Now that Bob was comfortably settled in an apartment a few blocks away, it was no longer needed.

When he had checked the wood for nails and splinters and carried it down to Children's Paradise, Dennis joined Edith and Laura in Kay's study. Edith brought up three large mugs of hot cider laced with dark rum. She put James Taylor on the small stereo. Feeling through the many pockets in his painter's pants, Dennis found his pipe and a tiny piece of hash wrapped in aluminum foil. He lit it, took a drag, and passed it on to Laura. Edith showed him the pigtails she had sewed on the children's Halloween costumes. With a solemn nod, he told her they were really heavy.

"How are you doing?" Edith asked, giving Dennis's knee an affectionate pat.

"Pretty loose, I guess," Dennis said, nodding thoughtfully. "I guess you could say I'm hanging pretty loose."

"Horny?" she asked.

He cocked his head to one side, and then nodded, almost in shame.

"How about you?" Edith asked, turning to Laura. Laura shrugged her shoulders.

They had discussed having a ménage à trois several times before, although they had never made any definite plans. Edith felt that they had to wait for a time when all three of them were alone together and feeling equally horny. It had to be spontaneous. Edith wanted to share her first sexual experience with a woman with Dennis, as it was something she felt a bit apprehensive about. And if Dennis were there she thought it would be much less traumatic and more "natural"-feeling. Laura had been looking forward to a ménage à trois with a mixture of excitement and dread. Excitement because it was such a daring thing to do (Stavros would have a heart attack if he ever knew) and dread, because she did not know if she had the necessary expertise to make love with two people at the same time.

The important thing was to look nonchalant, Laura decided. When they took off their clothes she looked casually out the window, at the soft yellow lampshade, the bright cushions, the cozy shelves of books, at the turntable under the brown plastic cover, and then when she couldn't put it off any longer, she gave Dennis a warm smile, as if she had run into him on the street, and stared into his eyes while she clumsily removed her jeans and pullover and socks and underwear. She was wearing a bra.

"That's the first bra I've seen for practically an Ice Age," Edith said. Blushing, Laura tried to explain it away by explaining that her pullover was itchy.

While James Taylor crooned away about sunshine and friends, they sat naked in a circle on the thick Flokati rug, sipping their second round of hot cider and dark rum. Laura glanced briefly at Edith's breasts. They were small and pretty, a completely different shape from her own, and for some reason they upset her, so she made a point of looking elsewhere. She did not look closely between Edith's legs. The only time she had looked between a woman's legs was in the movie *I Am Curious Yellow* and since she had never examined her own body very closely, it had been a great shock. She had been queasy for days. Now was no time to become queasy. She decided not to look at Edith closely until she was very aroused.

Edith crawled across the rug, rubbed her head playfully against Dennis's chest, and began to give him a blowjob.

Dennis shut his eyes, put his arms behind his head, and clenched his teeth, as children clench their teeth when they see a nurse preparing a syringe and the doctor tells them to be a brave soldier. Laura watched his armpits heave and fall. She tried to look serious, just in case he opened his eyes, because she didn't want to be the one to ruin the atmosphere. When the armpits grew too much to bear, she looked at the bookcase behind him and tried to read the titles. She was halfway across the first shelf when Edith sat up and fell on her back, a look of total abandon on her face.

"Oh, wow!" she said. She yawned, stretched out her arms, and then, very slowly, her legs. Dennis stared at her so hard that Laura thought he had gone cross-eyed. He put his hair behind his ears, and then, with a disturbing growl, he buried his head between her legs.

"Golly, Dennis, can't you hold your horses for a minute?" Edith said, sitting up. She turned to Laura. Dennis lifted his head obediently. "Do you mind if he does me first?" Edith asked.

Laura shrugged her shoulders, nonchalantly, she hoped. "Of course not. Go right ahead. I'm not in any hurry."

"Well, why don't you roll over here next to me and I'll try to see if I can get you going."

"Oh, never mind about that," Laura said, trying to sound off-hand although her heart was beating wildly. "I'm just happy sitting here and watching."

Edith gave her a strange look. "Okay," she said. "Whatever

suits you is cool." It was only when they had returned to their foreplay that Laura realized that Edith probably thought she was a voyeur.

A voyeur. That was terrible. Blushing, she turned away and tried not to look at what was going on less than three feet away. The noisy foreplay was coming to an end, and she could just see the noisy beginning of intercourse, the flash of frenzied naked bodies in the corner of her eye. Edith was shouting out breathless commands. It was impossible not to hear them, even when Laura nestled up against one of the speakers. She picked up the record jacket and tried to focus on James Taylor's bland, handsome face and perfect-fitting Levi's. "Faster! Faster!" Edith was screaming. "Slower! Roll over! Wait a minute! Over here a little. More! More! Higher, higher, right there! Oh! Wow! Now on the other side! Oh, wow! I almost came. Deeper, deeper, I'm almost there! Almost, almost, almost, hurry up and we can come together . . . No! Wait! Don't come yet! Slow, slow, oh, my God! Oh, my fucking God!" She screamed as if she had found a scorpion in her shoe. Then there was a silence. Dennis paused, and waited for her next directions. Laura could not understand why he had suddenly become so passive, so obedient, especially after all his lectures about how free they all were.

"Okay," Edith said in a matter-of-fact voice, "you can come now if you want." Right on cue, Dennis rocked her back and forth for a few seconds, and then he stopped, waited for Edith to scream her way to a second orgasm, groaned, rolled across the floor, and curled up into a fetal position next to the desk, leaving Edith panting next to Laura's outstretched feet.

Laura felt both apprehension and relief as she surveyed their naked bodies, which were painfully white even in the soft light of the desk lamp. Apprehension because instead of a love scene she felt as if she had witnessed a battle—a battle which was shortly to claim her as a victim. Relief, because the fact that she was not aroused meant that she probably was not a voyeur.

"Dennis?" Edith yawned, "how long will it take for you to get it up for Laura?"

"I don't know," he mumbled.

"Should I go ahead with her?"

"I guess so."

Edith cupped her hands around Laura's foot and began to nibble her way up Laura's leg. Laura closed her eyes and tried to become aroused, but her muscles were taut instead of relaxed, and instead of feeling spasms of warmth and pleasure she was highly aware of two lips and an annoying tongue traveling up her thigh, leaving a cold, wet path behind them, and the little pointed fingernails that were digging into her hips, and the ticklish swish of Edith's hair as she continued nibbling her way across Laura's stomach, finally reaching Laura's left breast, which she proceeded to lick like an ice cream cone.

Laura watched Edith lick her breast with detachment, as if the breast were not her own. She felt vaguely excited, but only vaguely. She closed her eyes, because the idea that she was about to make love with a woman excited her more than the woman herself. It was the same when Edith pulled herself up to kiss her on the mouth. It was all right, Laura supposed, it reminded her of the times she had kissed people good night out of politeness, after they had taken her to the movies or a party. The kind of kiss which makes you highly aware of the width of the lips, the activity of the tongue, the clanking of one set of teeth against another, because you're only kissing that person out of politeness, because you like him, or in this case, her, but only as a friend.

She was vaguely interested by the way Edith's nipples felt against her own breasts. This was interesting, and very new. She was beginning to lose her detachment when suddenly Edith lifted an arm and began to claw between her legs, and fumble, and tear at the delicate skin, like a dog tearing at the ground to uncover a favorite bone.

She pushed Edith off her and rolled over.

"What's wrong?" Edith asked.

"You're hurting me. You should cut your fingernails," Laura said.

"Sorry! I was just trying to orient myself, that's all." She rolled Laura over and began to feel between her legs again. By now Laura had frozen completely. "Is that your clit?" she asked, digging her fingernails into the lips of her vagina.

"Ouch! No, it isn't."

"Darn!" Edith said. "I was positive it was. Gee, this takes some getting used to." She felt between her own legs. "You know what? I think my clit is in a different place from your clit. Dennis, you're just going to have to show me what's what, that's all."

Dennis crawled wearily across the Flokati rug. Edith spread Laura's legs open sufficiently wide. "I wish you wouldn't make me do things like this," he said to Edith.

"Aw, come on! Don't be such a spoilsport."

He sighed. "That thing there is her clitoris, okay?"

"Right," said Edith, nodding efficiently, as if she were listening to directions to someone's house.

"I can't believe you don't know where her cunt is," Dennis said. The two of them peered between her legs. Laura's leg muscles tightened until they were as hard and inflexible as steel. She was trembling. It was worse than going to a gynecologist. She closed her eyes.

"Okay, okay," Edith giggled. "It's here, okay?" She poked her finger into Laura's cunt. Laura screamed. She rolled over into a ball. Edith crawled next to her and shook her gently by the shoulder. "Hey, I'm sorry. Did that hurt?"

"Yes," Laura said.

Edith brushed the hair off Laura's forehead. "You're not very turned on, are you?" Laura shook her head. She had a strong urge to put a thumb in her mouth and snuggle under a warm blanket and go to sleep.

"Maybe it would be better if Dennis did you first," Edith suggested.

Laura closed her eyes and nodded.

"I'm afraid you'll have to work him up first, though. He's just down to almost nothing." Laura sat up and dragged herself across the rug to where Dennis was sitting. "A blowjob is the quickest," Edith said.

"Oh," Laura said, "I don't think I'm up for a blowjob."

"That's cool! But just to speed things up, let me show how it works best for Dennis just in case you haven't tried it that way. Like this." She picked up Dennis's limp penis and held it in her right hand. "Two strokes, then squeeze with your whole hand, medium hard. Try and make it as rhythmic as you can. You see this crinkly area here? Well, that's the most sensitive part, so when you're doing the stroking part make sure you apply a little more pressure."

Stroke, stroke, squeeze. Laura followed Edith's directions with great reluctance. She resented the way Edith was bossing her around but could not find the courage to oppose her. She looked with great sadness at Dennis, who looked sadly back. His mouth drooped, his eyes had lost their rough-and-ready luster, the muscles in his arms bulged helplessly as Edith supervised Laura's efforts to give him an erection. They exchanged miserable looks. They were both helpless victims of Edith's leadership qualities— the same leadership qualities that had gotten her into college in the first place, no doubt, and had made her the best assistant editor that the college newspaper had ever seen, and had made her excel in countless volunteer projects, and would one day, no doubt, make her highly successful in one of the many professions she had already shown promise in—law, journalism, free-lance writing, social work, medicine, politics.

Laura had always imagined that Edith would be tender and loving in bed, perhaps because that was the way she was when she brushed other people's hair. She was surprised to see how bossy and rough she had become as soon as they had taken off their clothes. Certainly Edith had always been one to take the initiative, but never in this Hitlerian manner. After three unsuccessful attempts, Dennis was finally able to enter Laura with an erection he told Edith he thought he could maintain. Whatever illusions of sensuality Laura might have had by then, Edith destroyed by crawling around trying to find ways to get into the action.

She tried to crawl up from behind and put her fingers around Dennis's penis as he moved in and out of Laura. She tried to crawl on top of them and between them, knocking Laura's head when she tried to kiss Dennis, knocking Dennis's head when she tried to kiss Laura, pushing her strong white teeth against Laura's teeth so hard that she thought her mouth was bleeding. At one point she tried to sit on Laura's face. Laura thought she was going to smother to death. She tried to shake Edith off. She screamed. She felt her eyes, her mouth, and especially her nose being crushed by the firm white skin and bones above her.

Finally Edith crawled off her face and down toward Dennis's feet. Laura took in large gulps of warm air. Dennis was straining to keep his erection, but finally he gave up. He rolled off Laura panting.

"Did you come?" Edith asked.

"Maybe later," he choked.

"All that time and you didn't come?" Laura was trembling, too. Edith offered her a massage, but she turned it down. "Let me rest a moment," she said, and closed her eyes. Then she felt a wet finger circling her anus. She jumped up.

"What are you trying to do?" she screamed. Edith smiled. She waved her glistening index finger in front of Laura's nose. "Don't worry, I've covered it with gobs and gobs of Vaseline."

Screaming, Laura scrambled to her feet and ran into the bathroom, where she locked the door. Edith shook it and pounded on it and shouted at Laura to let her in. Laura drew a hot bath so she couldn't hear what she was saying. She poured a third of a bottle of bubble bath into it. When the bubbles were almost pouring onto the blue rug she turned off the water and stepped in. The bath was scalding hot. She stopped shivering.

When she had arranged herself comfortably and decorated her nose and cheeks with bubbles, she noticed that the intercom was on because she could hear metallic breathing broken by pathetic little sobs. It was Edith.

"Laura?" she finally said, "are you feeling okay?"

"I guess so," Laura said.

"Do you mind letting us in?" Laura didn't answer. "I really have to talk to you," Edith pleaded in a small, pathetic voice. "I . . . I . . . I promise neither of us will touch you. I just want to talk it over, okay?"

Laura was now resigned to the fact that you could not commit any sexual act without talking about it for hours afterward. She knew that if she did not make herself available now, she would have to make herself available tomorrow or the day after. She decided to get it over with while she was still hidden among bath bubbles.

She got up, let them in, and quickly took refuge in the hot water below the bubbles. They were naked and shivering. Edith put on Kay's HERS robe and handed Dennis Bob's HIS robe, which Bob had left behind and Martin was now using. They sat down next to the bathtub. Edith asked Laura why she had freaked out.

At first Laura offered her repertoire of disturbing childhood experiences and repressive parental attitudes, but when Edith pressed her she admitted that she hadn't wanted Edith's finger in her anus.

"It really upsets me," Edith said, "it really upsets me the way you refuse to open up to the possibilities of your body. I mean, it's so limiting. Do you really want to go through life being scared out of your wits worrying about someone wanting to fuck you up the ass? You have to get over this inhibition."

"I don't know why you're so worried about my inhibitions," Laura said. She felt braver under all the bubbles: surer of her own opinions. "I'm a free person. If I'm free, then I have a right to my inhibitions. And if I want to get rid of them, it's my decision, not yours."

Edith gave her that pained look that everyone who had taken a logic course or a philosophy course or participated in the campus revolution gave her whenever she made a comment on existence or freedom or basic rights.

"The thing is," Edith said, screwing up her face thoughtfully, "you can't ever expect to be an integral member of a close-knit group if you refuse to explore your body's needs in relation to the needs of everyone else in the group. I mean, it's almost a responsibility. You have to commit yourself completely, or else how can you expect to . . . to . . . *belong?*"

"Oh, I'm used to not belonging to things. That doesn't bother me a bit." Edith looked at her curiously. Then she grinned, as if Laura had told her a joke. She put her arm in the bath water (the bubbles were fast disappearing as she fished about and the water was less than lukewarm) and finally found Laura's hand. "I guess you need time to think it over," she said, squeezing it softly. "Maybe we can try it again next month sometime." Dennis gave Laura a sad look. He reminded Laura of an unfed dog. Edith's grip made her shiver. She felt as if Edith were trying to get under her skin.

It became apparent that they had left the intercom on when the girls started teasing her the following afternoon. "Did you have a nice bath, dear?" Sarah asked when she brought them their after-school hot chocolate. "Did you kiss Edith-poo nightie-night so she could feel better-wetter?"

Sarah tried to teach Nathaniel the school rhyme so that they could chant it all together:

"Laura and Edith, sitting in a tree,
K-I-S-S-I-N-G. That's how you spell kissing," Sarah explained.

"Girls can't kiss," Nathaniel protested.

"Laura and Edith can," Sarah said. "Laura kisses everyone she can get her hands on. She's a kissing maniac."

Nathaniel crawled under the table. "Don't kiss me, don't kiss me," he cried.

After they had finished their hot chocolate, the children went to try on their Halloween costumes. They ran about the kitchen, delighted with the way they looked.

Sarah and Bess were jittery, almost hysterical. Nathaniel was ecstatic that they were paying him so much attention. They made a great fuss about the way the corkscrew tails that Edith had sewed to their coral pink trousers dug into them when they sat down and the way they popped out again when they stood up. When Laura asked them about their day at school, they answered in oinks. They giggled a lot about the names Sarah had assigned them. Sarah was Petunia Pig, Bess was Ground Hog, and Nathaniel was Guinea Pig.

Nathaniel's name they found particularly hilarious. "You know what it means if your name is Guinea Pig?" they kept saying. They wouldn't tell him the answer. It was some sort of in-joke. They wouldn't tell Laura what the in-joke was, but she decided not to press.

25

The important thing was that they were being nice to Nathaniel after weeks of cruelty and threats so terrible that Nathaniel had spent the three previous afternoons quivering at the back of the tool shed, expecting meteors to fall out of the heavens onto his head and iron hands to drag him under the ground. It had been especially bad after the death of Flighty Angel, the small white kitten that Sarah claimed was Flicka's son.

For weeks now, Laura had been trying to convince the girls to admit Nathaniel to their club. They had continued to fight him away from the entrance. Even at meals they would treat him like a pariah. When Laura told her how lonely Nathaniel was now that his sisters would never play with him, Kay arranged for one of Nathaniel's classmates to come and play with him after school— a small silent boy called Sherman whose eyes seemed crossed, although they weren't, whose sole topic of conversation was milk trucks.

MOTHER'S HELPER

His father was some sort of graduate student and he lived in the graduate student housing development down the road. Although Sherman was the same age as Nathaniel, he seemed very backward in comparison. When Nathaniel discovered this he cast himself in the role of teacher.

He taught his new friend how cats and dogs mated, what went into an omelet, what turned raindrops into hail, what the difference was between wood and plastic that looked like wood. Kay was pleased. She said the peer-group aspect of the relationship was bringing out Nathaniel's latent leadership qualities. Everything was going very well until one afternoon Laura found Flighty Angel lying on the woodpile next to the fireplace, strangled.

Nathaniel said that Sherman had done it; Sherman blamed it sometimes on Nathaniel and sometimes on the trees. Kay decided it was probably Sherman because she had had a funny feeling about the boy from the word go. She quickly banned him. Just to be fair, just in case Nathaniel was the guilty party, she called up Nathaniel's teacher and warned her to keep him away from the hamsters.

The girls blamed it on Nathaniel. They were very upset. Sarah had been counting on Flighty Angel to open the gates of Heaven for all animals with initiative and inquiring minds, just as Jesus had once done for humans. After they had buried the kitten in a child-sized shoe box decorated with tinsel in a grave on the right side of Flicka, they dragged Nathaniel down to Children's Paradise and put him on trial. Laura didn't know about the trial, but fortunately she was sweeping the stairs to Children's Paradise when they found him guilty on two counts—being a murderer and being a boy—and condemned him to one thousand and thirty-nine lashes. Laura rescued him before they could administer the sentence.

Sarah went into a terrible sulk after that. At school she was doing a study project on the Constitution and the three branches of government. As usual, she had adapted what she had learned to her own purposes. When Laura tried to explain to her why they could not whip Nathaniel (she tried to explain this using Sarah's

— 303 —

frame of reference: she told her you had to have a jury), Sarah told Laura she was "uptrucking" justice and that she would take the case to the Supreme Court of Olympus. Nathaniel would be punished for his crimes, and unless there was a second coming very soon, the day of reckoning was at hand.

Days of sinister meetings and mysterious ceremonies followed. They never said anything in front of Laura, but Laura could tell that they were frightening Nathaniel out of his wits. He acted as if the whole world was out to get him: his daily meal of hot dogs, the refrigerator, the television bag, the voluminous parkas on the coat rack, the dead leaves, the sky. Laura began to worry what they were up to.

Now, as she watched them run around the backyard preparing for one of their interminable ceremonies, it looked as if the worst were over. Nathaniel was suddenly their friend again. The pig costumes had made the girls forget about the war of terror they had been waging on their brother. Or perhaps it had just become boring. It was like the old days at the arsenal. No whispers, no sinister, knowing smiles, no screams. Just laughter and frenetic action. Three little children in pig costumes running around the tree, decorating the three gravestone popsicles with candy corn, sitting on the old door that Sarah had dragged out of the tool shed, Sarah in the middle, Bess and an overjoyed Nathaniel at either side.

Sarah took the hand mirror out of the canvas sack where they kept all the props for their ceremonies, and went through the motions of pretending to send code messages to someone in the sky.

One of Laura's jobs that afternoon was to rake the leaves. Laura watched them curl their hands around their ears and pray in the same ritual manner they always used at the beginning of ceremonies. Then, as Laura raked the dead leaves around them, Sarah began to converse with the sky in pig latin, thinking, perhaps, that Laura would not understand her, not realizing that Laura had been a champion at this language in her own time.

"Ello-hay. Ee-way are-ay ee-thray ittle-lay igs-pay oo-hay ant-way oo-tay om-cay or-fay a-ay isit-vay. Ee-way ill-way oo-day anything-ay oo-yay ay-say if-ay oo-yay et-lay us-ay om-cay."

For the next hour the children ate the specified number of candy corns, ran around the tree the specified number of times, sang, "This little pig went to the market, oink, oink, This little pig stayed at home, oh yes, This little pig had roast beef, oink, oink, This little pig had none, oh no, This little pig went wee wee wee wee all the way to Happy Hunting Grounds. Oh yes, oink, oink, oh yes!", hosed specific sections of the garden, attempted handstands, snorted, rolled, and danced in any way that Sarah said the mysterious personage in the sky wanted them to. Nathaniel was especially eager to obey Sarah's instructions. Their acceptance of him had caused him to lose all his irrational fears about the sky falling in and the telephone wanting to hurt him and the quilt on his bed wanting to devour him whole, like a man-eating plant. He ran across the grass, oblivious to the hands that he once thought were lurking there. He threw his arms around the tree trunk, as if no one had ever told him that contact with bark would make his skin rot if he was a sinner.

Laura went inside feeling very happy that Edith had gone out of her way to make imaginative costumes. While she put a load of laundry in the washing machine and vacuumed the rugs on the top floor, she thought how it was just like the old days at the arsenal, before Sarah became so obsessed with punishments and rules.

Kay had bought a new kind of industrial cleaner that she wanted Laura to try out on the kitchen floor. When Laura went out to the porch to get the mop and bucket, she glanced over at the children to see how their ceremony was going.

Bess and Sarah were standing on either end of the door. Between them was Nathaniel. He was the only one with his pig mask on. The other two had their pig masks dangling down their backs. Nathaniel was lying on his side. He was tied to the door at his neck and his ankles. His pants and his underpants were lying a few feet away in the grass. His bare bottom looked as red and as raw as

Sarah's and Bess's cheeks. Both girls had their arms in the air. They were chanting some sort of gibberish. In Bess's hand was a cushion. Sarah was waving her arms round and round, as if in a trance. There was something in her hands that glittered in the weak October sun. It was a bread knife.

Laura stifled a scream. She ran across the lawn as fast as she could, as Sarah swung the knife around in wider and wider circles, first one way, and then the other, still chanting the strange staccato gibberish. The circles became figure eights, each one swinging closer to Nathaniel and the door. Coming up behind Sarah, Laura grabbed the knife out of her hand.

It took a moment for Sarah to react. Then she screamed. "She's attacking us!" They ran into the tool shed, leaving Nathaniel wriggling helplessly on the door. Laura chased them. The knife was still in her hand. "What's wrong with you?" she screamed. She started crying. The two girls huddled at the far end of the shed, tittering, their eyes following the path of the knife in Laura's hand as she cried and shouted at them. "What's wrong with you?"

Sarah ran to the front of the shed and slammed the door.

Nathaniel was crying too when Laura went back to untie him and get him back into his underpants and his trousers. "Don't hurt me, don't hurt me," he kept saying. When she brought him inside, he went straight under the table, where he continued to cry, off and on, miserably. When she tried to give him tissues, he screamed.

"Where's the girls?" he asked after a while.

"They're in the tool shed," she told him. He crawled toward the door and was fumbling at the doorknob when Laura lifted him away.

"I don't think you should go out there right now," she said. "You might catch a cold."

And the miserable crying began again. "But I want to be with the girls. Where are the girls? I want to play with the girls. What happened to the girls?" He wandered from room to room, crying, with his hand in his mouth. He pressed his face against the glass and cried at the tool shed. The door was still closed. "I want to be with the girls." He was all wet—his face, his hair, his eyes, his hands, his new pink shirt. He rolled under the table again. No matter what Laura did, he would not stop crying.

When Kay came home, Laura told her everything, perhaps in too emotive a manner. Kay listened with a stone face. Laura could not tell was she was thinking. "Dear me," she said, "this is disturbing news. I understand completely how it must have upset you." She put down her pile of papers, took off her orange parka, and went straight to the phone. "Where's Nathaniel now?" she asked while she was dialing.

"Behind the couch, I think."

"And the girls?"

"In the tool shed."

"Hmmm," she said, wedging the phone between her chin and her shoulders to write something down in the appointments book next to the telephone. "I don't know how you feel, but in my opinion it would be better for everyone concerned if we did not single this out as something extraordinary, at least in Nathaniel's presence. The last thing we want to do is create a trauma situation.

"Hello, Arlette? This is Kay here. Just checking to make sure it's still set for ten tomorrow . . . No, no, it's ideal for me because I have another appointment in that neck of the woods at noon . . . You'll be glad to know I picked up a few more juicy tidbits which will fit into the program very nicely indeed . . . No, nothing like that unfortunately, that would have clinched it, certainly . . . Will do, will do . . . Until tomorrow then. Peace!"

When she had placed the phone on the hook, she went out to the tool shed to fetch the girls, who came dutifully after her, their pigtails bobbing. When Nathaniel saw them come inside, he came tearfully out of his hiding place behind the couch. "Cocoa, anyone?" Kay said with a smile. Laura took the hint and went to the stove to make everyone cocoa.

At first Kay pretended that it was just a normal day, that it was not at all abnormal to carry on a conversation with three identical pig masks, two of whom refused to answer any questions and one of whom sank down from his chair and dissolved into muffled tears on the floor when she asked them if they wanted anything in particular from the supermarket. She told them about all the exciting things she had been doing at the network, and told them the good news that their father had agreed to take them trick-or-treating later that week. From the expression on her face you would have thought she was talking to three smiling children instead of three unsmiling masks.

Laura brought the cocoas to the table. Sarah lifted her mask so that she could take a sip, and that was when Kay looked her straight in the eye and said,

"Laura tells me you had a little ceremony today."

Sarah squirmed.

"Would you like to tell me what this ceremony was all about?"

"It's none of your business," Sarah said sullenly.

"Do you think so, Sarah? I tend to disagree. I tend to think this ceremony concerns me very much. I was very interested in hearing what you have to tell me about it. I am particularly interested to hear what you can tell me about this knife."

Sarah rubbed her eyes angrily. "We were just playing with it," she said, "just pretending."

"Pretending what, dear?"

"Just pretending. It was just an experiment."

"An experiment for what, Sarah?"

"To see if we could trick them so we could visit."

"Visit where?"

"There."

Kay stood up and walked to the fireplace. She turned around. "Where is there?"

"None of your business," Sarah said.

"Do you normally play with knives in this fashion?" Kay asked, folding her arms.

"Well, not always," Bess started to say, "but . . ." Sarah nudged her and she went quiet.

"Laura and I have been thinking," Kay said. "We've been thinking about that knife. And I've been wondering if you weren't intending to use it on Nathaniel in one way or another."

"What do you think I am, stupid?" Sarah shouted.

"No," said Kay in measured tones. "I just thought maybe you were thinking of hurting him in one way or another. And tell me if I'm wrong, but it just occurred to me that you two might have been playing with the idea of doing something to his penis."

Bess giggled. Sarah looked furious.

Bess giggled again. Sarah told her to shut up.

"You're telling me that wasn't what you had in mind?"

"We were just playing a game, stupid!"

"Well, I don't think it sounds like a very good or kind game, or even a wise game. *I* think it sounds like a bad game." She picked Nathaniel up from under the table and gently lifted the mask from his face. He put his hand in his mouth and stared at his mother with saucer eyes.

"Don't you think so too, Nathaniel?" Kay said, giving him a playful smile.

Nathaniel whimpered.

"I don't know what he thinks," Kay continued. "But I think Nathaniel is very lucky to have such a nice penis. If I were Nathaniel I would feel very mad indeed if my sisters tried to do something to it. I would tell them not to ever try that again. What would you do, Nathaniel?"

He took his hand out of his mouth, stared at her blankly, put his hand back in his mouth.

"You're just trying to blame everything in the whole world on me!" Sarah shouted. "It's not fair!"

"Sarah, please." She turned to Nathaniel again. "Aren't you proud of your nice little pink penis?"

Drooling, he shook his head.

"Don't you want to grow up to be a nice, big, peace-loving daddy and have lots and lots of lovely little girls and little boys?"

"Not like Daddy," he said hoarsely.

Kay laughed in the ultrasoft, ultracalm voice that she reserved for crises. "Hey, Nathaniel! You know there's nothing wrong with your daddy. I think your daddy is pretty neat myself. If I were you I would be proud of my daddy."

"Not like Daddy," he insisted.

"Well, then you can grow up to be a Martinlike daddy, or even a Dennislike daddy, if you wish."

"Is Martin my daddy?"

"No, but he can be your pretend daddy."

"Is Dennis my daddy?"

"No, but he can be your pretend daddy, too. You can have as many pretend daddies as you like."

"Well, I don't want any daddies," he said. He climbed off her lap and toddled out of the room. Kay sighed. She put her head in her hands and counted slowly to ten, while the girls squirmed in their seats, their faces behind the masks once again, their eyes glittering inscrutably above the two great snouts. "I don't think I have to list all the physical and psychological implications of what you two did to your brother."

"But we didn't do anything!" Sarah shouted. The mask made her sound as if she were speaking under a pillow.

"I'm sorry, I can't accept that unless you two can come up with a story that explains the knife and the rest of it. I just can't accept that. And I might as well add that I can't think of any explanation offhand that explains away the presence of that knife in a satisfactory manner. Game or no game, there is something about this ceremony that smells very bad indeed. I want you to consider terminating these ceremonies from now on. I only hope you haven't done your brother irreparable harm already."

She cleared her throat. "I want both of you to think very seriously about what you did. Tomorrow the three of us can put our heads together and see whether we can come up with a viable morality framework for the future." She paused and took a deep breath. "I feel it is only fair to tell you now that if I feel you are not providing sufficient input, or if I feel you have not been able to resolve this problem on your own, I shall seriously consider sending you both to some sort of psychiatrist."

Sarah made a noise under her mask. Bess giggled.

"What did you say, Sarah?"

Sarah made another noise.

"I'm afraid you'll have to speak louder," Kay said.

"I said OINK!"

Nathaniel returned to the tool shed. His fears about the earth and the sky and the machines and villains who were out to get him were stronger than ever before. He crouched under the work bench, crying, picking up nails and dropping them, screaming whenever Laura approached him.

He refused to go to school the next day, and the day after that. Laura had to skip her classes to be with him. He wandered around the house crying when she locked the doors to keep him from going out to the tool shed. Whenever he spoke, it was to ask about the girls. Where were they? When would they come home? Kay let him sleep upstairs with her in the master bedroom, but only when she came home, which was very late some days. Laura had to baby-sit until midnight or one in the morning, and it was very depressing to listen to him thrash and moan in his crib while his sisters' regular breathing came in waves over the intercom. Especially since Kay insisted that Laura continue to treat him as if nothing were wrong. "If he talks about monsters in the dark, tell him firmly that they don't exist. Under no circumstances should you make any concessions, like taking him upstairs or staying down there with him. If you do, then he'll think that monsters do in fact exist and you are trying to protect him from them. We can't let him think that his fears have any basis in reality."

When Nathaniel did not improve noticeably as the week wore on, Kay got in touch with her child psychologist friend at the university—the one who had been so successful at discouraging Nathaniel's gun-play earlier that year, if only temporarily. Kay thought very highly of her child psychologist friend. She said that if anyone was going to challenge Skinner in his own field, it was Eleanor in five or ten years' time. She was certain that Eleanor would be able to detraumatize Nathaniel. She had had amazing success with some very disturbed ghetto cases over the past two years.

When Nathaniel came home from his first visit to the child psychologist, his eyes and nose were dry for the first time in days. He was silent at dinnertime, and then suddenly he started laughing and gurgling like a baby. Kay said this was natural in the circumstances. He was regressing, but this would pass. It would take a long time for Eleanor's therapy to yield any results. She had only just started building the graph. "We just have to remember not to play up to him when he acts like this," Kay told her. But Kay was gone most of the time. She was working on some documentary. It was Laura who had to sit and watch him gurgling, and crossing his eyes, and clapping his hands like a spastic.

"What's wrong with him?" Sarah would ask.

"There's nothing wrong with him," Laura would say, trying to sound firm and indubitably in the right, like Kay, "he's acting perfectly normal."

And Sarah would say, "You're such a liar."

On Halloween he recovered slightly, although Kay wondered if it was a wise thing to let him go trick-or-treating. She was working at home that day, for a change. When the girls put on their pig costumes after school, she allowed him to put his on, too. They would see how things went, she said, and make their final decision later.

The two girls spent the afternoon trying to get Grosvenor to obey orders in pig latin. Grosvenor didn't seem to enjoy this game at all. He slinked from room to room with his tail between his legs, giving them doleful looks as they jumped around him, oinking frantically.

Nathaniel followed them at a distance, on his face the rapt and puzzled expression of a two-year-old watching something he has never seen before. The girls paid him no attention, but at least they weren't taunting him. That was all Laura cared about. He seemed happy enough. He wasn't clapping or gurgling. He seemed intent on the girls' game, and content to follow them at a distance, dragging his boy doll behind him, his thumb never far from his mouth, his mask hanging loosely from his neck, his pigtail sagging pitifully, hanging between his legs, just like Grosvenor's.

Kay had bought large quantities of raisins, breakfast cereals, and animal crackers for trick-or-treaters. When she came down to get ready for them in the late afternoon, Laura asked her if she knew where she might find a basket large enough to hold all the treats. Kay said she remembered seeing something that would certainly be large enough in the closet underneath the front staircase.

Nathaniel was coming downstairs at the time. When he saw his mother dart into the closet directly below him, he screamed, tried to run down the stairs, tripped on his doll, and rolled headlong down the stairs, hitting his head and denting the snout of his pig mask. When Kay tried to pick him up he became hysterical. "Don't!" he screamed, trying to kick her away. "Don't!"

That did it, Kay decided. He was in no shape to go trick-or-treating. When a very haggard Bob appeared at the door a few minutes later, Kay told him she was afraid it would have to be the two little pigs, not three.

"What's wrong with him?" Bob asked.

"We don't quite know yet," Kay said. "But one thing is sure. He certainly is in a state. And in no state to leave his mother for the time being, I'm afraid."

It was only later, when Bob and the girls had left without him, and he was standing on the couch, still crying, and screaming whenever a ghost or a devil or a witch or a lumpy horse or anyone in any sort of costume approached the house, that Laura remembered Sarah telling Nathaniel that stepmothers were mothers who lived under steps, and that if a mother went under a step, it was so she could grab her son by the feet and cut him into dog meat to send off to Happy Hunting Grounds.

She told this to Kay, who was helping her hand out the treats.

"I just didn't think that girl had it in her to tell such terrible things to her brother," Kay said, frowning. She went over to the couch and tried to reason with him. After a few screams, he let her hold him in her arms. She rocked him back and forth and told him that Mommy loved him more dearly than anything in the whole wide world, that she would never let any goblin or ghost or anything of the sort ever take him away, or his fingernails, or his curls, or his eyes, or his nose. The ghosts and goblins who kept coming up to the house were, as he knew very well, children just pretending to be ghosts and goblins. Just like he and his sisters were pretending to be pigs. They were little boys and little girls just like Nathaniel, and Kay would be very glad indeed if Nathaniel would help her give them treats.

He was calmer when she installed him next to the large basket of treats, though still quivering slightly. He handed out treats to Snow White and five attendant dwarfs, Marilyn Monroe, two pumpkins, a knight, and a demon. He was just beginning to act normal, more normal than he had acted all week, when three small ghosts rang the bell. They were accompanied by a grown man (their father, Laura decided) who was dressed up as the Green Giant. When Nathaniel handed them their raisins and animal crackers, the Green Giant suggested that they give him a special thank-you, and the three ghosts howled like wolves. Nathaniel screamed and ran down the hall. Kay went and fetched him back, but he had started crying again.

"Where's the girls?" he moaned.

"They went trick-or-treating with their father."

"I want to go with them. I want to go with them."

"Now, now, Nathaniel. I don't know about you, but I think we're having a dandy time right here in our nice warm house. I kind of feel sorry for the girls out there in that bitter wind."

Nathaniel was not convinced. The next trick-or-treaters were Frankenstein and Dracula. When he saw them he screamed and hid behind the couch. He wouldn't believe his mother when she told him they were two little boys about the same age as himself.

"Nathaniel, look at me," Kay said, kneeling down so that they were eye to eye. "No one wants to hurt you, do you understand? And you couldn't be in a safer place, right here next to your mother who loves you more than anything else in the whole world. Won't you come back and help me hand out treats? I'll be very sad if you don't." He took one look at the dragon who was standing at the door when they got there, and the witch with trick fangs and a glove that looked like a leper's hand who was standing behind the dragon, screamed, and ran down the hallway, out the back door, and onto the back porch. Laura went out to find him. She found him under the work bench in the tool shed, and when she tried to pick him up, he kicked and screamed. Laura went in and asked Kay to get him, but she said perhaps it would be better if they let him calm down in his own way. Perhaps she had been pushing him too much. "Let's wait until he comes back to us of his own free will," she said. "And anyway, I tend to doubt he'll want to stay out there when it gets dark." She sent Laura out with Nathaniel's coat and then turned on the intercom so that they would be sure to hear him when he came back in.

Twenty minutes later, they heard the back door open, and the sound of footsteps on the back stairs.

"Nathaniel, are you all right?"

He mumbled something.

"Nathaniel, come to the top of the front stairs so I can see you." Slowly, Nathaniel made his way to the front of the house. He stopped at the top of the stairs. He looked very, very sleepy. His eyelids drooped.

"How are you feeling now? Better?" He nodded. "Do you feel like coming down and helping us again?" He shook his head slowly from side to side and hiccuped. "Maybe later?" He put his thumb in his mouth and whimpered. "Good. Then you go ahead and have a good think and we'll be waiting here for you when you want to come down."

For a few minutes Kay wondered out loud about Nathaniel and the best way to deal with him, and the best way to deal with the girls. She just couldn't understand what had gotten into them. In the old days they had always been so kind to their brother, and she could not think what had turned them against him. She made a mental note to call their teacher. Perhaps the key to the mystery was something that had been going on in school. Laura suggested that the key to the mystery was in the girls' club.

"Oh, I agree with you there," Kay said. "But what I want to know is what spurred them into starting the club in the first place."

"Do you think it might have anything to do with the separation?" Laura asked.

Kay gave her a sharp look. "I've been fairly level with them on that score," she said, "and I have also probed their reactions for soft spots, but they've been pretty soldierly for the most part. No, I tend to think it is something neither you nor I know about, something they haven't mentioned to us. These ceremonies, for example. There's something about these ceremonies that smells very bad indeed."

"Oh, the ceremonies were okay in the beginning," Laura said. "I was just wondering if the separation had something to do with it."

Kay gave her another sharp look. "Gee, I can't see that at all."
She was silent for the next few minutes, and then she started to
tell Laura about her television job. While they stood at the door
handing out box after box of raisins and animal crackers, she talked
about the series they had been preparing on Roxbury housewives.
The experience had scarred her deeply, she said. In the course of
interviewing what they hoped would be a representative sample of
ghetto housewives, they had met with a number of community
organizers who had told her terrible tales of police harassment,
phone tapping, infiltration by the FBI. She said it made her wonder
where the country was going. She said it pained her that most
people were satisfied to sit back in their comfortably little lives and
let it all happen.

What depressed her even more than the laissez-faire attitude of
the bulk of society was the way the Establishment seemed bent
on perpetuating the misery of the ghettos. Her eyes gleaming
with anger, she explained to Laura how the welfare system actually encouraged fathers to leave home. Didn't the establishment
realize that they were encouraging broken families? Didn't they
realize that children from broken ghetto families were more likely
to suffer severe mental illness, less likely to succeed, and much,
much more likely to turn to crime for a livelihood? She was
thinking of writing a letter to *The New York Times* about the
whole problem. This benign-neglect attitude was eating a hole in
her heart. She was thinking of starting a pressure group for welfare reform, and she thought that if America was the country it
said it was, welfare reform should be the number one issue in the
next election.

Laura searched Kay's face for irony. She was surprised, almost
horrified to hear Kay talk about broken families in such broad
terms. Did she realize that her family could also be classified as a
broken one? Laura was disturbed by this gap in Kay's reasoning,
her failure to apply the rules she recommended for the rest of
society to her own life. Perhaps she thought that her background,

her education, and her wealth made her immune to the ills suffered by less fortunate broken families.

Toward nine o'clock the stream of trick-or-treaters dwindled. Kay and Laura went into the kitchen to heat up some cider. Laura turned on the radio. The announcer was warning parents to check their children's trick-or-treat bags for apples with razors in them, suspicious-looking cakes and cookies that might have hallucinogens added to them, bits of wire, chocolate-covered rocks, and many other varieties of cruel treats that had already been reported to the radio station by listeners that evening. The announcer also warned about car thefts, arson, broken windows, and child molesters. Kay said it made her heartsick to think of all the innocent little children who were walking through the streets of the country's ghettos unaware of the dangers that surrounded them.

Bob was supposed to have returned the girls by eight thirty. Kay wondered what was keeping them. "I hope he doesn't make a habit of keeping them out this late," she said to Laura. "It increases the worry factor by about ten times."

She decided it was time to get dinner on the road, even though it was possible that Bob had taken the girls to a McDonald's. "How does some cold chicken salad sound to you?" Kay asked, taking a chicken she had roasted a few days before out of the refrigerator.

Laura went out to remove the sign Kay had pasted to the back gate requesting that all trick-or-treaters come to the front. On her way out, she tripped over the plastic gasoline container that Kay kept on the back porch for emergencies. It was lying on its side, with its top off, and the whole porch smelled of gasoline.

"Golly gee," Kay said when Laura told her. "We'll have to do something about that right away. This house would go up like a tinderbox if a match ever got near that porch."

Nathaniel didn't answer when Kay called him over the intercom. They went upstairs to find him. Even before they reached the Thinking Room, Laura could smell gasoline. Kay smelled it at the same time. She ran the rest of the way, threw open the door.

Nathaniel was lying face down among the cushions. The stench of gasoline was overpowering. Kay knelt down and turned him over. His mouth was open and his face was glistening, his hair damp. When she sat him up his head swung to the side, as if he were fast asleep. Kay began frantically to pat his chest. She put her ear against his chest and listened for a heartbeat. She grabbed one of his wrists and checked his pulse. While she was holding him that way, she turned to Laura and told her to call the doctor.

26

Not everyone went to the funeral. There was only room for six people in the grandmother's car, and Kay did not want to make it any more complicated than the grandmother had already made it.

Laura had agreed to stay behind with the girls. Dennis couldn't cope with funerals anyway.

The weather that afternoon was clear and very cold, making the trees and bushes in the backyard look like nothing but sharp edges and loose ends. While they were waiting for the grandmother to come and take them to the funeral parlor, Sarah gave her mother a large homemade postcard and told her to put it on the grave. The postcard was addressed to Chief Justice Bacchus, Mount Olympus, Ancient Greece:

> How are you? I am fine. This is my brother down here. His name is Nathaniel. He can't read yet so make sure he goes to

school. Please send him there SPECIAL DELIVERY. I don't want him to catch cold. He needs a house. I think he wears size three.

Love,

Priestess Sarah

P.S. Forget all those things I said in my other letter.

When Kay read the postcard she gagged. Sarah was puzzled, and for the first time in the four days since Nathaniel's death, upset. "What's so funny?" she asked.

"Nothing," Kay told her, her face concealed behind a large pink tissue. She handed the postcard to Bob, whose face caved in as he read it. He handed it to Martin, who shook his head and passed it on to Edith, who shut her eyes as if in prayer. Louella read it over Edith's shoulder. "Oh!" she cried, squeezing her handkerchief. She lowered her head. Her long, gold earrings quivered as she sobbed.

"Now now, Louella," Bob said, patting her back. "It can't be helped."

"What's so bad about my letter?" Sarah asked.

"Nothing," Kay assured her in a shaky voice. "It's a very kind letter, and very thoughtful. I'll make sure it gets there."

The grandmother honked twice and they filed out the door.

Laura had work to do. One of Bob's graduate students was coming around for Nathaniel's crib between four and five. She had to get his clothes laundered and pack them into boxes for Goodwill. Then there were his drawings, his books, his toys. She wanted to get it over with as soon as possible.

The university day-care center was only interested in undamaged toys, so Laura took down large black garbage bags and filled them with broken Leggo bricks, splintered blocks, toothless combs, clay balls, headless teddy bears, one-handed clocks, contraband chewing gum, both chewed and unchewed, pencils mutilated by dog teeth, half-eaten crayons, the cracked rocking horse, the broken stethoscope, the three-legged stuffed dog, the one-armed boy doll, the countless scribble drawings and bomber-plane studies, the clothes that were too tattered to give away, the worn-out shoes. When she had closed the bags and put them against the staircase, she sat down and looked at the higher, deeper open shelves with great sadness as she repeated to herself her new discovery: the true meaning of life.

Life was just the fending off of death, that was all it was. When you sat back and looked at all the ways man tried to convince himself that he was permanent, you couldn't help but be sad. Futile was the key word as Laura reviewed the world through her new glasses. Factories were futile, houses were futile, drawings were futile, men were futile, children were futile, and especially life—life was futile, and so were funerals. What the grandmother hoped to achieve by having an Episcopalian funeral, Laura could not imagine, any more than she could imagine what a graduate student in pursuit of a futile degree would want with a futile crib for his futile son, especially since the crib was broken.

Nathaniel's death had made her understand the meaning of life. But no matter how hollow her laughter, no matter how superior her attitude toward the ignorant masses of the world who refused to see life for what it was, she found herself unable to believe that Nathaniel himself would never return. As she brushed his clothes off the open shelves and divided the tiny shirts and socks and underpants and trousers into whites and coloreds, she tried to convince herself that the boy who had worn them was now being lowered into a grave. A sharp pain, a flashing light, and then she couldn't believe it anymore. She just couldn't believe it. It wasn't true.

She still had the books to go through, but suddenly she felt tired, too tired to look through books. She put the white laundry pile into a basket and took it upstairs.

Bess was busy making yarn dolls at the kitchen table. In the past two days she had made close to one hundred yarn dolls. They were simple dolls. You could make them in five or ten minutes and they looked like scarecrows. Bess had suffered severe withdrawal after Kay had had the fight with the grandmother about the grandmother's decision to allow the people in the funeral parlor to put cosmetics on Nathaniel's face. Edith had taught Bess how to make the yarn dolls as a form of therapy. Still, the yarn dolls, though they seemed to make her happy, were becoming something of an obsession. They were now decorating every piece of furniture in the living room, every counter in the kitchen, every bookshelf, every flowerpot. If you tried to move even one, Bess burst into tears.

Now she looked happy, with her red, blue, and yellow yarn spead out before her, her scissors, and her latest creations. As Laura passed her, she looked up and smiled. The trauma had done something to her smile. Her eyes were glazed over instead of sparkling. Instead of showing pleasure or joy when she opened her mouth, she only showed teeth. The smile of one of those people who handed out Jesus pamphlets downtown: steady, strong, toothy, and completely devoid of affection. Kay said it would pass.

Dennis was in yoga position in the living room. He said everyone had to come to terms with Nathaniel's death in his or her own way. After Laura had the nightmare about Bob and Kay discussing the merits of a novel called *Nathaniel* in a literature seminar, Dennis had invited her to meditate with him. He told her she would find inner peace, but she must not have been sitting the right way, because that was the night she had realized that life was futile. When she fell asleep later, she had the same terrible fight with Bob and Kay in the seminar room. For the second night running, she told them to stop treating Nathaniel as if he were a symbol for modern man because he was real, or had been real until his death. And Kay smiled in the same mischievous way for the second time and told her in a voice that reminded her of a high school English teacher that this was a misinterpretation on Laura's part, as the protagonist's self-concept was not sophisticated enough to cope with a complex concept like Being as opposed to Nonbeing at the age of four, even four and three quarters. "Let's get down to brass tacks and look at it as an accident."

The dream made Laura feel very guilty because in real life Kay and Bob had been nothing if not dignified. From the way they had held each other in silence and shouldered each other's tears, you would never have known that they hated each other. They were very noble. They made Laura realize what a failure she was when it came to tragedies, emergencies, and deaths: anything in which laughter was inappropriate and well-contained grief the rule.

Laura had not been able to cry until hours after everyone had gone to bed that first night. And once, she thought it was on the second day, she had looked into the darkened living room and seen how nobly Kay and Bob and Martin were behaving toward each other—how civilized, how far above the petty things of life—and for some terrible moments she had hated them.

Hot and cold. Her moments of hatred were followed by great feelings of love for all of them, gushing love, the kind that made you feel you would never be worthy of your love object, no matter what you did. Dennis said she was working something out.

She left the laundry basket at the foot of the stairs. She had a headache suddenly, and she was tired, too tired to do a dead boy's laundry. There wasn't any rush. She went and sat next to the bay window and watched the dead leaves sail about the backyard.

Sarah was standing next to the popsicle grave markers, and scratching the earth around them with a stick. She was frowning, as if there were something about the popsicles she didn't quite like. She looked as if she were on the verge of a decision, but then she looked up and saw Laura watching her and she changed her mind. She turned her face to the sky and started to laugh. She started to run. Singing on the top of her lungs, swinging her arms, hop-jumping with a nonchalance that Laura found suspect, she ran around the oak tree in circles and figure eights.

27

On Thanksgiving Day the newspaper ran an article on Kay and her television program. There was a great commotion in the kitchen. Edith read it to the girls. Dennis rushed out to buy up extra copies. For the first time since Nathaniel's death, Kay seemed happy and full of her old energy.

The article was out of date, though no one mentioned this, of course. The picture showed a younger, plumper, more confident Kay. Her unruly hair was tied back with a piece of yarn and she was wearing a dark turtleneck pullover. It was a three-quarters pose. She was smiling thoughtfully and her eyes were looking up above the photographer's lights.

> Kay Carpenter is an attractive mother of three who objects to being referred to that way.
> Though recently separated, she and her husband are on amicable terms, and although she describes him as a "dear,

dear man" who should be better known for his works on the
Civil Rights Movement and undercurrents in twentieth-century U.S. politics, she was interested to know why I wanted
to know about him at all.

Was it because, she suggested slyly, I wanted to judge her
in terms of her man?

The article went on to describe Kay's background, education, and
accomplishments.

Though strongly committed to her maternal duties, Kay
Carpenter (her married name, which she no longer uses, is
Pyle) has remained in touch with the gnawing concerns of
contemporary America.

She was particularly involved in the Civil Rights Movement, state prison-reform, acted as a go-between for students
and administration during the campus upheavals a few years
ago, and has more recently involved herself in the fight to
modernize the welfare system.

On the university committee circuit she has acquired a
reputation as a lovable maverick.

The daughter of a judge, she returned to her alma mater two
years ago to complete her studies toward a degree in sociology. She was awarded her Ph.D. last June and Little, Brown
is currently considering her thesis, *Children: The Voiceless
Minority*, for publication. *The Minerva Show*, which will be
launched in January and broadcast in the afternoon every
weekday, will be primarily a talk show, with periodic docu-
mentaries on, and filmed interviews with, a representative
sample of women in Massachusetts.

When asked as to the kind of audience she hoped the program would attract, she said she was aiming for a mixed bag
of housewives, mothers, teen-agers, and professionals—serious women in all walks of life who thought it worth their

while to spend an hour a day trying to come to grips with the problems of the sisterhood in twentieth-century America.

Kay Carpenter sees herself as a "moderate" in the spectrum of American feminist thinking. She believes, for example, that the family, in one of its multitudinous forms, should remain the basic unit of society, though tasks within the family should be divided more equitably.

She believes in "people's rights" rather than "women's rights," although she concedes that the injustices publicized by the recent rise in feminism are the ones most urgently in need of attention in the America of today.

Kay Carpenter comes across as a dedicated woman with a highly developed sense of social duty and a wry wit which serves as a safety valve when conversation is in danger of becoming too serious.

She is one of a new breed of American women who are coming out of the woodwork after years of relative obscurity as mothers and housewives to take their rightful place in the limelight.

What were her long-term ambitions, I asked? The question brought a quick smile to her lips. A career in journalism would make her "as snug as a bug in a rug," she said, but she wouldn't go so far as to turn down a government post in the right kind of administration.

Serious once again, she stressed that the most important thing was to have a platform from which to speak on behalf of "The Voiceless Minority" (Kay Carpenter's jargon for children, also referred to as "The Tiny Minority" in her articles on the subject) and "The Powerless Minority" (women who are economically dependent on men) and, if she were convinced that she could reach more people by standing on an overturned box in a street in Roxbury, she would do that tomorrow.

Kay Carpenter is going places, and the Large, Powerful Majority had better watch out.

Kay was in such good spirits that she was even civil to the grandmother when she came to pick up the girls to take them to put flowers on Nathaniel's grave. It had been Sarah's idea, and Kay had been worrying about it all week because she couldn't understand why Sarah insisted on being taken there with the grandmother. She had even gone so far as to arrange for Melissa to accompany them, just to make sure the grandmother didn't try any of her tricks. But now she smiled and stood at the door waving good-bye as if they were off to a picnic.

While Kay and Edith went to work on the vegetables for the Thanksgiving feast, they joked about what would happen to them all if Kay actually did get a government post in Washington one day, impossible as it might seem that Nixon would ever leave the Oval Office.

"Well," Kay said, "if it ever happens I certainly won't have any lack of trusted staffers!" She put down the electric beater and looked at Edith, Laura, Dennis, and Martin, suddenly serious. She had lost ten or fifteen pounds since Nathaniel's death. The fat had disappeared from her cheeks, giving her face a new shape, and a vulnerable expression, not unlike a man who has just shaved off his beard. "That's not a joke, you know," she said in a low voice. "I mean it." She reached for Edith's hand on one side and Martin's on the other, and smiling at the others with a very sad smile, asked, "We'll stick together, won't we?"

Everyone said of course. Edith went back to basting the turkey. Kay went back to her vegetables. Martin went back to grading papers at the kitchen table. There was a festive atmosphere. Dennis was exuberant when he and Laura went upstairs to measure the walls of Bob's former study. "You know," he said, clenching his fists with joy, "I really think we're going to do it." Laura was not quite sure what he was referring to.

MOTHER'S HELPER

He had just returned from a five-day hike in Maine and New Hampshire with one of Edith's friends from the college newspaper. As they crawled about the room with measuring tape, Dennis told her how he had thought this friend of Edith's was a real drag the previous spring, when Edith had brought him home for supper. That was when Edith had been having a pretty heavy relationship with him, about the time the relationship was breaking apart, so the tension had been pretty hairy, Dennis explained. But recently he had gotten to know the guy on his own terms. He was really not bad.

During the hike they had some heavy raps about Edith and the system and life in general, and it was incredible how similar their reactions to similar situations were sometimes.

They hadn't brought enough food. The last two days they had subsisted on berries and mountain stream water. The combination of hunger and exercise had induced a sort of mystical trance, Dennis told her, a sort of exuberant sense of harmony with the natural world. He described the sound of leaves underfoot and the rustling of mountain streams.

They were sitting cross-legged on the study floor, knee to knee. Without even knowing how it happened or bothering to take off all their clothes, Dennis and Laura made love, so softly that it almost seemed as if they had no bodies, as if they were two spirits touching, merging, and becoming one. She came and came as if it were the easiest thing in the world. She gave Dennis everything she had, and he rolled onto the floor smiling. While she wafted slowly downward toward the facts of life, he stared at the ceiling, still smiling. Laura had never seen him smile so much.

"You know," he said slowly, "when we ran out of food and we still had thirty miles to go before we hit civilization, I had this sort of feeling. As if I was on the verge of some really unbelievable discovery. There was this barrier, see, and beyond it was everything I've been looking for—harmony, self-understanding, purpose, everything. But I just couldn't get over that barrier, see. But I got this sort of feeling that before I could do anything important, anything creative, I would have to get over that barrier. Well, now I'm over it, Laura. And if it weren't for you, it would never have happened. With Edith it would have been too complicated. I guess that's because there are so many associations with her. The whole thing about our relationship. But with you it's so straightforward. I guess that's because you're less of a vital figure in my life, so I can really see the act as apart from a particular relationship." He tapped his fingers on the floor. "I really think I've done it, Laura. First the hike, then making love with you. I really think I've finally been able to transcend sex."

"Really?" Laura said, trying desperately not to sound hurt.

"Like," Dennis said, sitting up and looking around the room with wild eyes, "like, I've had this sort of knot inside me fucking up my mind, but now it's gone, man, gone! I mean, now I can think clearly. I can really see where I'm going and not feel weighed down by needs or urges or anything. I can look at your body and I don't feel even the smallest iota of lust. It's just incredible," Dennis said, shaking his head in wonderment. "At the moment you could be a statue or a piece of wood for all the desire I feel for your body. Like, I don't even feel the slightest hint or suggestion of horniness. I guess you could say that as far as bodies go, yours is pretty okay."

"Oh, it is, is it?" Laura shouted. She buttoned up her shirt and pulled up her pants and bolted out of the room. Dennis caught up with her at the top of the stairs.

"What are you getting so uptight about?" he asked.

"Because! You were talking about me as if I were an object!"

"Hey! I'm sorry!" Dennis said. "I didn't mean to hurt your feelings." He sat her down on the top step and pulled her down beside him. "I didn't mean that I thought your body was an object. I was just trying to communicate how it feels when you have gone over your quota of sex and you no longer have the urge to deal with anyone on a sexual level. I mean, in that respect you aren't an object. But making love with you on this particular day turned out to be some sort of spiritual stepping-stone, if you know what I mean." He paused, and looked into Laura's eyes, to see if he was getting through.

"So you think I'm a stepping-stone. Well, that's an object."

"How can I explain to you that what I mean is spiritual?" he said, punching the palm of his hand. "Don't you realize what you've done for me? Like, now I really feel I have it in me to forget my personal needs and go out and do something really great, like fighting evil, or joining the Vietcong." He clenched his fist and stared at the wall with inspiration. "Or fighting forest fires in the Rockies. I really think I could do it now. Or making some sort of symbolic act against oppression, like assassinating someone where it would make a difference, like Ian Smith or that Spanish Fascist pig Franco."

He shifted his inspired gaze from the wall to Laura. Laura could tell he was looking beyond her, at mountains and heroes and raging forest fires and hated dictators falling from their balconies, the victims of an idealist's bullets. She wondered briefly if Dennis had become unhinged.

After the ménage à trois she had never been able to look up to him as she had before. She thought of him as a friend she could trust though not respect. Even so, it was insulting to be nothing more than a spiritual stepping-stone. She thought she had given him more than that.

She felt cheated. She felt as if she had gone on a long and painful journey to the end of a rainbow, only to find that there had never been a pot of gold there and never would be. All that, for nothing. After all her pains to try and discover where Dennis was at, she was beginning to wonder if he was nowhere.

When Sarah returned from putting flowers on her brother's grave, she went outside and dug up Flighty Angel's grave, and discovered that instead of flying off to the Happy Hunting Grounds faster than the speed of sound, the kitten had remained in its box and disintegrated, in the process creating an enormous stink. She very nearly ruined the festive atmosphere. Kay tried to remind her of the times she specifically remembered talking with Sarah about the disintegration of animal flesh—when the dog they had had before Grosvenor died, for example, and the time they had found the frog under the front seat of the car, and the conversation they had had about the stuffed elk's head in Grampa's study. Sarah refused to believe her, and Kay finally ran out of the kitchen in tears. Laura, who felt guilty for her own part in the misunderstanding, told Sarah about souls. That made Sarah even angrier. She said souls were the stupidest sounding things she had ever heard about in her whole life.

When Kay had recovered and they had gathered around the dining room table to sing "We Gather Together to Ask the Lord's Blessing," Laura looked at Sarah's pinched little face and tried to imagine what was going on in her mind: the gates of Heaven crashing closed, the mountain of Olympus fading away like a mirage; the river sticks, the fish that was the father of all mankind, the guardian of the road to Heaven, the fireflies that were from the right hand of God; Zeus, Allah, Buddha, Thor; all traitors who who tricked her into thinking that men and animals did not rot in their graves but lived forever in better places than earth; all traitors, even though she was the one who had made her religion up in the first place. It was her own idea, her own weapon, except this time she had chosen to turn the weapon against herself.

The dining room table was groaning. In the center was the twenty pound turkey, which Martin now prepared to carve. He scraped the carving fork and carving knife against each other, hit them against the small plastic bucket he had placed on his head, sang "I'm the Barber of Seville! I'm the Barber of Seville! Figaro, Figaro, Figarooooo!" and then proceeded to do his Julia Child imitation.

The meat landed sometimes on the plates, sometimes on the

table. Edith picked up whatever fell, saying, "No one minds if I use my fingers, do they? It's all in the family!" She dished out the chestnut-raisin-and-barley stuffing, the hand-mashed Idahos, the organic marshmallow-and-sweet-potato casserole, and the Greek string beans with garlic and corn oil that came from the farming cooperative where Edith's brother had been working ever since he had dropped out of Princeton. Dennis dished out the goat-cheese soufflé and the honey-glazed turnips, and Melissa served the spinach-carrot-and-bean-curd salad. Laura was in charge of the homemade cranberry sauce, which was brittle instead of jellylike and burned in places because Edith had insisted on using honey instead of sugar, and the gravy, which was grainy, almost the consistency of wet sand. Laura supposed that this was because of the things they didn't do to the flour at Edith's brother's farming cooperative. Kay put herself in charge of pouring the wine—dandelion for the truly dedicated, and Almadén for those who, like herself, thought dandelion was a little sweet to have with food.

When all the food had been served and all glasses, including the girls' Kool-Aid tumblers, were full, Kay stood up to make a speech. She was wearing a brilliantly colored Mexican robe that made her look even paler than she was and accentuated the red rims around her eyes. She was smiling weakly, like an invalid who has just returned from his first taxing walk down the hospital corridor. "I want to take this opportunity to thank each and every one of you for the support you have given me during this month," she said in a trembling voice, her eyes watering. "Friends in need are friends indeed. I could not have coped without you. I feel the worst is over. We are strong, we are together, we are a close-knit team, and in one way or another we are going to set this country on fire."

She gulped down some tears. "This feast marks the beginning of a new era, a new era of peace and productivity in the Pyle-Carpenter household, of which I consider each and every one of you a member." She lifted her glass. "A new era is not complete without a toast, so here I go. To the family! To Bess and Sarah and Na . . . and to my beloved sisters and brothers—Edith, Laura, Melissa, Dennis, and Martin!"

"Hear! Hear!" Martin said. "And here's to Julia Child, without whose help and guidance this bird would never have reached its present sorry state!"

Everyone laughed, except for Melissa, who had burned her fingers on a casserole and was busy licking them, and Bess, who was slouched down in her chair and singing a lullaby in a soft voice to two of her yarn dolls, and Sarah, who was glaring at her plate.

When the others began to wolf down their food, Sarah held her fork loosely between her thumb and her forefinger, and dragged it from one side of her plate to the other, over the string beans and hand-mashed Idahos and turkey slices, until there were little lines of gravy running through the clumps of vegetables, and little roads of white and red potato over the meat. No one except Laura noticed her. They were shoveling down the food so fast you would have thought they had not eaten for days, except for Bess, of course, and Laura, who could not bring herself to eat the honey-glazed turnips or the sweet-potato casserole (she hated marshmallow) and was in severe pain because of the little jagged pieces of cranberry sauce that had stuck between her teeth (it was like peanut brittle). When Sarah realized that no one was going to ask her why she wasn't eating, she pressed her fork against the plate so that it made an unpleasant screeching sound. When that didn't work, she grabbed her fork with both hands and began to combine all her vegetables together with furious energy, her teeth clenched.

Still no one noticed her. She cut her meat into little pieces and added them to the vegetable mixture. Slowly the eating frenzy came to an end. People sat back and Edith went around the table offering seconds. Dennis opened another gallon of Almadén and poured it around. While Sarah whipped her Thanksgiving dinner into a mountain of froth, Kay told the table how wonderful it made her feel to have such a wonderful and supportive family.

"I wish there was some way to make it legal," Edith said.

"Make what legal?" Laura asked.

"Just this free and easy feeling of being part of a family, you know, no one being married or obligated or related but just being around in case you need them, really sticking up for each other through thick and thin without any jealousy or anything."

"I don't know if I agree with you, Edith," Kay said. "I have the funny feeling that the stamp of the law would taint things somehow. I veer more toward simple pledges of honor between groups of people."

"Well, I guess you're right in that if the basic feeling of love isn't there, there's nothing a legal contract can do to make it be there. I know it's silly, but I was just feeling so happy that I sort of longed for some piece of paper that would make sure that we all stuck together forever. I don't know. I guess that's sort of the basis of law, the way it all began, I mean."

Sarah picked up her fork and dropped it into the mountain of mashed food on her plate. She did it again, from higher up. And again. The fork went crashing into the side of the plate, and then, accompanied by a fragment of the plate, it bounced to the floor.

"That's no way to treat food," Melissa remarked nervously.

"Well, it's none of your business!" Sarah hissed.

"If my mother saw the way you treat your food sometimes, she would dip you in batter and fry you with the eggplants."

"You're so ignorant," Sarah said, "eggs don't come from plants, you stupid dyke!"

Melissa was now used to Sarah calling her a dyke, but it still upset Kay. Her lips quivered as she looked at her angry daughter. She was too weak to handle this sort of crisis these days, so Martin took over. He threw her a glazed turnip. "Hey, creep! Catch!" Sarah caught it, then changed her mind and let the turnip roll to the floor. "What's your problem, cousin?" Martin asked.

"You're not my cousin. You're not my family either."

"Oh, so you don't want me hanging around."

"I couldn't care less."

"So tell us your problem, babe."

Sarah took a slow look around the dining room table, then bared her teeth and said, "You're all going to rot in your graves!"

There was a silence, broken only by a crunching sound as Melissa bit into a piece of cranberry sauce. "I don't get you," Martin said. "Are you trying to make me lose my appetite, or are you trying to lose *your* appetite, or are you trying to tell me that I can't wait for Judgment Day in an ice cube after all?" Sarah giggled in spite of herself. "That's better! Now we can sit back in our graves and rot in peace."

"Don't you think you're being unduly gross about . . ." Melissa began, but Martin put out his hand to hush her. "Now then," he said, "let's give the funky lady on your right an apology, and this famous mother of yours a big smile, so we can get back to serious problems like digestion and relaxation."

"She's not famous," Sarah said.

"Ah! But she's going to be famous soon, isn't she? Isn't that what it said in the paper this morning?"

"The person who wrote that article is a liar."

"Why so, Lois Lane?"

"She isn't the mother of three children anymore," Sarah said. "She only has *two.*" Kay made a strange squeak and covered her mouth. "And it should have said that in the article, too," Sarah continued, pleased at the attention she was getting, "it should have said two children . . ." She looked at her mother defiantly and stuck out her chin, "and ONE SOUL."

"Oh!" Kay cried. She burst into tears. Edith and Melissa hopped out of their chairs and went scurrying for tissues. Soon Sarah began to cry, too. It was the pathetic wail of a child who has been abandoned by her parents in a foreign train station, or condemned to five years of hard labor for something as petty as being late for school. Melissa nervously waved a tissue in front of Sarah's nose. Sarah looked through it as if it weren't there. Martin came around the table and knelt beside her chair.

"Hey, hey, hey. This is supposed to be a joyous occasion." Martin patted her cheek and gave her a puppy smile.

"He's rotting, isn't he?" Sarah sobbed.

"Who? That cat, kitten, whatever his name was?"

"No," she said, "Nathaniel." She put her fist in her mouth and gnawed at it anxiously as Martin took a deep breath.

"Well, his *soul* isn't rotting. I'm sure his soul is having a fine time wafting around up there. And I bet he can see us down here, too. Don't you worry your little head about it."

"You believe in souls?" Sarah asked in a quavering voice.

"Of course I do! What do you think I am, a numbskull?"

"YOU'RE A LIAR!" Sarah hissed. "Souls are the stupidest sounding things I ever heard about in my whole life!"

"Hey, come on! Give me a chance!" Martin cried.

"THEN PROVE IT TO ME!" Sarah screamed.

"Hmmm. This may prove challenging, but I think I can do it. Let me get my thinking cap on." He reached for the bucket that he had worn to carve the turkey, put it on his head, put his finger over his mouth, and pretended to think deeply. "Let's see. The last soul I laid eyes on was back in sixty-four in a suburb of Houston. I was standing at this door, see . . ."

"Martin," Kay interrupted. She was barely able to speak. Her voice, normally so loud and clear, was nothing more than a hoarse whisper. "I really don't think it's fair for us to confuse the girl any longer. I think she could use a good dose of scientific truth." She closed her eyes, and sighed, as if it were a superhuman effort to continue. "I think this is a case of overstimulated creativity. We have all been guilty at one time or another of"—she blew her nose —"of stoking the fire. I think we have a mind-reality problem here and should make a point of not making it worse than it already is. I can't help thinking that if Sarah hadn't scared him so, then perhaps . . ." Her lips quivered. ". . . perhaps . . ." She caught her breath and dabbed her nose with a tissue, then turned to Sarah and said in a firmer voice, "You were asking about Nathaniel."

Sarah gave her a sullen glance and said nothing.

"As far as we know," Kay said, trying to sound even-minded, "Nathaniel is right where we left him and where you went with your grandmother today, in the grave next to his grandfather and his granduncles and his great-great-grandmother." Sarah shrugged her shoulders. "As far as souls are concerned, well, it is a difficult question to answer truthfully. You see, we have no real way of scientifically proving the existence or nonexistence of souls, no more than we can scientifically prove the existence of heaven. Or God for that matter."

"What do you mean, or God for that matter," Sarah snapped.

Kay let out a shaky sigh. "What I mean is that we can't be sure if there is a God or not."

"I thought you said you believed in God."

"In a way I do, Sarah, yes."

"So why aren't you sure he exists?"

"I just don't know," she said heavily. "I just can't bring myself to be one hundred percent certain about something that no scientific tool has ever been able to determine or detect, Sarah. It's a difficult problem. And I assure you, Sarah, it is one that we all have to face up to sooner or later."

"Well, it's not fair!" Sarah cried angrily.

"Sometimes life," Kay gasped, putting her hand to her forehead as if to fend off a fainting fit, "isn't fair."

"I thought you said I could make up my own mind about God."

"Why, of course, Sarah, of course you can."

"THEN WHY ARE YOU TELLING ME ALL THESE LIES?" She took one of Bess's yarn dolls from the basket behind her chair and threw it into the sweet-potato casserole, then stomped to the door. "It's all your fault," she said, turning around. "And I WISH YOU ALL WERE DEAD." The door slammed.

MOTHER'S HELPER

They listened to her run down the stairs to Children's Paradise. There was another long, uncomfortable silence. Only Bess seemed unconcerned. She had rescued her doll from the casserole, and was brushing it off, saying "Poor baby, you've had a hard day, haven't you? It's lots of hot liquids and a beddy-bye for you!" She rocked it back and forth and sang it a French ballad her mother had taught her long ago.

Edith jumped to her feet. "I don't know about you, folks," she said, "but I think we should get the show on the road and hustle out some dessert!"

Laura, Melissa, and Dennis jumped to attention. While Martin held Kay's hand and Kay sobbed on his shoulder, Laura cleared the table and put the dirty dishes into the dishwasher; Edith set the table for dessert; Melissa arranged the pumpkin-and-molasses wholemeal-crusted pie, nuts, fruits, and cheeses on a long wooden board; Dennis carefully separated the biodegradable garbage from the nonbiodegradable garbage and placed the empty Almadén bottles in a sink full of water. You had to get the labels off before sending them to the recycling plant.

Bess lifted a handful of yarn dolls from what had formerly been a cat basket (now it was a "doll hospital") and arranged them on Sarah's chair. Bess had become a nurse. She said that when she grew up she was going to go to China and adopt at least one thousand and ninety starving children, and bring them to a beautiful hospital that was surrounded by beaches and flowers, and make sure that they were happy until they were twelve or thirteen, and then, if they wanted to, she would let them get married. Bess herself was never going to get married. Boys made her sick to her stomach, she told Laura.

While Edith sliced the pumpkin-and-molasses pie (she was having trouble cutting through the wholemeal crust), Dennis lit the three Christmas candles in the middle of the table. It was dark outside. The windows in the dining room rattled to the rhythm of the wind, making the candlelit table seem cozier than it was, and the faces softer. Conversation centered on the recent probe into the university's investment policies. Martin had had an extremely curious conversation with the dean of students on the subject only two days before that led him to believe that something fishy was indeed going on. While Edith and Kay discussed the sinister implications of this conversation, and Laura saw to the coffee, Dennis took a small plastic bag of grass out of his knapsack, some papers, and a joint-making machine. A few days earlier, Kay had decided that over the Thanksgiving weekend she would give marijuana a try.

Kay had never smoked before, partly, she said, because she was an "old fogey," but also because of the stories she had heard about how it caused brain damage, genetic mutations, psychological withdrawal symptoms, and impaired your distance perception if you were driving. But someone at the network had given her a pamphlet purporting that most of these stories were propaganda put out by the CIA. Some of her staidest friends from college days were regular smokers these days. It was time for her to see for herself.

It wasn't that she wanted to *escape* reality, she explained to Melissa as she poured out the coffee. Rather, she wanted to transcend it for a while and then return to her sober state, wiser for the experience, and better equipped to deal with the issues of the moment. No mind bending. She didn't think she was up to dealing with hallucinations or distortions of her environment. Dennis assured her that marijuana would not bend her mind any more than the glass of Almadén sitting in front of her. Especially not the joint he had just finished rolling. For later in the evening he had squirreled away some Colombian, but this stuff was from the marijuana plant he was growing in his closet. Fine, heady, but weak, he said. He used it primarily to take the edge off the morning gloom.

He lit the joint and then passed it along to Edith, who hogged it for about five minutes, as was her wont. Kay was next. Before she took the joint from Edith's hand, she informed Dennis that she had placed the family doctor's home phone number next to the telephone, just to be on the safe side. Dennis assured her that it was almost impossible to have a bad trip on marijuana that had been grown in a closet in Massachusetts in the middle of winter. Still, Kay insisted on telling him where she kept the Valium in the bathroom cabinet.

Dennis patiently instructed Kay how to inhale. She coughed the first two times but the third time she was able to hold it in for about ten seconds. "It smells very sweet," she said as she passed it on to Melissa, "is that normal for all kinds of hash?"

In his clean-cut hippy voice, Dennis explained that hash and marijuana were not the same thing. He went on to describe the difference between homegrown grass and South American grass, mescaline and peyote, hash and opium, cocaine and speed. He explained how heroin and barbiturates were the only drugs you had to stay away from, and then repeated the other favorite maxims of college drug lore. How hallucinogens, if used properly, could radically change your outlook on life in an extremely positive way. How marijuana caused so much less damage than alcohol. His voice reminded Laura of the voice the Ken doll would have if the Ken doll could speak. Or a NASA physicist describing the nature of moon dust to a visiting third grade class. And then, as he took a second drag from the joint, held his breath, and exhaled with a short, stoned chuckle: the Marlboro Man. The educated lumberjack relaxing after a long day at the foot of the Rockies, the cowboy with a college education who finds solace in wide open spaces while waiting for the revolution to start itself back East.

Kay listened carefully to what Dennis said. She made a note to get that book by Carlos Castaneda. Her second drag induced a terrible coughing fit, but on the third and the fourth rounds she inhaled without incident. While Dennis went through the roach-clip routine, she stared into her coffee cup as if to assess her high. Finally she said, "I don't feel anything."

"That's natural," Dennis said. "It takes most people a few times before they get the hang of it. But this Colombian I have stashed away is guaranteed to blow anyone away."

At Edith's suggestion they retired to the living room, where they sat cross-legged on the floor so as not to disturb the yarn dolls Bess had arranged on the couch and the easy chairs. They all knew from experience that, if they did, there would be a scene. Kay didn't look like she needed another scene. Edith put a stack of records on the stereo. The first to fall was the Rolling Stones. Full blast. Dennis laboriously rolled a joint of his Colombian, and they passed it around.

It was the kind of marijuana that made you feel as if you were balancing a cement block on your head, and brought out the sound of the bass guitar so thoroughly that it blotted out all lighter, finer sounds. Kay solemnly tested out her sensations to make sure they were all normal: the heightened awareness of sound and light, the dizzy feeling, the pleasant tickle in your chest, the sensuous attitude toward the future. She suffered a brief fright when Bess came into the living room to say good night to her dolls. Dennis assured her that this was natural, too. Paranoia was often a side effect of being stoned, he explained.

Bess moved slowly down the couch, kissing each doll. Martin turned down the stereo and went across the room to admire them. "What are their names?" he asked.

"Hatty," she said.

"But what about this one?"

"Hatty," Bess said.

"You mean they're all called Hatty?"

Bess nodded. On the other side of the room, Dennis guffawed. Bess looked puzzled. "Hey," Martin said, "that's pretty cool to have all your dolls with the same name." He started laughing, too, in the soft, secretive way stoned people laugh when they think something is absurd. Bess looked puzzled. She swept up all her dolls. "I'm taking them downstairs," she said. "You smell funny. There's too much smoke in here."

MOTHER'S HELPER

Martin turned off the overhead light, making the room look softer and more yellow. The only light came from a small lamp with a dark orange lampshade. Mick Jagger was superseded by an old Peter, Paul & Mary. They sat back on the cushions Edith had brought down from Kay's study, passing around joint after joint. Kay and Martin took turns leaning on each other's shoulders, Edith and Melissa had their heads on the same pillow and were caressing each other's arms, Dennis and Laura crouched beside them. Every once in a while, Dennis looked at Laura, shook his head appreciatively, and with a smile that disturbed her because it reminded her of Burt Reynolds, commented on the heaviness of his Colombian grass.

Simon and Garfunkel. Edith drew up her knees as she stared at the ceiling and repeated her pet theory about sexual taboos being holdovers from the Middle Ages. Sex was the only way two people could express themselves to each other in a completely honest and open way. Sex created a bond of love and understanding. Physical love vibrations, she called them. If you couldn't have a contract to bind people into blood-relation-free families, then you had to have physical love vibrations, and all possible combinations. Ideally, everyone should make love with everyone. If everyone had physical love vibrations with everyone else, then the "family" in question would be so interlocked that it would never dissolve.

It was a theory that made Laura wonder what Edith had talked about before becoming liberated from the possessive phase of her relationship with Dennis. It also puzzled her to see how eager Edith was to establish a network of commitments in the Pyle household while at the same time denying all commitments to Dennis in particular. There seemed to be a hole in the reasoning, but Laura did not bring this up because she didn't want anyone accusing her of being reactionary or spoiling the mood.

Making love was so much groovier when you were high, Edith continued. Edith suggested that they have an orgy.

Kay rubbed her head against Martin's shoulder and considered

Edith's proposal as if it were something as banal as a request for a paper extension. "You really think it would strengthen our commitments to each other," she said.

"Right, like getting rid of our inhibitions and then being able to treat each other honestly and like human beings instead of according to the dictates of an outmoded societal code. You know, all the roles they assign you. Mother, father, lover, fiancé, friend. It's all a load of bullshit, like I mean empty role-playing, because basically we're all people with animal and emotional needs and we should be able to relate to each other as equal human beings on all levels, including sexually."

Kay said she followed her line of reasoning and basically agreed with it, but to Laura's relief, she said she thought she had had enough new experiences for one day. It was an interesting proposal and she would think it over. Perhaps, if everyone felt the same as Edith, they could have an orgy over Christmas vacation.

"Now I don't want to put a damper on you younger people's fun," she added apologetically. "You go ahead and do whatever you like and forget about the momentary foibles of an old fogey like me."

Creedence Clearwater. Edith got up to do a dance. Eyes closed, she bounded around the living room in huge leaps, throwing her head and her amazing head of golden electric hair backward and forward, in her hands an imaginary electric guitar. Her dance was amazingly graceful in parts and amazingly clumsy in others. She was wearing her blue-and-white striped overalls and her usual flannel shirt. After one song she was covered in sweat, so she undid her flannel shirt and continued dancing in just her overalls.

Creedence Clearwater was monotonous after a while. Edith made the stereo skip to the middle of the next record. The Rolling Stones again. "Wild Horses." She bent down and pulled Melissa to her feet. Hugging each other tightly, eyes closed, Melissa's mouth clamped shut in the usual thin, crooked line, Edith's mouth hanging open in the usual abandoned manner, they moved around the room in little box steps. Laura knew from Dennis that they had been sleeping together on and off for the past three weeks or so, but the only evidence Laura had seen of this until now were the special smiles, the hand-squeezing, and the occasional intense eye contact that sent Melissa off balance but that Edith could sustain indefinitely. As Laura only knew too well.

This was the first time they had embraced in public. They were holding each other tight and nuzzling each other's necks. Dennis nudged Laura. Grinning his silliest grin, he pointed at Melissa's hands, which were squeezing Edith's ass and kneading it as if it were a loaf of bread. Laura did not see what Dennis thought was so funny about it. Nor did she understand his helpless belly laughs when Edith and Melissa began to kiss each other passionately, or the way he rolled on the floor clutching his stomach when they fell on the couch.

"Ahem! Ahem!" Sarah was standing in the doorway. She was wearing a long, off-white nightgown. Her arms were hanging limply at her sides and she was angry.

Kay opened her mouth to say something, but she had a coughing fit instead. So Martin took over. "Hey, what's happening?" he asked. "Are you feeling better?"

"No," Sarah said.

"Gee, that's terrible," Martin said. "Anything we can do for you to make you feel better?"

"No." She looked around the room suspiciously. "What are you doing in here?"

"Just relaxing after that groovy meal, that's all."

"You never relaxed like this in here before."

"Gee, Sarah, we're usually too busy to do any relaxing at all. I guess this is an exception."

"Why is there so much smoke in here?"

"We were doing a bit of smoking a little while back."

Sarah rubbed her eyes angrily. "What are Edith and Melissa doing on the couch?"

"Well, to me it looks like they're just playing friendly happy puppy games," Martin said with a smile.

"It doesn't look that way to me."

"Gee, Sarah, you look so glum that if I didn't know where you've been all night I would say you'd just seen about nine hundred and fifty ghosts."

Sarah dropped her head. "You don't care about him, do you?" she moaned. "You just care about yourselves. Well, you know what I think?" she looked up and screamed. "I THINK YOU'RE ALL WHORES!" She slammed the door and ran downstairs.

Kay stopped coughing and stared at her feet with a childish frown. Then Dennis giggled. Looking at Dennis with a mischievous grin that did not befit her, Kay began to giggle, too. Dennis lit up another joint and passed it to Kay. Kay tried to hold in her smoke but she started to giggle again and the smoke came pouring out in one great gasp of helpless laughter. Dennis pointed at Edith and Melissa, who were thrashing about the couch. Kay, Martin, and Dennis looked at each other and laughed. Laura felt as if someone were tightening a metal band around her head.

There was something wrong with the stereo. It turned itself off in the middle of a song. Laura closed her eyes. Wet kissing sounds alternated with ripples of laughter. Laura couldn't stand it anymore. She walked through the front hallway into the dining room. The Christmas candles were still burning. The table was covered with empty coffee cups, nutshells, orange peels, bits of cheese, and large hunks of the pumpkin pie's wholemeal crust, which no one had been able to eat. Bess had arranged some of her dolls on the empty chairs and the Christmas candles cast them in an eerie light.

She opened the door to Children's Paradise, walked down the dark stairs. The only light came from the purple plant-lights which they still kept on even though Nathaniel had broken the last of the flowerpots months before. Tripping over a book and what felt like a child's alarm clock, Laura went to Sarah's bedside, patted her lightly on the back, and told her not to cry. Sarah was choking on her tears. Her back was shaking, as if her anger were too much for her small frame to bear.

Laura wanted to tell her that she understood what it felt like to discover there was probably no God, that when you died you probably went nowhere. She knew how it felt when you took enormous pains to construct an elaborate explanation for life and then discovered it was all wrong because you had based it on wishful thinking or lies. She wanted to tell Sarah that she knew how terrible it was to walk into a living room late at night and see your parents and your parents' friends making fools of themselves. It had happened to Laura often as a child. It had not been unusual to find men lying on the floor with their heads under couches on mornings after parties, or see fifteen men in tuxedos jump off a first floor balcony into the sea, or people pouring cheap champagne on other people's heads. She wanted to explain to Sarah how alike the two of them were under their shells. But empathy was a clumsy emotion, and Laura could not bring herself to tell Sarah anything.

"After all the prayers I wasted, and all the letters I wrote to the Chief Justice, and all the ceremonies I had for him, and everything else I did to make sure he was happy there, it's just not fair." Sarah began to sob again. Laura patted her on the back. She waited for the hiccuping and quivering to come to an end, and then she said, "Don't worry. I know how you feel. I'm ready to help you and I want you to know that no matter what happens, I'm your friend."

Sarah sat up abruptly. Her face was gray and purple in the purple light, and her lips were shaky and black. "You are not my friend," she hissed. "You're worse than all the others put together. You lied to me. You told me Flicka would go to Happy Hunting Grounds, and he didn't. And you knew it, too. You were just trying to oppress me. You're a warmonger. I didn't think you'd be so mean to do that to us, but you did. You killed my brother. And I know how." Breathing deep and fast, her hair wild, she stared at Laura defiantly. Laura was too stunned to say a thing.

Sarah dived under her covers, groped around for something,

found it, and crawled down to the end of the bed, where the light from the plant light was strongest. There was something in her hand the size of a calculator. She pressed it.

And then, somewhere in the central playing area, there was a round of machine-gun fire, an explosion, a grenade whistling through the air, a plane diving to earth, a siren, the steady drone of a powerful machine, the familiar red glow of the cockpit as the tank rolled past the column and into view.

"That's how you killed him, you warmonger murderer. I should have known from the very first day."

"Give me that!" Laura lunged across the bed but Sarah was too quick for her. She darted into the central playing area. Laura ran after her. She caught her by the end of her nightgown. There was a ripping sound as Sarah hopped over the tank into the blackness beyond the column. "You think you can murder me, but you can't! I'm too fast for you. I'm not dumb like Nathaniel." Laura chased her around the column. She grabbed Sarah by the waist. But she broke away screaming "Murder! Murder!" at the top of her lungs. The tank continued its erratic course across the floor. The red light glowed, the gun revolved, the sounds of battle continued.

"Murder! Murder!" Around the column again and again, changing direction every few times, until Sarah tripped over the child's clock. She went flying over the tank and onto the floor. Laura pinned her to the ground. "Help!" Sarah screamed. "Murder!" Laura gripped her shoulders and shook her as hard as she could.

"Why are you doing this to me, Sarah?" She was shaking her so hard that Sarah's teeth were chattering. "Why are you trying to do me in? You know I didn't kill your brother! You know it! Why are you trying to put the blame on me?"

"You're a warmonger!" Sarah screamed.

Laura shook her even harder. She felt a thrill, an electric current, as she did so. "Don't you realize I'm the only real friend you have in the world?"

"Don't hurt me! I have a fever!"

"Don't you realize that I'm the only one who really cares about you around here and understands you? You need me! You need someone in this house who can be on your side against the rest of them! Don't you understand? I'm your *friend!*"

Sarah stopped struggling. She turned her head to one side and began to cry very softly. She was saying something. Then she cried a little harder. Laura took one of her hands from Sarah's shoulders and pushed the hair away from Sarah's face. "What's wrong, Sarah? Tell me what's wrong."

"I miss him," she said.

The light clicked on. Looking behind her, Laura saw Kay staring at her from the top of the stairs. Then Dennis, Martin, Edith, and Melissa crowding behind her, all aghast at the scene below them. Sarah sat up suddenly. "She's trying to murder me!" she screamed. She was trembling and sobbing and pale, pale white. Her hair was wild and the front of her nightgown was torn. The expression in Kay's bloodshot eyes was one of horror. She was not looking at Laura anymore but beyond her, at the tank, which rolled out from behind the club cubicle into the central playing area. With a clatter of gunfire, an explosion, a final blast of siren, it rolled into the open shelf that marked the beginning of Bess's bedroom cubicle, where it tried to continue, without success.

28

When Laura woke up the next day in Bob Pyle's former study, she felt very happy without knowing why. When she remembered what had happened the night before she felt embarrassed, but happy nonetheless. Sarah's accusations, Kay's ominous decision not to talk about It until the next day, Edith's reproaches ("After all the things she's done for you," she had said), the fact that to an outsider it would seem as if she had been trying to beat Sarah up instead of trying to convince her that she was her friend. And the tank—the tank was especially embarrassing, but Laura didn't care. It had been worth it. She had gotten through to Sarah, shaken it out of her. She had shaken through the barrier and reached the real Sarah underneath: the dreamer, the fighter, the Sarah who still had a heart.

If everyone was going to run around making love with everyone else as Edith suggested, then they had to be able to touch each other in anger, too. Laura had gotten angry at Sarah, and shaken her, and told her the truth—that she was her friend, that she was on her side, that sometimes she understood her better than her own mother (although she hadn't put it that strongly). That she was probably the only person in the world who knew what kind of person was hiding behind that bratty facade, because she and Sarah were so much alike. And if she hadn't said that in those precise words, she had said it by shaking her. Physical vibrations, not of tenderness but of anger, which Laura now decided was the most intense form of love.

Looking outside, Laura saw that it was snowing. It was the first snow of the year and the drifts were already a foot or two deep. She put on her heavy flannel shirt and her blue-and-white overalls that she had bought during the summer in order to look like Edith, and went downstairs with her head high. She was ready for the inevitable Family Council meeting. If they banned her, she would make an eloquent final statement, explaining her own position and pointing out everyone else's faults. She would shake their hands, take Sarah aside for a private talk, and make arrangements to meet with her later in the week and every Friday afternoon thereafter. Then she would put on her coat, tell them that she was sorry it had to happen this way, and leave through the front door.

If they didn't ban her, she would consent to stay on, but not until they had thoroughly discussed the terrible pressure Kay's new life-style was putting on Sarah—not to mention Bess—and come up with reasonable suggestions for the future so that no more damage would be done.

She had been the silent observer too long. It was time for her to speak out. She strutted into the kitchen ready for anything.

As she turned the corner into the kitchen, a conversation came to an end. Edith, Melissa, Martin, and Kay turned around and greeted her with steady, almost glassy smiles, the kind of smiles people wear when they are waiting for an amateur photographer to finish adjusting his lens.

"Good morning!" Kay cried. "Did you see the lovely snow! Help yourself to some lovely bacon and eggs, or some lovely leftovers!" Laura filled the kettle with water and put it on the stove. As she did so Martin got up and stretched. "I guess I'd better start shoveling the blizzard off the path," he said. Edith jumped to her feet. "Well, I'm off now!" Without explaining where she was off to, she turned to Laura and asked, "Do you need anything?"

Laura said no.

"Did you know it's noon already?" Kay said in a loud, cheerful voice. "Gee, what I would give to be able to sleep until noon these days." Laura made her cup of instant coffee and brought it over to the kitchen table. There was a fire raging in the fireplace. Outside Sarah was making a snowman, angrily. She had made the basic snowman shape and now was trying to add arms to the torso, but they kept falling off. Each time they fell off Sarah kicked it.

"How do you like the fire?" Kay asked.

Laura said she thought it was very nice.

"We had a fire going the first day you ever worked here, didn't we?"

Laura said yes.

Kay chuckled. "Funny, isn't it."

Laura agreed. She walked over to the bulletin board, her head less high. She looked for some announcement of an emergency Family Council meeting to discuss her status but she could not find anything on the bulletin board that she had not already read a hundred times.

Melissa was sitting with her arms crossed, staring at the table. When she did that she looked ten years old. It was as if she were afraid to look Laura in the eyes. Laura suddenly felt sorry she had ignored her, had even dismissed her as a loudmouth, and had even ganged up on her with the children. When she rose to make her second cup of coffee, she asked Melissa if she would like one, too. Melissa stood up, suddenly very nervous, mumbled something about the slave-labor typing she had to do, and left the room.

Kay was trying to interest Bess in origami, but Bess wasn't

interested. Bess was busy attaching tinsel to lines of Scotch tape, which she then attached to the heads of her yarn dolls to serve as hair. She showed little interest in the creases and folds Kay was making in the little squares of thin red and blue paper and did not seem at all surprised when they turned into horses and cranes. "Oh, Bess," Kay kept saying, "I do wish you would look and see how I do this! It's such fun!" And each time Bess would answer, "Just a minute."

Laura looked out of the window and watched Sarah throw the snowman's head across the yard and stamp on top of it until it was a small white mound covered with bumpy boot prints. She stomped onto the porch and into the kitchen. When Laura smiled at her, she scowled. She threw her coat and boots on the kitchen floor and stomped down the stairs to Children's Paradise.

"Gee," Kay said, looking up from a half-made crane, "I'd be awfully grateful if someone would give the bathrooms a quick vacuum!" Laura got the vacuum cleaner out of the closet and lugged it up the stairs.

On her way from the blue bathroom to the green bathroom Laura passed Dennis, who was crouching outside the Thinking Room studying a set of directions. Dennis was turning the Thinking Room into a sauna. Due to the circumstances of Nathaniel's death, the girls had decided that they could do longer think there. Kay had bought a do-it-yourself sauna kit from Sears Roebuck. Two or three other closets, as well as the unutilized space below the stairs to Children's Paradise, were being considered for the new Thinking Room.

Now Dennis was trying to figure out what paneling went where and how the heating unit could be fitted in. His face was wrinkled in thought. There was a pencil behind his ear. As she passed him, Laura tapped him on the shoulder. "How are you feeling today?" He nodded in his usual fashion, his eyes still on the set of directions, then gave her a quick, reproachful look.

"Fine."

She went to vacuum the green bathroom. It was covered with Band-Aids and condoms and cat litter as usual. While she vacuumed she thought about the strange way everyone was treating her. As she carried the vacuum cleaner down the stairs, she decided it could not go on any longer. She couldn't take it.

Kay was still trying to interest Bess in origami. "Bess dear," she was saying, "it's not that I don't want you making dolls or playing with them or making believe you are running a hospital. Not at all! I only felt that the game is becoming a bit obsessive, that's all! And I thought origami would be a good way to broaden your horizons."

Bess looked at her mother suspiciously, as if broadening one's horizons were a dangerous sport in which ninety percent of the participants broke their necks.

Laura had worked out what she was going to say to Kay. "Kay," she was going to say, "I have the feeling that you have made up your mind as to what happened last night without even asking me for my side of the story. I respect you and your ideas very much, but in this instance I am afraid that I do not approve of your tactics. I am sure, for example, that you do not know when or why I bought that tank. Or that Nathaniel did not show the slightest interest in playing with it. Yes, I agree that as toys go it is a fairly disgusting toy, but I was merely reacting against what I felt at the time was the way you were ruining the children's harmless games of imagination by trying to make the games reflect your own liberal and feminist morality. I would be happy to air my feelings on this subject with you at greater length whenever you feel you have the time."

But when Kay looked up and gave her a warm, almost glassy smile, she forgot her speech. All she said was, "I'd like to apologize about that tank."

Kay laughed and returned to her folds and creases. "Come, come, now. There's no need to apologize."

"I know you must think I was encouraging Nathaniel all along to play war games, but actually Nathaniel didn't even like . . ."

Kay put her hand over Laura's mouth. "Please. Let's forget about the whole thing, Laura. The sooner we all do the better. What's done is done."

"But I only wanted to explain the whole thing to you so you don't misunderstand what was going on when you came down . . ."

Kay pressed Laura's hand and looked tearfully into her eyes. "Laura! We *understand.*" A glassy stare. A fixed smile. A silence. Laura tried to grasp what they had understood. It made her uneasy to think that Kay had taken time out to think about her, understand her, and probably discuss her with other people who had also taken time out to think about her.

"As a matter of fact," Kay said, still pressing Laura's hand, "Sarah here has something to say to you. Sarah?"

Sarah was hunched over the fire. Next to her was a cardboard box full of papers which seemed to all have something to do with Sarah's former club. She was throwing them one by one into the fire. Her eyes were full of hate and anger. She spat out her words.

"I'm sorry!"

"And I want to . . ." Kay prompted.

"And I want to make up for all the cruel things I said to you," she recited in a loud voice.

"So could we . . ." Kay prompted again.

"So could we do something together this morning," Sarah yelled, throwing a large pile of papers into the fire. Sparks flew into the air. "And be friends again like we used to be!"

"How about some butterscotch fudge?" Kay suggested.

"I don't *like* butterscotch fudge."

"Then how about a nice spice cake?"

"I don't *like* spice cake."

"Chocolate, then." Sarah glared into the fire and shrugged her shoulders. Kay rummaged through the drawers, found a brush, brushed her hair into a tight ponytail, and announced that she would be working in her study if anyone needed anything. "Gee,

Laura, I really appreciate this." Laura did not know what she was referring to. Kay winked as she turned toward the stairs. She gave Laura a special smile, a new smile that Laura had never been subjected to before, a fixed, toothy smile that made Laura feel as if she were an escaped convict who was known to be dangerous or an Alsatian watchdog who had been trained to understand directions only in German.

Making a cake with Sarah usually meant that Laura did the work and Sarah licked the spoons, beaters, and bowls when she was done. Laura didn't mind this, as she enjoyed making cakes. When she made a cake without licking any bowls or spoons she felt very thin. She leafed through the *Joy of Cooking* until she came to her favorite recipe for chocolate cake. She got the ingredients out of the refrigerator and the cupboards. Under Sarah's curiously hostile gaze, she chopped the cold butter into small pieces and began to blend in the sugar. Now that Kay was gone, Laura expected Sarah to change and start acting like her friend.

Sarah was sitting on the counter over the dishwasher, next to the sink. "Give me that," she said when Laura was halfway through blending the sugar and butter. She grabbed the bowl and started hacking at it with the fork. When Laura tried to look over her shoulder, she covered it with her left arm. "Are you sure you blended it the right way?" Laura asked. "Don't you want me to check?"

"It's none of your business," Sarah snapped. "Just give me the eggs."

Laura gave her the eggs. Casting sideways glances, Sarah cracked the first egg into the bowl. Very slowly. She threw the empty shells over her shoulder. "Oops! Missed the garbage can!"

"Throw the eggshells into the Disposall."

Sarah cracked the second egg and threw the shells over her shoulder. They landed next to the other shells on the floor. "Oops, missed again." She reached for a third egg.

"You only need two eggs," Laura reminded her.

With an arch smile, Sarah cracked a third egg into the bowl, then a fourth and a fifth. Why was she acting this way? Why did she want to hurt her only friend? Laura decided not to show that her feelings were hurt. "I hope you're going to pick up those eggshells," she said in a cool, stern voice.

"That's what you think," Sarah said.

"We'll see about that," Laura said. She realized that she did not sound as cool or as stern as she would have liked.

"Now what?"

Laura handed her the flour. "Blend those eggs with the butter and sugar mixture, then sift two cups of this flour with one teaspoon of baking powder, one of salt, and one half of soda. I'll tell you again if you want me to." With a snakelike smile, Sarah poured a large and indeterminate amount of flour over the unblended butter and sugar, and unbeaten eggs. She then free-poured the salt, added a dash of baking powder instead of a teaspoon, added water instead of milk, and added the cocoa with such violence that the air filled with brown dust.

"Give me the baking pan!" she snapped.

"Are you sure you don't want to mix it together before you bake it?" Laura asked.

Grabbing the fork from the sink, Sarah whipped the contents of the bowl with five violent strokes, sending the flour and cocoa and a thin brown liquid sloshing everywhere.

Then she grabbed the large rectangular baking pan Laura had gotten out of the cupboard and poured the contents of the bowl into it.

At that Laura lost her temper. It was not the clean, cathartic anger of the previous night. Something snapped inside her head, like a wire that has been pulled too far, or a floor board that has been danced on one time too many, or a roof that has had to endure more rainstorms than it was made for.

"Do you really want me to bake that?" Laura shouted.

"Yes!"

"Well, I hope you're prepared to eat the whole thing all by yourself! You know why?"

"Why?"

"Because it's going to taste like dog food!"

"How do you know?"

"Because I know better than you! I'm a grown woman! I've made thousands of cakes in my life and I can tell you right now that this is going to taste like a barrel of shit."

"That's a lie," Sarah said. "You're not a grown woman, you're an immature adolescent."

"Who says?"

"My mother says." Sarah looked at her triumphantly.

"Oh, she does, does she?"

"Yeah. And do you know what else she says? She says you're not ready for adult responsibilities."

Laura calmly put the cake pan into the oven. "How interesting," she said with a smile.

"Edith said Mommy should sue you for neggel-gence," Sarah continued, "but Mommy said she couldn't do that. And you know why? Because *she* says you didn't know what you were doing, because *you* are sort of *disturbed.*"

Laura bent down to pick up the eggshells Sarah had thrown on the floor. She had never gotten used to the new biodegradable, nonbiodegradable garbage system, so she absentmindedly threw them into the large garbage can that was exclusively for nonbiodegradable refuse. Underneath the bacon wrappings and soup cans, she saw the tank.

"And you know what Mommy said to Martin this morning?" Sarah continued, pleased at the effect she was having on Laura, "she said that if you weren't a scholarship student, she would recommend you to a *shrink.* And you know what she made me promise? She made me promise to be nice to you, or else you won't ever get better, but you know what? I don't *care* if you get better, and you know why? Because I hate you."

Laura walked over to the fire. Looking into the flames, she tried to think clearly. All the time and energy she had wasted on Sarah and Bess and Nathaniel, only to have Nathaniel die on her and Bess turn into a doll-making machine and Sarah abuse her. She couldn't believe that Sarah hated her.

On her way up to Kay's study she felt completely free. It was the first time in months.

Kay was bent over a yellow legal pad, scratching the bottom of a Magic Marker against the back of her neck. When Laura entered the room she looked up politely. Her eyes said please do not disturb, I am deep in thought, but she gave Laura another one of her glassy smiles.

"Yes?"

"Why did you say all those things about me?" she almost shouted.

"What things, Laura?"

"That I'm insane!"

Kay looked puzzled. She stared at Laura for a few seconds. Then she frowned. "Oh, dear. Oh, dear." She rushed across the room and put her arms on Laura's shoulder. "Sarah told you that, didn't she?"

Laura nodded.

"Dear me, what must you think of us. I hope you believe me when I tell you that I did not in fact tell anyone that you were insane. Sarah got things mixed up, that's all."

"You mean she was lying to me?"

Kay looked compassionately into her eyes. "No," she said slowly. "Just jumping to conclusions, that's all. As you know, her imagination has been a bit overstimulated lately." Kay smiled. Her hands pressed into Laura's shoulders a little harder. She was leaning on her, almost pressing her into the wall.

"In a way you could say that was the whole problem, couldn't you?" Kay said softly. "There's such a thin line, isn't there, between playing imaginative games and telling people calculated lies." She gave Laura a tight, trembling smile, and looked at the corners of Laura's eyes, her nose, her mouth, and then her eyes again. Full blast. Laura tried to move but she couldn't. Kay had her pinned.

"You know what?" Laura said, trembling. "I think you're the one who's lying to me, not Sarah. You think I'm insane! You really do!"

"Hey, hey. Laura, calm down. Let's get the record straight for once and for all. All I recall saying is making an offhand comment about how nice it would be if you could go to a psychiatrist once in a while."

"If I weren't a scholarship student," Laura said.

"That's right," Kay said softly. She paused. "It's terrible, isn't it, the way the medical profession discriminates against the vast majority who cannot afford their exorbitant fees. But to set the record straight, let me tell you that the only reason I mentioned psychiatry in the first place is because I am one of those crazy people who think that, ideally, everyone should undergo psycho-analysis at one time or another." She smiled. "So you see? Sarah was just exaggerating, as I said."

"You think I'm sick."

Kay sighed. "That girl." She shook her head. "No, Laura, I don't think you're sick. Not any more than anyone else, that is. It's been a difficult year, and I guess we're all a bit jumpy as a result. But we'll pull through. That's why we have to forget about what's happened, and concentrate on the future. Let's try and forget what you said and what I said, and for goodness' sake stop feeling guilty. That's what families are for, to forgive and forget and to live with each other through thick and thin. It's hard for me to know how to put this, Laura, without sounding corny, but please believe me when I say that I love you. That's why I understand what you're going through and why you did what you did and forgive you completely."

Her voice was soft and her eyes full of compassion. Perhaps it was her iron grip that made Laura feel as if Kay were trying to smother her. She tried to push her away, but Kay held her tight. "Don't, Laura, don't. Just be patient. Love will find a way. Don't make things worse than they already are. I really do look on you as one of my own children."

"GET YOUR HANDS OFF ME!" Laura screamed. Kay didn't. Laura struggled under her iron grip. "You don't love me! You don't love anybody! You don't even love your own children!" She spat her words into Kay's face as she struggled to get free. Kay held her shoulders firmly, the same way she held Sarah's shoulders when Sarah had one of her tantrums. Her face showed no expression. "You've never loved anyone in your whole life!" Laura screamed. "All you want is to control people, and have your own way, and make everyone think the way you think. Well, you know what? Maybe you can tell all those other idiots what to do and what to think, but YOU CAN'T TELL ME!"

She began to cry, in great violent gasps, while Kay held her firmly, her eyes compassionate once again, as if Laura were a dog dying of a disease for which science had no cure.

"Are you finished now?" Kay asked when Laura could almost breathe regularly again.

"Yes."

"Now, that's better, isn't it?" Kay smiled.

"No, it isn't," Laura said. "I'm leaving!"

"Leaving where?"

"Leaving this house. I quit this job."

"Oh, dear." Kay let go of her shoulders and took her hand, which she patted several times. "Are you sure?"

"I'm sure."

"I hope you don't think I have in any way pressured you into this decision." She searched Laura's face anxiously.

Laura shook her head, still fighting tears.

"As far as myself and the girls are concerned, the Pyle-Carpenter household is your home as long as you want it to be."

"Thank you."

"There's nothing to thank me about. We talked it over and it's how we feel." Kay took Laura's hand and squeezed it with emotion. A rehearsed emotion. It was a rehearsed speech, Laura suddenly realized. She had been having second thoughts, wondering if she had acted rashly, but when she saw how thoroughly prepared Kay was for what Laura thought was a spur-of-the-moment decision, she was angrier than ever.

"I guess I'll pack up my things," Laura said finally.

"Will you at least stay for tea?" Kay asked with a beseeching smile. Laura disengaged her hand.

"Well, you got what you wanted," Laura said to Sarah when she went downstairs. "I'm leaving."

And Sarah said, "Good riddance to bad rubbish."

Laura went from room to room collecting her books, her letters, her records, her hairbrushes, her clothes, her underwear, her toilet articles, her hats, her gloves, her jackets, her sunglasses, her flashlights, her bracelets, her notebooks, her pictures. She was wearing Edith's horseriding boots. To make herself feel worse than she already did, she took them off and put on a pair of sandals that she had left there during the summer and forgotten to take back to the dorm. If word reached them that she had pneumonia, then they would feel very guilty.

After she had double-checked the living room, the bathrooms, the kitchen, and Children's Paradise, she went up to Bob Pyle's former study and looked under the couch. There was nothing there. Then she went to the Thinking Room to tell Dennis what she had decided to do, and to say good-bye.

He reacted to the news with a resigned nod.

"Will you call me?" she asked.

Dennis went very red and threw his hammer on the floor. "Why do you make so many demands on me?" he shouted.

MOTHER'S HELPER

"I'm not making any demands on you. All I asked is if you would call me."

He closed his eyes and rubbed a clenched fist against his forehead as he counted to ten. "Listen," he finally said. "I wish I could say this to you in a nicer way. But you've got to realize that I don't have any obligations to you just because we've had an off-and-on sexual relationship for the past few months."

"That wasn't what I asked you. All I asked was if you would call me."

He closed his eyes. "There you go again. Making demands."

"You're out of your mind!" Laura cried.

He hit the floor with his fist. "How many times have I told you not to interfere in the private relationship between Edith and me?"

"You *never* told me!"

He glared at her. The veins in his neck and his forehead stuck out. "Edith and I have a very special relationship."

"You could have fooled me!" Laura shouted. She had lost all control of her temper. "I don't know how you stand that girl. She walks all over you, and you don't do a thing about it."

Dennis let out an exasperated sigh. "Edith is a woman," he said in a tired voice, "and a very fine woman at that. I wish you would learn to say *woman* instead of *girl,* Laura. If you don't learn soon, you could find yourself in some pretty hairy situations."

He picked up his hammer and went back to work.

"Well, good-bye," Laura said.

He put his hammer down again.

"Look," he said. "I'm sorry. I'm into some pretty heavy self-evaluation these days, like I told you yesterday, so don't take it personally. Listen. If you really have a strong need to see me, like if you're in a heavy emotional rut or something that you don't think you can get out of without some outside help, then I guess you can reach me here or at home. Then we can meet at a coffee house or something. But no promises. It depends on where my head is at, so I can't give you any guarantees."

Downstairs the others had assembled in the kitchen. Melissa was busy looking something up in the phone book; Martin was trying to interest Bess in a game of Blockhead; Edith, her cheeks still red and her parka speckled with snow, was talking with a friend on the phone; Kay was looking through the box of undamaged toys that Laura had prepared for the university day-care center which the day-care center had not picked up. She was probably looking for war toys. Sarah was sitting on top of the refrigerator, looking smug.

During the year she had worked for the Pyles, Laura had kept a record of her working hours on a chart on the inside of one of the kitchen cabinet doors. Laura now noticed this chart lying on the floor. Someone had crossed it out with a big red "X". On top of the pile of odds and ends that Laura had put on the kitchen table was a green plastic garbage bag.

"I thought you might find that that bag would come in handy," Kay remarked, searching through the drawers for her checkbook. Laura loaded her odds and ends into the bag.

"It's amazing how much you can accumulate in one year," Laura said.

Yes," Kay said in an absentminded voice as she wrote in her checkbook. "It's absolutely supercalifragilistic." She handed Laura a check for twenty-seven fifty to cover the hours she had not already been paid for and put her checkbook back into the drawer.

There was a burning smell in the kitchen. Sarah's cake was cooling on the rack.

"Are you sure you won't stay for tea?" Kay asked, examining a ring she had found in the drawer.

"Thank you very much," Laura said, "but I think I had better go."

"It just occurred to me that that dorm of yours will be darned lonely and empty and gloomy this weekend."

"It doesn't matter," Laura said.

Kay went over to the cake that was cooling on the rack and cut out a large rectangular piece. She pressed this charred hunk into

Laura's hand. "For dessert," she said in a soft voice. The cake was
white and powdery where the flour had not blended with the liquid,
and on the bottom was something that looked like a fried egg,
except that the egg white was brown.

"Let me wrap that up in some aluminum foil for you," Edith
said. She took it away. Laura put on her coat, her mittens, her hat.

"Hey," Kay said, "why don't you take those old snowshoes of
mine. Those sandals look deadly. I don't think they can stand up
to more than one second of snow."

"Oh, I'm used to walking in the snow in sandals," Laura said.

Kay put her hands on her shoulders and looked into her eyes,
her forehead wrinkled with concern. "Listen, Laura, I'm serious.
If you ever have second thoughts . . ."

"Of course," Laura said.

"I hope you believe me when I say that you are free to continue
to use this household as a home base, *especially* if you are feeling
low, and . . ." Kay let go of her shoulder and grabbed her hands.
There were tears in her eyes. ". . . help yourself to whatever you
may find in the refrigerator. Gee, I'm sorry it didn't work out."

Laura thanked her anyway. By now she was feeling quite
numb. She picked up her green garbage bag and headed toward
the door. Edith darted in her path and kissed her on the mouth.
"Listen!" she said, flashing one of her perfect smiles. "If you're
ever lonely . . . Hell! No matter *how* you feel! We've only just
begun to get to know each other! Why don't you give me a call in
a week or so and you and I can meet at a coffee house or something?"

Laura said she would do that. She tried once again to make it
to the door, but this time Melissa blocked her way. "Good luck for
the future," she said solemnly, offering her hand. "I hope you do
well in whatever career it was you told me you were going into."

Kay laughed. "Why does Melissa always make everything sound
so Melissa-ish?"

"Well, good-bye," Laura said.

"Bess?" Kay said, turning around. "Aren't you going to say good-bye to Laura?"

Bess glanced up from her doll basket. She was feeding one of them imaginary milk from a tiny plastic milk bottle. "Isn't she coming back?"

"We certainly hope so!" Kay said.

"Then just a minute."

"Sarah? Sarah? Where are you, Sarah?" Sarah was clinging to the coats on the coat rack. "Aren't you going to say good-bye to your good friend Laura?"

"Good-bye!" Sarah said. "And don't bother to come back either!"

Kay gave her daughter a sad look, then turned to embrace Laura. "Gee, I want to thank you for the invaluable help you've given us over the past year."

"Hear! Hear!" Martin said. He was standing behind Kay, the familiar clown grin on his face.

"We really couldn't have made it without you," Kay said.

Once again Laura said thank you and good-bye. This time she made it out the door. Her green garbage bag slung over her shoulder, she trudged down the porch steps into the snow. Three or four inches had fallen since Martin had shoveled the path, and by the time she reached the gate, her sandaled feet were already frozen. Each footstep was like plunging into freezing water for the first time.

Opening the gate took some doing. She had to kick the snow away to get it to move, numbing her toes even further. Just as she managed to open it wide enough to get her garbage bag through, the kitchen door opened.

"Laura?" It was Kay.

"Yes?"

"Forgot to ask you. How are you fixed?"

"Fixed for what?" Laura asked.

Kay mouthed the words "For money."

"Oh, fine."

"Oh, wonderful. I just wanted to make sure. Well then! See you soon!" Kay shut the door. They were all standing in the bright yellow light of the doorway, smiling and waving as if they were seeing someone off at the airport. Except for Sarah.

Laura waved good-bye and went through the gate and closed it. Leaning against the fence, she looked at the black snowcapped trees and the white road and the deep snowdrifts before her. It was getting dark and the lights were on in all the mansions and frame houses that weren't offices. Their windows were little yellow boxes of fire and they made Laura feel even colder than before.

She opened the gate again to take a last look at the Pyle house and the warm yellow life inside it. At the kitchen and the hallway and the living room and the master bedroom and the two studies. As an outsider, instead of a member of the family whom no one could do without. The grown-ups had scattered. Laura could see Kay's head in her study, the top of her bookcase and the colorful book bindings, the shadows that the desk lamp cast on the ceiling. Kay had given her every opportunity to stay if she wanted to. So why did I leave, Laura asked herself. And why do I hate her so? She could see Martin's back as he climbed up the back staircase: his ragged mop of dirty-blond hair, except in this light it looked almost golden, his heavy gray sweater, then just his Levi's, his work boots. In the kitchen she could see the tips of the flames in the fireplace and Bess's downturned head at the kitchen table, the counters, the edge of the oven, and next to the refrigerator, Dennis yawning. He was probably making himself a cup of coffee. Melissa was standing in the middle of the living room, her head framed by the bookshelves where they kept the serious books: Sir Walter Scott, the poetry of Heine and Goethe, *The Collected Works of Shakespeare, Don Quixote,* Paul Tillich, Tennyson, *Beowulf, The Decline and Fall of the Roman Empire* and *The Rise and Fall of the Third Reich, Bleak House, The Pickwick Papers,* and *Growing Up Absurd.* She was staring at Edith, whose head was just visible above the back of the couch. Edith was waving her hands around in the air. When her face came into view for a brief moment she saw that she was laughing.

Dead people probably felt this way, Laura said to herself, when they came back to haunt their former lives.

Only Sarah remained in the doorway. Her eyes were blank and far away, her cheeks wet with tears. She was crying. Laura wondered what she was crying about.

Her lips were moving, but Laura could not hear any sound. She pressed her face against the glass door, flattening her nose and her lips. She pressed her hands on the glass above her head and let them slowly slide. Through her own frozen breath, Laura watched Sarah's face disappear behind the clouded glass, until there was nothing left except two pink hands slipping downwards, a pink spot of nose, two nostrils, and two lips moving, thicker than life, and sadder. Laura wondered what she was saying.

She closed the gate.

One summer in Eressos, when she was still a child and too young to know not to poke her hands into holes when she was swimming around caves, Laura had been attacked by an octopus. It was not a very big octopus but it clung to her shoulder so firmly and sucked against her skin with such force that it took all of Laura's strength to wrench it off. Then it had clung to her hand. By the time Laura was free of it she had swallowed so much seawater that she thought she would drown.

To get back to the cove where her parents were waiting, she had had to swim fifty feet out to sea along a ridge full of sea urchins and dragonfish and mussels and swaying sea plants that she had never learned to trust and her mask magnified vastly. She had to swim along that ledge, even though she was full of seawater and thought she was dying. Her shoulder ached as if the octopus still clung to it, and when she looked at the brilliant blue haze of the water out to sea she was sure there were sharks there, and moray eels, and huge schools of overgrown dragonfish, and Portuguese men-of-war waiting to kill her. But there was no way out except along the ledge, so Laura had swum into the treacherous blue haze as fast as her flippers could take her. It sped past her: this luminescent fog that hid every monster and every form of torture and death that she had ever imagined. Two streams of blue on either side of her head as she swam with determination into the unknown. She reached the end of the ledge and then the cove without incident, but she had never forgotten the color of the sea that day.

Now, as Laura turned away from the gate and looked over the snowdrifts, she saw that same color at the end of the road. The snow and the trees and the sky had mingled to become that same brilliant blue haze of deep water. There was that same hush, that same premonition of terrible danger, and the same hazy blue of the unknown. It reminded Laura of that day in Eressos when she thought she would die. She remembered the red spots left by the octopus and how much they had hurt, how quickly they had gone away, how everyone had laughed when she told them how brave she had been to swim out to sea along the treacherous ledge. "We've *all* swum along that ledge thousands of times," they had told her. "You're just imagining things. People have been swimming here for thousands of years. There's no way in the world you could have been in danger."

Her feet were freezing cold by now, as was the section of neck that her scarf did not cover, and the half inch of bare skin between her coat sleeve and her glove. Plunging through virgin snow in sandals was painful, so when she set off down the road to her dorm she took care to step in other people's footsteps as often as possible.

MAUREEN FREELY

was born in Neptune, New Jersey, in 1952, the eldest of three children. When she was eight, her family moved to Istanbul, Turkey. It was here that she spent the remainder of her childhood, with the exception of one year in London, one year at a boarding school in Beirut, and many summers with her family on the Greek island of Naxos. After graduating from Radcliffe College in 1974, she returned to Europe to live with her husband, the American writer Paul Spike. Their first child was born in late 1978.